The Espion Series, Book One

IMPERFECT WEAPON

by A B Potts

To John
Best Wishes

Published in 2012 by FeedARead.com Publishing – Arts Council funded.

First Edition
Copyright © Anni B Potts, 2012

www.abpotts.co.uk

PROLOGUE

Myth, legend and prophecy feature in every culture, be it humanoid or otherwise. Some of these tales are filled with words of wisdom and some are just downright odd.

Far, far away, on a little blue world called Mona, the inhabitants speak of the Tinnin: a collection of three beings who control and shape the worlds in which we all live with their constant meddling. They have no names; they have no need of them. They know who they are.

In the gloomy darkness of their cave, these three cold shadows sit peering into a fire. The flames lick the air with an eerie, unnatural orange glow, and the red smoke that it exudes twists and twirls leisurely into the air, not dispersing, but winding itself into an ethereal rope that reaches eternally into the vault above where it undulates like seaweed in the currents of a quiet sea.

As the wisps of smoke wind themselves into the rope, they are momentarily unravelled, showing the hazy crimson visions of which they are formed. Visions fashioned from memories and history, of current events, and of that which is yet to be or may be. Visions that, as they touch each other, react with each other, evolve and are ever changing, entwining themselves into newer and stronger ropes until, under the strain of their own volume, they break apart, snapping like strained string.

The shadows watch and occasionally snatch a thread of smoke, pulling it from its natural path. They examine it as it twists and writhes like a small snake in their gnarled, elongated fingers and then, having studied the surrounding visions for a suitable place, let it go to reintegrate itself back into the fabric of time. Occasionally it takes an extra prod with a bony digit to make the smoke attach itself to the place they want it to go, but finally, once it has caught, they can watch it return to the column and fully re-entwine itself back into the rope of scarlet, smoky visions.

These are the Tinnin—watching, waiting, keeping, nurturing, and reading the signs; but this story is not about the Tinnin. It is about the finest little thread of smoke that is floating almost insignificantly in the air, so pale and fine that it is barely visible—but the Tinnin have seen it and are watching it as it hovers tantalisingly just out of their fingers' reach. Every now and then, it comes just a little bit closer to them, so close that they stop. Even their breathing stops as they are mesmerised by it, waiting to see if it will come close enough to them this time.

"The time draws near," gasps the First, breaking the silence.

"Yes, I can feel the beginning," quivers the Second with excitement.

"And the end," says the Third with great sorrow in her voice.

"The beginning comes first!" snaps the First. "It starts with the beginning."

"No," corrects the Third, "every beginning is the aftermath of an end, and every end is the dawn of a new beginning. It has always been this way and always will be. One man's end is another man's beginning. This is the way of all things."

The First and Second ponder the sentiment as they have so many times before. It is an old argument and once more, they nod reluctantly in agreement, all the while watching the smoky threads.

"But how many ends have come to pass for this one beginning?" ponders the First.

"And how many more are yet to come?" adds the Second.

The Third suddenly lurches upwards and oh! Such joy on the Tinnins' faces, for she has it at last, in her grasp...

CHAPTER 1

Kyamena looked up into the night sky towards the place where the stars no longer shone. She knew that it was there and if she squinted her eyes to look, she could just make out the inky blackness of its outline: the thing that now hung in front of the stars stopping them shining through. It had arrived just a few weeks ago and had been barely noticed at first as it sat so quietly in the sky. But then had come the chaos and the war. It had been a short war—a war that they had lost.

Now she understood her enemy and she knew that on this battlefield, she and her people had never stood a chance. Yet she wasn't filled so entirely with despair because she had been raised an optimist, and she wasn't dead yet. Not yet, although she feared there wasn't long to go.

A sharp nudge in the small of her back shunted her forward. She turned and glared at her oppressor as she was shuffled forward with the rest of the throng of people to whom she was bound. The Sallow Warrior stared back at her through its cold, hell-fire red eyes.

"You may have won this war, but there is always another day," she hissed at it, although even she knew that her words were empty. As for the android, it certainly felt no fear or trepidation at her words. It jabbed at her again, and she stumbled onto her knees but quickly brought herself back to her feet despite her hands being tied behind her back. She had started this trip with five people behind her in the throng, but as each of them had fallen, the Warrior had held no hesitation in putting them out of their misery with one quick blast of the weapon built into its arm.

It was ironic that something as beautiful as the Warrior could be so deadly. It was tall and strong, yet incredibly nimble and agile—out of all proportion to its bulk—and it shone like polished gold with brightly coloured enamel inlaid into the headdress that surrounded its face. It reminded her of the sarcophagi of the ancient Pyranian kings that she had seen as a child when her father had taken her on one of his archaeological digs, but that was so long ago and where was her father now? Was he already dead? Probably. The cities had been struck first and he was a lecturer at the *University of Archaeology & Heritage* in the capital.

As they crested the hill, the valley below was not as she had last seen it. The last time she was here, in the early spring, the meadow that had stretched out before her had been filled with tall fresh grasses, and a myriad of little flowers had speckled the
60
snowstars had dotted the landscape. Butterflies had hovered above the meadow too, dancing from flower to flower, competing with the bees for the nectar. Now, it

was a black place despite the intense lighting from the spear-lamps pushed into the ground. The grass had been scorched away leaving just the dry earth, and it was scattered with huge metal containers. Some were only about ten metres square but others were much bigger, up to five times as big. These were the ones into which the Warriors were herding her people, cramming them in tightly before sealing the doors.

As the Warriors traipsed back and forth, she could also make out the ships that had brought the Warriors down from the thing above, the same ships that would carry them away again once they were done. In between them, she could see another type of android, a very different type to the Warriors. It had none of the armaments of the Warriors and was much more humanoid in its stature being tall (although not as tall as a Warrior) and slender. It was dressed in simple white linen robes and it wasn't gold either, or even metallic. It seemed to be coated in a flexible white plastic material that had an odd translucency to it. As it passed in front of one of the spotlights, she could see into its head; and then she realised, as she was looking directly at it, that it was looking directly at her. Its face was moulded with human-like features but they were cold and expressionless, and its eyes looked at her out of colourless eye-sockets as blank and white as a shop window's mannequin.

She did not drop her gaze, and nor did it. It ceased its dialogue with the Warrior that was by its side and walked towards her. Another sharp jab on her shoulder caught her off guard. She lost her balance, stumbled and fell forward, smacking her face into the cold, hard dust. Urgently she began trying to get to her feet. She could hear the motors of the Warrior as it brought out its weapon. Her feet slipped on the dry dust as she scrabbled. She heard the click as the gun snapped into place. She knew that the fizzling sound it made as it was fired was just a moment away. She'd heard it five times before, but still her feet couldn't get a grip on the loose earth.

"Come on then, you bastard!" she screamed. "Finish the job!" and she stopped struggling. Perched on one knee, with one leg splayed out beside her, her head bent down and her forehead touching the earth, she closed her eyes. She had no desire to stare her executioner in the face.

But the shot didn't come. She could feel her heart pounding in her chest and the adrenalin coursing through her body, but nothing happened. Slowly she opened her eyes. On the ground in front of her were firmly planted two white feet. The long, white linen robe wafted around them in the gentle night breeze, flicking at its ankles. Slowly, her eyes moved up the figure to greet the face of the android looking down at her. It tipped its head to one side and spoke in a soft, round voice.

"Hello."

For a moment, she said nothing. What was there to say?

"Hello," she finally said, rather dumbly.

"My name is Mela-14. I am a Scientific. What are you?"

"I am... Kyamena. I'm a bookkeeper." It sounded a really stupid thing to say under the circumstances. What relevance was it that she was a bookkeeper? What use is a bookkeeper to anybody in a time of war?

"Ah! A mathematician, a thinker like myself—and a rather spirited one too. I think you will do very nicely."

It turned from her and made a brief gesture to the Warrior beside her. It lurched forward, grabbed her by the shoulder and lifted her effortlessly, as though she was nothing more than a rag doll, and threw her onto her feet. From its free arm, a blade unpeeled and flicked out deftly. Kyamena flinched but it didn't touch her. Instead, it cut her bonds, freeing her from the line of captives. The blade was re-homed, and she was pushed away from the others towards the space ship. As she was shoved through the doors, she glanced back to the throng of people with whom she had travelled to this god-forsaken place and saw the horror in their eyes as she was dragged away. Little did they know that of the two parties she was the safe one—for the time being at least. The throng of people were pushed into one of the containers and the doors sealed. It was the last time they would ever see light.

* * * * *

Kyamena sat in the ship amongst the Warriors. Her hands were still bound behind her so she couldn't lean back properly, and the seat wasn't designed for comfort.

The ship was quite large inside, about the same size as one of the public buses that ran in the cities, and it was as crowded too. Behind her was a legion of about forty Warriors that stood to attention. In the bright lights of the interior, she could see that they were dusty and bloody.

She was sat amongst another legion of about twenty Warriors in the middle of the ship. Forward of that was a deep arch and beyond that, the cockpit of the craft. There she could see more Warriors seated at the control panels, or at least what she assumed were control panels. They were completely flat like monitor screens and apparently blank, but the Warriors' hands moved over them quickly and deftly as though something were there. No words passed between them, but it was obvious that they were communicating somehow. They worked together as a team to launch the craft and take it up into the night sky, through the atmosphere and towards the great darkness that lay beyond.

A small noise behind her made her turn. It was the Scientific, Mela-14. The Warrior to her right rose and vacated the seat so that Mela-14 could sit down beside her. It did so in an oddly human-like way, slapping its palms on its thighs as it sat, but said nothing. She stared at its hands and looked up into its face that was fixed, staring on a point ahead of it. She felt strangely at ease with the android that had saved her from the Warrior, although every fibre of her being kept reminding her that it was still a cold machine that had no better-nature to it, that she was in as much danger now as she had been back in the meadow with the Warrior towering over her, its weapon locked and loaded.

"Excuse me," she ventured after some time.

Mela-14 turned and looked at her.

"Yes?" it replied very matter-of-factly.

"Where are we going?"

The android leaned into her and pointed out of the forward window. She peered down the line of its finger to the blurry black orb that lay ahead.

"What is it?" she asked.

"That, my dear, is a DaerkStar: the DeathMaker in fact. That is where I live."

The conversation had clearly ended and silence fell again, but Kyamena was still curious. As she saw it, there was very little to be lost by asking a further question, except perhaps her life, but she doubted that a few questions would have any real impact upon her longevity. After all, why would the android have separated her out from the others just to kill her now? No. She was here for a reason. Was that

7

reassuring or did it fill her with more foreboding? She wasn't sure.

"Why have you come here? To my world, I mean. What do you want? Where do you come from?"

"We come from everywhere. We have no homeworld of our own. We come to conquer."

"Could you not have come in peace? We could have given you a place to live, if that's what you needed—and food, but..." her voice trailed off. What food do machines need?

It was as if it had read her mind.

"Machines do not need food, but the Council members, the blood-Sallows, they do; but no, we could not have come in peace. We came to annihilate your kind, to exterminate you from this place and that is what we have done. That is what Sallows do. All Sallows throughout the galaxies have sworn to destroy you and your kind wherever they may be."

"You have destroyed other worlds like mine before?" she exclaimed in horror.

"But of course."

"How many worlds have you destroyed?"

"The DeathMaker alone or the sum total of our fleet?"

"There are more of you?" she gasped.

"Oh yes! But the DeathMaker is one of the most successful DaerkStars in the Sallow fleet—the second highest ranking in fact. We have vanquished twice as many worlds as the BloodLust and Vanquisher combined, and not because we have picked smaller targets. In fact, we have often picked larger and more difficult targets. We are simply more..." it thought for a moment, "...efficient than most Sallow Councils. We expend more energy and resources on scientific research and development, which means that we are more advanced than they are. We have... the edge," it finished with great pride.

Silence fell again and she thought about all that the android had told her.

"You have a council?" She was thinking of her own society's council. Perhaps if she could gain an audience with them, maybe she could persuade them to leave her planet alone. "Are you a council member?" she asked hopefully.

"Good grief, no! Only the blood-Sallows are Council members. I am a mere android. The blood-Sallows are our creators, the original Sallow race of flesh and blood."

"Like me?" she exclaimed.

"Goodness! No!" exclaimed the android in controlled horror. "Not like you. You are a goyeme, a humanoid. The Sallows are the pure race, the superior race."

Kyamena was reminded of the race wars on her planet three thousand years ago. The races from the north thought themselves superior to the races from the south and set about their annihilation. Souths were rounded up and executed in their hundreds of thousands just for being a South or just for looking like a South with their paler skin and unusual fashions. Just as then, she doubted that any such plea would be worthwhile, but she continued anyway.

"And you work for them?"

"Yes."

"Are there many of you? Androids I mean?"

"Oh yes. Well, Warriors, yes," it corrected.

"I'm sorry, I don't understand. What do you mean?"

"We are three castes: Scientific, Warrior and slave. I am a Scientific. We are the thinkers, the designers and the creators who develop the weapons and technology to aid in the war against the humanoids. The Warriors..." it pointed around itself to its shining golden comrades, "...outnumber us significantly. These are our legions that fight the battles. They are our battle fodder on the front lines, the snipers in the hills, the fighter pilots and the commandos. Are they not a glorious sight?" it said proudly.

"And the slaves?" Kyamena asked. "How many of them are there?"

"Oh them! They do not matter!" Mela-14 waved a hand dismissively at the mention of their name. "I have no idea how many of them there are. They undertake all the menial tasks of maintenance, housekeeping, that sort of thing," and it pointed dismissively over to a small alcove in the sidewall. There, stashed away like a discarded vacuum cleaner, was a flimsy, skeletally-framed little android. It seemed to have been very carelessly built with the barest minimum of parts for it to function. Its simple metal frame was rough and dull, and it was short and thin with limbs that consisted of little more than metal rods. It had no protective coating to cover its mechanisms and gears. It was an entirely less sophisticated machine than the Warriors or the Scientifics.

"Stupid creatures really. They have no powers of independent thought or speech and lack any strength in their bodies, but they serve a function."

She thought again about the ancient Pyranians and their pyramids that she had helped her father excavate, and the hundreds of slave bones that they had found. *'Obedient, servile, disposable and irrelevant'*, he had described them as. She thought of them now and felt a vein of pity for the thing in the cubbyhole.

"And that," said Mela-14, puffing itself up with pride and pointing towards the front window, "is DeathMaker."

The DaerkStar still sat quietly in the sky, just as it had done over her homeworld, but now its immense size impressed itself forcefully onto Kyamena. It was a huge thing, camouflaged against the blackness of space, a shadowy burst of darkness between the stars. It revolved gently on its axis like a big spiky ball.

"My god, it's huge!" she exclaimed. "How many of you live there?"

"Well, there is the Sallow Council of five and over four hundred thousand androids."

She gasped and her gaze travelled across the ship, exploring its exterior.

There were no lights on it. It was completely black so its detail was blurred against its background, but as they got nearer, she could make out the intricate details of the outer hull criss-crossed with pipes and conduits. She could see what looked like big obsidian panels in the tips of the spines of the orb and dotted along its lengths. As they approached the tip of one spine, the obsidian window evaporated and soft white light spilled out towards them. Effortlessly, the ship glided into the hanger deck.

The first thing that struck her was the whiteness of it all. None of it was brilliant white on its own, but when all the whiteness was put together it was blindingly so. It was such a stark contrast to the blackness of the outside.

Having successfully docked, Kyamena was led out of the ship and onto the hanger deck. It was huge and so busy that she couldn't make out the end of it. Other ships were coming and going, and she could see the huge crates that her people had been herded into, stacked like the containers on the docks in the shipyards back home. She had expected it to be noisy with the cries of the people inside, but it wasn't. Only the hustle and bustle of the androids and the noise of the ships' engines could be heard. She slowed as she passed by one of the containers to listen, but the Warrior behind pushed her forward through some doors and out of the hanger deck.

They seemed to be walking forever down the stark white corridors, and each one looked the same as the next to Kyamena, barring the strange black patterns that ran along the ceilings and walls. Some of it looked like writing but she couldn't be sure. Mela-14 walked ahead of her and now, when she tried to talk to it, it completely ignored her.

Suddenly, they turned off sharply and a set of doors slid open allowing them entry into a room. Inside was a laboratory stacked with a whole plethora of scientific equipment, monitors and tools. There were specimens of things in jars and pictures of things she couldn't identify. Kyamena felt sick. She began to wish she'd stayed with the others. She had a horrible feeling that whatever their fate was, it would have been better than this.

A scraping sound made her jump with fright, but it was just Mela-14 pushing a stool across the floor towards her.

"Sit," it commanded. She sat.

Looking around her, there were whole banks of monitors stretching around the room, angled at forty-five degrees. Most of them were blank and the android switched the rest off as she settled herself on the stool somewhat apprehensively. For a moment, she wished she'd seen what was on them before it had turned them off, and then she thought it was probably best that she hadn't.

Mela-14 took her by the shoulders and swivelled the stool around so that one monitor was immediately in front of her. It turned it on and the image of two humanoids came to life. They were sat together in an empty room, as cold and white and sterile as the corridors she had just walked through.

Although humanoid, the woman was very different to herself. She had beautiful, dark Nubian coloured skin and a very delicate build. Her face was long and triangular with a prominent brow, high cheekbones and a narrow, delicate chin. She stared at the camera that watched her, with deep, soft brown eyes. She had long, straight ebony hair that trailed over her shoulders and onto her companion's fair arms. She was very slightly built and she wasn't tall. Kyamena wouldn't call her short as such, just childishly un-tall, but then she couldn't have been more than fourteen or fifteen years old.

She sat with her slender legs folded to one side of her, with her companion, a small white child, perched on her lap.

The boy was very different to her, and yet so alike. His skin was ashen and his hair so fair that it was almost white. He was just a toddler, little more than a year old she guessed, and he sat patiently on his mother's lap with his head resting on her breast, listening to the sound of her heart beating gently in his ear.

With his finger, he was absent-mindedly tracing the white tattoo on the girl's arm. It seemed to tickle her a little because Kyamena saw her shudder slightly at the touch, but she didn't stop him doing it. She looked away from the camera and smiled down at him, and despite her obvious sadness, the smile lit up her face. For a moment, her eyes beamed with joy and the little boy looked back at her. She thought he was about to giggle at the girl, but he didn't. The girl took a deep breath, so deep that even though Kyamena didn't hear it, she saw it, and then the girl stroked the boy's arm. He had a tattoo as well, but his was black upon his fair skin.

In response, he looked up at the girl again. This time his whole face became visible on the monitor, and Kyamena gasped at the sight of him. He had lovely rounded features and brilliant, cat-like emerald-green eyes that flashed with life and shattered the monochromaticity of the cell like a hammer smashing a glass pane. He was absolutely beautiful, angelically so.

The girl swept the boy deep into her arms and held him very close. He snuggled into her and she bent her head right down to him so that her mouth was just over his ear.

"I don't understand," said Kyamena turning to Mela-14. "What do you want with me? And what do they have to do with anything?"

Mela-14 gently took her chin in its hand and directed her face back towards the monitor.

"Watch him, Kyamena."

"Why?" she puzzled. "Who are they?"

"She is the mother of Death; and he is Death. He is the Destroyer, and he will help to destroy you and every other goyeme in existence."

"But he's just a little boy, a baby."

Mela-14 stepped in front of her and bowed down so it could look directly into her eyes.

"Surely you had criminals on your planet?" it asked. "Surely the most heinous of these started life as a mere babe in arms?"

"Yes, but as children, we did not know what they would become. How do you know what he will become?"

"Because I have made him, and I am still making him." Somehow, its voice had changed. For the first time in the android's company, she felt deeply intimidated. She realised that whatever happened to her next would be completely and totally as the android desired. She was just a toy for the android, a pawn in its game. She felt powerless and afraid.

"He will walk amongst your kind. He will infiltrate your deepest resistance groups, and he will betray you."

"My people are already dead," she braved. Her voice was shaky, trembling with her fear.

"Yes," replied Mela-14 softly. "Your planet is already plundered and your people plunged into extinction, and we shall continue to do that to planet... after planet... after planet." Mela-14 rose and had began to walk around her, circling her like a vulture. "And he will help us."

"So..." she hardly dared ask, "what does this have to do with me?"

"You are going to stop him. Or at least you are going to try."

"But he's just a kid!"

"Now? Yes, but he will grow up and while he is growing, you will watch and learn everything he learns. You will learn all the tricks he learns, and when you are ready, I will pit you against him."

"Why?"

"Because I will need to test him, and to do that I will need a worthy opponent—one that will appeal to his sense of humanity (if he has one), and one that is trained. At present I do not have such a thing available to me, so I must make one."

"And what if I refuse?"

"Then he will kill you."

"But I'm not a killer!" she exclaimed. "I'm not a soldier! I'm a bookkeeper!"

"You—" Mela-14 placed itself strategically by the side of Kyamena, knelt down to her level again and whispered in her ear, "—are whatever I want you to be. Yesterday you were a bookkeeper. Today you are just someone with a good instinct for survival. Tomorrow I will have honed your skills and you will be a Warrior. You will have two choices. You can either live or you can die." And with that, it placed a finger under her chin and redirected her gaze back up to the monitor.

"Know your prey," it finished.

* * * * *

In the cell, the girl had begun to whisper softly. So softly, her mouth barely moved, and so quietly, it wasn't even audible enough for her son to hear; but he heard her. For him the silence shattered amongst her words, but no one else heard them. Her words were only for him.

CHAPTER 2
Five years later

Walking down the corridor of the DaerkStar, the boy was accompanied by a Scientific at his side and two Warriors behind. The Scientific was Mela-14, his guardian and mentor. Indistinguishable from any other Scientific to most, ATB-80 knew him so well he could pick him out of a room full of identical Scientifics as easily as a parent can identify one twin from the other. And that's a good analogy to make because Mela-14 has raised him, taught him everything he knows and guided him in his studies, so much so that ATB-80 even calls him *'Father'*.

Like his android brothers, ATB-80 looked perfect. He was beautifully groomed. His short ash-blond hair was firmly stuck in place and the deep-blue military uniform that had been especially designed for him was immaculate with not a single crease out of place. His heavy black boots were so highly polished that the corridor's lights shone brightly in their toes. He looked like a perfect little soldier at an award ceremony, and as he walked, his footsteps were in perfect tune with his escorts', but his feet made no sound as he trod; only the footsteps of the Warriors could be heard.

Suddenly, the boy reached up and slipped his tiny hand into that of his father. For the android, it was a practice that it found foreign, but it was a convenient one and so it humoured it. Mela-14 looked down at its ward, unwittingly squeezing the boy's hand reassuringly. ATB-80 smiled at the android's expressionless face and, although there was no physical change in his father's features, he could feel the android smiling back at him. As they walked down the corridor, ATB-80 continued to peer up into Mela-14's face. The lights of the corridor exaggerated the translucency of its skull so he could see the components in its head and sense all the electronic impulses coursing through them.

Mela-14 did not look back at him. Its thoughts were far away. It was thinking about the latest conundrum that the boy had presented it with: an apparent lack of fear that threatened his very existence. It recalled the events of the previous day when they were on the flight deck.

They had just finished a piloting lesson, had left the Targa behind and were walking back across the deck. A weapons shipment was being delivered and ATB-80's attention was drawn by the Warriors that were orchestrating its arrival. Some seven metres above them, the cables that held one of the loads began to creak. Mela-14 had glanced up to see the cable protesting and beginning to shear. Instinctively, it had reached for ATB-80's hand, but it was too late. He had already gone. Like a panicked parent, Mela-14's head had whipped around frantically searching for its ward. Its eyes had found him quickly, but it didn't calm it. In fact, it was horrified.

ATB-80 had run into the area directly underneath the shipment and was stood gazing up at it, watching the steel threads of the cable twang free. A Warrior, also seeing the predicament, shot forward to grab the boy, but just at that moment the cable snapped, the cage broke open, and the containers rained down. The first hit the Warrior squarely from above and crushed it into the floor like a tin can. Broken plates of gold-coloured metal exploded off it like a firework going off and smaller bits of Warrior pinged across the floor. Then the bullets began to fly, discharging from the crushed Warrior's in-built weaponry. As they ricocheted off the walls, the aircraft and other Warriors, the cage relinquished more of its load. Its containers beat against the floor, bouncing and breaking open. The missile cartridges, bursting from the containers, were catapulted high into the air and across the floor. More Warriors leapt in to try to reach ATB-80, but they too fell foul of the downpour. One Warrior was thrown backwards by a small explosion. Another lay face down on the floor, both its legs blown off. The remains of one arm hung limply from its shoulder. Bits of wiring and mechanism trailed from the bottom of its body like bloody intestines, with red oil spilling out of its guts. Yet still it followed its directions to save the boy, dragging itself across the floor. A cartridge finally finished it off, crashing down in between its shoulder blades. The remains of its body folded up around the impact point like a pie casing, and the lights of its eyes were extinguished.

Beneath it, amidst it all, ATB-80 dodged and ducked the projectiles. He was laughing and shrieking with excitement all the while.

And Mela-14? It couldn't move. Its feet were fixed to the spot, and its limbs would not respond to its commands. It felt like every fluid ounce of lubricant had been drained from its systems. Nothing would move. Nothing would respond. All the alerts its systems had seemed to be going off at once, but none of them were. It felt... but androids did not feel, and that was part of the quandary. That, and the boy itself.

Any normal child would have been terror stricken, but ATB-80 was not a normal child. He was raised amongst androids as an android; 'manufactured' without fear—a choice Mela-14 now questioned. Fear kept 'blood-things' alive. It told them when to run and when to hide, but ATB-80 had none of that wisdom. He was not a machine like Mela-14; he could not simply be downloaded back into a new body to pick up from where he left off. Blood-things had to be grown from a single cell, and that took time. What odd things blood-things were, but the world was ruled by blood-things—the blood-Sallows, the Sallow-Council that were his creators and his masters.

The boy squeezed his father's hand and Mela-14 felt a small surge of something. Was it an energy spike, a lubricant issue? It ran its diagnostics again but, as usual, nothing showed up. It was probably just its processors working overtime, trying to work out what its ward was thinking or doing or planning, trying to get to grips with the child's logic—or lack of it.

Suddenly, they stopped. They'd arrived at the cells on the Training Deck and a third Warrior stepped out from the doorway to greet them. ATB-80 leant into Mela-14's bodywork and placed his hand on his father's chest, just above its main processor unit. It was an odd gesture even for ATB-80. One might have thought that ATB-80 felt some fear of the Warrior that towered in front of him and was seeking

14

reassurance, but Mela-14 knew differently. It looked down at its ward and was not disappointed. There was no fear in him. He stood looking at the Warrior with nothing in his eyes, nothing whatsoever. So what was he doing? What was the meaning of the gesture? And then Mela-14 brushed it all aside as nonsense. It was being paranoid.

That worried it too.

The Warrior held out its hand to ATB-80. In it was an Uldaker, a type of handgun, and one of the many weapons that ATB-80 had been trained to use. This one fired bullets of hard blue light. Its advantage over a traditional handgun that fired metal projectiles, was that its bullets would not penetrate the walls of the ship where a breach could be catastrophic, but it was equally as damaging as metal bullets to a living organism, if not more so. It could even take out a Warrior if you hit it in the right place.

This Uldaker was smaller than normal having been especially designed for the small hand of ATB-80, but it still retained all the power of the full-sized model. ATB-80 took it and his hands moved swiftly over it, checking it like the trained soldier that he was. He knew the weapon well; he used it daily during practise sessions. Once he had satisfied himself as to its fitness, he looked up at Mela-14 who gestured for him to enter the room. He obeyed, and Mela-14 followed in behind.

Inside, sat a little girl in the middle of the floor. She looked lost and alone in the otherwise empty room, as empty and sterile as the one in which he himself had been born, but he didn't remember that, or the woman with whom he had shared his cell.

The girl was probably about the same age as he and if she was afraid, she didn't show it, but there the similarities between them ended. She had gypsy-black hair and olive skin, but little else in the way of beauty about her. Her mouth was thin, her nose slightly crooked and her eyebrows were uneven. She had dirty bare feet and wore layers of ragged clothing to keep her decent. As they approached, she looked up. Her eyes flicked across the two of them in turn, and then they fixed upon him. He could see the side of her neck now and, although the light was meagre, he could make out a mark there. It wasn't a finely etched tattoo like the identity marking on his own arm, but a handmade one scratched amateurishly into her neck with ink and a sharp object. It was the letter 'V' written in Arabidan, an ancient language from an ancient people; but she was not an Arabidan, so why the letter? And in the same instant that he asked himself the question, the answer came to him.

It was the sign of the Vaigrani.

The Vaigrani were considered a very powerful and dangerous people because of what they were. They were not a race and they were not a society. They were a faction of people, usually nomadic, borne out of wars. They were those who had nothing more to lose other than their own life. Torn by the grief of their losses, they had sworn to help others to keep that which they had once cherished and were prepared to lay down their lives for that cause. Thus, driven by their own sadness into foolhardy errands for others, they were the strongest of Warriors and the most formidable of foe; but they were not a threat to the might of the Sallow Empire because they lacked organisation and ambition.

The boy pondered how he knew these things but then, as the girl moved and the mark disappeared into the creases of her neck, he resurfaced from his reverie. She continued to look directly at him, directly into his eyes. For a moment, they captured him, and then he heard her voice in his head.

15

He knew it was her voice just because he did, and he knew it was in his head because her lips didn't move. He felt something stir within him, something from the past—a memory perhaps, but like a wisp of smoke in the air, as the fingers of his mind reached out to grasp it, they passed through it, and it was gone.

Yet her words were crystal clear: *'One man's end is another man's beginning...'*

ATB-80 shivered. The cool hand of Mela-14 fell gently upon his shoulder and he was startled, just a little. He began to turn to look at his father and then he felt the gentle kick of the Uldaker as it went off.

With his enhanced reactions, his head snapped back towards the girl and he saw the ball of blue light cross the room. He saw it smack into her forehead. He saw her body thrown across the floor like a rag doll, spinning, with blood spraying out of her head and spiralling into the air like a Catherine Wheel until she impacted against the far wall and came to rest. Her limbs were twisted unnaturally about her, and her body twitched violently for a moment whereupon the two sides of her head separated, split in two like a melon cleft in half with a machete. Then she lay still, and he could see the whitish-grey of her brain matter doused in red blood. One of her eyes rolled out across the floor. She'd had blue eyes.

It had happened so quickly and yet, for ATB-80, it had happened so slowly.

"Very good, child," said Mela-14, and indeed, the android was pleased. It was a nice, clean, deliberate kill. It helped to prove that the prototype, despite its appearance, was not humanoid and that it remained detached from humanity. Mela-14 took the boy's hand and began to lead him away. As they passed the Warrior, ATB-80 disarmed and secured the weapon and handed it over. The Warrior tipped its head subserviently.

On the way back to his quarters, ATB-80 was silent and methodical. He hadn't meant for the gun to go off, but it didn't bother him that it had. It didn't bother him that he had taken a life. He didn't understand what life was. What was bothering him was that little bit of familiarity. He was still clutching for that wisp of smoke, but no matter how hard he tried, he just couldn't quite grasp it. So engrossed was he in this that he didn't register the second Scientific that joined them in the corridor, or the conversation it had with his father who confirmed that they were ready for the next stage and to start making the necessary preparations.

* * * * *

That night he dreamt. ATB-80 had never dreamt before, not as far as he was aware anyway. He dreamt of flying horses with eyes that shone like stars, wings that beat like thunder and golden hooves that struck lightning as they dashed across the skies.

CHAPTER 3

Next morning, ATB-80 awoke with a headache and while he usually awoke with a headache, this one was different. It was more severe. It was pounding. As he lifted his head, waves of nausea washed over him and drove him to bury it back into the pillow. He made a couple more attempts but each time suffered the same effects and slumped back. After the third attempt, he just wanted to give up but he kept reminding himself that the sooner he was up and in the shower, the sooner it would go. He always felt better after a shower. It was as if the pelting hot water purified him, washing away the pain, so gingerly he made a final attempt. Gently, he swung his legs over the side of the bed and sat up slowly, scrubbing at his face with his hands as he did so.

He felt awful—much, much worse than usual. Every time he moved his head, even just a little bit, the room whizzed around uncontrollably, continuing to spin long after he'd stopped turning his head, and then suddenly, it would jerk violently back into place. The whole experience was very disconcerting but, in rather the same way that you keep prodding a mouth ulcer with your tongue even though you know it's going to hurt, ATB-80 kept moving his head in experimentation. It was, after all, a most peculiar sensation.

Finally, having determined that the effect hadn't diminished and probably wasn't going to, he decided that he really, really needed to get into the shower. ATB-80 began rising to his feet but another rush of nausea took hold of him, and he fell heavily back onto the bed. He closed his eyes, took some long, deep breaths, and lay very still to try to keep the room steady. As he lay, his thoughts began to wander back into the night before and suddenly, his dream was broken. He remembered the story of the horses of Igdaleana, with *'eyes that shone like stars, wings that beat like thunder and golden hooves that struck lightning as they dashed across the skies'*. He smiled to himself. It was a happy memory and in his mind's eye, he could see the fantastic beasts once more, rearing up and pawing at the air with their golden hooves. Bearing in mind he'd never seen such beasts, the detail he recalled was incredible: the long, fine silky whiskers around their muzzles, the feathery socks that draped like curtains around their hooves and the chestnuts by their knees. How could he have imagined creatures in such detail? He hadn't. He knew he hadn't. The horses of Igdaleana were real. Just as real as Arcus...

'Beware Arcus, the beautiful, olive-skinned goddess of the Giarrri people, with her burning red hair. She carries a huge longbow across her shoulders and travels the

17

lands alone, but even a warrior needs the company of a mate from time to time and so, when the desire takes her, she selects a single arrow from her quiver, shoots it from her bow and races after it. It doesn't matter in which direction she aims because the arrow will always find its way and lead her to her next suitor. Having found him, she will seduce him and then, after her night of passion, she will abandon him to bear and rear her child alone. Beware of women with burning red hair!'

No, that wasn't right! Arcus wasn't real! Arcus was a legend! A story told by generations of Giarrri, told from parent to child—but how did he know the story? Nobody here told him stories. Here, he learnt only facts—cold, hard facts. Yet this story? He remembered it exactly as it had been narrated to him, and remembering gave him a warm, comforting feeling inside; but attached to it was another more wispy memory. Just like the one that had haunted him yesterday when he had remembered the Vaigrani.

'Tatoom has three suns. It orbits two of them while the third sits on the edge of the solar system, in one of its own. It is a bizarre arrangement with the two systems' planetary paths weaving in and out of each other, pulling and tugging at each other's planets and moons. Their varying sizes and masses form equilibrium in the gravitational pulls so that all the planets in the systems follow their paths without collision, but it's a very delicate balance, and the result is that the seasons vary in length from one cycle to the next, as do the years and the days. Each day has twenty-two hours and each hour, eighty-eight minutes. A minute is divided into seconds that are measured against the heartbeat of a cow at rest, and so a minute may be as short as eight or as long as sixty-six seconds. Time is a very complicated affair and only for those who can afford experienced mathematicians to calculate it—namely the Emperor.

'They say that Tatoom's mathematicians are the greatest mathematicians of all time, and this is probably true. They sit, forecasting the calendar for the years ahead; for hour upon hour with abacuses, pencils and charts, determining the length of each day; calculating how to fit the twenty-two official hours of the Imperial Calendar into those days. At the beginning of each year, the calendar and clock are published and sold to the people, and the revenue pays the mathematicians' wages and fills the Imperial coffers. This is the way it has always been, for a thousand centuries, in all its absurdity.

'However, there is a second clock at work: the Common Clock. A clock where the minutes and hours are of fixed length and only the number of hours in the day varies. It is one that can be measured by an affordable and easy-to-understand timepiece ticking away the regular hours and minutes: a minute lasting seventy beats of a resting cow's heart, and an hour, seventy minutes. As soon as the rim of the sun no longer touches the horizon, the day has begun and so has Hour One. The number of hours in the day has thus become the variable.

'But it raises no revenue for the Emperor and thus it is illegal despite its popularity, every citizen becoming a criminal with its use. So when the Emperor Frollandicus decided to abandon the Imperial Calendar and legalise the Common Clock, you would have thought the people would have welcomed it with open arms, but no. Tatoomians are sticklers for tradition and the Imperial Calendar is one of their oldest traditions along with the Imperial mathematicians. There were riots in

the street and protests, and eventually a coup. The common people stormed the Palace and hung the Emperor Frollandicus from the hands of his new clock and, the following day, his younger brother Eradicus became Emperor. The Imperial Calendar was reinstated and everything returned to normal—or so it seemed. The irony is that when the mathematicians started their calculations again, they found that they had made an error. They had miscalculated the year by two whole days. The mistake was hastily debated and the days 'lost' in the chaos of the coup. They claim that nobody outside of the mathematicians' circle ever knew, except for the Emperor of course—and he knew better than to argue the point.'

So many stories, legends and myths filling his head, all being recalled just as he had been told them, but where had he heard all these tales and when?

Their recollection made him feel safe and secure; sensations that he had not felt in a long time—if he had ever felt them at all. Yet he did remember these feelings from somewhere deep within his past, and so he kept reaching back, clawing desperately at his memories to try to place them. But, like the familiarity he had felt after yesterday's kill, he couldn't quite grasp it, and as each tale finished, the warm and comfortable feeling dissipated until he recalled the next tale, and so he recalled them one after the other.

'There are two forces at work in our existence—the forces of Lite and the forces of Daerk; but do not confuse them with gods, for there are no gods, only entities who believe themselves to be such.'

ATB-80 sat up. That was not a story. That was... philosophy? Yet it belonged with the stories. It was part of them.

His mind was spinning. He still felt nauseous and peculiar. Even his thoughts were odd—as though they weren't his own. He was a six-year-old boy and these thoughts were too complex and too deep to be his. He was reasoning things through in a more sophisticated fashion. He was searching his mind logically for the source of the stories, and...

His head hurt so much.

ATB-80 shook himself intentionally to exacerbate the pain and break himself free from the train of thought. He looked around his room. That was strange too and yet, still the same.

It was the same bed and next to that was the same living area with two comfy chairs and a small table. This swept around the corner into a range of storage cupboards fitted with shiny white doors that included his wardrobe and then a further door into the bathroom. On the next wall was a study area with computer consoles, a swivel chair and workbenches with various half-finished projects strewn across them. They were spacious quarters... although not quite as spacious as they had seemed yesterday. The room felt to have shrunk, except for the floor, which seemed to be further away than usual. The ratios were all wrong!

With his temples still swathed in the palms of his hands, he stood up. The floor zoomed even further away from him and he lost his balance. ATB-80 swayed erratically and his arms flailed about furiously to steady himself. Display activated— an assortment of readings and monitors that flashed before his eyes overlaying his normal vision. Indicators of roll, pitch and yaw helped him regain control and steady himself until the sensation passed. He looked at his feet. Distance indicators showed that they were 0.732 metres further away than yesterday. That couldn't be right. His eyes swept the room again and Display calculated its size. It was the same as it had always been, so he looked back to his feet—still 0.732 metres further away.

Another deep wave of nausea swept over him, and he felt hot and sweaty. Display initiated more indicators, this time for temperature, both internal and external. He was one degree above norm. Nothing serious but he felt the urge to cool his face and wash away the wooziness, so he made his way to the bathroom somewhat gingerly, like a kid with his very first hangover.

Having reached the sink, he ran the cold tap and began to splash his face in handfuls of water. It was as cool and refreshing as it had promised. He filled the bowl. Even that was different. He seemed to be looking down upon it. It made him feel sick again, so he turned Display off before it could register anything else. Display was useful, but it also got in the way and was irritating. All those numbers, readings and indicators overlaying his normal vision, half of which he didn't understand anyway.

Once full, he dunked his head into the sink and held it there, breathing in the crystal cool freshness of it, letting it bathe him inside as well as out, and then he pulled his head up and wiped the streaming water from his face with his hands. His mouth filled with de-oxygenated water, painlessly and effortlessly regurgitated from his secondary gill-lungs. He spat it into the sink. The light-headedness was beginning to wane. The nausea was subsiding and the headache was finally diminishing, but he still felt... different.

He opened his eyes, looked into the mirror and gasped.

Yesterday morning, when he had looked into the mirror, he had been greeted with the familiar reflection of a little boy with neatly groomed, ash-white hair, but what looked back at him now was the face of a virtual stranger.

In the mirror was a teenager with long, tangled light blue hair. The face was pale like his and the eyes—the deep emerald green eyes with the slightly elongated pupils—they were his too, but the rest of it was barely recognisable. He re-initiated Display to measure the relational distances between his own features and those of the reflection in the mirror, comparing them. Conclusion: the face was his, but older!

He leant closer into the mirror and pulled at his chin with his fingers, turning his head from side to side, examining himself more closely, and then he pulled up the sleeve of his shirt to expose the tattoo on his arm, his identification number— ATB-80. Yes, this was definitely him, but how much time had passed since what seemed like yesterday? Had he lost his memory? What was the date? He prompted Display to access the DaerkStar's main computer to check date and time. Server responded instantaneously. Three days had passed! A whole three days! Just three days?

ATB-80 heard the door to his quarters slide open and started at the noise. That would be his father. He went to see.

Indeed, it was his father. Mela-14 had entered the room with two boxes in its arms. It gave a fleeting glance to ATB-80 but said nothing as it carried the boxes across the room to the wardrobe and set them down on the floor. It lifted the top box, which was empty, and placed it beside the other, which was sealed.

"Are you well, child?" it asked.

ATB-80 said nothing. Was the android completely stupid? Had it not noticed its son's physical change? He strode purposefully back into the bathroom to check his reflection in the mirror. No, he wasn't imagining it; he had definitely changed. He went back into the main room.

Mela-14 had opened the wardrobe door and was removing his clothes from it. Each piece it folded neatly before placing it in the empty box, and then, having finished removing every last item from the wardrobe, it closed the box and sealed it. It then took the second box, opened it and began taking out new clothes, bigger clothes, that it placed on hangers back into the wardrobe. That could only mean that Mela-14 not only knew what to expect when it came into the room that morning, but had prepared for it too.

Having finished its chore, Mela-14 placed the full box inside the empty one and turned to ATB-80. It was still waiting for a response to its question.

"I asked if you are well?" it repeated.

"I don't know," said a man's voice. ATB-80 stepped back, putting his hand to his throat. He crashed into the swivel chair behind him, stumbled and fumbled as he steadied it. It wasn't his voice either!

"What's..." He cleared his throat and began again. "What's going on?" he asked, still trying to clear his throat but to no avail.

His voice was deeper and fuller than it used to be, the voice of an adult male instead of that of a little boy. He was confused and disoriented. Was this him, or was this someone else in him, or was he in somebody else?

Mela-14 picked up on his distress and approached. From within its robes it produced a medical scanner and swept it up and down ATB-80, hovering momentarily at his head and chest. It studied the readings and then reported, "There is nothing to be concerned about. Everything is as it should be."

ATB-80 felt his mouth open and words tumbled out indiscriminately.

"As it should be?" he squealed indignantly. "Have you taken a look at me this morning? I'm about ten years older. I've grown up overnight! I'm a bleeding adult!"

Along with his youth, his self-control was gone. Mela-14, on the other hand, remained composed.

"Yes, I have looked at you this morning, and yes, you have grown up, but not overnight. The accelerated growth process has taken place over a period of three days, but no, you are not an adult, not yet. You are, as you pointed out, just ten years older—approximately that is. That makes you an adolescent, a juvenile—a developmental stage at which I personally believed it was a mistake to pause the process at."

"A mistake? A mistake? Who are you bleeding kidding?"

"That is not a tone to which I am accustomed, child," chided the android stiffly.

"Well, get accustomed to it!" he shouted and stomped off into the bathroom, slamming the door behind him. He slumped over the bathroom sink and began to sulk. After a few moments though, he realised the absurdity of this action. He was now shut in his bathroom with Mela-14 in his living room. It didn't matter if he stayed in there for a minute, a day or a month. When he left the bathroom, the android would still be there, as if no time at all had passed. ATB-80 bent down, rested his elbows on the vanity unit and buried his head between his forearms. He laughed weakly to himself and stood up. The mirror over the sink reflected his image back at him. He grinned at himself. He was quite tall and, actually, he liked what he saw. He smiled, but that didn't resolve the predicament that he was in, so he turned, perched on the edge of the sink and thought some more.

His brain was in turmoil. He couldn't think straight. He felt angry, and thinking about that anger made him more so. He was tense and agitated and had to force himself to think logically.

He wanted answers and Mela-14 had them. He could waste a few hours sitting in here sulking, which would get him absolutely nowhere, or he could go out and ask his questions. And, if time was slipping away from him this fast, the sooner the better.

"Oh, bollocks," he mumbled to himself, and opened the bathroom door.

On the other side, it was just as he had expected. Mela-14 was sat in one of the comfy chairs waiting for him, looking somewhat smug. Anger rose in ATB-80 again. He forced it down inside of himself. It was not something he was used to, neither the anger nor the smugness of the android. Suddenly he wanted nothing more than to wipe that silly grin off that damned android's face with one quick smack of his fist. In fact, why not, and he found himself striding over to the android and grabbing it by the lapels, lifting it easily to its feet.

"Okay, let's get one thing straight," he hissed. "I'm not happy, and I want an explanation."

"Hmm," buzzed the Scientific thoughtfully. "As I say, this is a stage in humanoid development that I suggested we by-pass for these very reasons," and with that, it placed its hands firmly around ATB-80's wrists and skilfully twisted his hands away from itself, driving him effortlessly down onto his knees. ATB-80 squealed in pain like a dog. With a final flourish the android flung ATB-80 backwards, releasing its grip. ATB-80 fell awkwardly and landed painfully. He twisted clumsily on the floor to untangle his legs from beneath his body and lay nursing the small of his back with his hand.

"You know, my spine isn't designed to bend that way," he snapped.

"Of course I know, child. I also know exactly how much force is required to break it. Perhaps you should remember that next time you wish to assault me?"

"What a loving parent you are," ATB-80 sneered sarcastically.

"I believe there is a humanoid expression: *spare the rod and spoil the child.*"

"*He that spareth his rod, hateth his son,*" ATB-80 corrected, still wincing. He sat up, arching his back to relieve the pain there. "Go on then, spoil me," he challenged. "Tell me what's happening."

Mela-14 tipped its head to one side expectantly.

"Please," added ATB-80 begrudgingly. The word burnt like acid in his mouth— and his pride. If the android had a mouth, it would have smiled with it, but it didn't. Not that it mattered. ATB-80 felt it smile.

"You grow too slowly," the android began as it sat back down into the comfy chair. It took the scanner out again, but this time it placed it on the table in front of it and crossed its legs. ATB-80 noted that it had left the scanner open and that it was continuing to take readings. Mela-14 waved a hand at the second, vacant chair, and ATB-80 knew that this was the cue for him to join it, but he was reluctant to do so. He didn't want to obey, so he sat on the floor, propping himself up, leisurely. Somehow though, he just knew that he would end up sat in the chair, but he really, really wanted to resist if only to show Mela-14 that he couldn't be bossed about. How stupid was that though? What the hell was he thinking?

Mela-14 interrupted his thoughts.

"I can wait all day if need be."

ATB-80 raised an eyebrow and scowled.

"And exactly how much older will I be at the end of the day if we wait all day?"

The android buzzed oddly, a sort of a cross between a cackle and a voice synthesizer with feedback. Was it laughing at him? ATB-80 continued to scowl, and they sat in the stalemate for a while.

"You know that if you want answers, you will have to oblige."

Nuts, thought ATB-80. His father was right.

"Let us not forget our manners, ATB-80. We are a civilised people. Come. Sit. Let us discuss the issue in a civilised fashion."

Reluctantly, ATB-80 got up and slunk over to the chair. He dropped down into it with his buttocks on the very edge so that he could lean back as sloppily as was possible. He rubbed his chin nervously with his thumb. Mela-14 smiled at him despite its inanimate face, and all the more smugly it seemed. It glanced at the scanner and then began.

"As I say, a very difficult stage in humanoid life. From my studies, I understand that puberty is a very troublesome time for most species. A time of change that affects both body and mind. Hormones aiding the physical development from childhood to adulthood, that also confuse and confound. A time when the young feel they are competent and capable but are, in fact, at a point when they have the most to learn. A point when they are mentally at their most vulnerable."

Mela-14 unwittingly began to mimic ATB-80 and rubbed its chin with its thumb thoughtfully.

"You may conceive," it continued, "that you have the body and mind of an adult but what you actually have is a most volatile concoction of hormones and pheromones coursing through your veins, and at highly elevated levels, I might add. It is a side effect of the accelerated growth process. It should settle down in the next few days. For the moment though, this, coupled with your lack of experience and wisdom, makes you not only vulnerable but also highly obnoxious."

"Fuck off," said ATB-80.

"Yes, I believe profanity is the standard retort for a young man in your position."

"Fuck off!" he repeated.

"Very well. I shall leave you for a while to allow you time to recompose yourself."

"No!" shouted ATB-80 in frustration. That wasn't what he wanted at all! What he wanted was answers.

ATB-80 leant forward in the chair. He rubbed his eyes with the palms of his hands. He felt so out of control.

"So when you say fuck off, you do not actually mean fuck off?"

ATB-80 smirked. Hearing an android swear was rather like hearing a vicar fart—not that he'd ever met a vicar or even knew what one was, yet he did.

"I am curious," said Mela-14. "What is it that makes you use profanity?"

ATB-80 sighed.

"I don't know," he replied truthfully, frustration high in his voice. He flopped back into the chair and sighed heavily. He looked like a rag doll that had been thrown there, with his legs splayed apart and his back so badly positioned in the seat that it couldn't possibly be comfortable.

"Is it really agreeable, to sit like that?" Mela-14 asked, and then raised a hand to silence ATB-80 before he could respond. "Try," it advised, "thinking before responding. You need to start thinking before you speak. You have to regain control of yourself. A lack of self-control is a defect in an android that cannot be tolerated."

ATB-80 conceded. He reluctantly repositioned himself in the chair, casually crossing his legs so that the ankle of one rested on the knee of the other. As he did so he realised that, yes, it was a lot more comfortable, but he hated himself for having admitted it, even to himself.

"You have been flooded with ten years worth of hormones in three days but none of the knowledge or experiences that would normally be associated with them. A whole wealth of data has been downloaded into you that you have yet to organise and process. You have to adjust to these new circumstances and assimilate the new data. Thus, for the moment, while you are doing this, I shall forgive you your outburst, but you must regain your self-control if this project is to continue."

ATB-80 gave a deep rumbling noise borne out of his frustration and anger. He felt really tense and irritable.

"So, are you saying that I feel like this because of what you've done?"

"Yes."

"But I will adjust?"

"You are already adjusting. You have assessed the situation. You are responding and rewriting your program to take into account the new parameters of your condition. Biologically, your adrenalin and hormone levels are returning to normal— normal for an adult male, not a child, that is. You will find some differences. You have a complicated set of data to analyse and a whole new set of emotions and thought patterns. With this highly complex combination of events, you are currently pondering the situation and feeling angry, irritable and frustrated. You know that any effort to resist or protest will be futile, no matter how ardent and fervent, but you also wish to set a stance. You do not want to lose face and thus feel that you must stand by your initial outburst and continue, but you also know that to pursue that course of action would be illogical, unbeneficial and quite probably lethal. What an extraordinary dilemma that must be for you?"

"Yes, thank you, it is," ATB-80 replied somewhat sarcastically. He closed his eyes and leant his head against the back of the chair. After a few moments, he opened them again and looked at his father with its head tipped slightly to one side, smiling back at him with that faceless android smile. Despite everything, he could not help but smile back at his father. He really did love this damned android that had taught him everything he knew and who understood him so well.

"So tell me, Father," he grinned, "what's it like being a smug bastard?"

"Very nice, thank you. What is it like being a little shit?"

ATB-80 laughed. "Touché," he added.

"Pardon?"

"Touché—it means... oh, never mind. It's all a bit *'et tu Brute'*."

"I am sorry, I don't understand."

"No, neither do I," ATB-80 sighed despondently. "It's just crap in my head. I've got a headache and I'm talking crap. You were saying?"

"If you have finished digressing?"

"Yes, I've finished digressing, thank you."

"Then I may continue uninterrupted?"

ATB-80 opened his mouth to let out a smug remark like *'depends how much shit you gonna talk'*, but then thought better of it. He made a motion with his hand for his father to continue.

"As I was saying, personally, I would have taken your accelerated development beyond puberty and kept you in an unconscious state until you reached full adulthood, allowing you to stabilise, but there were other risks to consider. The advancement was simply too big to undertake in one bound. This is new technology and your mind, as well as your body, needs time to adapt to the changes before moving forward further. You need time to acclimatise before further acceleration."

"Further acceleration?" he exclaimed. "You mean you're going to do this to me again?"

"Yes, but not for a while. You need time for your neural pathways to adjust and redevelop, and for your programming to update... and the blood-Sallows felt you should experience some of what it is to be a blood—a humanoid."

"Humanoid?" he repeated the word softly. His father had been referring to him as that all morning but he wasn't humanoid; he was a Sallow. But as he caught sight of his reflection in the shiny glass surface of the door, his heart sank. It was true. He was not built of metal and plastic like his brothers, he was flesh and bone like the blood-Sallows of the Sallow Council. Yet he was not a blood-Sallow either. They were hideous creatures: flesh as black as coal and cracked like dried mud, with red eyes that burnt from deep within their skull and rows of needle-sharp teeth spilling from their mouths.

Suddenly, the physical differences between him and his Sallow brothers, metal or blood, were obvious to him. He looked more like the prey he hunted on the training decks and in the maze than a Sallow; and yet he thought like a Sallow, and he felt like a Sallow.

"Human," he repeated reluctantly.

"Yes. Well, let us say humanoid because you aren't actually human, are you? Your heart is Sallow."

"But my body isn't."

"No. We made you humanoid in appearance."

"So, I'm a skunk," he said with disdain in his voice.

"Yes, if you will, but a very special skunk."

ATB-80 huffed in contempt. Was it worse to be a skunk than a humanoid? Yes. He had been raised to despise humanoids all his life, but skunks he hated because they were impure. Skunks were the Sallow hybrids that contaminated his race. They were a mistake, created on the Science decks. They were the failed experiments from another era, bred to try to restore the Sallow physique that had been lost in the Sallow/Tarrow-Man wars—

—and suddenly ATB-80 was somewhere else...

He could hear Mela-14's voice distantly in the background, but it was fading away fast, and now he was now stood in the middle of a silent battlefield—the aftermath—filled only with the dead of what he knew were Sallows and Tarrow-Men.

The Sallows were tall and muscular beings dressed in gladiatorial finery, not like the squat, hunched over, puny little Sallows of today. Their black flesh, greased with sweat, shone like obsidian in the sunlight, and their deep red blood, splashed across their muscular torsos, was seeping away into the sand. Their red eyes no longer shone with life but stared blankly upwards into the sky, and the ravens scavenged upon their perfect bodies.

The Tarrow-Men were tall also, but more slender with long, lean limbs. Their heads were squat and fat like toads and balanced precariously on top of long, thin necks decorated with dozens of neck rings. Their eyes, too, gazed blankly in death: bulging, straw yellow eyes, spliced in two by a black pupil that in life had constantly dilated and contracted. The one at ATB-80's feet had its mouth open. It was such a big mouth, spanning the whole of its swollen, flat head and filled with rows of uneven, sharp, needlepoint teeth and a spongy, swollen green tongue. Its flesh was khaki-green, camouflaged with shots of blue and red veins.

Their bodies trailed down into great holes dug into the sandy earth, into the Tarrow-Men's burrow-cities. This was the land of the Tarrow-Man: a desert-like region where they could bask in the sun during the day and hunt the warm-blooded creatures that formed their prey after dusk; prey so often eaten alive.

'Once, they found their perfect union with the Sallows, but it was not to last. Both desired to be the Masters of their lands, and so it was that the marriage became an imperfect one, and they battled against each other for divorce and supremacy; a battle that neither race won.'

"ATB-80? ATB-80? Can you hear me, child?"

ATB-80 broke from his reverie to find his father waving its hand before his eyes.

"Huh?"

"Child, you did not seem able to hear me?"

"Uh. No. Sorry. Just thinking, that's all," he said, still distracted. He brushed the images aside and continued as though nothing had happened. "But Sallows hate skunks."

"Yes, but some are special, and you are a very special skunk. You are the *Destroyer Series, Mark-I (Espion)*—a prototype hybrid."

"Oh."

Mela-14 looked at him quizzically. A little red signal from Display flashed in the periphery of ATB-80's vision. It was annoying and aggravated his headache, so ATB-80 ignored it and turned it off.

"That is odd. Are you not familiar with the term? You should know all this. Can you not access Server? Your access should have been updated."

ATB-80 tried his access, but it made his head hurt to try and the pain showed in his face. Mela-14 looked at him, concerned, and then picked up the scanner. It studied it and then ATB-80.

"No," he finally replied. "Display isn't responding well. I don't have access at the moment. It hurts when I try."

Mela-14 pulled itself forward in the chair until it was poised on the edge of it.

"Hmm," it said. "That means something is wrong. Your access is automatically updated as you progress. If your access has not been updated then Server may have detected an anomaly in your systems. Run Data-Access Diagnostic Program Four."

Obediently ATB-80 accessed the code—and then screamed in agony!

His head was filled with a sudden bolt of pain that shot behind his eyes. Display cut in again, but this time the information was overwhelming. Display had taken over the whole of his vision, blinding him with its brilliance and sheer quantity of data.

Information was scrolling frantically from side to side and from top to bottom, layer upon layer of data. Too much to analyse! Too much to handle! The light! The data! The information! There was screaming in his ears. The buzz of electronic transmissions pounded against his eardrums from inside his head. He was vaguely aware of Mela-14's voice in the background, but he couldn't make it out. He could hear his own voice screaming, but it was almost drowned out by the transmission noises, and then...

* * * * *

"ATB-80! ATB-80! ATB-80!"

As he awoke, he found that his father was bent over him, cradling his head in its hands and staring into his eyes. The world was dim, grey and unfocused. He was oddly aware of how plain, blank, cold and colourless the android's face was, and yet he could see—no feel—the concern in its mannequin eyes.

"Child? Can you hear me?"

He could hear the words, but his ears were still ringing.

"Yes," he murmured and began trying to get up, but Mela-14 held him down, shushing him, encouraging him to stay still.

"Child, what happened?" it asked.

"I think..." he started.

Display cut in with a few choice words. He simply read them.

"Re-indexing in progress," and then he passed out again.

27

CHAPTER 4

When consciousness finally returned to ATB-80, it was dark. Was it night-time? Where was he? In the background, he could hear voices. They were arguing.

As he became more lucid, his systems reactivated. Display responded with night vision and began a reconnaissance of the area. His night vision was poor, its ability diminished by the lights at the periphery of his sight. He activated his echolocation software and began scanning the room for its boundaries.

The room was large and circular. There were two exits from it: one behind his head and slightly to his left, the other below him and to his right. He was laying 1.07 metres from the floor and the ceiling above him was domed. The lights and voices were coming from the exit towards his feet.

That was more than enough information for him to identify his location. He was lying in one of the surgical facilities—a theatre with an observation deck above. By the dimensions of the room, it had to be one of the larger facilities in the labs on the Science Deck, more often used for the dissection of specimens. How many times had he dissected a life form on one of these tables? He'd never anticipated being *on* one though.

He tried to turn his head, but it wouldn't move; but not due to any physical restraints. He couldn't feel any bonds or other forms of constraint holding him down, but he could feel the device resting on his forehead. A synaptic dislocation unit. Emitting a harmless electronic impulse, it isolated the messages from the brain to the body, rendering him paralysed.

"Father!" he called.

"I am here," droned the soft voice of his father. He heard his father's footsteps approach and felt the cool of its hand on his cheek.

"What is this? Why am I here?"

"We are running some tests on you."

"But why here?"

"We need to find out what happened to you, and the facilities here are better than..." Mela-14 fell silent.

"That sounds a little ominous."

His father smiled at him with its immovable face.

"And anyway, I know what happened to me."

There was a rustle of movement as the other androids approached and the lights above him exploded into full brilliance, blinding him. ATB-80 snapped his eyes shut against the pain and winced. He tried to turn his head away, but couldn't. Mela-14 saw his reaction and shouted furiously to its associates. Immediately, the lights were dimmed again.

Three faces lent down over him—Mela-14, Jordan-4 and Jordan-5. It was very claustrophobic and intimidating. His systems reacted, analysing the situation, identifying the potential dangers and entered battle-mode. Was he here to be fixed or dismantled? The Sallows had wanted an android that behaved like a human but having got that, was he too human for them? Should he point out this irony to the Sallows and share his concerns, or would that be too human? Perhaps he should behave more like an android, but if he were more android-like he would not be able to infiltrate the humanoids and the project would be a failure. He would be useless. He would be terminated. This was a lose-lose situation, and it felt very bad indeed. His analysis continued.

The Scientifics, seemingly unaware that his systems had activated and that he was assessing them, also continued.

As ATB-80 thought through the options, another part of him was uploading the schematics of the synaptic dislocation unit, trying to work out how to disable it. He was also prioritising the attack order on the androids. He should take out Jordan-4 and Jordan-5 first. Mela-14 would be slower on the uptake because of its emotional attachment to him and that would buy him time.

What was he thinking? These were his brothers! And his own father!

"Well? What happened to you?" asked Jordan-5.

"Father?"

"Yes child. I am here."

ATB-80 paused. He had made his assessment and made a decision.

"This is not a good situation to place me in."

"What do you mean?"

"I asked a question," snapped Jordan-5, gently but forcibly pushing Mela-14 aside. It leaned closer over ATB-80's face, as though trying to look into his mind via his eye sockets. The urge to surge forward and take a chunk out of the android's face with his teeth was almost overwhelming. ATB-80 closed his eyes against the android and desperately pushed the urge back down inside him. Inside though, he knew that one day he was going to rip its head off with his bare hands and smash it against some hard, inanimate object. He smiled.

"It is smiling!" exclaimed Jordan-5. "Why is it smiling?" it demanded of Mela-14.

"Why do you not ask him?" suggested Mela-14. "After all, he is right there."

Jordan-5 jerked its head mechanically to one side in surprise and then stood erect.

"Hmm!" it puffed, and then turned back to the juvenile on the table.

"Why are you smiling?" it demanded.

Inside ATB-80's head, things were happening. His brain was 'tingling'. It was a queer mixture of numbness and over sensitisation. Rather like when you've been sitting on your leg for too long. When you get up, for a moment, your foot is numb and then, just as the pins-and-needles start to set in, it becomes highly sensitive to everything. You can feel the numbness and the pins-and-needles and everything else that touches your foot all at the same time. It made him feel slightly light-headed too.

The synaptic dislocation unit worked by disrupting the flow of the electrical impulses from the brain to the body, but it had to be specific. It had to permit certain instructions to pass: instructions to breathe and for bladder and bowel control for instance, otherwise he would have suffocated by now or be lying in a pool of urine. By rerouting the signals from his brain, could he regain some movement? No, not rerouting, otherwise he'd stop breathing. Could he piggyback signals along the same pathways as those for breathing? And having got the signals past the synaptic dislocation unit, could he reroute the right signals to move limbs? Schematics of nerve pathways were flashing through his head as he traced and retraced pathways, but could he even do this? Humans, he knew, couldn't, but he wasn't human. He was an android. Surely, it was just like rewiring a machine.

"ATB-80? Can you hear me?"

"Yes, Jordan-5. I can hear you."

"Then why are you smiling?"

"Because I am pleased."

ATB-80 grinned all the more. Jordan-5 was confused. It looked up at Jordan-4 and Mela-14, but neither of them could give it any indication as to what ATB-80 meant.

"Why are you pleased?"

ATB-80 thought he could move his fingers but wasn't sure.

"Because, my dear Jordan-5, your experiment is a wonderful success."

"It is a shame that we are not convinced."

"Then allow me to enlighten you. You—we—" he corrected, "—desire a weapon that looks and behaves like a humanoid, but isn't. A weapon with the heart of a blood-Sallow and the ruthlessness of an android-Sallow, and that is exactly what you have, but you are just too android to understand it.

"A humanoid would be lying here in fear, but I am not afraid, so I am not humanoid. An android would be lying here... well, what would an android be doing? Erasing its databanks for security purposes? It appears that I can't do that either. So what am I? Am I so human that I am untrustworthy, or so android that I can't fulfil my mission? What do you think, Jordan-5? What do you see when you look into my eyes? Humanoid or android? Come on, Jordan-5. Don't be shy. Come closer. Look at me. Take a really good look at me. Look really, really closely."

ATB-80's words ran slower and slower as he spoke.

"What do you see? Come on Jordan-5. Are you frightened to look at me? Do you find me that disturbing?" he goaded hypnotically. "Come on, Jordan-5. Closer, Jordan-5, closer." His voice had dropped to a whisper and the words were extra slow and deliberate, enticing Jordan-5 to lean in nearer to hear. "Closer... closer..." he said slowly, mesmerically.

Jordan-5 leant in closer still and whispered, "I am not sure I can get any closer ATB-80, not without cracking your skull open and crawling inside it, so what is it that you want to tell me?"

ATB-80 laughed lightly at it.

"You'd like that, wouldn't you? To crack my head open? Because you don't like this. You don't like this project. You don't like me, and you don't trust me. I'm just *too* humanoid for you, aren't I? I behave just *too much* like a human, don't I? And it worries you."

Jordan-4 and Mela-14 whispered concernedly to each other. They couldn't quite make out what ATB-80 was saying. He was talking too quietly, and his speech was quite hypnotic.

"And so here we are. Me, restrained on the very same table upon which we—yes, you and I—have dissected other humanoids. I am paralysed, and you want me terminated. You are relishing the opportunity to cut open my head and see just what work your little huma-nanites have done for you; and yet I do not fear you. I should do. You are a threat to me. You want me dead. Tell me I'm wrong, if you can."

"I cannot tell you that you are wrong because I believe that this whole experiment was a mistake," replied Jordan-4, equally as softly. "I do not believe that we can create anything as sophisticated and ruthless as this out of blood and tissue. I believe that blood and android are mutually exclusive. You are nothing more than another mistake in the Sallow history of genetic engineering. Of all the skunks, you are the king of skunks, a half-breed mistake; neither fish nor foul, and impure. Your very existence is an insult to the Sallow race. You should be terminated and all evidence of your ever being, destroyed. As an android, you are wrought with illogical programming errors from the blood-side of you. You are like a bug, a virus in our systems, a threat to our security and our very being. As a human, you are insane. You are nothing more than a machine, a defective machine that should either be fixed or turned off, and I have no desire to fix you. You are, at best, an abomination to our race and an insult, and at worst, you are kylem!" He spat the last word out.

"Kylem?" asked ATB-80. "Hmm. That's not a term with which I am familiar."

"It is a very, very old word from the days of the ancient blood caste system. It means literally nobody or nothing. They were the people at the very bottom of the caste system, not considered to be people at all. Untouchables. And that is what you are. Nobody. Nothing. Kylem."

"Thank you for telling me that. Now, tell me something else, Jordan-5. What would you do in my place?"

"Disabled as you are? In enemy hands? I would initiate self-destruct and destroy myself and my assailants, but you are not an android and are not equipped with a self-destruct mechanism, so I am quite safe."

"Safe? You're safe, are you? Are you really? Are you absolutely sure about that?"

"Absolutely positive, thank you."

"But would it please you to be wrong? Would it please you if your toy proved to be the efficient fighting machine that you want it to be? That it can be programmed and reprogrammed to deal with different circumstances? That it can learn from its mistakes and evolve into the best fighting machine the Sallow Empire has ever known?"

Jordan-5 was now so close to ATB-80 that it could feel the boy's breath on its face.

"No," it hissed.

"Then I'm sorry that you cannot terminate happy."

"Pardo—" but Jordan-5 never finished the word.

ATB-80 lunged forward. Jordan-4 and Mela-14 lurched back in surprise, knocking over the instrument trolley behind them as they stumbled, but not Jordan-5. It was too near to ATB-80.

Although still half paralysed, Kylem's right hand had sprung out and folded around the back of the android's head with a vice like grip. His taloned fingers crooked firmly under its chin, and he pulled the Scientific onto his chest, flipping it over so it was face upwards. Its feet were scraping across the floor, gaining no purchase, and its arms waved frantically in the air. Its neck was fully exposed as the boy's jaws wrenched themselves wide open. Huge canine teeth unsheathed like a snake's, and he lunged forward into the Scientific's neck, burying his teeth into the machine's throat. His hand released its grip momentarily. The talons withdrew back into the tips of his fingers for a moment, but then extended again as he lashed them back into the androids neck, ripping and shredding as they passed. The automaton froze, suddenly rigoured by death. Noise whizzed from it. Sparks popped and flashed like a Catherine Wheel. There was a hiss and little curls of smoke exuded from the huge hole rent at the base of its neck. There was a final twitch as ATB-80 wrenched its head free from the body. He let the corpse go, and it fell to the floor. Blue and green electric flashes spiralled from the huge gashes ATB-80 had made in the body, buzzing and screaming, burning out every circuit, melting components and wires. Small explosions split the Scientific's casing, and bits burst free to tinkle across the floor.

ATB-80, free of the weight of the scientific on his chest, sat upright with the head of Jordan-5 still in his hand. He was panting heavily. Red lubricant was smeared around his mouth like smudged lipstick. He wiped his mouth on the back of his sleeve and spat a mouthful of red oil onto the floor. He stared at Mela-14 and Jordan-4.

Mela-14 was on its feet helping Jordan-4 up, but both now froze to look at ATB-80. What would he do next? Which of them would he attack next?

Slowly, stiffly, ATB-80 turned on the bench to face them properly. The head was still in his hand. It buzzed and ATB-80 dashed it repeatedly against the corner of the bench. It was just as he had imagined it would be—him pounding it madly until the white plastic coating was shredded and burnt away, leaving only the shiny metal workings of the scientific gleaming in the bright theatre lights. With each blow, Mela-14 jerked in reaction, but Jordan-4 simply watched on.

Finally, he was done. Exhausted, he dropped the remains of the dented and bashed head onto the floor. Gently, he pulled the synaptic dislocation unit from his forehead and control rushed through the rest of his body. The surge of adrenalin sent his head spinning. He closed his eyes, threw his head back and drew a huge, deep refreshing breath of air. His head spun as chemicals kicked around his brain, and then, slowly, he opened his eyes and got off the table. He stood shakily in front of the two androids.

"And that, my dear friends," he breathed, "is how the *Destroyer Series, Mark-I (Espion)* reacts when you threaten it. And trust me, my dear friends, humanoids cannot reroute their synaptic pathways like that. Now, does anyone else fancy a pop?"

The two Scientifics looked on, still rigid with shock.

"No," Jordan-4 finally said, pulling itself to its feet.

"No, I didn't think so," hissed ATB-80. "Now if you'll excuse me, I've got a few neural pathways to route back to... well, wherever it was they grew in the first place."

ATB-80 got painfully off the bench and began to make his way unsteadily to the door, still panting heavily. His feet didn't seem to want to move as they should.

"I have not dismissed you!" boomed a voice from the observation lounge above. ATB-80 stopped. He knew the voice. It was Doobee, one of the blood-Sallows. He looked up, and the lights in the observation lounge brightened. Sure enough, the blood-Sallow was there looking down upon him. For a moment, their gazes fixed upon each other, and then the Sallow turned and disappeared from view. A few moments later, he appeared in the doorway. He entered the room with his eccentric, gory black robes glistening and swishing about his ankles as he circled the young man before him.

"Congratulations," he said. "I am both impressed and disappointed."

"Why disappointed?"

"You have destroyed a perfectly good Scientific."

"No, I destroyed a defective Scientific."

"How was it defective?"

"It doubted the wisdom of the Sallow Council in the approval of this project. It sought my destruction, solely to fulfil its own self-satisfaction. It underestimated the ability of my makers, and it underestimated me. *'Never underestimate your enemy'*— that is what I have been taught, and if I have learnt it, why didn't Jordan-5?"

"Jordan-5 is... was... not a Warrior."

"But I am."

"Yes," he said, still circling ATB-80. "I heard your conversation with Jordan-5. Some very interesting points made there. A very interesting perspective and one we shall enjoy discussing at dinner tonight."

"Eat well," said ATB-80, quoting the traditional Sallow regard.

"Yes, we shall. Don't be late," and he smiled grimly at ATB-80 and pushed past him, rows of little white needlepoint teeth flashing briefly in his mouth. He made as to leave the room, but at the doorway stopped and turned back to look at the boy again.

"Kylem?" he said thoughtfully. "Yes, I like that. The name fits. Perhaps it will remind you who... or rather what... you are. Don't be late... *Kylem*," he said, emphasizing the name, and then he was gone.

Kylem puffed himself up and smiled broadly.

Mela-14 came to his side.

"I would not smile if I were you, child. It is intended as an insult."

"I don't care," and he beamed with joy. "I have a name. Doobee has given me a name." He turned and looked into his father's eyes. "What did he ever give you? What's he ever given anybody other than a death warrant?" he asked triumphantly. "No, precisely. He's never given anybody anything, but he gave me a name—not a designation!—not a breeding number! A name!"

"Yes. Well. Congratulations then," said Mela-14 sarcastically, and stepped over the remains of Jordan-5. "Do not be late for dinner though," and it swept out of the room.

CHAPTER 5

Mela-14 scurried down the corridor towards his laboratory. He was deeply troubled by the events that had unfolded, and that was troubling in itself. Scientifics were designed to think independently, to problem-solve and to create, but not to feel. Was this a defect?

As the years had passed by perhaps the experiences and knowledge he had gained had made him a little more sentient, but what was it that defined sentiency? That when a being exceeds the sum of its parts it has gained sentiency? Or was that sapiency? The definition varied from culture to culture which meant that whilst one culture would call him sentient, another would just call him a machine, but how would his fellow Sallows categorise him and would the blood-Sallows want a sentient Scientific? Had Jordan-5 also displayed signs of sentiency by wanting the destruction of the Espion? If so, was the Sallows' android race developing into a sentient race of its own? And would the blood-Sallows permit that to happen? Would they want their servants to be more knowledgeable, stronger and thus more powerful than they were?

Androids could survive without blood-Sallows. For them—for him—they served no purpose. But could the blood-Sallows survive without the androids to serve their every whim, to fight their wars and harvest their food for them? Simply put, no, they couldn't. And these thoughts troubled him all the more. They were blasphemous.

Having reached his laboratory, Mela-14 went into his study area. He sat down in his big, comfortable chair, put his feet up on a little footstool and prepared to run diagnostics from Server. They were more thorough than his own internal diagnostics and being independent, if he had been compromised, Server would find the problem and rectify it. And then he stopped and reconsidered.

If he ran diagnostics from Server and there was a problem, it would be logged and then Doobee, as Head of A.I., would see it. Server would alert the blood-Sallows as to what he was, what he had become, but what had he become? Why hadn't it already been noticed?

But he knew why not, because he suddenly realised, he had ceased running the normal routines of an android. Yes, he ran regular internal self-diagnostics, but he had stopped Server diags, downloads and software updates. But when?

He accessed his personal databanks for the history, but there wasn't a definitive answer there. It had been a gradual process over the last few years, with him running those routines less and less frequently and deselecting more and more options.

The only thing that had changed over the last few years was—the Espion?

Was ATB-80—Kylem—the root of the problem? Was Jordan-5 right to be afraid of the project? Was the Espion's software defective, and was it making him defective? Machine and blood were, as Jordan-5 had so often said, mutually exclusive, and the attempt to make them meld was an ambitious one. After all, what they were attempting to do was take a blood-thing and turn it into a machine that would do their bidding, and that was a contradiction in terms. It would never be a machine. It would always be a blood-thing that could feel physically, if not emotionally. It would be susceptible to heat and cold, pain and comfort. It would live and die as all blood-things do. It might even procreate. Who knew? These were all things that he, as a machine, could not do. It was a huge divide to attempt to cross. Or was it? And he fidgeted at the arm of the comfy chair in which he sat. Why did he even *have* a comfy chair?

Mela-14 sat up, rummaged in his pocket and pulled out the medical scanner from earlier. He opened it to study the readings and sighed. They were odd. He took the scanner over to the big workbench in the middle of his lab, the tabletop of which was a large monitor, about two metres by four, surrounded by instrument panels. It was the height of computer technology and linked into almost every system on board the DaerkStar.

Slowly, deliberately and carefully, he disconnected the worktop from Server and then connected the scanner. The readings were anomalous to say the least, and disturbing. The Espion had changed its programming. It had instigated new firewalls and defences and had even changed the format of its files. That meant that the data downloaded during the accelerated growth process, had not instantly been added to its library. Kylem would have to access each file individually, categorise it and assimilate the data one piece at a time. How human, but why had it done that? By adding those constraints, the Espion could no longer assimilate data quickly, receive updates to its program or add new command structures.

Mela-14 buried his head in his hands as he realised that was exactly why Kylem would have done it. To stop the Sallows from changing it, from controlling it.

Not *it! Him!* Why did he think of Kylem as *'it'* and not *'him'*? Kylem was male and therefore a 'he', unlike himself who was genderless. Yet, he suddenly realised, he thought of himself as 'he' rather than 'it', but why? He didn't have a gender. Only the boy gave him a gender by calling him Father, and why was that? The boy had not been ordered to call him Father, but then the boy did many things he wasn't supposed to do. Playing dodge the exploding missiles on the flight deck, for instance. Where had the project gone wrong? And when had he become infected by this... virus. Was it a virus though, or was it evolution?

Mela-14 began to think back to the very beginning and called up the image of the first-born, the predecessor to the project: the foetus that should have been the Espion, but that had failed so miserably.

This child had been genetically engineered in exactly the same way that Kylem had but incubated in an artificial womb. The result had been horrendous. The foetus's DNA, engineered from numerous different races, had struggled within itself for dominance, and the huma-nanites had only exacerbated the situation. The resulting child was 'born' deformed and twisted, a small, puny albino hunchbacked boy. (It was still around somewhere. Perhaps he should take a closer look at it sometime.) And that was why it was decided the surrogate should be used. The genetic material was flawless upon conception but became unstable as the foetus developed. What was needed was something to give the foetus stability, and thus a young girl from the Tatoomian race was chosen. Her genetic makeup gave that added genetic stability and protection to the unborn child through a complex exchange of genetic material and antibodies in the amniotic fluid. And indeed, from that point of view, the experiment had been a success. The next child had not mutated, and its DNA had stabilised and remained stable throughout incubation, even when the huma-nanites were introduced.

Mela-14 studied the data twice to be sure, but still he could see no defects or anomalies.

He jumped to the records of the child's birth and the issue of the First Command—the very first instruction given to the Espion to ensure his allegiance to the Sallow race. It had been chosen with great care. They needed to pick a single word that would set the path and the way forward, a word that would bind it unerringly to the Sallows. That one word was 'OBEDIENCE'.

As soon as the child was born, it was extracted from the parent and, already flooded with huma-nanites whilst in the womb, the First Command was issued via its very first download. It had been such a simple process, and he recalled how the baby had stopped crying as the download started. It seemed to be mesmerised by the input, and then it had scowled before recommencing its crying. That done, the child was given back to the girl to nurse and feed with her milk rich in the natural antibodies that would help the child's immune system to develop.

Perhaps something had happened then that had compromised Kylem? Perhaps she had done something? But how could she have compromised the First Command? With a countermand before birth, perhaps?

Mela-14 checked his data, the videos and the readings. He checked the brain waves recorded from the foetus in the womb and saw the consistency throughout. The blank canvas waiting for the first brushstroke, and there were no anomalies. These recordings went right up to the birth itself, only ceasing once the child had left the womb, so he knew that nothing had happened prior to birth.

The birth then? Now, that had not gone according to plan. Mela-14 summoned the image of the prodigy's entrance into this world and watched as the girl birthed in complete silence with her back to the cameras, hiding the event from view. She had held the infant in her arms for only a few moments before Mela-14 had realised, entered the room with two Warriors and taken the child from her. Well, not *taken*, for as he watched the screen, he noticed now that as he had entered the room, she had held the child out to him.

This was a point he had not noted before. He had not had cause to. Initially, he had been concerned that she might try to hurt the child once it was born, but his worries were soon allayed by the care with which she had tied the umbilical cord with strips of her clothing and cut it with her teeth. She had swathed the boy in yet more of her clothing and kissed him gently on the side of his head before handing him over.

He replayed the scene repeatedly. Something wasn't quite right, but Mela-14 couldn't place what it was, so he rewound it and played it again and again. He became transfixed by the moment of the kiss. The one haunting kiss she had given her newborn just before they had taken him from her. The kiss ended up on a continual looped playback, and Mela-14 watched it repeatedly.

It was an odd sort of kiss, a little clumsy perhaps. He froze the video at the point where her lips were poised for the kiss, zoomed in and dimensionalised it so that the image was displayed, suspended vertically in the air in front of him like a frameless window. He stepped back and crossed his arms thoughtfully, tapping his chin with his forefinger. Her face now filled the screen in front of him, but it was not enough. He zoomed in twice more until just her mouth was on the screen and then, frame by frame, he played it again, straining to see what was so odd about the kiss. Was it really a kiss?

He zoomed in further still, but the definition was degrading. He began tapping furiously on the instrument panels to enhance the image and watched it again, peering even harder at it. Were they words?

There were just four barely distinguishable movements to her mouth, possibly syllables, but why couldn't he hear her voice? In all the time he had worked with her, he had never heard her speak, but that didn't mean that she couldn't speak; only that she didn't speak to him.

He ran a further search of the audio files on another console from the bench behind. He turned the volume fully up, but still he heard nothing more than dull background noise. He loaded the wave pattern onto the worktop. It flickered below the image of her mouth as he synchronised them. He could see some very subtle changes in the wave detail but it was little more than minor background noise, so her words—if they *were* words—were voiceless. But that would have been an impossible communication. They had tested the Espion for a telepathic link when she was terminated. That test had shown conclusively that such a link had not been established, so, if she had communicated anything, it must have been verbal.

Mela-14 began calling up images of other humanoids onto the surrounding monitors, zooming in on their mouths as they spoke. He was attempting a comparison. If he could isolate the mouth movements, could he isolate words?

The deafening babble of humanoid voices and the cacophony of images around him became excessive, but slowly, he narrowed down his search. Abruptly, Mela-14 cut the other monitors and the noise shattered into a deafening silence.

He was still not convinced that it was possible for her to have communicated a message to the boy, but if she *had* said something to him before the First Command was issued, could a simple instruction have been sufficient to be interpreted as the First Command? In which case, the Sallow command of obedience would have become the second. Was this why the project was failing?

He swapped the images around so that her mouth was on the flat worktop and the waveform on the vertical display. He compared the tiny peaks and troughs of the waves to her lip movements to isolate them visually, matching them to the other humanoids in an attempt to create a substitute sound track. By mirroring her lip movements and then matching the incredibly subtle changes in the waveform, could he do that? He tapped on the instrument panel again to discard all the unwanted parts of the waveform and then enhanced what he had left, playing with the controls to add definition to the words...

And then he had it! Her words—quiet, slow and deliberate; each one spoken by a different voice patched in from the other recordings:

"*Do... as... you... please.*"

Horrified, Mela-14 stepped back. If his mouth could have fallen open, it would have done. As it was, he could only stand in dumbstruck horror at the realisation.

The project was a failure! The Espion had been contaminated at birth. He should arrange for Kylem's immediate discontinuation and erasure of his software! But he didn't want to do that.

It was an emotional response; one he suddenly believed he had contracted from Kylem, so he too should be destroyed; but he didn't want to die. Could androids die? Was there an android heaven? He laughed feebly and then stopped abruptly, realising that androids don't laugh, can't laugh, shouldn't laugh.

He was a failure. The Espion was a failure.

Or was it? Was this the natural progression of things? Was this evolution? The Sallow race had once been strong and full of tonicity, but now, after the wars, they were weak and feeble beings that had developed the androids to serve them. Was it a form of natural selection? That the weak blood-Sallows were dying out and the androids were becoming more numerous? If the blood-Sallows did die out, who would lead the Sallow race of androids, or would they simply fall into disrepair? Was this why he was becoming sentient? And what about Jordan-5? It had certainly been emotional about the boy, but it had not had the same contact with Kylem that he had. Perhaps the experiment should continue. Perhaps he shouldn't be so hasty to terminate himself or the boy. Perhaps he should investigate further before making a decision. Perhaps there was something to be learnt from this after all.

Mela-14 accessed the worktop again. His hands moved swiftly over the keyboards, minimising the audio wave patterns and the images of the girl. He called up the original files from Server and transferred them onto the worktop. Then he reached for the medical scanner and docked it into the console. His hand hovered over the keyboard and then he pressed 'TRANSFER', then 'SAVE'—and then he pressed 'DELETE'.

CHAPTER 6

Kylem made his way back to his quarters slowly and somewhat painfully. He'd begun to wonder just how much damage he'd done to himself in mounting his rescue. More to the point, could he undo it? He'd used his huma-nanites to reroute his synaptic pathways down routes that were not designed to take them and these little gems of technology had done him proud at the time. Shamefully though, he'd neither backed up nor properly mapped out the original pathways. He'd not had time and he wasn't even sure what he'd done in the first place, let alone how. He'd sort of done it subconsciously, yet consciously.

So besides the emotional and hormonal upheaval of growing up ten years in three days, he had terabytes of data awaiting analysis and assimilation. He also had a sophisticated software system that he hadn't understood when he was six years old, but now, a mere three days later, he was supposed to be completely au fait with. Display seemed to be doing its own thing, and he had a set of huma-nanites that he still didn't really know how to control. On top of all that, there was the issue of simply staying alive and a dinner date with the Sallow Council. What else could there possibly be?

He determined that once back in his quarters he'd have some quality quiet time to start sorting things out. He'd have a proper look at Display and its functions, start indexing his new data ready for a detailed analysis and access the database on huma-nanite technology. If he had them, he should at least know how to use them properly, and then perhaps he could sort out the mess he'd made in his head and get his feet working properly. If he mastered all that, stopped behaving so erratically and employed a bit more logic, the Sallows might feel a little more at ease with him, and then he could get on with his life.

The door to his quarters opened and Kylem stumbled inside, heading straight for his bed to lie down and start the process, but no sooner did his head hit the pillow than sleep wafted over him and swept him down deep into its murky depths.

Kylem looked out over the emerald plain and surveyed his homeland—the land known as Glyder. Only he wasn't Kylem. He was Jaëdah.

Jaëdah was at that age when he considered himself to be no longer a boy but, although he was approaching manhood, he still had a good way to go before he would be a man. He was tall for his age though, and as he stood looking out over the Underlands, he cast a graceful silhouette against the morning sky. It was a beautiful place, best appreciated from the rocky heights upon which he stood. As he looked down his toes overhung the edge, but they did not impair the view.

The cliff face dropped away severely beneath him and far below, the thick canopy of the vast forests stretched out as far as the eye could see. Animals flitted from branch to branch in a world of wooden bridges and exotically coloured birds fluttered about in the clean and unspoilt world above. What lay beneath the green, cushioned floor, he'd seen only once when he was very young and had entered the Underlands on a dare. It had been cold, dark and dank. Long, slender translucent lizards scuttled blindly in the darkness amongst the trees, and the smells were strange and unwelcoming. There were no flowers there either for they only grew on the top branches of the trees where the light showed off their brilliance and insects could buzz about, pollinating them. He'd felt deeply uncomfortable in the forest's depths and so had stayed just long enough to fulfil the dare. Then he had left and never ventured there again.

A strong wind blew up that tried to push Jaëdah over the edge, but he was used to such gusts and held his ground well. For this is where he and his people lived, on these tall reaching and rugged pillars that rose forcefully from the Underlands, in aeries that hung off the sides of them like swallows' nests.

The wind howled again, whistling about his ears, and Jaëdah swayed as it caught him and made a more determined effort to sweep him off his feet and over the edge. It felt good when the wind was like this. It made him feel free, as free as a bird.

Jaëdah closed his eyes and drew a long, sharp breath, pulling the air deep into his lungs and held it there, savouring it—and then he let himself fall into the wind, surrendering to it and toppling over the edge.

He opened his eyes to see the forest hurtling towards him. He was spinning as though on a spiral of air. Round and round! Faster and faster! But Jaëdah wasn't afraid. When he had fallen as far as he wished, he spread his huge, sleek, ebony wings, caught the air and glided gracefully over the domain like a giant raven.

This was the 'light' of the Glyder people. Humanoid in appearance, they were avian, bearing huge wings. Jaëdah himself was a beautiful example of his people, with a wingspan of five metres or more. His soft, black feathers shone brightly in the morning light. They covered his scalp, cloaked his shoulders and carpeted his wings with their glory before petering out in the small of his back. His skin was a deep, rich brown and his eyes as black as a raven's too. The Glyder people had no meaning to skin colour as you or I despite their varied shades. Some, like Jaëdah, were as dark as the night; others, dove-white or speckled brown like a sparrow. And just as a black cat may bear white kittens, so the Glyder people were. There were no races to fight amongst, there was ample food and shelter for all, and so the Glyders knew nothing of war. There were no battles, no disputes and no crimes. Everybody came and went as they pleased and even the children of Glyder could fly all day, as far as they wished, without raising concern for their safety. Villagers would welcome them along the way, share food and water with them and then, as the day began to wane, they could head back home again. It was a blissful existence.

The winds were always strong this far above the ground but today the currents were particularly excellent and held Jaëdah well. It took little effort to fly when the air was this good, and he felt adventurous. He could glide for a hundred miles when it was like this, and he was happy to let the winds carry him over the plains.

As he flew, he played in the currents, swooping and diving like a bird displaying. He ducked and dived out of one current and freefell into the next until he spread his wings again, banked and was caught in its arms to be carried further still into the distance.

As he travelled, he passed by many of the tall rocky pillars upon which his people settled. Some of the settlements were active; others had been abandoned for more favourable positions long ago. As he passed the inhabited ones, he waved and shouted greetings to them, occasionally stopping for water and refreshment.

As the morning drew on the currents became calmer, and Jaëdah could no longer perform his little tricks in the air. He had to be satisfied with the one gentle stream that carried him sedately across the sky, but it was not the same. It was monotonous to simply float upon the air, and so he turned his thoughts elsewhere. He began to look for the next settlement, that he might land, quench his thirst and pass the time of day with the villagers there until the currents picked up again, but he could see no one. At the beginning of his flight, he had seen many, many people, but now, reflecting upon it, he hadn't seen anyone for some time.

Jaëdah tipped forward and gently dived towards the forests below. As he did so, the fresh scent of the flowers and trees rose up to greet him—and then another smell invaded, one that he couldn't place. He dropped lower and the odour became stronger. It was a sickly smell, sweet and unpleasant. The lower he dropped, the stronger it became until the smell jarred in his nose and throat, and then finally he recognised it. It was the smell of dead things: the smell of carrion. But why could he smell it this far up? And why was it so strong?

Jaëdah felt uneasy. He could see nothing that moved below, nor could he hear anything—no Glyders, no birds or beasts of any kind. The usual chatter of birds and animals calling from the forest canopy was absent. There was just a deathly hush.

Anxiety began to breed within him. Closing his wings, Jaëdah dropped from the air towards a low plateau. With the agility of an eagle, he brought his wings forward to slow his descent and came neatly to rest upon the rock. He flicked his wings gently against the air and then folded them behind his back. He stood for a moment and listened. Not a sound could be heard. With caution, he bent down, crept on knuckles and toes towards the edge, and peered down into the nests below, but there were no signs of life. He looked further down to the forests and there he could see something, something different, but he couldn't quite make it out. He tipped his head and swayed softly from side to side to aid his focus. He could make out the shapes of the trees with ease, but their leaves were different. They glistened with an unfamiliar ruby brilliance. Never had the trees borne red leaves before!

Puzzled, Jaëdah rose to his feet and looked further into the distance for any sign of life, but still nothing stirred; not a single bird in the air nor a single creature in the forest below. There was only horrid silence.

The sun was high in the sky and the day was warm. Sweat began to gather on his forehead and formed into a single droplet that ran down his nose to the tip. With the back of his hand, Jaëdah wiped it away, but as he did so his nose wrinkled in disdain at the smell. He looked at his hand. His fingers were coated in a thick, sticky, red liquid. He looked to his feet, and it was there too. Blood! He was standing in puddles of blood congealing in rocky pools! It was blood that had painted the trees in such a glorious crimson!

Panic began to rise within him and he felt sick. He was frightened. His breath became fast as the full horror dawned upon him, that the trees were painted red with blood. But what could have done this? What could have brought such death and destruction? The world began to swim and spin around him, and he wanted to vomit. His breath came in shattered bursts and he slumped onto his buttocks in dismay. What should he do? And then he realised—he had to go back. He had to go back and warn others.

Recomposing himself, he rose to his feet and leapt from the stony precipice, hurling himself into the winds; but whereas the currents had brought him easily to this place when that was their direction, now he had to struggle against every breeze. Never had he had to fly so hard against his element. Never before had the currents seemed so against him.

Far across the plains in the place from whence he had come, the Sallows had arrived. They came in shiny, black birds with wings that did not hug the currents as the Glyders did. Nor did they have their grace, but they flew with similar ease and at this, the Glyders marvelled.

They came to see and watched with awe as the Sallows landed. The bellies of the birds split open and from within people came, a people they had never seen before and one whose ways they did not know.

The Glyders ran to greet them with gifts of flowers and fruit, and their offerings were returned with streaks of light that burnt their path through all they touched. The slaughter had begun.

The Glyders fled, taking to the air but the invaders shot them down. Some plummeted to their death in the Underlands, while others fell onto the plateau where the Sallows tore their wings from their bodies and threw them down into the forests below.

The emerald forests turned red, painted with the Glyder blood that showered from their bodies as they were dashed and smashed against the rocks. When the slaughter in the skies was complete and Glyder limbs, barely recognisable for what they were, decorated the trees like Christmas decorations, the invaders climbed back into their cold and stainless birds and moved on. But it had not ended yet.

Having conquered the skies, the Sallows knew the Glyders would seek refuge in the Underlands, and this is where their allies were waiting: the Tarrow-Men. Running through the forests, they shot at the Glyders as they panicked and fled. Those that flew high met the Sallows' gunfire and dropped like stones to the ground to be splattered across the earth. Those that flew through the trees of the Underlands found their wings being shredded by the dense branches. Once disabled, they fell to the ground whereupon the Tarrow-Men leapt upon them with their cries of triumph and war that could not touch the constant screaming—the cries of Glyder agony—or the screech of the Tarrow-Men's weapons. For hours the slaughter continued, until the sun began to sink with a red glow that was unable to stain the lands any further with its colour. Darkness set in and an eerie calmness settled.

But still, it was not over.

Deep within the Underlands, the invaders had cleared an area in which to celebrate their victory. Noisily, they drank and jeered and ate with rebellious disarray. They were gathered about a huge table that was once a tree, five metres across and as old as Glyder herself. They laughed and pointed to the centre of the stump finding great amusement in the entertainment there. For in the centre, swimming in a claret soup of blood, Glyder children writhed upon their bloody alter. Limbless bar a single wing, they squirmed and span, pivoting upon their pained and mutilated bodies. For those that screamed, never could their cries have been heard above the party's clamour. For those that lay, now too exhausted to cry out, whose screams had died in their despair, these tiny children no longer with energy enough to form a tear, prayed only for a speedy death to end the torture they endured. Such a pitiful prayer for tiny innocent children, and as the children ceased to be so entertaining with their hopeless attempts to crawl away, Tarrow-Men shot forward with wide and gaping jaws and gouged a chunk of tender flesh. Sallows, not equipped with such mouths, simply pulled the prey towards them and carved their slice of meat with long and slender blades.

Kylem awoke with a violent start. His hearts were pounding in his chest and he was covered in a cold sweat.

It had started as a dream and ended as a nightmare. It had begun with him playing the part of Jaëdah and ended with him seeing the events through everybody's eyes, or so it seemed. But it was just a dream. No matter how vivid it was, it was just a dream. Or was it?

He lay quietly for a few moments, recomposing and calming himself. What time was it anyway? He accessed Server.

Shit! He had just twelve minutes until dinner.

He leapt off the bed, ran into the bathroom and showered as quickly as he could. On his way out, he grabbed a comb and ran it through his hair where it caught fast. His hair had grown so long overnight and with the events of the day, and his tossing and turning in bed, it was a horrible, tangled mess. In frustration, he grabbed a pair of scissors and hacked the comb free. Then he hacked at his hair some more to even it up a bit. He stood looking at the result. It was a mess, but it was okay. It would do. And then he became aware of two new things.

First, he didn't have a headache anymore; and second, it was the *first time* that he didn't have a headache. He realised that, in the past when he'd thought he'd not had a headache, he'd been wrong. There had always been a dull pain throbbing somewhere behind his eyes. It had just been less prominent at times. Now there was no pain at all. His head was quiet, serene and pain free. There were no lights, no symbols, no readings and no Display.

No Display? That couldn't be good. He tried to activate it and, to his surprise, Display instantly and happily flickered into place. That was interesting. He accessed the list of files awaiting his attention and there, at the top of the list, was *'Data-Access Diagnostic Program Four'* marked as deleted. But he hadn't deleted it— although bearing in mind what happened the last time he'd run it, he probably would have done so. Display, however, had already taken that step. So, was he running Display or was Display running him?

He suddenly caught sight of Mela-14 in the mirror, standing behind him in the doorway, watching him. It startled him, and he knocked the shelf below the mirror as he turned. An assortment of toiletries tumbled into the sink and rattled around it before finally coming to rest. Kylem made no attempt to catch them.

Mela-14 had the medical scanner open in his hand. They stared at each other for a moment, like two guilty parties caught in the act of doing something they shouldn't. Then Mela-14 leant casually against the doorframe in a most un-android-like manner. Kylem became aware of the scissors still in his hand and his fingers twitched around the handles.

43

"Do you intend to stab me with those, child?" asked Mela-14.

Kylem looked down at the scissors.

"What makes you think I'm thinking about it? Can you suddenly read my mind?"

"No, I cannot read your mind," he admitted. "But I know you."

The silence was awkward.

"And what does your little toy tell you?" Kylem asked after a few moments.

Mela-14 snapped the scanner quickly shut.

"Nothing. Only that you have changed." He seemed sad. "That you have evolved past that which we designed and developed. You have..." he stopped talking and looked around him as if searching for the right words on the walls, "...exceeded the sum of your parts."

They stood and studied each other silently.

"Is that a good thing?" asked Kylem, but Mela-14 did not answer.

"Hurry up. You are going to be late," he said finally.

CHAPTER 7

As he entered the dining hall, it wasn't at all as he had imagined it would be. He'd pictured another large, sterile room with a roughly hewn table surrounded by the blood-Sallows, gorging themselves upon copious amounts of meat with a complete lack of table manners and cutlery. What he found was an elaborate, well-sized room in excellent taste. It was decagon-shaped and each snowy white wall had two ornate panels inset into it with deep borders broken in the middle by a wave pattern. The heavily moulded edges of the panels depicted rampant ivy heavily veneered in different shades of gold leaf.

In the centre of the room stood a fantastically carved hardwood table with the grain of oak but the red hue of mahogany. It was big enough to seat at least ten people around comfortably, and its ornately carved central leg mimicked a whimsical tree trunk with ivy snaking up it. As the wooden leaves reached the table platform, they embraced the lip before lapping over the edge onto the polished surface.

Above it, a glorious crystal chandelier hung with a storm of brilliantly clear, heavily faceted crystal droplets that caught the light and refracted it into a rainbow of colours on the domed white ceiling above. That too had mouldings that rose from the corners of the decagon walls to the centre point. They had the same ivy leaf design but faded from gold to white as they climbed to meet the chandelier, giving the impression of snow-covered leaves. Below that, in the centre of the table, stood a solid silver candelabrum fashioned as an ancient oak adorned with finely cut crystal leaves. Small, snow-white candles were perched upon the ends of its branches, and the little flames flickered gently in the breeze from the open door and then settled again once it had shut. Mela-14 directed Kylem to a chair and began to leave.

"No, Mela-14," commanded the blood-Sallow at the head of the table. "Sit. Join us."

Kylem felt his father's discomfort as he hesitated and reluctantly sat down next to his prodigy. The eyes of the five blood-Sallows rested upon them both. For a moment, Kylem again felt like a naughty schoolboy in front of a disciplinary panel of teachers, with his partner in crime by his side, but Kylem had never been to school. He wished he knew where these sensations were coming from, but now was not the time so he turned his attention back to the dinner party.

The table setting did the room justice. It was laid with immaculate, pure white china, equally as tasteful in its design as the room itself. Three little white butterflies perched on a delicate ribbon raised themselves out of the porcelain and ran around one side of the egg-shaped plate. The drinking glasses were of fine, long-stemmed crystal, again with a butterfly motif cut into the glass, and the highly polished silver cutlery had long, elegant blades and handles. In the centre of each plate was a little white bowl that matched the butterfly plates, and to one side, a pure white serviette was neatly folded. Each place setting rested on a silver placemat, an etched silver platter with a highly polished silver rim.

Around the table stood seven chairs, one for each place setting. Each was as ornately carved as the table, with a high back, long arms and a sumptuous, white cushioned seat. With Kylem and his father now at the table, every seat was occupied.

At the head of the table was Emoth: the head of the Sallow Council and captain of the DeathMaker. According to his reputation, he was a particularly ruthless and sly individual who took great pleasure in the discomfort and suffering of others. It was said that Emoth made sadists look like saints, but Kylem wasn't sure whom it was that had said it, nor did he know what a saint was.

To his right were Mada and Jurrish and on his left, Doobee and Rathan. Kylem also knew each of these Sallows more by reputation than personal intercourse. Bar his meeting with Doobee earlier, he'd not formally met any of them before and knew them only by sight; but he had learnt a little about them from his father over the years. He resolved he should make it his business to know them better. *'Know your enemy'* whispered in his mind, but he cast the thought aside. After all, these were not his enemies. Were they?

Doobee was a philosopher, Head of Artificial Intelligence and the mildest of the blood-Sallows. He was quiet and rarely voiced his opinion, but very thorough in his work. He'd had a lot to do with Kylem's programming, and his connectivity to Server and the other androids.

Rathan, who sat between him and Emoth, was a scientist with a special interest in chemistry. He didn't look at his best. His skin had an unhealthy pale hue to it. He was greyer than the other Sallows, which made him look old and decrepit. He sat with his head nodding gently as he dozed in and out of consciousness. His eyes were puffy and swollen, and the veins on and around his forehead were pumping, making his whole head appear to pulsate.

"You must excuse Rathan," boomed Emoth. "He's been at the Agaratax again."

"Agaratax?" queried Kylem

"It's a brain steroid he's been experimenting with," explained Jurrish. "He claims that it enhances the thinking processes, but it appears to be packed full of side effects. If you ask me, he's been taking far too much of it for far too long."

"Yes," agreed Emoth. "His sanity is doubtful to say the least, but his brilliance far outweighs his oddities."

"Sadly," Jurrish added quietly, under his breathe.

Jurrish sat immediately to Emoth's left. He was probably the most intelligent of the blood-Sallows (bar Rathan) and was an engineer who oversaw the design and construction of the android Sallows. He preferred to work more in metal and plastic than with blood, so Jurrish was to be treated with care until his true feelings regarding the Espion Project were known.

Finally, there was Mada. Mada was potentially the most dangerous of the blood-Sallows as far as Kylem was concerned, because he was a purist who hated all skunks with a vengeance. He was a biologist and headed the Regenesis Project in its bid to rebuild the physical strength and stamina of the Sallow race. In the process, he had bred lots of skunks, all of which he despised; but one day one of those 'skunks' would be declared the mother of the renewed Sallow race. Perhaps it was the irony of his work that made him so bad-tempered. Perhaps it was his own physical inadequacies, having been born of the same Sallows he was trying to repair; tainted and withered by the genetic war with the Tarrow-Men.

All these Sallows, to one degree or another, had a hand in Kylem's creation and his continued existence. All had to be humoured, but what was it they were hoping to see? Something Sallow or something humanoid?

Three slaves approached the table and poured ruby red wine into the glasses. Kylem tipped his head in thanks at the slave and noted the blood-Sallows' reactions—disapproving and curious. He wasn't sure that the blood-Sallows knew themselves what they wanted to see.

The slaves, having finished filling the glasses, began to serve the first course. It was soup which was ladled expertly from large tureens into the neat little bowls. Kylem looked at the cutlery. He'd never seen so many different shaped knives, forks and spoons, each no doubt having a different purpose. So which should he use?

Emoth raised his glass and his companions did the same. Kylem picked up his glass and followed suit, but Mela-14 did not. He was an android without a mouth and thus unable to make the toast. Emoth scowled at him.

"What's wrong, Mela-14? Will you not toast the Empire with us?"

Kylem looked at Mela-14 who seemed unsure what to do. Then, hesitantly, he picked up the glass and raised it. Kylem looked quizzically at him and then at the blood-Sallows, so obviously enjoying this moment of confusion for the android. They wanted to see what it would do. Would it pour the wine down itself in an attempt to drink it, or would it simply raise it, say the appropriate words and replace the still full glass on the table? That's what Kylem would have done, but he was programmed and trained for espionage, to fit into situations such as this, calmly and coolheadedly. In fact, he surprised himself just how calm and self-assured he was. Mela-14, on the other hand, was not a spy, nor was he comfortable, and that was what this test was about. The blood-Sallows wanted to see Kylem's reactions; how he would blend in when in the company of strangers, how he would react to awkward moments and, perhaps, how he would bend the circumstances to his own ends.

"Glory be!" screamed Emoth loudly.

"Glory be!" shouted the others and threw the contents of their glasses into their mouths. Kylem took a generous mouthful, held it for a moment to savour it and then swallowed. He was keenly aware that all eyes were upon him.

"Hmm," he said, raising his eyebrows appreciatively. "Very nice indeed. I congratulate you upon your excellent choice of wine."

It was the right thing to say because the Sallows' gazes quickly transferred away from him to Mela-14 who was sat frozen in his chair, the glass still in his hand. Aware that he was now the centre of attention, Mela-14 moved the glass nervously to his inanimate lips.

"Glory be," he said clearly and tipped the glass, knowing full well that he was about to douse himself and his fine white robes in red wine; but just as the liquid was about to pour over the rim, a hand reached over and pulled the glass, gently but firmly, from his. Mela-14 looked aghast as his son set the glass back down upon the table.

"Now, now Father," he chided politely. "It's a beautiful sentiment but we all have our limitations, and it would be such a shame to spoil the upholstery of such a fine room. Would you not agree, gentlemen?" and he smiled with sweet smugness at his hosts.

Silence gripped the room icily and held it for some minutes. Then Emoth burst out in deep, noisy laughter. His companions began to laugh with him, more out of politeness than genuine amusement.

"What an odd creature you are, Kylem," declared Emoth loudly. "But why did you choose that course of action?"

"It seemed... appropriate."

More laughter.

"Yes, yes, yes, but why?" Emoth pushed. "Of all the things you could have done, why did you do that?"

Kylem set his own glass back down and leant forward, placing one elbow carefully on the table so that he could rest his chin on his knuckles without upsetting the china. The blood-Sallows leaned closer to hear what he had to say.

"Gentlemen, to understand that you'd have to be a humanoid, and that is my curse, not yours."

"Oh, Mela-14," began Emoth, "I must congratulate you. You seem to have developed a very convincing spy for us. He answers our questions and yet he says nothing."

"That's what worries me," muttered a Sallow to his left.

"Enough, gentlemen," shouted Emoth boisterously. "Let us eat!" and he picked up a large round-bowled spoon, watching Kylem all the while. Kylem selected the very same instrument.

"Very well done," said Emoth, smiling wildly with his uneven, prickly, little teeth flashing. "But of course," he began, beaming wickedly at Kylem, "if I had picked up the wrong spoon to test your knowledge, the game would be up by now, wouldn't it?"

"Maybe so, maybe not. I am merely a humble peasant who is unaccustomed to such finery. Are all men well educated in table etiquette? I doubt it, and I doubt that many men have been hanged for their poor choice of cutlery. Besides, I didn't realise I was on trial."

Emoth laughed heartily and then stopped abruptly. The laughter fell from his face and his features became hard and cold.

"Of course you're on trial, you bloody idiot!" but Kylem was not flummoxed. He smiled cheekily back at Emoth, raised his glass again and took another mouthful. Emoth's face twisted as he thought; was the boy playing games with him?

"Enjoy the soup," he snapped coldly. His tone was worrying.

Kylem looked at the soup and then cast his eyes around the room. All five Sallows were looking at him, spoons poised in their hands ready to eat, except Mada who was ignoring him and had begun to eat.

"Is there something wrong?" asked Emoth.

"I don't know. Is there?"

"No," he snapped. "Eat the soup!" he commanded, but Kylem didn't.

"Will it kill me?"

"And what makes you ask that?"

"I have a naturally suspicious nature."

Emoth emitted a hard, forced laugh. The other Sallows joined in, somewhat faint-heartedly.

"We are all eating the same soup," hissed Emoth and he took a mouthful.

"But not from the same bowl," and with that, Kylem picked up his dish and swapped it with Mada's. Mada, who had a spoon laden with soup half raised to his lips when Kylem snatched the bowl from under him, gawped in surprise and gazed at the new bowl of soup thrust in front him. Was Kylem right to think the soup might be poisoned? Kylem, meanwhile, dipped his spoon into the soup and began to sip it from one side of the miniature ladle. It was a lovely golden colour and tasted golden too, steamy hot and slightly spicy. Emoth roared with laughter.

"It's okay, Mada," he reassured him. "You can eat it. I have no ill intentions towards our guest. Not yet."

The room relaxed. The Sallows tucked into their first course and the conversation soon turned to more mundane matters. Kylem sat, ate and listened.

Most of the conversation centred around him, which was no bad thing. It gave him an opportunity to learn more about himself.

It transpired that the Espion Project had been conceived by Rathan, and that it was his creativity and genius that had seen it come to fruition. He was the one who had cajoled the others into partaking in the project on the basis that it could run parallel to the more important Regenesis Project. Mada, with his knowledge of biology and genetic engineering, was credited with the creation of his physical body and had helped to overcome the problems of rejection and mutation. Doobee had developed the huma-nanites—the microscopic robotic devices that had buried themselves in his brain, cutting his biological synaptic links and replacing them with their own to 'upgrade' his systems. They gave him his intelligence and his programmable android mind. Jurrish was responsible for his training as a Warrior amongst the Warrior class, whilst taking into account his fragility as a blood-thing of course. And Emoth? Well, Emoth's only input seemed to have been in supporting Rathan on the premise that, if the project failed, it would be fun to see the Espion pitted against the Warriors in battle. He would make a most worthy opponent for a Sallow Warrior.

Throughout the meal, Rathan sat with his head nodding gently and the Sallows, basically, ignored him. Occasionally he would jerk awake and begin to rant about something. The Sallows would cease their conversation, listen attentively to his ravings and then, once he fell silent again, continue their own conversations exactly from where they had left off. For all his peculiarity, and contrary to their derision, it was obvious that all four of them held Rathan in very high regard. Mela-14, meanwhile, sat statuesque with his hands folded neatly in his lap.

Eventually the conversation turned from Kylem to other matters, whereupon Kylem discovered that Sallow dinner topics were not quite as refined as their immaculate table manners. In fact, they happily discussed all sorts of topics with no regard as to the suitability of the subject matter. They had no concept of poor taste, discussing everything from the dissection of live specimens to sex. They recounted past battle conquests with crude humour and referred often to the Feast of Galmatek, which, Doobee reckoned, was probably the best feast since the legendary Feast of Glyder.

Kylem was startled at the mention of Glyder and dropped his fork. It clattered noisily against the plate and ten eyes were suddenly cast upon him.

"My apologies, gentlemen, but I am unaccustomed to such fine tableware."

Emoth grunted and the conversation continued.

They remembered the fresh meat still quivering with life, the sweetness and tenderness of it, the like of which they could only rarely experience on the DaerkStar where it was farm-bred and dead; but Kylem didn't hear this. His thoughts had wandered to his dream about Jaëdah and the planet Glyder. These were not ordinary dreams woven from imagination and fiction. There was more to this. It was something else he would have to find out about. Kylem looked at the steak on his plate and wondered what it was, or even *whom* it was, that he was eating.

"You're very quiet, Kylem," said Emoth after a while.

"I'm enjoying the company and the conversation. It is a pleasant change. Usually I eat alone."

"So you appreciate being invited *for* dinner then?" said Mada slyly, believing his pun to be rather clever. The other Sallows giggled at the play on words, but Kylem was not impressed by his childish humour.

"Yes, I'm sure you would have preferred having me *for* dinner rather than *to* dinner, but you will have to wait until I have outlived my usefulness." Kylem cringed at the basic fact he had just voiced.

"Well, you are a new race. I wonder what you would taste like," tormented Mada. "Are you not curious about such things? Do you not wonder what I would taste like? What pleasures the flesh of a Sallow might conjure in your mouth?"

Kylem did not wonder at all. He did not share the Sallows' lust for good meat, nor their adventurous nature in trying new flesh, but it would be un-Sallowlike to say so. On the other hand, he could hardly say yes, say that he wanted to eat his masters, but what could he say?

Kylem placed his knife and fork together on the plate to indicate that he had finished his meal and dabbed his mouth politely with the napkin before setting it down. It served to buy him time to think.

He took his empty wineglass and held it aloft. A slave scuttled forward and replenished it, and Kylem leant back in his chair, watching as the Sallows waited upon his response. He took another mouthful of wine. He had never consumed alcohol before and the effects were beginning to take hold. His face felt warm and he was feeling a little light-headed.

"To be honest," he began, "I'm not sure that I like the taste of meat. Perhaps that's a flaw in a Sallow, but is it a flaw in an Espion? What would you say, Doobee?"

Kylem had picked upon Doobee as the philosopher, the one Sallow who could perhaps appreciate the subtle nuances of his character and help excuse his humanlike flaws.

Doobee took a sharp intake of breath and thought for a moment.

"He has a point," he said finally, nursing his glass in both hands.

"But every Sallow loves good meat," pointed out Mada.

"Yes, but he's not a Sallow, is he? And, allegedly, every Sallow loves good sadia."

"Every Sallow does!"

"No," said Doobee. "I don't like sadia at all, if I'm honest."

His four companions glared at him, some in surprise and others in disappointment. Sadia to a Sallow was like poitin to an Irishman, or a fine, twenty-year-old single-malt whisky to an Englishman. Every Sallow was predisposed to enjoyed sadia.

"Sorry," apologised Doobee, "but it's true. I can't stand the stuff."

"But you drink it," retorted Jurrish.

"Well, it's expected, isn't it? You said it yourself: what self-respecting Sallow doesn't like sadia? So I drink it, but I'd rather not."

Emoth threw his cutlery onto his plate. It bounced angrily against the fine bone china. He stood up sharply, scraping his chair over the polished floor and marched over to a slave that stood obediently in the corner. It had a tray in its hands, bearing a decanter and half-a-dozen small, empty liqueur glasses. He whipped the decanter off the tray and returned to his chair, the slave scuttling along behind him like an obedient puppy. As he slammed the decanter onto the table, the slave whizzed into action and set an empty liqueur glass before each blood. Emoth poured himself a generous helping of the sadia and passed the bottle to Jurrish on his left. Jurrish also poured himself a glassful of the black, inky liquid, then passed the bottle to Mada who did likewise before passing the bottle to Kylem. Kylem took it, poured himself an equal helping and handed the bottle to Mela-14 who passed it to Doobee. Doobee poured himself a glass of equal proportions, knowing that he would not get away with less. He smiled to himself as the bottle finished its round with Rathan who, predictably, threw the last of his wine down his throat and proceeded to fill the wine glass to the brim with sadia, the wine glass being a much bigger vessel than the liqueur glass provided.

"Glory be!" screamed Emoth.

"Glory be!" screamed the blood-Sallows, and they each threw their sadias down their throats.

Kylem did not. He more sedately lifted the glass and studied it. The liquid was black, quite opaque and it clung to the sides of the glass like good sherry. He smelt it, took a sizable mouthful and held it on his tongue to extract the full flavour of it before swallowing. It burnt comfortably all the way down in the same way that a good whisky does, warming your belly and giving your head that gentle, friendly whack.

"Well?" asked Emoth.

Kylem smacked his lips and pondered for a moment.

"Well, I hate to disappoint you, Emoth," he began, "but I rather like that," and he sat back in his chair, nursing the glass and took another mouthful. "Very good, in fact."

"You're supposed to knock it back in one go," rebuked Mada.

"Well, my mouth isn't quite as big as yours so it presents me with a small problem there," smirked Kylem.

Kylem felt Mela-14's horror but didn't care. Fortunately, the remark delighted Emoth who rose from his seat, clapping and laughing raucously. Jurrish and Doobee followed suit, although somewhat nervously. Rathan was too smashed to notice, but Mada was seething.

Still laughing, Emoth walked around the table to refill Kylem's glass, and Jurrish took the opportunity to change the subject and move the dinner party on.

The plates were cleared away and desert was brought. It consisted of some small orange fruits decorated with little white blossoms and a light dusting of icing sugar; simple, sweet and light. More after dinner drinks came and the seven of them sat at the table as the slaves cleared away the last of the detritus from the meal.

"This is kara," Doobee said as he poured the new drink. "It is made from the nut of the karam tree, but not an ordinary karam nut. To make kara, the nut has to be eaten by a slent, an animal with a very poor digestive system. The nut is only partially digested and thus passes through the animal relatively intact. The droppings are then collected, the nuts separated out and cleaned before being used in the fermentation process."

"Sounds delicious," replied Kylem dubiously and he smiled at Doobee. Doobee looked coldly at Kylem, and then his face warmed with a smile and he shook his head affectionately.

"I find it highly preferable to sadia. I would be interested in your opinion."

Kylem took a sip and gagged. It was like drinking paraffin and being smacked in the face with a bowling ball at the same time. He swallowed hard and slammed the glass on the table before pushing it away. The Sallows giggled as his face twisted in distaste.

"Obviously an acquired taste," he coughed, as it burnt the back of his throat like stomach acid.

"It's an insult not to drink it," said Mada, his face contorted with joy at Kylem's discomfort.

"Then I have not insulted you but," and he coughed all the more, "it could be lethal to drink! Christ! And I was worried about the soup!"

The Sallows laughed heartily (except Mada of course) and Kylem rubbed his forehead and blinked. The room was starting to spin.

Without warning, Mela-14 broke his vigil. He'd been watching Kylem closely. He'd witnessed drunken Sallows before, and he'd seen them pay the price of a tongue loosened by alcohol. He'd let Kylem push his cheek and luck as far as he dared but the limit was reached. As he hastily stood up from the table, all eyes turned to him.

"Gentlemen," he began. "I fear my ward has become intoxicated. He is unaccustomed to such beverages. I therefore propose that I take him back to his quarters so that he may retire for the evening."

"Oh, nonsense," shouted Kylem who stood up a little too hastily and knocked over an unfinished glass of wine. The liquid splashed over the tabletop and the glass broke.

"Oops!" said Kylem and looked up to see Rathan, now fast asleep and snoring gently, with his head resting in his dinner plate (the slaves having been unable to clear it away). He stared at him for a moment, debating his own state.

"Second thoughts, maybe you're right." He backed away from the table as gently as he could but felt the chair against the back of his knees too late. As it fell, he swung about trying to catch it and missed horribly. He ended up on his knees, with his head buried in Mela-14's stomach.

"Sorry," he whispered to Mela-14 as he straightened himself up. He tried to recompose himself as best he could and tugged at the bottom of his jacket to straighten it. The room was spinning uncontrollably now.

"If you will excuse me," he said as elegantly as he could and backed slowly away from the table. He turned for the door and then realised that the door was so beautifully tailored into the walls that he couldn't actually see it.

Never mind, he thought, the door will open when I get there but having completed a full circuit of the room, the door remained concealed from him.

Slowly and drunkenly, he made his way to Emoth and leant over to whisper in his ear, in the way that only drunks do, in what he thought was a quiet tone but most certainly wasn't.

"Uhm, sorry about this, but," his words were slurred. "But, uhm, where's the door please?" and he slid down Emoth's arm, collapsing into a tittering heap on his knees.

Emoth was no longer amused. He made a gesture for Mela-14 to take the boy away.

Mela-14 had been forced to stand by and watch as Kylem made a complete fool of himself, so at Emoth's signal he eagerly hurried over and took his son, summoning a Warrior from beyond the door at the same time. The Warrior entered, swept up the barely conscious lad, threw him over its shoulder and left the room. Mela-14 followed behind, bowing low to the Council as he departed.

As the door shut, much to Mela-14's relief, he heard the blood-Sallows laughing. All except Mada, of course.

CHAPTER 8

When Kylem regained consciousness barely an hour later, he was alone in his quarters and he couldn't remember how he'd got there. He was lying face down on the bed with his head buried in the pillow, in almost exactly the same position in which the Warrior had dumped him.

He called up the lights and found that he was still fully clothed. He rubbed his thick, muggy head with his hands and began to recall the events of dinner. He felt like shit and recalling only made him feel even worse through sheer embarrassment. He'd got drunk and behaved carelessly with the Sallows. It was a shame too because it had started out so well. He sighed deeply and began to wonder how to right the mess.

To start with, he needed to clear his head and his body of the intoxicating chemicals he'd imbibed. He accessed Server for details on what he had consumed to find a solution. A pain shot through his head rather like a javelin being thrust through his temples. Display and alcohol didn't mix well apparently, but he needed a cure so he pursued the information despite the pain.

He got rather more information than he'd hoped for.

The array of beverages he had consumed contained a wide variety of substances, of which alcohol was the predominant.

'Alcohol has an almost immediate affect upon the central nervous system affecting balance, speech and vision. It often induces heavy sweating and the dulling of physical sensation such as pain, and disrupts the brain's judgement of distances and heights and the ability to reason. It is also a diuretic causing dehydration,' which explained his raging thirst. *'The after affects, known as a hangover, include headache, dizziness, more thirst, paleness and tremors. Alcohol also interferes with sleep rhythms,'* hence his current wakefulness. The long-term effects, he ignored, not intending to repeat the experience.

His head was pounding all the more now, with someone apparently twisting the javelin inside his skull, so he shut off all his android systems to lessen the torture. The pain subsided into a dull but persistent thudding inside his head, but his thirst became more urgent. He needed to rehydrate and as quickly as possible so he staggered into the bathroom.

After a shower and four pints of water, he was feeling more coherent if not a little bloated. His head was still spinning though, so he decided to go for a jog around the deck. This would help clear his mind and speed the drugs through his system.

He dressed in fresh clothing and opened the door out of his quarters but was stopped dead in his tracks by a Warrior blocking his path. It was one of the older-style Infantry Class, Mark-IX's that was being phased out in favour of the newer Mark-X's. They looked very similar but the Mark-X featured inbuilt weaponry. Either way, anger rose in him at the sight of it.

"Get outta my way," he snapped at it.

"You are restricted to quarters," hummed the Warrior.

"You reckon?" he challenged.

"Yes. You will remain in your quarters."

"And how much force are you authorised to exert in order to enforce that order?"

(In an instant, the Warrior had connected to Server and asked the question. In his laboratory, Mela-14 received the query and responded. He got up and began making his way back to Kylem's quarters. He just knew there was going to be a problem.)

"I am not authorised to release that information to you," the Warrior replied.

Kylem smiled wickedly at it and made to push past it on its left-hand side. As the Warrior reached out, he deftly ducked under the Warrior's right arm and was past it in an instant. It swung about, expecting to see Kylem disappearing down the corridor, but Kylem had not fled. Instead, he was standing just out of arm's reach, looking at it, waiting. The Warrior straightened up, repositioned and then lunged at him. Kylem darted nimbly off to one side and around behind the Warrior. The Warrior straightened up again, turned about and took a step towards Kylem. Kylem took a similar step back, remaining just out of arm's reach. The Warrior flexed its long, spindly fingers and lurched forward, swiping at him with its left arm and then its right, but Kylem dodged them both beautifully, somersaulting low across the floor, although he misjudged the distance (being bigger than he was used to) and smacked clumsily into the far wall. Seeing its opportunity, the Warrior leapt forward, throwing its whole body onto the boy but only met the floor. With very little elegance, Kylem had rolled awkwardly out of the way and scrambled to his feet. He laughed at the Warrior poised on all fours seeking him out. Despite his clumsiness and his intoxicated state, it seemed he could still outsmart and outmanoeuvre a Warrior.

"Is that the best you can do?" he taunted.

The Warrior leapt to its feet and broke into a run towards him, but he was already off, tearing down the corridor with the Warrior in hot pursuit.

He passed a couple of slaves in the corridor and grabbed one of them to use as a pivot, circling around it to monitor the Warrior's progress as it hurtled towards him. The Warrior crashed into the walls at every turn of the corridor. When it got to the slaves, the Warrior ploughed into them, smashing them asunder like skittles. In the aftermath of its wake, only one slave stood up. Bent and distorted, it picked itself up and limped over to begin cleaning up the mess that had once been its comrade.

Coming to the next junction, they were now beyond the outer ring of the DaerkStar and travelling down a corridor that led only to emergency airlocks and maintenance hatches. After a few hundred yards, Kylem found himself at a dead-end facing the airlock doors. He stopped and turned. He could hear the Warrior coming long before it appeared, by which time Kylem had activated the door control and ducked inside an airlock. He didn't seal the door behind him though. That would be silly. It would leave only one way to go.

Kylem looked out of the airlock's outer hatch, out into the void of space and when he turned back, the Warrior was at the door. It was the end of the line.

For a moment, it stood in the doorway with one hand on either side of the doorjamb and its legs splayed to bar the way, staring at Kylem. Kylem could feel its sense of triumph. It looked at the door controls and then looked back at him.

"We are done," it hummed. "You have lost this chase and you will return to your quarters,"

"You gonna make me?"

"Affirmed," and deftly the Warrior activated the door control and slipped inside before it closed, to trap the two of them in the confined space. At the same moment Kylem threw himself to the floor and slid like an arrow between the Warrior's legs, only just clearing the door as it slammed shut.

He stood up, dusted himself down and turned back to look at his prey in the airlock, the Warrior now trapped on the wrong side of the door. He gave it a cheeky salute and lifted his eyebrows playfully as his hand hovered over the external door control. He flexed his fingers teasingly whilst he played a psychological game of 'shall I, shan't I'.

"I would not do that if I were you," boomed a voice from behind. Kylem's head swung about but his hand remained poised over the button. Mela-14 was stood looking at him like the disapproving parent he was.

"Emoth is right. You are an idiot."

Kylem took a sharp, deep intake of breath as he considered it. His father was right. This was stupid and would earn him no *Brownie points*. He allowed his hand to drop from the controls, turned and pushed his way past Mela-14, heading back down the corridor towards his quarters.

* * * * *

"What the hell did you think you were doing, child?" shouted Mela-14 once they were both safely inside Kylem's quarters and could not be overheard.

"I don't know," he replied despondently, throwing himself onto the bed. He felt exhausted.

"That Warrior could have killed you."

"No, it couldn't," replied Kylem dismissively. "It wasn't fast enough and anyway, you told it not to use unreasonable force so it was never gonna hurt me!"

"How do you know that?" There was an element of shock in Mela-14's voice.

"Know what?"

"How do you know what I told the Warrior?"

Kylem covered his face with the palms of his hand and yawned.

"I..." but he wasn't sure exactly how he knew it, he just did, but he shouldn't have been able to intercept that communication. He half sighed, half yawned and turned onto his side. He puffed up the pillow and snuggled into it, blinking drowsily at the Sallow.

"What happens now?" he asked.

Mela-14 shook his head. "I do not know," he said, but Kylem didn't hear him. A drunken sleep had already stolen him away.

He lay on his belly, in a landscape filled with the dead of his tribe as far as the eye could see. In the distance were seven huge golden men standing by a container. They were Sallow Warriors, but Kylem didn't recognise the class or type. He had never seen the like of these Sallows before. They were less skilfully worked than the ones he knew and lived with, more bulky, simpler in their design and with less ornamentation.

There was a mound nearby, silhouetted against the artificially low horizon. The Sallow Warriors kept walking between it and the container, picking things up from the mound and throwing them into it. Kylem wanted to move away but his legs wouldn't work so he simply lay and watched as the mound shrank away until it was gone.

The Warriors spread out over the battlefield. The urge to run filled him again, but still he couldn't get up. He looked down at where his legs should be but saw only ragged edges halfway down his thighs. Shock and horror filled him but, strangely, there was no pain. He felt nauseous with the realisation that he was crippled. Vomit suddenly filled his mouth and spewed out. He was helpless. He began scrabbling around, searching for a weapon, but there was none. There were only the bodies of his tribe. He looked back to the Warriors spreading out in different directions. One was coming his way, looking directly at him. It stopped about ten paces in front of him. He looked into its eyes, and it into his. It drew a long, curved blade and held it to the light, and then it bent down. As it rose up again, something screamed. It was holding a man by his scalp. His arms were waving frantically in the air. He could see the whites of his eyes, hear the panic in his screams. The Sallow raised the body high and plunged the blade downwards into the shoulder joint of the man. There was a cracking sound as it wrenched the blade sideways and split the joint, severing the arm. The man screamed more and more, the pitch getting higher and higher. The Warrior let go and he dropped to the floor. His wails suddenly grew faint and turned into sobs. Taking the blade in both hands, the Sallow plunged the blade in again, this time deep into the man's body. The sobbing stopped but still the blade went down again and again. With the proficiency of a master butcher, the Warrior carved limb from limb and flesh from bone. It macheted open the chest and began to cut the organs free, tossing them onto the pile of dismembered limbs for collection. And when finally it was done, it dropped the carcass and stepped forward... towards him...

Kylem awoke screaming. He was flailing about in his bed, his bedclothes were everywhere and he was knotted in them. He was hot, sweaty and confused. The terror of the dream faded fast and the confusion broke as Kylem realised where he was.

He lay there, gasping for breath and shaking, and then he went into the bathroom and vomited. The room was still spinning, and then he passed out on the bathroom floor.

57

CHAPTER 9

It was late morning when Kylem awoke again. He still felt like shit, probably worse than before. His head was pounding, and he felt dizzy and nauseous. Even with his eyes closed, he could feel the room spin sickeningly around him. It was even worse than when he had awoken from the accelerated growth process, if that were possible.

He was lying face down on his bed, which was strange because the last thing he remembered was chucking up in the bathroom. He turned his head and cautiously opened one eye to find Mela-14 sitting in the chair, looking disapprovingly at him. Kylem buried his head shamefully back into the pillow to avoid his gaze.

"The Sallow Council is waiting for you. You have an hour to make yourself decent. I shall be back for you then. Please be ready," pleaded Mela-14, standing up.

"I've really screwed up, haven't I?" mumbled Kylem.

Mela-14 stopped and sighed deeply.

"Yes, child," he said. "It cannot be denied."

* * * * *

When Mela-14 returned, he did not cross the threshold but stood expectantly in the doorway. Kylem wiped his palms anxiously on his thighs, pulled at the edge of his jacket and composed himself with a sharp jerk of the chin. He cleared his throat nervously, crossed the room and exited through the door to join the contingent waiting for him. He fell into the middle of a three-by-three formation of Warriors led by Mela-14. They marched noisily in unison towards the Council Chamber, and as hard as Kylem tried to resist, the little soldier in him ran a quick assessment of the party. Eight Warriors: five Infantry Class, Mark-IX and three Mark-X's—no additional armament—low risk. The escort was purely formal.

It was not long before Kylem found himself in areas of the DaerkStar that he had never seen before. He wondered just how big this bird was and made a note to download the schematics of the ship when he got back to his quarters—if he ever got back to his quarters. In fact, perhaps he should do it now, just in case he needed them, so he did. His head protested and he squirmed at the pain, but he persisted.

The Council Chamber lay near the very centre of the ship, along with Server and the blood-Sallows' private quarters, all three areas receiving maximum protection in the event of an attack by the physical presence of the outer decks as well as a sophisticated array of security devices and measures.

Kylem felt a little more in control now that he knew exactly where he was headed and mapped their progress on the plans as they worked their way along the corridors, deeper into the ship. Finally arriving at the Council Chamber, the great arched doors opened gracefully to greet the party.

Unlike other doors on the ship, these were hinged doors that stood some five metres high and were made of a rich, deep brown wood. They had three moulded panels inset into each, the middle of which was circular, and each panel held a different design. It seemed to Kylem that they were cartouches and he half recognised the writing, but not enough to decipher them. They entered the room.

If Kylem had thought the dining room was beautiful, elegant and ornate then the Chamber was equally as impressive with its oligarchic décor. It was much, much larger than the dining room and circular with a domed ceiling. It was completely colourless bar the doors, its decoration founded in texture and tone. A beautiful relief of a Sallow battle scene encompassed the top half of the walls. Expertly carved, the characters lifted themselves off the mural into the battle with intricate detail and design.

The judicial bench that stretched beneath it was broken only by the huge doors by which Kylem and his contingent had entered. It stood some three metres from the floor and was adorned with simple white panels, one for each seat that stood behind it. There must have been room enough for fifty Sallows.

The domed ceiling stretched high above with huge, backlit, triangular white glass panels set into it. The lighting it gave was bright, too bright, almost washing out the mural's effect.

The floor also was in shades of white. A glossy, white marble path led from the doors, crossed the middle of the room and then wrapped itself back around the perimeter of the Chamber. Finally, in the centre was a white floor-lit glass platter: the dock upon which Kylem now stood.

As Kylem positioned himself in the centre of it, the Warriors passed him by and continued on the path to the end. They branched off to take their places at arms length from each other, with their backs against the bench.

They stood in silence and waited.

After a few moments a door revealed itself in the mural behind the bench, and the blood-Sallows filed in and took their seats. The door closed seamlessly behind them as they made themselves comfortable, and Kylem noted that the seating order was identical to that at the dinner table. He accessed Server to enquire about this curiosity and discovered that it was of great importance at any Sallow assembly, each position signifying rank and status. He also noted the distance between the Sallows and wondered how they could confer quietly to each other when they needed to.

A gong sounded, interrupting his thoughts, to announce the start of the proceedings. Kylem found it a little melodramatic and had to stifle a grin.

"You are hereby accused of the treasonous act of Imperial vandalism. How do you plead?" boomed Emoth.

Kylem noted that the acoustics of the room were quite operatic and again wondered how, or if, they could talk quietly amongst themselves.

"Not guilty," said Kylem.

Emoth raised an eyebrow.

"You attempted to destroy a Warrior, a symbol of the Empire," he reminded Kylem.

"It was not an attempt. An attempt suggests that I failed in the task, which I did not. I just... changed my mind."

The Sallows touched their ears with their forefingers and mumbled into their hands. Of course! They were each equipped with a discreet headset: a simple earpiece and microphone activated by touch so that they could confer amongst themselves.

"You deny failure," stated Emoth finally.

"I do."

"You do not accept failure well."

"I am a Sallow. Show me a Sallow that accepts failure well and you show me an insult to the Sallow race."

In unison, their hands went to their ears again and the whispering continued. Emoth listened to his peers quietly and then declared, "The charge of treason stands."

Kylem thought for a moment, raising his eyebrows as he did so. He wondered if when one Sallow killed another to gain the captaincy of a DaerkStar, if that was treason or promotion, but that was a side issue.

"Still not guilty," he retorted.

"Defend," commanded Emoth, and so Kylem began his defence.

"It was not attacked because it was a symbol of the Empire and thus, the act was not treasonous."

"It is a Sallow—"

"No. It is not a Sallow. You are a Sallow. I am a Sallow, but these things made of metal and plastic are not. They are just... tools... like slaves and doors, just tools and instruments."

The reaction was instant. Mada, Jurrish and Doobee stood up protesting loudly, angrily shaking their fists. Emoth hammered on the bench and the gong boomed untidily with every punch. Kylem grinned. The gong operated via a sensor trained on Emoth's movements, a method of operation that should have impressed with its apparent sounding at the mere will of the judge, but that now only served to ridicule the court with its erratic interruption.

"Silence!" screamed Emoth at them. "Silence!" he boomed again. His angry glare flashed at his comrades and Kylem knew he'd put the cat amongst the pigeons. Sallows, by their nature, were quick to anger. Those that rose above those tendencies and harnessed them were the Sallows that rose to power—like Emoth. He could tell that Emoth considered his comrades to be idiots that should be reprimanded for their uncontrolled outburst, but Emoth couldn't do that in front of him. That would belittle them and Emoth couldn't afford to do that. Sallows took offence easily and mutiny was not uncommon, with many a ship's captaincy changing hands in that manner. Although since the Sallow/Tarrow-Man Wars and the enfeebling of the blood-Sallows, it had become a much rarer occurrence. The blood-Sallows numbers were few and losses could not be afforded.

As order returned to the room and the Council sat down again, Emoth bade him to continue.

"Warriors are made by Sallows to do the Sallows' bidding. They are engineered to fight and to die, and they do it very well but that's all they are. They are as disposable as a slave and are nearly as lacking in intelligence. They are just 'doors' that open and close, allowing you access to your desires. They are just instruments and equipment, and thus they are no more 'Sallow' than those most splendid doors by which I have just entered this room."

"Actually, those doors were designed by Ragatan, a blood-Sallow and thus are Sallow by design," corrected Doobee.

"With all due respect," and Kylem bowed his head courteously to Doobee, "but the design is Daltanian. The words written upon them are Daltanian and they were carved by Daltanians. I think we can therefore safely assume that Ragatan simply removed them from Daltan and had them installed here."

"And when did you become such an expert on Daltanian architecture?" asked Doobee. "Do we have a Daltanian library on board that I don't know about?"

"Yes, we do. Server holds the libraries of many races." Kylem was amused and baffled that Doobee didn't know this. "It's where I get all my information from."

Suddenly, Doobee's annoyance dissipated. He leaned forward, piqued with curiosity. He had always doubted that the Espion could master the androids' code effectively enough to communicate with them and Server on an at-will basis—and even if he could that any such communications would be long and drawn out affairs, hindered by the slow learning process of an organic—but suddenly there were indications to the contrary. Mada opened his mouth to speak but Doobee raised a hand to silence him.

"And when exactly did you access that piece of information?" he enquired.

"Just now."

"This very minute?" His face contorted with curiosity.

"Yes."

Doobee shuffled with excitement in his chair. Emoth stood up and beckoned to Mela-14 to approach the bench. He did so and Emoth leant over it to confer with him. As Mela-14 stood looking up at Emoth from the bottom of the three-metre cliff face and Emoth looked down upon him, Kylem found himself, again, having to stifle a grin.

"You had not reported that the Espion's access to Server was quite so developed," Emoth whispered.

"It was always designed to be that way, but that he has mastered it? I was not aware of that myself," replied Mela-14 softly. "You must understand that his neural pathways and the huma-nanites are still bedding in. He is still growing and developing, and learning how to use his features."

"Is this a controlled development or are there concerns we might need to consider?"

Mela-14 cast a nervous glance back to Kylem that Emoth noted.

"Is there a problem?" asked Emoth.

"Not at all. It is just..."

"Just what?"

"Well, his hearing is enhanced, probably more so than even a Sallow's, so he can no doubt hear every word that we are saying despite our whispering."

Emoth raised his eyes to Kylem who was stood with his arms akimbo.

"Well?" he asked the boy. Kylem smiled.

"Well, what?" he asked in return, but even Emoth knew he was lying.

Emoth sighed deeply and sat back down, waving Mela-14 away.

"Are we not straying from the point?" demanded Mada impatiently. "He was in the middle of telling us what makes a Sallow a Sallow."

"Yes," agreed Emoth, "but Mela-14, I would like to see a full report on the

61

Espion's access capabilities immediately after this hearing. In the meantime, Kylem, continue. Tell us what you believe it is that defines a Sallow."

Kylem waited for Mela-14 to return to his post before continuing. He took a sharp intake of breath and began again.

"To be a Sallow, you must have the heart of a Sallow."

Doobee, Jurrish and Rathan nodded in agreement without realising it.

"Warriors have no hearts—"

"Nor do Scientifics," reminded Mada coldly, "so why speak of Warriors alone?"

"True, but this only serves to make my point. Scientifics do not have physical hearts, no, but it is not physical hearts of which I speak. I have two hearts and am Sallow, but that does not make me twice the Sallow that any of you are. Scientifics, like you, think for themselves. They are designers and have creative abilities. They love their race, the Sallow race, and will fight and give everything they have for it. They have aspirations and..."

Mela-14 went rigid with fear.

What was Kylem saying? Did Kylem know about his defect? Did he know of his sentiency? Mela-14 felt sick to the pit of his stomach. He glared at Kylem, thankful that his face was fixed and could not betray his emotions to his masters. Damn the boy! Damn these feelings! Damn this sentiency!

Inexplicably, Kylem looked over his shoulder directly at his father.

Mela-14 felt more alarm. What was that look in his eye? Was it query? Was Kylem confused? Why was he confused? Because the little shit could read him like a book! The little shit was inside his head! In the same way he could access Server, could the little shit could get inside his head? And why was he swearing?

"Kylem?" said Emoth. "Are you suggesting that the Scientifics are... sentient?"

Kylem felt Mela-14 baulk at the word. He turned back to Emoth but hesitated before he spoke. Something was wrong. He could sense it in his father. He wasn't sure what it was but the suggestion of sentiency had sparked it. Was that it? But now was not the time for this internal debate. Now was the time to back-pedal.

"God, no!" he exclaimed. "Dedication, devotion, loyalty maybe, but not sentiency."

Kylem took a step forward, inadvertently leaving the dock. All eight Warriors immediately took a step towards him in unison, stamping their feet noisily on the floor. Kylem stopped, rolled his eyes impatiently at them and took another two deliberately large and exaggerated steps forward. The Warriors mirrored his steps.

Kylem accessed Server, notifying it of his intentions. The Warriors received commands. Seven of them took three steps back and the eighth stepped forward so that it was just an arm's length away from Kylem.

The blood-Sallows were aghast and Kylem instantly knew he'd slipped up. The Warriors should not have stepped back like that. As part of the contingent, their duty was to protect the blood-Sallows and thus, they had mirrored every step of Kylem's advance towards the bench. Stepping back was not in the protocol.

The blood-Sallows' eyes bulged in horror at Kylem's control of the Warriors and Mada rose, speechless. He stood with his arm outstretched, pointing at Kylem with his mouth open.

"Don't look so worried," assured Kylem, seeing the alarm on the Sallows' faces.

As if in response and to reassure them, Uldakers unfurled from the forearms of the Mark-X's and locked into place, targeted upon Kylem.

"I'm sorry. I did not mean to alarm you," but the blood-Sallows found little reassurance in his words. Kylem, on the other hand, felt a rush of exhilaration at the control he had over the blood-Sallows—the emotional control he had over them. He'd actually frightened them, but that was not a good idea. The blood-Sallows would never let him live if they thought he had any control over his android brothers.

"Hey, I simply accessed Server and notified it of my intentions. *It* gave the instructions and clearance, not me!" he assured them.

"And the arming of the Sallows?" asked Emoth.

"They reacted to you, not to me!"

"So you did not do this?" Emoth demanded, pointing at the Warriors.

"God no! Of course not! My access might be better than you had anticipated but it's still just access. I can't control the Warriors any more than a slave can."

Emoth looked at Mela-14 who stood motionless for a moment.

"I concur," he stuttered. "He is just an android with a lowly status. He has no control over Server or the Warriors."

"Are you sure?"

"Yes," and he fumbled in his pocket for the scanner. He pulled it out, looked at it dumbly for a moment and then flicked it open and passed it over Kylem. He looked at the readings and nodded in affirmation.

"Diagnostics confirm it. Server confirms it. Circumstances may have generated the illusion of him having control, but he has none."

Although reassured, the blood-Sallows still seemed uncomfortable but they re-seated themselves, glaring at Kylem all the while.

"May I continue?" asked Kylem. Emoth signalled his approval with a simple eye movement. Kylem began to circle the Warrior.

"As I was saying, this has no heart, no passion—or whatever else you want to call it. It is nothing more than an inanimate object," and he came to stand directly in front of it. It looked down upon him with its cold red eyes and Kylem felt uncomfortable. Kylem looked back at it. It was inexplicable but... there was something there. Something sinister that unnerved him.

"Kylem?" prompted Emoth, breaking Kylem from his reverie.

"It is dead," he continued. "It is lifeless... passionless... compassionless. It is a lesser thing than even I," and he looked back up into its cold face, still searching for the oddity whilst his words trailed on.

"Emoth, when you kill, you kill for pleasure. When Mela-14 kills, he kills to sate his curiosity, but this? Why does this kill?" and he walked around it one more time. "It kills because you tell it to, not because it desires it or wants it. It doesn't feel such things. It doesn't feel. It doesn't want. It has no curiosity. It does what you have designed it to do. No more. No less. And for that you think that this *thing*—" he emphasised the word with scorn, "—is a Sallow? It is not a Sallow. It's just something made by Sallows, to serve Sallows. It's just a machine. Nothing more and nothing less."

"Not like Jordan-5 then?" retorted Mada.

"Jordan-5 sought my destruction!" shouted Kylem angrily. "It sought the termination of the Espion Project and the future of the Sallow race! If you wish to charge me with the destruction of a Sallow, charge me with his destruction but not that of a stupid Warrior that I never laid a hand upon!" His eyes flashed angrily at the Sallows, and the Sallows conferred again.

"Some very valid observations," announced Jurrish, "and perhaps the charge regarding the Warrior is incorrect, but you mustn't be so disrespectful of them. It may be that, one day, your model supersedes them but they have served us very well for many years and have fought our battles admirably. They are stronger and faster than any humanoid species we have encountered and thus we have great pride in them."

Kylem smiled disdainfully back at the Warrior and shook his head in disagreement.

"No. I disagree," he said, locking eyes with it. He raised his eyebrows mischievously at it and began to circle it again. The Warrior's eyes followed him. As Kylem began to disappear from its view, it shifted position, swivelling about to maintain the lock. At just the point when it was stood on one leg, Kylem's right foot kicked out and punched into the back of the Warrior's knee, guaranteeing its passage to the floor. It hit the deck hard but, being as agile as Jurrish had promised, it flashed around, quickly recovering its feet, spinning into a crouched position with one hand on the deck, ready to pounce. He heard the buzz of Uldakers powering up. Kylem stepped back, his hands raised in surrender but still glaring at the Warrior. Kylem laughed.

"Faster than any humanoid species?" repeated Kylem mockingly. "I don't think so."

He turned his back on the Warrior as a final insult, secure in the knowledge that it wouldn't be permitted to strike. He returned to the centre of the dock and placed his hands neatly behind his back to stand at ease, and waited.

Emoth took a deep breath and again conferred with his colleagues. Kylem watched as the Sallows, with their heads bowed, nursed their earpieces.

Was the Espion the success they wanted or was this machine running rampant?

After a few moments, the blood-Sallows straightened themselves in their chairs and Emoth placed both his hands flat on the bench in front of him.

"You have some very high opinions of yourself. You obviously think yourself better than a Warrior, do you not?"

"Yes."

"But that is a position you must earn. You have also raised a number of questions regarding your functionality. You have, in the space of one day, destroyed a Scientific and plotted the destruction of a Warrior. That, at the very least, shows disrespect for the property and achievements of the Sallow Empire. These are acts that concern us—"

"I do not disrespect the achievements of the Sallow Empire," Kylem interrupted.

Emoth raised an eyebrow disapprovingly. He wasn't used to being interrupted, but Kylem was oblivious to him. He was in full flow.

"I merely know that the Empire is on the brink of something new. The Warriors have taken the Empire as far as it can go. Now you need something new and something better. With the Espion, you have this new tool, and the Empire will rise to new heights. I merely look upon your old tools as the relics that they are."

Mela-14 wished he'd just shut up but knew he didn't stand a hope of that wish coming true.

Rathan activated his earpiece and whispered to Emoth. Emoth looked disturbed for a moment, then quizzical and then nodded his approval at Rathan. Rathan leaned forward.

"So tell me, Kylem. Here we are, with an untested prototype that is behaving in an unpredicted manner. You could be malfunctioning."

"Or I could be exactly what you desire. The object of the Espion Project is to create a new Sallow Warrior that appears humanoid. To appear humanoid, one must look and act humanoid. My outward appearance is not under scrutiny, but to act humanoid? Does that mean I am humanoid? That is your concern. Are my hearts and my head Sallow or humanoid, and what are my physical capabilities as a Warrior? That's a very high and varied specification for one android."

Emoth leant back in his chair, folded his arms and cradled his chin in one hand whilst he thought.

"We shall adjourn for a moment," and with that he stood up and left the room. His four companions followed.

* * * * *

"He is still erratic," argued Mada in the private rooms beyond the Chamber.

"Yes," agreed Doobee, "but let's look at the facts. He is an android with humanoid tendencies programmed into him. That is what we sought and that is what we've got."

"But he is unstable!" repeated Mada.

"No more so than any other adolescent. Come on, Mada, you're surely not going to tell me that you never had a tantrum as a child."

"But he's not a child!"

"Six days ago he was!"

"But not now! Now he is an adult!"

"Wait a minute," interrupted Jurrish. "Doobee has a point there."

"Yes," cried Doobee again. "What about all those hormones that a pubescent body produces? That his body has produced in bulk over a very short period of time?"

"What hormones?" shouted Mada.

"Oh come on, Mada. You're the biologist," said Rathan. "All those hormones that turn a boy into an adult, physically and mentally; that make his voice break and develop his sexuality. He has ten years' worth of that stuff pumping through his veins all in one go. And let's be frank, Mela-14 did express his concerns on this matter several months ago."

"So are you suggesting that we forgive him these misdemeanours? What about his appalling behaviour at the dinner table last night?" cried Mada.

"We must accept some of the responsibility for his behaviour ourselves," said Rathan more softly. "We gave him the drink. We placed him in a position where he had to drink it. Between that and the accelerated growth treatment, what we got was an over-emotional, hormonally driven juvenile with pubescent outbursts, fuelled by copious amounts of alcohol that he was unaccustomed to. And now we're sitting here wondering at his behaviour. We have to accept some of the blame."

"Yes, well you would find such behaviour forgivable, wouldn't you?"

"Now, now!" bellowed Emoth. "Stop it. We're arguing like children and bandying insults between ourselves now. How can we slander the boy for behaving so badly if we cannot behave amongst ourselves?"

"So what do we suggest?" asked Jurrish calmly.

* * * * *

Time seemed to stand still as the silence stretched out. Finally, the door opened and the blood-Sallows returned. They sat and recomposed themselves with great dignity and after a few moments, Emoth spoke.

"We could very well be, as Kylem claims, at a turning point in our history, but we don't know that. We do not know that the Espion is going to be an effective weapon. Unlike our Scientifics and our Warriors, we do not know what it 'thinks' or 'feels'. We cannot download its archives as we can a Warrior's. Nor can we wipe its memory and completely reprogram it. So how do we know if it is fit for purpose?

"We must test it. We must test you, just as we must test every weapon and every other advancement in our technology before rolling it out for general distribution. We must test your physical abilities, your stealth and strategic cunning against those of our existing Warriors, because you must be at least as good as, if not better than, our existing Warriors. We must test your ability to infiltrate a humanoid settlement so that when we send you out into the field, you will not be discovered. We must test your mettle and your soul, and this we shall do. And as we test you, as you prove your worth, you will earn your position in our society. Today you stand before me as a skunk. Tomorrow you may be seated at my dinner table as a true blood-Warrior or you may be at my dinner table as part of the main course, but until then, you are a skunk. Do you understand me?"

"Yes."

"Mela-14, step forward."

Mela-14 bolted to attention and stepped forward onto the dock.

"Yes sire," he said meekly. 'Sire' was not a word that was used often and that Mela-14 used it made Kylem aware of the importance and severity of what was being said.

"You will teach it manners. You will teach it how to behave in the company of Sallows as well as in the company of humanoids. I will not be insulted by this thing again, do you understand me?"

"Affirmed," and he bowed his head subserviently.

"As for you," and he turned again to Kylem. "Your first test will be tomorrow. You will prove your mettle against the Warriors."

"Okay," he said, and felt a sharp nudge from Mela-14. "Sire," he added quickly.

"This Council is dismissed."

Emoth placed his hands on the bench and the gong sounded. The blood-Sallows ceremoniously left the room. The Warriors, ignoring Kylem and his father, fell out and also departed. Only Kylem and Mela-14 remained.

"How'd you think it went then?" Kylem asked humorously. Mela-14 stood fumbling with the scanner that lay in his pocket and felt angry with himself.

"Well?" prompted Kylem.

"I hope you like a challenge," he replied.

"Why?"

"Because tomorrow you are going into the maze."

Kylem thought for a moment.

"That's okay. I like the maze. I like hunting with the Warriors."

"Not with them, stupid!" shouted Mela-14. "Against them!"

"Oh."

"Yes, 'oh!'" he mimicked. "They will slaughter you!"

Kylem sighed, took a sharp intake of breath and smiled. He slipped his arm playfully through his father's and began leading him out of the Chamber. The doors closed majestically behind them as they ambled slowly down the corridor.

"No, Father, they're not gonna slaughter me," he assured him and tugged affectionately at the android. "'Cause I'm gonna smash the mother-fuckers out of existence."

Mela-14 turned and looked at Kylem who was smiling devilishly at him. The child was insane.

"Now, if you don't mind, I need to prepare."

He released Mela-14 and broke off into a canter down the corridor, leaving Mela-14 alone and somewhat confused. What was he going to do with the boy?

CHAPTER 10

Mela-14 was deeply troubled. He walked back to his laboratory, all the while toying with the scanner in his pocket. Having arrived, he sat at his desk and pulled the scanner out. He laid it down purposefully in front of him, lining it up so that its edge was parallel to that of the desk and stared at it as the instrument of his deception. When the blood-Sallows had asked him to verify Kylem's claim about accessing Server, he had pulled out the scanner, pretended to use it and then lied. It wasn't even the right sort of scanner for heaven's sake—it was an engineering scanner for testing electrical circuits. But why then, had he lied to the Council? Was he protecting Kylem or was he protecting himself? Was he in fear of his own life? Was he even, technically speaking, alive?

He picked up the scanner and threw it angrily into the back of his desk drawer, slamming it shut and buried his head in his hands.

The Espion Project had just begun to come to fruition. He had waited years to get this far; before this it had all been preparation. First, there was the gene selection process which had required the analysing and classifying of hundreds of humanoid species. After that had come the selection process, followed by the cutting and splicing of the genes ready for the blending to create, what was supposed to be, the perfect hybrid. Once the hybrid had been formed, new problems had emerged. The foetus had rejected the huma-nanites and mutated, so the genes chosen for cutting and adaptation had to be reconsidered. Then there was the unforeseen necessity for a surrogate to aid the foetus's development, and that was just to obtain the organic casing for the Espion.

As for the technological part, the artificial intelligence, it had soon become apparent that you couldn't just download a Warrior's program into an organic. Besides its behaviour betraying it as being just another android, the technology had to create a bridge between the organic part of the android and the machine part; thus they'd had to develop a suitable programmable material to blend with the organic, namely the huma-nanites. They had to be similar enough to existing Sallow technology to ensure compatibility, but different enough to be able to manage the organic. Then there was the question of how and when to introduce them into the foetus. Extensive experimentation proved that it had to be a gradual process, with each stage being monitored to ensure that the huma-nanites were properly accepted and integrated. As they destroyed the organic brain matter, they had to simultaneously assimilate the brain's information, learn how to use it and take control otherwise the organic would forget how to do even the simplest of things, like breathe.

Having achieved all that, the child was supposed to have been born by caesarean section and removed from the surrogate, but he had arrived early.

Prematurely born, he was small, puny and lacking in natural defences. It became blatantly obvious that androids did not know how to care for the young of organics. Insufficient means had been prepared for the baby and even less for a premature one. It had therefore been more practical to allow the surrogate to care for the infant and to feed him, thus providing him with antibodies from her milk to strengthen him. The solution had seemed to work. The child had grown stronger with each day and her nurturing had helped him with his social development with humanoids. After all, he was supposed to be able to live in their company, in the guise of a humanoid— although, first and foremost, he had to be a Sallow, and so he had to be removed from her care, but how soon?

Yet more choices followed. When to start his education, how to educate him and then, with regards to his physical training, did he need practical training where he could learn by doing—learn from his own experiences and mistakes—or like a Sallow Warrior, by downloading programs into him overnight as he slept?

In the end a combination of the two methods had proven to be the most successful, but with an organic body there were more difficulties. The blood-thing was so fragile. Test it too hard and you could hurt it, break it or kill it. Don't test it enough and it would not know its limits or learn how to care for its own fragility.

The same care had to be taken with the programming. Program it as a Warrior and all you'd have is a ruthless killing machine in an organic skin, with no ability to infiltrate and spy. Program it as a blood and you might end up with an emotional humanoid, with super strength and intelligence, working for the enemy. So which programming to use and which to reject? When to accelerate the development and by how much?

Ten years of hormones and teenage temper-tantrums, all abbreviated into a few overnight events, had given him an insight into the pitfalls. Every step of the project had been an experiment and now, finally, he was so close.

He knew that the Espion was still just a prototype. He knew its development was controversial. He knew that to be successful in its mission it had to be so heavily disguised as a humanoid that it would unnerve the blood-Sallows, which it did. So was it a success, or was it a failure?

If they terminated the project now, he'd never know so he had to keep it going. Not for himself though, not for his own survival, but because he was a scientist. He had to know. That's why he'd lied to the Council. That's why he'd hidden the data about the child's birth on the medical scanner, and that's why he would continue to protect him. Blood-Sallows were volatile creatures, erratic and indecisive, changing their minds again and again, so Mela-14 had hidden the data. He determined that only he was suitably equipped to decide when and if to terminate the project.

But there was still one problem—the one that he had discovered when the boy had collapsed in his quarters. He was having difficulty accessing the unit. The Espion had changed his access codes and built new firewalls. It was understandable though. He'd done a very similar thing himself, to prevent Server from learning of his plans.

The Espion was designed for one purpose and one purpose alone. To achieve that purpose, he had to have a well-defined sense of self-preservation, a persecution complex and a deeply suspicious mind. Without those things, he could easily be compromised and fail in his mission; and so it was that the Espion was suspicious of its own creators. He was obviously aware of his status, that he was just a prototype and an experiment that could be scrapped. That would make him want assurances, wouldn't it?

But that didn't solve Mela-14's problem: how do you infiltrate a unit that you don't have access to? Simple. You have to gain its trust.

* * * * *

Kylem had a thousand questions that he wanted answers to but for now, he had to prepare for the maze. He hadn't been long in his quarters when Mela-14 arrived. Kylem was surprised to see him.

"I told you I have to get ready," he said.

"I know we do."

"We?"

"*Know your enemy,*" he quoted.

"Sorry, but what do you mean by 'we'?"

"If you fail at this, I fail too and as a true Sallow, I do not accept failure well. Now, we have work to do."

CHAPTER 11

'Know your enemy.' Kylem knew this was true which was why when the Sallow Council arrived at the maze, they found him already there waiting for them.

The maze was a challenge. It wasn't a simple two-dimensional puzzle where you ran from corridor to corridor until you found the exit. It was a three-dimensional structure with moving walls, stairs, ladders, pits and slides. It contained a variety of 'dens'—large areas themed around different scenarios: a village, a wooded copse, a derelict mediaeval style church, a cavern and so on. A puzzle that could fox the most experienced of hunters as well as the prey, with its floors and ceilings that could open and close before your eyes; sideways, upwards, downwards or diagonally; opening your escape or sealing your fate; and if you should get trapped within the door, it would hold no mercy. It would simply crush you.

It was a place where the Scientifics tested their prototypes with new subroutines, pitting them against existing tried-and-tested models as well as the *'most resourceful of humanoids'* taken from the battlefields. It tested the cunning and skill of new models and helped in the development of the Warriors' programming because they all had the ability to learn as well as to share their knowledge and expertise.

With such fine sport available to entertain the blood-Sallows, adjoining the maze was the cinema. With its domed, bubble-like construction, the walls and ceiling formed a huge panoramic view screen allowing the voyeurs to fully immerse themselves in the hunt without any personal danger. It was carpeted in deep sapphire blue and furnished with an eclectic collection of chairs and chaises longues, each with brilliant white, curvy frames and deeply upholstered in various shades of blue velvet.

For Kylem, the maze was a familiar training ground where he had been taught to hunt, learning both from his prey and the Warriors that accompanied him. He had also witnessed its secrets from the cinema as part of the audience and studied the methods employed by his metal counterparts. Today though, the test was to be the Destroyer Series, Mark-I (Espion)—*'a prototype hybrid—a cross between the organic and the machine'.*

The excitement of the event filled the air as the blood-Sallows rendezvoused. They were chattering away excitedly like schoolchildren going on a trip because whichever way the test went it was bound to be entertaining. Kylem, despite his young age of six, was a trained Sallow Warrior. Now with the physical presence of an adult, it would be interesting to see what he could do. If he won, he would have proven his strength. If he lost, then the Espion Project would be deemed a failure but even then, nothing would have been lost. Much of the technology used in his creation was also being utilised in the Regenesis Project.

"You're early," pointed out Emoth.

"I'm punctual," corrected Kylem.

Emoth scowled. "Do you have any questions?" he asked, examining the weaponry Kylem had chosen.

From one hip, cradled in a holster, hung an Uldaker. Not the little one he had trained with as a child, but a full sized weapon. At his waist was a serrated hunting knife and on his back, a pair of swords were crossed: one a light scimitar affair, the other, a heavier machete type.

Emoth wondered what else the Espion had hidden about him.

"Oh, I think I know the rules by now. More to the point, is there anything new I should know about?"

Emoth laughed heartily.

"No, no, I don't think so. I wouldn't want to spoil the surprises. In you go then," he said chirpily, and Kylem entered the maze.

* * * * *

Kylem was enclosed in the 'lobby', an area about three metres square that served as the waiting room. He was a little nervous but healthily so. He limbered up by shaking his hands and flexing his fingers. He jogged gently on the spot, blew out some long breaths and rotated his head to relax his neck muscles. He had an advantage over many in that he knew the maze well despite its ever-changing layout, and he knew the enemy even if he didn't know their numbers.

He gently touched the Uldaker at his side and then craned his head to listen. He had particularly good hearing for a humanoid, thanks to his Sallow breeding. He could hear the partitions moving in the distance. Sometimes they moved softly, at others they banged and screamed noisily. Soon one would open for him. Which one would it be? —And at that moment, the partition in front of him dropped. It hit the deck below with a thundering crash that echoed furiously through the chambers, but still he waited.

He could see only a few metres ahead and then there was a left-hand turn. What lay beyond that he didn't know. Only the blood-Sallows, sitting in the cinema, knew that and equipped with their remote controls, each had the ability to activate the partitions; each could seal him into a dead-end with no escape, or open the way up for him. They could just as easily guide him into the path of his executioner as lead him to safety.

Cautiously, he took his first steps out of the lobby to the corner where he stopped. He took a daring glance around it, pulling his head quickly back before he'd properly had a chance to register what he saw there. It was just as well. A blast of light flashed, noise screamed past his ear and he felt the hairs on his head singe under the heat. Instinctively, he pulled back, pressing himself hard against the wall, which suddenly gave way behind him. He stumbled back into the void and although still dazzled by the light, took the opportunity offered to him. He turned and ran as far and as fast as he could. If he were going to fight a Warrior, he would need strategically better conditions than this. A good Warrior knew when to run as well as when to fight.

Another corner, but he had no choice. He had to go on. He could hear the Warrior's feet pounding up behind him. Then he heard a partition moving. He glanced back to see the way close in front of the Warrior. He wondered which Sallow he had to thank for that and which one to curse for having sent a Warrior to greet him so soon in the game.

He moved swiftly down the corridor, deeper into the maze, eager to put some distance between him and the lobby. Soon it would open up into the central labyrinth where the partition matrix was bigger and more open, with fixed stairways and ladders. If he made it that far, there would be more cover and more path choices. It would be a classic game of hide-and-seek and dodge-the-bullet, neither of which worried Kylem. He was well armed and experienced enough to tackle a Warrior, but he had to get there first and the corridors from the lobby to the central labyrinth still ran a long way. He'd always hated this first bit of the maze with its lengthy corridors.

In between the partitions moving, he could hear at least one Warrior's footsteps. They were agile creatures but not quiet, and these corridors only served to accentuate the noises. Kylem looked down at his boots and smiled. They weren't his usual ones. These had softer soles and although they were less durable than the ones he had been issued with, this gave him an advantage against the Warriors: silent running. Thank you Father, he thought.

Suddenly he stopped, waited and listened. There was a Warrior close by, very close by—just on the other side of the partition in fact. Another wall was moving. Was it the one between him and the Warrior? No, it was ahead, just beyond the corner—but was it opening or closing? A faint vibration in the partition between him and the Warrior sealed the decision. This one was about to open. No time to think— just run! He ran.

He rounded the corner. It was another long, clear run ahead, about fifty metres of uninterrupted corridor with no cover. He continued to run, glancing behind him. The familiar forms of two golden Warriors were there and closing fast, weapons drawn. He could hear the walls moving furiously around him, forcing him to take just one path, the noise drowning out the sounds of the Warriors' footsteps. He picked up his pace, but glanced behind again. They were still there. He looked, again, in front of him to the open corridor ahead, but it was gone!

He hit the wall with the full force of his speed behind him and bounced dully off it like a poorly inflated football. Another wall closed in behind him. He hit that too. Reeling from the double blow, dazed and confused, he swung about with the Uldaker in his hand waiting for the stars to clear. He was now in a tiny cubicle... trapped.

* * * * *

"For goodness sake, Mada! Give the lad a chance!" exclaimed Jurrish.

"I thought he was supposed to be clever! This should be easy for him!" he retorted.

"He may be clever but you're just throwing him to the lions. There's no sport in this. You've manoeuvred him into the arms of two—"

"Three," corrected Doobee disapprovingly, and pointed at the screen. Jurrish looked and scowled.

"—three Warriors!"

"I agree," said Emoth. "I can see an execution any day of the week. If we test him fairly, if he's a viable Warrior, he'll do well. If not, I at least want a little bit of entertainment for all our troubles."

Mada scowled at his companions, nodding reluctantly in agreement.

"Right then. Mada—stop it!" and he snatched the remote control from Mada's hand. "Rathan, call the Warriors back. Give the boy a few minutes to recover, then give him the start he should have had in the first place—and no more of this nonsense, Mada!"

* * * * *

The minutes seemed endless as Kylem waited. He desperately needed an advantage. It seemed as though the blood-Sallows were out to kill him so he'd have to be spectacularly good to impress them enough to save his skin. He closed his eyes, activated Display and accessed Server. To his delight, the pain was minimal. Perhaps his huma-nanites were getting to grips with things again. Using the access codes that Mela-14 had provided him with, he hacked his way into the traffic: the communication highway used by all the artificially intelligent. All of the androids were equipped with transceivers to communicate wirelessly with each other over short ranges, and through Server for longer-range transmissions. For the purposes of this exercise, his own link had been severed—but not for long.

The traffic indicated that there were Warriors barely a spit away, and they were synchronising their movements against him. No, wait a minute. They were receiving new instructions. They were retreating. They had been recalled by... Rathan! He listened some more. It seemed that Mada was the one seeking his demise. No surprises there then, but what had changed? Why were they being recalled? He opened his eyes and lost the link. That was a nuisance; something he would have to address, but not now.

He drew his breath slowly and purposefully, making as little noise as he could. Between the thunder of moving doors, stony silences fell. Kylem held his breath to listen and then, in the mute punctuation between the doors' groans, he heard it again: footsteps, but not a Warrior's footsteps. They were irregular. They were humanoid. So he had humanoids, as well as Warriors, to deal with.

He dared to close his eyes once more to re-access the Warriors' traffic. He was painfully aware of how vulnerable he became with his eyes closed and how little he could hear around him when he was monitoring traffic. He filtered the transmissions down to those of the Warriors in the maze but it was harder than he'd anticipated. He counted four, maybe five or even six, but he couldn't be sure.

Without warning, the floor beneath him gave way and he plummeted down to the level below on the newly formed slide. With the added momentum from the slope, he hit the deck running and leapt forward into the corridor beyond, only pulling himself to a halt when he was satisfied he was clear of immediate danger.

He measured his breaths—long, quiet, deep. He couldn't afford to start panting noisily. It was a flaw in humanoids he had used to his advantage when he was a hunter. He wasn't going to give the Warriors any advantages if he could help it.

A partition suddenly and silently swung up into place in front of him, sealing the way. That was inconvenient. He turned to face the way he had come. There was now a crossroads ahead. He took a step towards it and stopped dead as the tip of a shadow fell across the junction. He held his breath and waited as it lengthened. There was nowhere to go. He raised his Uldaker and braced it with both hands. He'd only get one shot at this. What surprised him most though, was the lack of noise from the Warrior. Was this one of the new models his father had told him about? Or was it just an ordinary Warrior being unusually stealthy?

The shadow now spanned the whole of the junction. He could hear its footsteps now it was getting closer, which answered his question. There was a brief flash of gold as it waved its arm in the abyss, but Kylem didn't flinch. That was an old trick to draw the prey out, to fool it into giving away its presence, but he wasn't going to fall for that one. He was going to wait for his shot, his one and only shot.

Suddenly, the Warrior sprang into the junction with its Uldaker raised, pirouetting guerrilla-like, checking all the corridors in every direction as quickly as it could. It spun clockwise, as Kylem had predicted. Kylem was in the corridor to its left giving him the maximum amount of time possible. Perfect! Kylem's shot rang out. One shot directly into the back of the neck, perfectly aimed between the skull and neck plates. The Warrior spasmed and fitted, its arms shaking epileptically. The Uldaker dropped from its hand and it began toppling forwards onto its face. The floor beneath it gave way and it was swallowed up into the chasm. Kylem ran up to the gaping hole, but it resealed itself before he got there.

That was too convenient—or maybe it was lucky, but he doubted it. As for the Warrior, it was doubtful that the blast had been enough to deactivate it but it would be heavily disabled. If this were on the battlefield, it would simply lie and wait wherever it fell in case an easy target passed by, but once the battle were over, it would deactivate itself and shut down. Kylem sighed and looked around, taking his bearings, making a note of where the injured Warrior lay on the floor below. Where next?

Not far from here, about eighty metres to his left, there was a permanent cavity in the decking. It was about four metres wide, six metres across and six metres deep. In it was a series of static, white poles about twenty centimetres in diameter and over a metre apart. Each one sank lower, forming a set of steps if you could leap from one to the next. If not, it was a full twenty-foot drop to the floor below. Kylem smiled. This was a section he knew well and a section he liked, so he headed towards it.

He got there with relative ease and effortlessly leapt from one step to the next to descend. As his feet hit the deck, a doorway opened up in front of him and he entered willingly, knowing that a den lay beyond that would offer much better cover—and much better sport.

* * * * *

The den mimicked a town razed to the ground by shellfire many years ago. The streets were deserted and the buildings reduced to remnants of brick walls. Tumbleweed lolloped down the street in the gentle breeze generated by Server. Weeds encroached and grew along the kerbsides and out of the debris. In the middle of the street, a burnt-out old van lay rusting on its side. It might have been red once. Even the light-blue sky had little, puffy white clouds floating gently across it. This was more like it.

He hurriedly sought cover in the pathetic remains of a building and waited. He closed his eyes and dared another listen in on the traffic. Yes, there was a Warrior close by. He could read it clear as day and he could identify it too. Mela-14 had taken great pains to show him the new Warrior prototypes that were currently being tested and from its registry, Kylem could tell that this was one of them: the Chaser.

The Chaser was revolutionary in design. Jurrish had almost taken a step back in time, utilising an earlier model from several hundred years ago that had been much nimbler and quieter on its feet, and then completely redeveloping it with modern, stronger and more resilient materials. He'd added to the specification and refined the aerodynamics of the Warrior to give it a stealth, speed, accuracy and silence that none of the current models enjoyed. It had lost its golden lustre and was instead, the dull grey colour of base metal. It was tall with spindly-looking arms and legs that misrepresented the power and strength within it, and it had a short, horn-shaped head that curled down towards the back of its neck and housed the traditional glowing red eyes. The abdomen and chest were trapezium shaped with their smaller edges marrying up via a complex web of cables and conduits that formed the spine. The abdomen was small and the chest broad and fashioned like a gladiator's breastplate. Its arms were abnormally long to match the length of its legs, enabling it to move with the same stealth on all fours as it did on two legs. Its left hand had an Uldaker built into its wrist, and its fingers were comprised of an impressive array of long jointed blades like filleting knives.

Kylem knew that to disarm it, he would have to aim between the trapezoids, at the trappings of its spine. He opened his eyes, listened again and began activating some of his own features. His software reconnoitred the area. It noted the cover and the open spaces, the vantage points and the potential pitfalls, and his heat seekers came on-line. The Chaser would not register as warm as a humanoid but it would generate some heat. Would it be enough for him to pick it up, though? Oh yes, it would! Glory be!

It was not a brilliant signature by any means, but a faint heat signature from beneath the breastplate was visible. He made a mental note to recommend more shielding be applied if the model were to be a viable one, and then he began to formulate his attack.

He was crouched down behind a somewhat unstable, crumbling wall that had once formed the corner of a building. An ivy-like plant had taken hold over the remains and wrapped itself around the brickwork. The ground was rough and strewn with blasted building materials, concrete and tarmac. Part of a rusty, old bed frame lay behind him and what could have been a cooker.

Kylem moved cautiously out from his hiding spot, keeping the Chaser in his sights all the while. Momentarily, it disappeared from view behind a wall, and then it sprang up from behind it like a cat and sat perched on all fours, with its comma-shaped head looking around, scanning the area. Its stealth was certainly impressive. Suddenly, its head stopped moving and became fixed upon Kylem's position. It had heat-seeking equipment too.

It moved like a spider over the wall, hunting with long, spindly limbs that gently touched the surface, testing it before committing to each movement. One long, twig-like arm reached out and then the other, followed by its left foot and then its right. It manoeuvred itself off the wall and onto the floor. The Espion's heat signature was strong. He had been running so he was hot and his signature glowed like a beacon in the night to the Chaser.

It crept slowly forwards towards the wall behind which Kylem was hidden and craned its head first to the left and then to the right. Its neck stretched as it did so, to enhance its range. Then it looked up and coiled itself, wriggling its bottom like a cat preparing to jump, and sprang silently up the eight-foot wall, landing on top of it with legs splayed to either side of its body. It looked down to where Kylem should have been but was disappointed to find that the space was vacant. Kylem had gone.

Its head slowly rotated, searching afresh for the signature and found its mark to the right, taking refuge behind the remains of the upturned van. It crept across the top of the wall. A brick dislodged and fell to the floor. The Chaser watched it as it crumbled into large lumps and then looked back to its mark. The wheel on the van was turning slowly where the runner had disturbed it. The mark had moved further off. The Chaser scanned again and found the signal behind another wall. It was a little hotter. It was probably scared. When humanoids were afraid, their hearts pounded, their muscles tensed, they sweated more and became flushed. They ran 'hot'.

It dropped silently from the wall and stood up to its full height, its long, gangly arms hanging limply at its sides. It walked over to the van with long, deliberate footsteps that made no sound, and its arms swung gracefully as it trod. It dropped back onto all fours and crept around the vehicle.

It moved more slowly now and peered cautiously around the wall. Behind it, a makeshift hideout had been erected. There was a pile of debris with a sheet of rusty corrugated iron propped up in front of it and behind that, poorly masked, was ATB-80's hot signature.

It tipped its head almost sympathetically as it considered the poor, frightened humanoid hiding there and crept towards it. It flexed the long, knifey fingers of its right hand and clawed them into a deadly five-pronged weapon ready to thrust into his flesh. With its left hand, it wrenched the iron free and plunged its fingers forward, slamming them it into what lay beneath, and then drew back somewhat perplexed.

Kylem could actually feel its disappointment at him not being there, and its puzzlement as it stared into the flames of the small fire he had set behind the sheet of rusty iron. He savoured it for a moment, but just a short moment. Then he rose up from the shadows behind the Chaser, with the machete held firmly in both hands. He thrust it as deep and as hard as he could into the crevice between its trapezoids.

The scream that it hollered from its alarm system was bestial, wailing high and long. Its back arched and it fell forward, but Kylem was prepared for that. He fell with it, ensuring that the blade was caught in the main spinal conduit. He twisted it to left and right, paralysing limbs and severing the main artery. Lubricant sprayed out in a huge arc and the Chaser's systems lost pressure. Kylem continued to twist the blade, but it wasn't necessary. It was already incapacitated. The Chaser's fate was sealed. As the last of its lifeblood dribbled from its spine, its skeletal frame relaxed and gave a final sigh. The lights in its eyes dimmed and died.

Kylem straightened up to admire his handiwork and then he looked up into the camera. He couldn't see it but he knew exactly where it was having watched from the cinema so many times before. He licked his finger, chalked the number one in the air twice and then he winked at it.

* * * * *

Inside the cinema, the whoops and hollers were deafening. Mela-14 stood on the periphery of the room smiling quietly to himself. Jurrish, Doobee and Rathan were hugging each other, jumping up and down like excited school children, their robes flapping clumsily about them, and Emoth was grinning so broadly that it looked like his face might break apart.

Mada sat stony faced.

"I don't know what you're so happy about, Jurrish!" exclaimed Mada. "He's just buried your Chaser project."

"No, no, no, he hasn't," bubbled Jurrish, breaking free from the group. He ran over to Mada and bent down to draw level with his face.

"Don't you see?" he beamed. "He's better than the Chaser. The Espion is *better* than the Chaser, and I've already tested the Chaser against our Warriors. It's an absolute success. Once Kylem is debriefed, I can make a few minor modifications and the Chaser can go into full production. Both the Espion and the Chaser are successes!"

"It's not over yet!" mumbled Mada begrudgingly.

* * * * *

Kylem left the den and re-entered the corridors of the maze. He was now on the outskirts of the central labyrinth where the terrain was more amenable to him. The corridors were shorter with side junctions every couple of metres and as the open areas grew more abundant, more partitions were fixed. It was a more stable environment and Kylem felt more relaxed. Nevertheless, he proceeded cautiously, hugging the walls, with his Uldaker at the ready.

He came to an open crossroads in an area that he knew to be exposed, but he had to cross it. He drew his second Uldaker, the little one that he had trained with as a child and had hidden inside his jacket. It was tiny in his hands now but wonderfully easy to carry and conceal. He calculated his move, prepared and then tumbled across the floor in a forward roll that an Olympic gymnast would have been proud of. His arms were crossed in front of him, bracing the Uldakers steady against his chest, their barrels pointing to left and right. Having traversed the intersection, he rolled neatly onto his feet and ran on without delay. No time to stop and inspect, to see if anything were in pursuit, but with no repercussions it appeared to have been clear so deeper into the maze he ran.

He knew the instant that his foot touched the floor that something was amiss. The floor panel gave way beneath him, dropping into a slide but that was not the problem: that eventuality he had trained for. He knew how to land and how to control his sliding descent, but as he began to plunge, he heard the scream of sheering metal and the panel's hinges tore free. The slide collapsed and as the whole panel crashed down to the floor below, Kylem fell backwards, smacking his coccyx hard onto the surface. He landed badly and yelped with pain but he had no time to spare. He was too vulnerable, so he spun around onto his feet and ran off into the corridor, limping badly as he went. Having put some distance between himself and the panel, he stopped for the luxury of rubbing his wounds and winced at the pain. He swore quietly under his breath and then carried on. He never saw the Warrior crushed beneath the panel.

Kylem was moving more slowly now, pandering to his bruises. He had no idea how long this test would last. He had to pace himself.

The wall behind him opened and Kylem turned sharply with both Uldakers extended, but the corridor was clear. He listened.

In the silence of the maze, every sound was poignant; every footstep announced its owner's location. Even the partitions spoke their own language, scraping when they slid like doors, thudding as they opened like trapdoors, crashing as they freefell to the floor below and gently whirring as they were raised. He could also pick out the gentle vibrations that they so very often made just before they moved.

He felt one now, on the wall behind.

He swung about as it slid swiftly to one side and fired his Uldaker into the void beyond. It was an insurance shot, but as Uldakers blasted out and light exploded, burning everything into a confused white mass, he was thankful for his prudence. Blinded by the light, he heard the crash and the grating sound as the Warrior slid down the wall. He glimpsed it as a faint, golden haze through his baffled eyes. He blinked wildly to clear the shock to his eyes, the light blindness, and then looked at the Warrior. The red eyes still glowed faintly and the Warrior twitched. Kylem fired another shot into its eye. The glass shattered but the other eye still shone. Should he risk a final shot? He didn't have to. The eye faded and died.

* * * * *

"Oh, come on! The slide shearing off like that was just sheer luck!" laughed Jurrish, half-heartedly protesting.

"Luck had nothing to do with it!" giggled Rathan.

"Well, what else do you call it?"

"Poor maintenance."

Jurrish shook his head good-humouredly.

"He has the luck of the devil, that boy!"

"Maybe, but he has taken out three Warriors fair and square," Doobee replied and raised his glass in a toast. Rathan and Jurrish joined him, glugging merrily.

"Yes," agreed Emoth far more sedately. "It was a good show of reaction and stealth there—not quite as entertaining as the Chaser but very well done nonetheless," and he too, raised his glass with his comrades.

Mada sat sulking, silently swilling his drink around the glass. Emoth watched him thoughtfully.

"Do you know, I think I've changed my mind," Emoth finally said. "I don't think I want him to die today."

"You wish me to end the game?" blurted Mela-14, his heart soaring at the thought.

"Not quite. I'd still like to see him tackle the Hunter. Recall the other Warriors by all means, but I'd like to see him outwit that."

Mela-14 immediately sent the recall instruction. "What about the humanoid?" he asked.

"Humanoid?"

"Kyamena," he explained.

"Oh, yes," pondered Emoth.

"What's that doing in there?" asked Rathan.

"I threw it in for good measure," said Emoth. "Well, if ATB-80 wasn't going to last the day, not much point in keeping it alive; and this is what it was trained to do—to be pitted against the Espion."

* * * * *

Kylem lowered the Uldaker and listened. His eyes still hurt from the flashes and watered profusely. He wiped them on the back of his sleeve and blinked until they eased. How many more Warriors were there? He couldn't go on indefinitely.

He closed his eyes and listened to the traffic again, intercepting the last transmissions of the deactivated Warrior in front of him. It was a standard Warrior, Infantry Class, Mark-IX. How quaint, he thought.

Judging by the damage to the Warrior and the blackened, buckled wall behind it, one of his shots had caught it a glancing blow in the chest area. Another shot had hit it above the left breast, near the base of its neck.

The wall behind him suddenly screeched with protest as it tried to open. Kylem winced at the offence to his ears. The wall panel was jammed. When the Warrior had fired, it had aimed at the left-hand side of the opening, predicting that he would move to his right. The Warrior's judgement would normally have been correct. He would have moved to his right but as it was, he'd lurched to the other side because of the pain in his buttocks. He rubbed his coccyx again and scowled with irritation. Only his injury had prevented his death. He made a note to be less predictable in future.

He relieved the Warrior of its Uldaker on the basis that you can never have too many weapons and moved on.

There was another crossroads ahead. Kylem walked lightly on his feet. He still hurt and it was affecting his concentration so he stopped, closed his eyes and issued a command to override the pain. It worked but he knew that he'd pay a price for that luxury later. He opened his eyes and considered the crossroads.

The panel in the floor at the centre of the crossroads was missing leaving a wide, deep hole. A gentle whooshing sound behind him told him that pathway was now closed. He had no choice but to go forward. He sheathed all his weapons and studied the chasm, then with a hop, skip and a jump he ran at it and cleared the gap. On the other side, he just ran like hell. He didn't have time to stop and investigate what may have lain in wait for him there.

Kylem knew that he was approaching another den and he was looking forward to it. His eyes moved quickly about, continually scanning in all directions. The ceiling above opened and he turned swiftly upwards, throwing himself onto one knee, Uldaker aimed, but nothing emerged. He took a sharp intake of breath and continued on his way, gliding silently like a ghost down the deserted corridors. He came to another corner and tucked himself into the edge of it before poking his head around for a quick inspection. It was a dead end!

He looked back the way he had come, his only route, but the path was closing. He started a dash towards it but stopped abruptly. It was closing too fast, even for him.

A whirring sound and the wall behind began to open. Kylem turned and rolled agilely underneath it before it was even a foot off the floor. It was the only way to go and he knew it was an entry into the den. Getting in before it was fully open might provide him with the opportunity to get to cover before anything could take a shot at him.

80

No sooner had he cleared the door than the mechanism reversed, the gears graunching angrily. The door slammed shut but Kylem had already turned his attention to the scenario.

He was inside the ruins of an old warehouse or factory, albeit a rather glorious one, it having once been a church. Two rows of tall, thick pillars lined the central aisle in varying stages of decay. Perhaps, once, they had held up a second floor but now they stood redundant. Kylem tucked himself in behind one of them and continued his reconnoitre.

Little had changed since he was last here.

At the far end, the wall was furnished with a set of church windows: three high arches devoid of the stained glass that had once adorned them and with only parts of the mullions remaining. On either side of the aisle, small, functional square windows had been punched into the walls. Set high up, they were also devoid of glass and gaped gormlessly out into the evening sky. About halfway down the long room were the remains of a mezzanine floor supported by a row of finer pillars no thicker than a man's arm. The stairs leading up to it were gone.

The floor of the building was uneven. Once, it had been an impressive and colourful combination of tiles that bordered sophisticated mosaics, but now the mosaics had been destroyed by nature's reclamation of her ground. Weeds had pushed up through the gaps between the little tiles, spreading them asunder. Only the bigger border tiles remained sort-of intact.

The ceiling was supported by a skeleton of metal joists, rafters and purlins, quite ornate with Victorian swirls and flourishes cast into the metal. From that hung another structure: a large grid of iron, the bars of which were about three metres apart. It stretched from one end of the warehouse to the other and virtually its full width. Its original purpose was beyond Kylem. Perhaps it was part of a false ceiling or perhaps it was part of the machinery that had been housed there before it had been stolen from whichever world it came.

The sound of movement distracted Kylem. It emanated from the far end. Kylem closed his eyes to access the traffic, only to confirm what he already knew: that a Warrior was already in the den. He managed to snatch enough information from it to determine that it was a Hunter, another of Jurrish's new prototypes. He opened his eyes. He wanted to get a better look so gently, he slunk down the pillar and then peered gingerly around its side.

The light was beginning to fade as the simulation mimicked dusk, and the far end of the warehouse was heavily draped in shadows and darkness. Amongst the shadows, Kylem could just make out his adversary.

The Hunter also lacked the golden lustre of the traditional Warrior. This one was bathed in the grey, khaki and green shades of woodland camouflage but it was also destined to be produced in desert and urban camo. Much stockier and heavier than the Chaser, it didn't have the same vulnerabilities. It had, more or less, the same ratios as the traditional Warrior and thus was of more humanoid proportions although larger, standing over two metres tall. Its limbs were bulked out with bulletproof armour plating that concealed hidden compartments and housed additional weaponry. As standard, it was fitted with an Uldaker built into the underside of the left wrist, and in its right arm a crossbow and machete were neatly folded away like a Swiss army knife. Its thighs would normally be packed with hand grenades, fresh power packs, spare bolts and other ammunition although Kylem doubted it would have grenades on the DaerkStar. Its hands were large and powerful with elongated fingers, and its armour plating covered the whole of its chest and spinal areas. It didn't have the same cat-like agility of the Chaser, but nor did it have its weak spot at the base of its torso.

Cover in the room was basically limited to the remains of the columns. Kylem reckoned that whilst he was probably as fast as the Hunter, in the confines of the den, he would tire before it did. However, he was lighter and nimbler and to take best advantage of this, he should head to the higher ground.

Kylem crouched down and re-holstered his Uldakers. He flexed his fingers in preparation and then gripped the column. The claws, hidden deep in the tips of his fingers, extended and bit into the stone and gave him adequate grip as he scaled it. He just hoped that the column was as sturdy as it looked and not invisibly crumbling away. Getting to the top was not effortless. The stone was hard and smooth, not like wood, the substance for which his animal claws were designed. At the top of the column, he sat perched upon his tiny island of stone.

He pulled up Display and began to compute the distances between the columns, comparing them to his own physical stature (he'd fallen foul of that error once before). If he'd been in this body a little longer, he would have known precisely what his own capabilities were. As it was, he had to rely on guesswork. Could he make the leap to the next column or not? He doubted it, so he turned his attention to the metal ironwork just above his head. As his eyes ran along the grid tracing its path, he judged its stability.

The sound of movement caught his attention. The Hunter had spotted him and was emerging from the shadows. For a moment, their eyes met and they stared at each other as if sizing each other up. Kylem wondered if the Hunter could climb.

The gentle hum of hydraulics signalled that it was engaging its crossbow. It was quite impressive the way it unfolded so neatly out of its forearm and sat on the top of it. The first thirty-centimetre bolt was already loaded, but subsequent bolts were stored in its left thigh. It was quite a primitive weapon really, slow to reload and with a limited range. He appreciated that it was still in the developmental stages but with manual reloading—well, personally, he would have resolved some of those issues before installing it in a Warrior.

Kylem stared hard as the Warrior aimed the weapon at him, his eyes narrowing in concentration. He focused upon the release mechanism.

As he concentrated, the world entered a state of slow motion. He saw the trigger squeezed, the tickler sprung and the string snap forwards, thrusting the bolt down the tiller and into the air. His eyes focused on the bolt as it approached and he adroitly tilted his shoulders to one side. The bolt sailed past him. There was a dull ting as it struck the wall far behind him and embedded itself into the brickwork.

Kylem raised an eyebrow at the Hunter and sneered. The Hunter considered the situation and then lurched forward into a sprint towards the column. Kylem did not hesitate. He leapt forward off his column, arms outstretched, reaching for the nearest metal bar of the mesh frame—and missed!

He went crashing to the floor but realising his error, rolled expertly as soon as he hit the ground. Rubble jabbed into his back. He sprang to his feet and began to run, zigzagging in and out of the columns. He cast a quick glance back to the Hunter, which was lurching after him. As it ran, it held out its arm and fired the Uldaker. Bullets of blue light whizzed past him, and he ducked and shied away from the shots.

All the while, his brain was analysing the Hunter's reactions and responses. He concluded that its armoury was clumsily arranged. The Uldaker was badly positioned on the underside of its arm, which hindered its ability to fire and made it impossible to use the weapon when climbing. It couldn't even reload its crossbow whilst on the move. Unlike the Chaser, this model would need a lot more work before going into final production. In the meantime, these flaws were the ones he was going to exploit, and to do that, he needed to get the Hunter off the ground.

The end of the warehouse was fast approaching. The wall with the huge multi-arched window was ahead. Kylem braced himself in readiness with his hands outstretched and claws extended. As he hit it, he leapt, drove his claws as deep into the brickwork as he could and yanked himself viciously up its face and onto the sill. Without pausing, he turned and leapt again for the grid, throwing himself almost sideways at it. This time his hands caught fast and the momentum began to swing him upwards. With his legs, he exaggerated the movement so that he swung up and over the bar. Rusty flakes drove themselves into the palms of his hands as he did so, but he paid them no heed. Then he let go and flew towards to the next bar of the grid. He kept the momentum going and flew from bar to bar like a gymnast, Display continually recalculating his moves, telling him where and when to let go.

At the fifth bar, as he reached the pinnacle of his swing, he pulled himself to an abrupt halt atop of it and perched. Crouched, with his legs straddled either side of his hands, he quickly glanced below to confirm that the Warrior was following at floor level. He stood up and ran the length of the bar towards the mezzanine floor, the metalwork bouncing gently beneath his weight. Reaching the end, he launched himself off it and came to land neatly upon the remains of the deck.

Deftly, he turned and looked for the Hunter. It was still running towards him. It looked up, pointed its Uldaker and fired. Kylem ducked and dropped from view. He drew his own Uldaker, took a deep breath, held it and then stood up. The Hunter saw him and fired again, but Kylem dodged to one side, running and letting a string of shots ring out in quick succession, all concentrated on one point—the Hunter's Uldaker.

A blast of brilliant, white light blossomed from its arm as the Uldaker's power pack exploded. The blast threw the Hunter backwards. It rolled across the floor several times but recovered its feet and stood with its shooting arm hanging limply by its side. The plating had been stripped away, wires were straggling and lubricant dripped from the severed pipelines. This would have been sufficient to disable a normal Warrior but the Hunter was better designed. It would not 'bleed' to death, because as the pressure dropped from its compromised lubrication system, cut-off valves activated and isolated the limb. It took a few moments more for additional fluids to be pumped back into its system and pressure restored, but not long. In the meantime, it undertook a damage assessment. The Uldaker was completely gone and the arm a useless stub. As for Kylem, he had run out of floor.

The Hunter's eyes searched for Kylem again and it lowered its good arm to its thigh. There were gentle clicking sounds as the arm docked onto its thigh and a fresh bolt loaded. It seemed that it was not quite as clumsy as Kylem had assumed. It looked up at the mezzanine floor but it was empty. Its eyes moved along the path upon which Kylem had been travelling and followed it through and over the edge. The Warrior deduced where he would have landed and made its way around the pillars.

It was suitably rewarded. There on the floor, stunned and dazed, was Kylem. He was on his hands and knees, reeling giddily as he pulled himself to his feet. He turned towards the Hunter but didn't actually see it. He was an easy target for the Hunter. It raised its arm and fired.

The bolt flew through the air and punched into his left shoulder. The impact threw him back against the wall; the long bolt skewered his flesh, pierced through bone and drove itself deep into the wall behind, impaling him upon it.

Kylem squealed like a dog and grabbed at the bolt, trying to pull it free but the bloody, smooth shaft just slipped through his fingers. He looked at the Hunter, slowly approaching, and snarled furiously at it. He was trapped. He was beginning to panic. His eyes turned red with rage and his hair stood on end. His claws and fangs extended, and he shook his head, roaring like a huge, angry lion, all the while fumbling at the bolt, but still he couldn't get a grip on it.

The Hunter stopped, just an arm's length in front of him, to savour the moment for its blood masters. It regarded its prey, trapped, pinned to the wall and panic stricken—but Kylem wasn't about to give up.

Suddenly, he wrenched himself forward, yanking himself off the bolt, pulling it right through his shoulder. He roared and screamed in agony as he ripped free of it and fell into the arms of the Hunter.

The Hunter seized the opportunity, grabbed him by the front of his jacket with its good arm and twisted him around. Kylem lost his footing and was dragged across the floor, his feet scrabbling against the loose mosaics. The Hunter pulled Kylem to his feet and slammed him against the nearest concrete pillar. Using its chest as a weapon to punch him with, it hurled itself at Kylem, slamming into him with its body. Kylem gagged, winded. The Hunter relaxed, backed off and then slammed into him again. Kylem's head flopped forward against the Warrior's chest. The Warrior backed off and repeated the exercise again and again, each time winding Kylem some more. The world began to darken, his arms dropped to his side and his head lolled as the last vestiges of consciousness left him. The Hunter felt him collapse, lifted him off his feet and threw him violently to one side, like a child throwing a toy onto the floor in a tantrum.

Chunks of rubble punched into his arms and chest, but it didn't matter. In that instant, free of the Hunter for one short moment, he gasped in the air he so vitally needed. Registering the gentle whirr of the Warrior changing its weaponry, loading the machete, Kylem scrabbled to his knees and fumbled at his thigh for the hunting knife. His fingers closed around the handle, hesitantly at first and then, remembering the dream—the carnage and the butchering on the battlefields, his fingers fastened into a steely grip.

The Hunter raised the machete high over its shoulder to make one final diagonal swipe and sever his head from his shoulders. Kylem saw the flash of the setting sun on the blade's edge as it came down hard and fast. He arched backwards and the blade swished by in front of his face, nicking his cheek as it passed. He lost his balance and hit the floor again. Another lump of rubble punched into his back like an iron fist. He dropped the knife and rolled off the rock, pain cannoning into his spine. He kept rolling haphazardly across the floor, trying to favour his ripped and bloody shoulder but failing miserably. As soon as he was able, he rolled onto his feet and then ran as though the devil himself was on his tail. But there was nowhere to go.

At the far wall, he stopped and turned. The Hunter hadn't followed. It didn't need to. It was stood where he had left it, watching him with its cold, blood red eyes assessing his condition. Kylem bent down, exhausted, resting one hand on his knee as he tried to catch his breath and carried out a similar damage assessment. He wished he hadn't.

He was tiring. His clavicle had been punctured and was badly splintered. He had several broken ribs that threatened to puncture a lung and countless other minor fractures. He was feeling faint as shock and concussion took hold, and he was bleeding internally as well as externally. He had lost a lot of blood and was still losing it. The Hunter, on the other hand, had only lost one limb. Other than that, it was relatively intact. It had no sense of exhaustion and was not 'bleeding' to death. In short, the Hunter didn't need to do much else to achieve its kill. It could just stand there and watch him exsanguinate if it pleased, but Kylem knew that it wouldn't because that wouldn't entertain the bloods. It would come to him soon enough, to finish him. The thought angered him. He wasn't going to die that easily for them.

Kylem drew a long, deep, painful breath and held it for a moment before exhaling. He gathered his thoughts and made a resolution: if he was going to die, he would die a proud man and he would die fighting like a true Sallow.

He straightened himself up and stood tall and proud despite his injuries. He pursed his lips and his eyes narrowed to slits. His injured arm felt cold. He nursed it, cradling it against his chest and tucked it inside his jacket to keep it out of the way. He then reached behind him to draw whichever blade came to hand, hoping that at least one of them was still there. His hand reassuringly found the machete.

Inside his jacket, his fingers touched upon the warm surface of the little toy-like Uldaker. Warmed by his body, it felt unusually hot in his cold and bloodless fingers, but they managed to wrap themselves around it.

Now the two of them stood, face-to-face, ready to dual. They moved away from the columns into the centre of the room where it was clearer and began circling each other. The Warrior flicked and twirled its blade as a gesture of intimidation. Kylem considered making a similar gesture but decided that it was probably not the best time for showing off. He momentarily wondered, how could he be so flippant at a time like this, but the thought quickly died as the Warrior lunged forward with its blade raised and brought it down hard. Kylem parried the blow skilfully although his knees buckled slightly under the impact. The blades rang out and sparks of metal flew as they struck. The Warrior stepped back and prepared for another blow. Kylem knew that he would not be able to parry many blows like that. He had to think of something. He had to take control of the situation.

As the Warrior raised its blade again, Kylem stepped back and off to one side, just enough to place him out of reach. The Warrior had to reposition itself for the blow so stepped forward. Kylem stepped back again. The Hunter glanced behind Kylem and smiled to itself. The stupid boy was backing himself into a predicament. Behind him were the remains of a concrete pillar that stood about a metre high, well below Kylem's eye-level. It manoeuvred itself around a little and then stepped forward, herding Kylem unwittingly back onto the pillar.

Kylem retreated again. Another step and Kylem's buttocks touched the pillar. It unbalanced him and he ended up sat awkwardly upon it, with his legs straddled on either side of it.

Kylem felt the Hunter smiling at him as it brought its blade down again. Kylem parried but it was badly judged. The Hunter's blade smashed into Kylem's and the machete leapt from his hand, somersaulting into the air. It clanged noisily as the pommel struck the floor, and then it bounced and tumbled through the air giving a dull ting each time the blade hit the concrete.

Both Sallows watched the machete spin and bounce further and further away. The Hunter lowered its blade triumphantly. Slowly, sadistically, it turned back to Kylem to grin at him as best it could with its cold, inanimate face.

Kylem could actually feel its disappointment when it found itself looking down the barrel of his tiny Uldaker. His hand was shaking slightly with weakness, but he was not too weak to grin back at it.

"Game over," he said and pulled the trigger.

The Uldaker, firing on automatic, released a fusillade of shots. As the first one struck the Warrior's face, Kylem pulled his own back, knowing all too well what the blasts could do at such close range. As they began stripping the face off the android, sharp shards of metal and splinters of glass flew through the air. Electronics sparked and screamed as the bullets penetrated deeper. The face began to erode, its plastic components melting away under the heat.

The blue light bullets intermingling with the multi-coloured sparks and golden confetti made an impressive firework display as the Warrior's face was sheared off, but Kylem knew that this wasn't necessarily the end. Taking the head off a Warrior wasn't like taking the head off an animal. Warriors didn't keep their brains in their heads, only their eyes and their sensors. The Warrior lurched backwards like a headless corpse, with its arms flailing wildly. It tripped over a lump of rubble and fell backwards onto the floor. It started to turn over but seemed to have forgotten that its arm was gone. It scrabbled about, blind and disabled. Kylem limped over to it.

The Hunter didn't hear the gentle shush as he drew the scimitar from its scabbard.

Standing over it, Kylem bent down and picked up a palm-sized chunk of rubble. Blood dripped off the ends of his fingers as he carefully positioned the tip of the blade under the edge of the Hunter's armour plating. He wiggled it gently, to ease it into the narrow gap between the plates and then, taking a calming breath, he raised his arm and smacked the rock hard against the pommel, driving the blade deep into its spine. He pounded on it a second time and then a third, and with each blow, the Warrior jerked and spasmed. When the blade would finally go no further, Kylem dropped the rock, took the grip in both hands and rocked it from side to side, using his knees to help force the blade. The effort and pain showed visibly in his face but didn't stop him. The Warrior struggled a little, but not much. In truth, it was too badly damaged and had already begun shutting down. The blade being wedged into its chest and severing its systems was little more than euthanasia. Kylem knew all this but he didn't care. This was symbolic.

Satisfied that it was dead, Kylem withdrew the scimitar. It screamed in protest against the metal as it came free, and he dragged its blade across the floor as he stepped back, exhausted. He looked at his handiwork for a moment, then threw his head back and opened his mouth wide to draw in deep, noisy, revitalising breaths. His body hurt, but it was time to move on.

Kylem sheathed the scimitar and walked over to his machete. The blade was hacked and dinted but he sheathed that too. He looked for his other weapons, kicking the rubble aside with his feet to reveal them. Having collected them all, he recomposed himself and approached the Hunter one last time. He relieved it of its extra power packs and checked its thighs for additional ammunition. He was right, though—no grenades.

He made his final assessment. It was not as effective as the Chaser in its current form but had the potential to be so with some modifications. The Uldaker needed remounting on the arm to enable it to fire whilst climbing or gripping. The power pack should be better protected and... Oh, what the hell! He hurt.

He was tired, he was bloody and he was weak. His wounds throbbed but the bleeding had slowed. His huma-nanites, it seemed, had finally started the healing process but his blood loss would take a while to resolve. He was still disadvantaged but it didn't matter. He was not going to quit now.

He walked up to the door of the den but it didn't open. He hammered on it angrily but weakly with the butt of the Uldaker.

"Open the fucking doors, you morons!" he screamed, but still it wouldn't open. What the bloody hell was going on? He closed his eyes and accessed the traffic. There was a message waiting for him. It said, "GAME OVER".

"Thank fuck for that," he mumbled to himself.

* * * * *

Having finally received Kylem's acknowledgement of the message, Mela-14 deactivated the doors and opened all the partitions.

"Excellent!" beamed Emoth. "Absolutely superb!" He took a sharp intake of breath and held it. He was brimming with emotion and quite tearful.

"And that, my dearest friends," he said proudly, rising to his feet, "is the embodiment of a true Sallow hunter. That's what we, as a race, used to be like."

"Shame he looks so human," sighed Mada.

"Yes," Emoth agreed, "the appearance is all wrong, but the heart! The heart is most truly Sallow!" He clapped his hands together and clenched them close to his mouth as if praying.

"Gentlefolk, let us stand and honour our Espion," he said dramatically, and all five Sallows stood and watched in silent wonder as the Espion limped through the maze, making his way home. Even Mada was somewhat in awe. He was actually considering using more of the Espion's genetic sequences in the skunks, to rebuild the Sallow race's former strength and stamina. These were certainly admirable Sallow qualities that the skunks were lacking in and, seeing as so much of the Espion's DNA was of Sallow origin, it would be quite acceptable to integrate more of it into the skunks' genetic makeup.

"Hmm," mumbled Emoth, considering Kylem's condition on the screen. "Mela-14, I think you'd better go and fetch him. He looks like he could use a hand— and take Mada with you. He's the nearest thing we have to a proper surgeon, and I'd like a full assessment of his condition as soon as possible."

Mada tutted softly to himself but made no other protest.

"Come on then," he sighed to Mela-14 and led the way.

87

CHAPTER 12

As Kyamena stalked the corridors, she thought about the Warriors she'd seen so far. She'd been told that they wouldn't hurt her unless she got in their way and so she didn't. Even when she'd found herself caught in a dead-end with the Chaser, it hadn't turned upon her. It had walked casually up beside her and stood patiently waiting for an exit to open. It had towered over her with its long and lanky limbs and when it looked down upon her with its fiery red eyes, she was unnerved.

"You know you're not supposed to kill me," she reminded it.

"As long as you kill the Espion."

Its voice was similar to Mela-14's but whereas Mela-14 spoke with expression and intonation, the Chaser's voice was cold and toneless. She didn't mind that so much. It was its words that disturbed her, reminding her once more of her objective. The door opened, the Chaser dropped on all fours and cantered off. Kyamena watched it disappear.

Since then, she'd come across the ruins of two Warriors, one of which was the Chaser. It made her feel even more anxious and quite rightly so. For the past five years she had been trained as a Warrior and instructed in all the affairs of the Espion, especially his strengths and his weaknesses. She had seen him grow and watched him kill. He was a cold but merciful killer with a morbid sense of curiosity. He would stand over the corpse of his prey and study it with his cool, grey eyes. Often on the videos, she had zoomed in on his face to watch his expressions but she could never see any emotion there, no guilt or remorse anyway—just curiosity perhaps. So she knew what he was and what he was capable of. That didn't trouble her either. What concerned her most was her part in all of this.

She had come to realise that she was little more than a toy for the Sallows to play with. Despite all that she had seen and experienced, she still couldn't believe that anyone would put such a lowly value upon life or take such great pleasure in the suffering of others. It was inhumane. She laughed feebly to herself at the thought. They weren't humanoid so of course they weren't humane, but somehow humanity was not the same as humanoid anymore. To her, humane meant all of the characteristics of a sentient, caring being. It no longer related to a species or a race. She knew dozens of skunks and other aliens that were humane despite their lack of humanoid DNA. Kyamena had redefined her concepts to try to make sense of the madness because, in spite of everything, Kyamena was still a humanist, which begged the question: what was she doing cooperating? They were making her like him, asking her to kill as coldly as he did and she didn't like what they were turning her into; but there was no alternative that she could see, other than death.

Once upon a time, she had been a simple bookkeeper whose biggest concerns were her prepayments and accruals. Now she had been driven down a path she didn't choose, a path she hated, doing things she didn't want to do. It wasn't fair. It wasn't right.

A sense of complete desolation rushed over her. Perhaps death was the answer she was looking for. She stopped walking. Her arms dropped to her side and she closed her eyes. She could end this now if she met the Espion, simply by letting him kill her. She knew he would be quick but...

She had that one nagging doubt that she knew would stop her. She knew that she might well be the last hope to save her people from him, or if they were all gone, to save everybody else from him; so she at least had to try to defeat him, but she didn't like it.

Mela-14 had told her she could live if she killed the Espion but if she did kill him, would the android keep its word and if it did, where would she go? Her world was gone. Wherever the Sallows went, they destroyed lives and ravaged worlds. There was nowhere to go. If the android let her live, it would be here, on the DeathMaker. Was that even life? It certainly wasn't living.

She leant against the wall and slid despondently down to the floor.

If the android let her live, she would not be able to stay in the Bio-Labs with her friends. She didn't know where it would put her but it wouldn't be there. Despite what the priest said, what would her friends think of her, protected from death whilst they were experimented upon and killed in the name of research? No, she would be alone.

Silent, hopeless tears began to roll down her cheeks as she debated the options.

* * * * *

"I sincerely recommend that you slow down," said Mela-14 as Mada stomped hurriedly through the maze.

"Really, and why's that?"

"Because we are not alone."

"Kylem knows the game is over."

"I was thinking of Kyamena."

"Kyamena?"

"Yes, the humanoid. She is still in here."

Mada stopped so sharply that Mela-14 almost ran into the back of him.

"You were told to call them all off!" he shouted.

"I was told to recall the Warriors, which I did, but she is humanoid. I have no method of communication with her."

"Humph," blurted Mada. He sneered. "You may have a point," and he stepped back, waving Mela-14 ahead of him. The android looked blankly at him, so much so that Mada felt forced to explain his cowardice.

"I am not a Warrior, you know. I'm a blood, and I'm not replaceable!"

Evidently, thought Mela-14, considering the long and honourable line of blood-Sallows from whom his master had been born. He could feel their shame of him.

* * * * *

Kylem was in a bad way and he knew it. His body ached, his shoulder in particular, screamed with pain and he was weak from blood loss. He had to stop every now and then to regain his senses, ease the dizziness and fight off the shock. An organic body would react in this way. With dropping blood pressure, his vital organs wouldn't be properly oxygenated. His breathing was fast and shallow, and he felt nauseous. He didn't usually feel the cold, yet now he felt chilled and clammy, but he felt comforted by the thought that Mela-14 was coming to fetch him. His father would take him home, tend his wounds and help him heal. So why, exactly, was he trying to walk out of the maze when help was on its way?

Having realised this point, Kylem stopped and lowered himself gently onto the floor. He sat cross-legged with his back against the wall. He placed his hands neatly onto his knees and closed his eyes, but not to access Server. He just wanted to sit quietly and wait for his father.

It was a very peaceful, tranquil feeling just sitting there alone. His mind began to wander, gently sweeping him away to a quiet place. The urgency and danger of the maze melted away as his thoughts centred within him. His breathing slowed becoming longer, deeper and more revitalising. He found himself in an almost dreamlike state, meditating upon his own being: what he was, his design and his huma-nanites—how they had been programmed and how they were developing.

As he drifted further into the meditative state, he became 'at one' with himself. He felt himself floating through his code effortlessly, like a feather on the breeze. It wasn't like Sallow code at all. It was very different, built in an entirely different way and yet similar. It had originated from Sallow code but since its conception, it had evolved. It had become more sophisticated and yet simpler. It distinguished itself from the Sallow code by calling itself K-Code. Reading it was both easy and painless, unlike Display and Server, both of which still caused him problems when he used them for any length of time; and then he understood why. Display wasn't part of him anymore. It hadn't been generated by him or his huma-nanites. It was, in fact, the last vestiges of the Server's programming. That's why it hurt so much to access it, and having understood this, the huma-nanites set to work upon it.

It was rather like watching a jumbled up Rubik's cube being solved but not by twisting the various sides. The huma-nanites literally disassembled it and then recompiled it. The end result wasn't even a cube any more. It was a different shape— better, clearer and more beautiful. More so, it was painless to use.

He thought about the way he accessed Server and the Warriors, the pain it caused and watched as his huma-nanites began their work on a new translation matrix, using their own unique K-Code. All they had ever needed was a little bit of quality, quiet time to operate in, time without distraction.

* * * * *

Kylem was awoken from his reverie very suddenly. His eyes snapped open. What had awoken him?

The cold of a gun barrel was pressed against his temple but he was not afraid. He was never afraid. Cautiously, he looked up out of the corner of his eyes towards his assailant. A pair of delicate, girly hands held the gun. They were shaking slightly. Beyond the hands was a dark-haired woman of about forty, staring at him with deep concentration. Her face bore many scars. She looked harrowed and uncertain.

"Well?" prompted Kylem, but she did not reply.

Slowly, Kylem turned his head so that he could look at her properly. Her eyes were pale, crystal blue, a stark contrast against her dark hair and olive skin. He felt that they were not the eyes of a killer, so very gently Kylem reached out and placed his hand lightly over hers. As they touched, in that instant, in the flash of that moment, he saw something. It wasn't like the dreams or the waking dreams that he had. Those were like a story, a film, and took time to run their course. This was just a snapshot—a hazy, crimson vision of a reality—one that was yet to be. It was just a flash in his mind's eye and was over in less than a second.

"Give me the weapon," he said, his voice barely above a whisper but she didn't release it.

"I can't."

Her voice was weak and her forehead furrowed as she fought with her conscience. Her eyes were strained and he could see her pain in them.

"Yes, you can."

"No! I have to do this. I'm sorry but... I have to think of the greater good," and her whole body tensed as she prepared to pull the trigger. Her hands quivered as she tightened her grip, but still she couldn't fire. She wanted to shoot him. She really, really wanted to but he looked so harmless, so innocent, and he had no fear. He seemed so angelic, so naïve.

"I have to," she repeated, telling herself rather than him.

Kylem shook his head and sighed sympathetically.

"No, you don't," and he smiled gently at her. She noticed how one side of his mouth rose higher than the other and how it made a little dimple in his cheek. Even now, even having seen him kill as many times as she had, he still looked like an angel.

"I have to!" she hissed angrily, "If I don't, you will destroy us all." Her voice faded away at the end of her sentence, and he could see the desperation swelling within her. Her eyes became red rimmed with tears ready to brim over the edges and her mouth quivered with unspoken words. She drew a long, sharp breath and held it... staring at him... still braced ready to fire, but she couldn't.

She realised he was right. It wasn't in her!

Suddenly, she exhaled with a deep, desperate gasp, yanked the weapon away from him and stepped back. She pushed the barrel of the Uldaker hard up under her chin, gritted her teeth and closed her eyes.

"May god forgive me," she cried, but it was too late. The decision was taken from her.

Kylem had stood up so quietly that she'd not heard him, and he pulled the gun from her hands. She'd thought she'd had a good grip on it, but he took it from her so easily and so softly. Dismayed, she watched him disarm it and let it drop to the floor. She started to sob piteously. Her hands were still clenched before her as though she was praying, and as her crying intensified, the tears ran freely down her face. She sank onto her knees, weeping wildly now. She didn't actually care anymore that she was about to die. She didn't care that she was never going to get out of there. She only wanted it to end, and to end quickly.

Kylem had never seen anybody cry before but he understood the emotion. He sat down and pulled her towards him, putting his arms around her and cradling her. He felt her body stiffen with uncertainty and it made him feel sad. He'd never held

91

anyone before and he didn't know why he was doing it now. All he knew was that it was the right thing to do. He wanted to make her feel better and then he realised he could, because he knew the truth.

"You don't die here," he whispered softly to her.

She fought against his embrace, pushing herself away from him with her hands against his chest until she was looking into his eyes. They were such deep, rich, emerald green eyes now.

"You don't know that," she sobbed.

"Yes, I do," he said. "I don't know how," he explained, "I just do. I've seen it." As the words left his mouth and he heard them, he knew just how weird it must sound, but he also knew that he was telling the truth.

"You die an old woman, sitting in a rocking chair, watching the rain fall outside your window."

Kyamena's mouth fell open slightly as she felt the fleeting hope that his words brought her. She so wanted to believe him.

* * * * *

When Mela-14 and Mada found Kylem, he was sitting on the floor next to the disarmed Kyamena. They sat regimentally, side-by-side. She looked up sharply, sheer terror in her red-rimmed eyes. Kylem, on the other hand, was relaxed. He didn't bother to move or even to open his eyes at first, and when he did finally deign to open them and look up at the two of them, he merely smiled. His eyes were calm and steady.

"This one will be useful to me. She mustn't be harmed," he instructed them. "I have need of her."

Mela-14 and Mada shot bewildered looks at each other and then back at Kylem.

"Do you understand?" he stressed the question.

Mela-14 nodded in acknowledgement. Mada made to protest but Mela-14 pulled him to one side.

"Forgive me, but he will have his reasons. He can explain himself later but for the moment we need to tend to his wounds."

Mada reluctantly agreed.

CHAPTER 13

Kylem looked up from his book and scowled with irritation.

"You should knock," he chided, taking his feet off the desk and returning his chair onto all four of its legs.

"You look well," commented Mela-14, and it was true. Only a couple of days had passed since Kylem had left the maze but he was already feeling much better, and not just physically. He was in an excellent frame of mind since his huma-nanites had begun their updates, work they were progressing well with in the luxury of this 'down' time.

"I said: you should knock."

"Why?" asked Mela-14.

"Because it's customary to knock before entering a room."

"Why?"

"To ask consent to enter."

"I do not need your consent and you were expecting me. In fact, you asked me to come."

"Yes, but you should still knock."

Mela-14 was puzzled.

"Why? What if the room was empty?" he asked.

Kylem buried his head in his hands in mock despair and laughed, "Okay, I need you to hold that thought."

"Why?"

"Because it'll help explain why I'm asking what I'm going to ask. It's all to do with cultural differences."

Mela-14 was deeply confused.

"I really do not understand what you are saying, child."

"No, and that's the whole point."

Mela-14 pulled up a chair and sat opposite Kylem, eager to find out more. That's when he registered the book in Kylem's hands.

"What *are* you doing!" he exclaimed, snatching it from Kylem's hands.

"Reading!" he exclaimed back, and lunged after the book. He winced as a spear of pain shot through his shoulder in protest at the sudden movement.

"I can see that, but what—and why?"

"Because it's pleasurable," glowered Kylem, rubbing his wound.

"But you can download anything you need from our databanks so much faster. You do not have to resort to *reading*," he scoffed.

"That's not entirely true. Yes, I can download faster but the data still has to be accessed and assessed. The information may be in my databanks but it's a bit like a library—I might have the book but unless I read it, I don't know what it says and anyway, this sort of stuff isn't in the databanks."

"Why? What is it?" he said studying the cover—*A Kiss Beyond Midnight* by Eileenia Brooga. Kylem felt him scowl with disapproval and had to suppress a smile.

"It's a crap book, I'll grant you, but interesting in its own way."

Mela-14 looked dubious.

"How so? What can you *possibly* learn from it?"

"Oh, so much!"

Kylem leaned forward in his chair, resting his elbows on his knees. His eyes were alight in much the same way as when he was about to get up to mischief. Mela-14 wondered what was coming next.

"You've no idea how much I don't know."

The statement intrigued Mela-14. "Go on," he urged.

Kylem leaned back in his chair, returning his feet to the desk and leisurely crossed his arms behind his head.

"Well," he began, "the write-up on the back tells me about the author, so I know it's a fictional story written for pleasure, to be read for pleasure."

"You mean, it is a lie."

"No," sighed Kylem, absent-mindedly picking a long, white hair off his trouser leg and flicking it onto the floor. "It means it's something made to entertain,", but he could feel the lack of understanding exuding from his father. "Look, ignore the story—"

"The lie," corrected Mela-14.

"No, the story! A lie is told with the intention of deception. There is no deception here, thus, it is a story—a piece of fiction designed to entertain and amuse."

"Ah! Rather like the maze!" exclaimed Mela-14.

Kylem tutted.

"Not the best analogy in the world, but it'll do for now. Anyway, as I was saying, if we can ignore the story and examine the interaction of the characters instead, we will find a whole array of customs, behaviours and everyday things that humanoids take for granted."

"Such as?"

"Knocking on a door before entering a room."

Mela-14 obviously didn't have the gist of it yet.

"Apparently—and this makes sense so I would surmise it is the same in most cultures—it is customary to knock before entering a room, to alert the occupants of your desire to enter."

"Why does one need permission?"

"Because the occupants might be involved in something that's none of your concern."

"Conspiring you mean? All the more reason not to announce yourself!"

"No."

"No? Well if not conspiring, what then? What could they possibly be doing that they want kept secret?"

"I'm talking about privacy, not secrecy." Kylem looked long and hard at his father. He could appreciate his confusion. He often felt a similar confusion.

Androids had no sense of privacy, having no intimate relationships. As for blood-Sallows, they did have intimate relationships but historical archives showed them to be very public affairs, and monogamy was not a word in the Sallow dictionary.

"The reasons don't matter," he concluded. "It only matters that that is what they do. Now, can you please try to bear with me for a bit?"

Mela-14 nodded so Kylem continued.

"The plot is thin but it's about three friends—two brothers: Vore and Radus, and a girl called India. All three of them have been firm friends since childhood. They have grown up together, been to school together and even went on to college and university together, and both boys love India, but India only has eyes for Radus."

Kylem could see the vacant look in his father.

"School, college and university are all educational bodies for different age groups. Bear that explanation in mind too. It is also relevant to my point. Anyway, Radus and India plan to marry but there is a shuttle accident and India is tragically killed. Vore blames Radus for the accident and his hatred blossoms when, within a few months, Radus marries another woman. Vore is crushed. He feels hurt and that India has been betrayed by Radus's actions. Then his business collapses leaving him with huge debts. His world is reduced to nothing. Radus, on the other hand, becomes a very successful man with a beautiful wife and child—a little girl, called Serena. Anyway, the years pass by. Serena grows into a young woman of great beauty and intelligence. Vore meanwhile becomes obsessed with thoughts of revenge. Finally, he abducts Serena with the intention of destroying Radus by torturing and murdering her. What he doesn't bank on is her charm. As a result, during her captivity, they develop an unspoken attraction for each other that neither party can act upon, both recognising that they are captor and captive."

Mela-14 shook his head. "I am sorry child but I still fail to see the connections here."

Kylem sighed deeply.

"I know and that's the problem. You don't understand humanoids. This story tells me so much. For instance, it shows me that humans are such deeply hopeful creatures filled with moral codes."

"Hopeful?"

"Well, yes. The writer has written something that inspires the reader to hope for a particular outcome. The story itself depicts moral codes. They may not be written down but they have obviously set their own moral standards, which can be unique to an individual or shared amongst many. Further, these standards can clash with each other, being completely contradictory in the same person..." his words trailed off. He could see that Mela-14 still didn't follow.

"The book is giving me an insight into the human psyche," he concluded.

"Oh, I think I see."

"And there's more. Just as the blood-Sallows have customs and etiquette, so do humanoids; like knocking on a door before entering a room."

"Ah!" said Mela-14, finally getting the drift.

"Then we have education, money—"

"Yes, I know about money," interrupted Mela-14.

"But I don't. I had to find out about money from a work of fiction. Do you not think that alone would give me away when I'm in the field? And what about music and singing? What are they? And humanoid courtship? Humanoids often pick their own mate through, what seems to be, a very complex series of time-consuming rituals— and they are, apparently, monogamous. They have a very complicated set of fixed family relationships, way beyond the Sallow understanding—aunts, uncles, grandfathers, nieces, cousins and so on."

"And you have learned all this from a book—this book?" he said waving it in the air.

"I've learnt *of* it, not about it. The author assumes prior knowledge of the reader, just as the humanoids will assume prior knowledge of me."

"I see!" said Mela-14 and began flicking through the pages of the book, snatching brief passages of it.

"And where did you get this?" he asked curiously.

"Uhm, well, from you," Kylem admitted, looking suitably shame-faced.

"What!" Mela-14 was startled by this revelation.

"It was just lying around in a box of stuff," explained Kylem.

"So you just took it?"

"Yes."

"You stole it from me!" his mood was quite stern.

"Yes, but who did you steal it from?" Kylem demanded, snatching the book back from his father. "You obviously didn't pay the three... whatever-it-is... cover price!"

Mela-14 scowled but decided that it was a point not worth pursuing.

"So what are you suggesting?" he asked returning to the subject. "That you want access to more of this sort of material?"

"Well, yes, if you have more. I need it to learn from."

Mela-14 sat back and considered the request.

"I am not sure," he said thoughtfully.

"Do you have more then?"

"Oh yes, lots."

"Then I need to see it!" Kylem was growing impatient.

"You do not understand."

"Make me understand."

Mela-14 thought some more and then began, "It is in the miscellany."

"The miscellany?"

"Yes, but I do not know if I can get you access."

"Why not?"

"I do not know that the Sallow Council will want you to dig up things they have buried."

Kylem frowned.

"Buried in the miscellany?" He didn't understand.

"Yes. You see, long ago, in ancient times, long before the androids were created, when the Sallow race was strong and healthy, it was very different indeed," he paused.

"Go on," prompted Kylem.

"I do not know if I should tell you this."

"Why not?"

"Because it involves you."

96

"How?"

Mela-14 shook his head and sighed.

"You will not find this in the archives."

"Why not?"

"The blood-Sallows buried it."

"In the miscellany?"

"I am talking metaphorically."

Kylem was intrigued and puzzled.

"Are you going to talk any sense at all today?"

Mela-14 smiled to himself. How often had he wondered that of his son?

"Have you ever heard of Taxana?" he asked.

Kylem accessed his databanks.

"No, I can't find any reference to that at all."

"No, it does not surprise me. More than two thousand years ago, before the time of the androids, the Taxana Research Station was the scientific laboratory at the forefront of Sallow research. They had, in their time, developed a complete barrage of weapons that they continually added to and updated for use in their war against the humanoids. Their experiments led them down the path towards the gateway of genetic engineering. They had explored chromosomal manipulation and broken DNA coding, deciphering many of its inner secrets. They even delved into the chemical compilation of DNA codes and learnt how to build new codes, giving control over the matter they were creating. They were at the dawn of a new era, one where they were designing blood-Sallows engineered for specific purposes."

"Like me?"

"Yes, but something went horribly wrong. Somewhere in the process, whilst tangling with nature's secrets, they inadvertently created something else—a type of virus, we think. It was so strong and virulent that it swept through the Sallow Empire in a matter of months. It eroded Sallow DNA, mutating the race beyond recognition, destroying it from within. The effects were devastating and the Sallow race perished within a year, all except those in Taxana. We do not know why they survived, but they did. At the onset of the outbreak, Taxana went into an automatic lockdown—quarantining the area and entombing over three and a half million scientists and lab technicians inside. Again, many died, but many also survived and over the coming years the mutations became all the more devastating, transforming the tall, strong, muscular, obsidian-skinned warriors and hunters of our legends into the small, feeble, cracked-skinned specimens we see today."

Mela-14 leant back in his chair having reached the end of the first chapter of his tale.

"But it was an accident," exclaimed Kylem. "Accidents happen. Why's it such a big deal?"

"The accident is not what shames them. It is what happened next—the aftermath." Mela-14 leant forward again, placing his elbows on his knees and sighed deeply.

"They were trapped within Taxana and should have worked together to find a resolution and move forward, but they did not. There were no Sallows left outside of Taxana to help them and they could not get out so, for three hundred years, the Sallow race was relegated to the confines of Taxana."

"Wait a minute. If they knew the Sallow race outside of Taxana was dead, then they'd know that it was most likely more lethal outside Taxana than in. Why would they want to get out? Surely it would be safer to stay in Taxana?"

"Food. There were no long-term food sources."

"And what about the Tarrow-Men? Wouldn't this have been at the time of their alliance? Didn't they help?"

"Ah! So you know something of ancient Sallow history. I did not think there was anything in the databases about the Alliance."

Kylem suddenly realised that this was information gleaned from his dreams, like the one about Jaëdah and the invasion of Glyder. Did it mean that the dream or some of it at least, was true?

"There is mention of them in the invasion of Glyder," he braved, knowing that every invasion would be logged even if the details were exaggerated in the Sallows' favour.

"Indeed, there is mention of them in that invasion, although it is not in the databanks. Oh, but wait, it is one of the scenes depicted on the Council Chamber walls," he said accessing Server, "yes, there it is. It is mentioned in the history of the relief installed in the Chambers. My, you are observant."

"But the Tarrow-Men?" Kylem prompted.

"The Tarrow-Men did nothing. It was at the end of the Alliance."

"So it might have been the Tarrow-Men's doing?"

"It might, but we will never truly know."

"Okay. So what happened in Taxana?"

"The Sallows split into two factions: the Jabberhans and the Mobans. The Jabberhans tried to reinstate a sense of order and build a new society. They set about finding new methods of growing foods artificially in the laboratories. The Mobans, on the other hand, preferred to hunt as they had always done, but prey was limited. They lived upon their wits, raiding the Jabberhans, cannibalising them and thus destroying any possibility of a new and ordered society within Taxana. The Mobans hunted the Jabberhans into extinction."

"And then what?"

Mela-14 shrugged. "And then they turned upon themselves. Their numbers dwindled even further and, it is said, they ate their own children and even bore children purely for that purpose."

"But that couldn't go on forever? Statistically speaking, you can't breed faster than you can eat."

"Well that depends. Amongst the mutations, the Sallows became... well, not entirely a single-sex race. Individuals developed both male and female genitalia, and some had the ability to self-impregnate."

Kylem visibly shuddered at the thought. Mela-14 laughed.

"You find the thought of self-impregnation more disturbing than mutation?"

"The mental image of mutation, I can handle. The mental image of a Sallow..." Kylem shuddered again, "...let's just say, I don't wanna go there, okay?"

Mela-14 considered how human a thought that was, smiled and continued.

"Well, it meant that the race could continue for an awfully long time—if it was regulated, and it was because the Mobans had to react or die out. Finally, order had come to their society. They had breeding programs and selection processes to choose which infants would live and which would become food. The stronger, more Sallow-like specimens would live and be allowed to procreate while the lesser specimens would be raised and slaughtered. At the same time, they began working on a way to get out of Taxana because, to continue, they had to get out and find better sources of food, and eventually they did.

"Four hundred Sallows walked out of Taxana to find a new world in readiness for them. Their technology had been patiently waiting for them all that time, and it was easy for them to pick up the pieces their ancestors had left behind. Only their numbers hindered them and their physical weaknesses."

"So they built the androids."

"Yes. We do all the things for them that they used to do. They hunt through us and see through our eyes."

"And that's why there are still ground missions."

"Yes. The blood-Sallows could easily eradicate a planet from the stars but the thrill of the hunt is missing, and they do like to hunt. That is the reason behind Regenesis; why they are experimenting with the skunks. They are trying to re-engineer the Sallow race back into its former glory. They are desperate to recapture their vitality and former physique so that they can experience the true thrill of the hunt again."

"But after their last foray into genetic engineering, they are cautious."

"Yes, and that is why they are so nervous of you. You too are a skunk with Sallow DNA. You have the tonicity, strength and vigour their race once had, and you are part Sallow. You could be, not just a new series of Warrior, but also one of the building blocks of their new race. On the other hand, you could be their final destruction, a harbinger of some new virus or disease. That is why they call you the Destroyer Series. They are just not sure what you are going to destroy, them or the humanoids."

Kylem bit his bottom lip thoughtfully.

"That explains a lot."

"And that is why the miscellany is so big. You may not have realised this, but the Mobans did not build the DaerkStars. They were built by the original Sallows who went on conquests and invasions. They were the hunters who loved warring. They pillaged and plundered thousands of planets and took trophies to display in their quarters. Have you never wondered why this ship is designed the way it is? Why there are so many quarters such as yours, lying empty? This ship was built, not for an army of androids, but for an army of bloods. These ships are thousands of years old and were filled with the spoils of war."

"Which are now in the miscellany?"

"Yes."

"Why are they there? I mean why pack them all away? Why not just leave them where they were? Or why not dispose of them?"

"I do not know. Perhaps they do not want to be reminded of what they once were, not until they have regained their former physical glory. I do not know."

"So how big is the miscellany then?"

"Kylem, I am really not sure that the miscellany is such a good idea."

"We don't have any choice, Father. If you want the perfect spy, you *must* give me access to the tools I need to become just that. Otherwise, I'm not going to last five minutes in the field. The first time I open my mouth and shout *'Glory Be'* or curse like a Sallow, it'll be *eghhhhhh*," and he drew a finger across his throat to illustrate his throat being slit.

Mela-14 considered the boy's point and had to admit that he was right. Kylem gave him a wry, little one-sided grin.

"I will talk to the Council about it," he relented. "Is there anything else?"

"Yeees," Kylem said drawing the word out, "but you're not going to like this either."

"Why? What is it?"

"Kyamena. I need access to her. I need to interact with a humanoid to avoid peculiar conversations such as the one you had with me when you came in."

The silence that followed was long, but Kylem was determined he was not going to break it. He began picking at the spine of his book, waiting for his father to speak. Mela-14 folded his arms and thought.

"Why Kyamena?"

"I have the beginnings of a rapport with her. I can manipulate her."

Mela-14 remembered how he had found Kylem and Kyamena sat side by side in the maze.

"What happened in the maze?" he asked.

Kylem grinned widely.

"You thought you could turn any humanoid into a killer, didn't you?"

"It is within all of them."

"Yes and no, but you won't appreciate that. That's why I am the Espion and you are the Scientific. At this moment in time, I have a hold over her. She is emotionally indebted to me. I can use that to my advantage and gain the knowledge I need from her."

"We can extract—"

"No! No! No!" interrupted Kylem. "You cannot *extract* that kind of information. What I need has to be given freely. Information gained under the duress of torture is rarely reliable. You taught me that!"

Mela-14 didn't reply.

"I'm sorry," said Kylem. "I shouldn't have shouted at you, but—"

"—but I do not understand?" Mela-14 finished the sentence for him.

"No, I'm sorry but you don't, and you never will because you are..." His words trailed off.

"...just an android?" finished Mela-14 again.

Kylem sighed deeply.

"If the Sallow Council wants the Espion Project to succeed, they must help me. If all they want me for is to aid them in the reconstruction of the Sallow race, then I need never see combat and we can lay the matter to rest. The choice is ultimately theirs, but there is no point sending me out into the field as badly equipped as I am now. I won't last five minutes."

"I believe they want both."

"And they can have both, but only if they give me the tools I need to succeed."

"I shall ask," conceded Mela-14, "but I cannot promise anything. I am not sure that they will understand your reasons." Mela-14 got up and made his way to the door.

"Father," called Kylem.

Mela-14 turned and looked at his son.

"They will understand because they are not androids. They have emotions and they are not stupid, so you can make them understand."

Mela-14 nodded and left.

CHAPTER 14

Mela-14 hadn't expected Emoth to say yes and he hadn't, but he hadn't said no either. It was probably due to Kylem's performance in the maze that Emoth had been so amenable, and thus he had listened attentively as Mela-14 put forward both of Kylem's requests. Then he'd sat very thoughtfully rubbing his chin before suggesting that Kylem come and ask him himself. That was a good sign, but when Mela-14 realised he meant alone in his quarters and not a formal meeting of the Sallow Council, well, that was just downright odd.

* * * * *

Emoth stared at the door as it closed behind Mela-14. A frown was cut deep into his forehead, crinkled and cracked like aged, black rubber. The request it had made on behalf of the Espion was bold, but the boy had a valid point. Whilst he had considered the aesthetics of the project and tasked Mada with the necessary arrangements for the surgical procedures that would be required before each mission to adapt the Espion's features to match the humanoid race he was to infiltrate, he hadn't really considered the finer details that Kylem had raised. Only now was he beginning to doubt the wisdom of the Espion Project and to see the grandiosity of the scheme. Had he been too ambitious? He hoped not. The thought of a spy amongst the enemy—and not just any spy, *his* spy—it thrilled him!

Besides, there was always the other option. Having been engineered from Sallow DNA, Kylem's genetic material was viable and acceptable in the reconstruction of the Sallow gene pool. If it transpired he couldn't use the boy as an Espion, he could use him as a donor in Regenesis, and he had shown some remarkable and highly desirable Sallow-like traits, both physically and mentally. He was tall, muscular and bold like the ancient Sallows, and he was cunning and deeply manipulative. All of these were traits that needed to be reintroduced back into the Sallow race, although he had an equal number of undesirable ones. He was humanoid in appearance and thus such an ugly, pale creature and yet, there was something morbidly attractive and fascinating about him. Perhaps it was because he was a single sexed creature and so obviously male.

Emoth sighed. He envied him that. Cursed as he was by the body into which he had been born, Emoth had never been able to enjoy proper sexual relations with another being. His genitalia, it seemed, were quite unique. His encounter with Egomara was the nearest he'd ever been to proper intercourse but even that had been

102

fraught with difficulties despite the two vaginas she had to offer. The fact that he was not alone in that department, that all blood-Sallows had similar difficulties to one degree or another, gave him no solace.

Once upon a time, the Sallows had been a virile race with almost insatiable sexual appetites. Sallow history was laced with stories of victory orgies in the middle of blood-soaked battlefields, where males and females would strip naked to masturbate and copulate openly with each other, in groups and with the dead of their enemies, but those times had gone. Sex was... difficult, but that didn't stop his desires and yearnings. The thoughts of naked, buxom, glossy black, female warriors with their slick bodies pressed hard against their muscular male counterparts had aroused him. He slipped his hand inside his robe and pushed his fingers into that little spot he knew so well. A thrill of excitement rose sharply within him. A shiver quivered up his spine. He gasped and slid deeper down into his chair opening the gap wider and as his fingers worked, he thought of Kylem and groaned with pleasure.

* * * * *

Jogging was not Kylem's favourite pastime. In fact, he found it extremely dull and boring, but it was a necessary evil if he were to achieve full fitness again. He tried to fill the time by processing and cataloguing the vast amounts of data that had been foisted upon him, but that was tedious in itself.

He was on his third lap when his knee suddenly gave a little crack and a sharp twinge of pain pricked it. It wasn't serious but, nonetheless, he knew he should pander to it if it were to heal properly, so he pulled himself to a halt and raised his knee, flexing and massaging it. After a few moments, the pain died away into a small, dull ache so he gently lowered his foot back onto the floor. He'd not actually dislocated it when he'd fallen off the mezzanine floor in the maze, but he had wrenched it badly. He'd not noticed it at the time, he'd had other things on his mind and more serious injuries to worry about. Now that his more serious wounds were dressed, soothed and healing though, it was the smaller injuries that seemed to nag him the most.

The pain had gone so he stood upright and yawned widely. This was so boring that even while jogging he felt like his body was going to sleep. He linked the fingers of both hands together, placed them behind his head and arched his back, stretching and flexing his spine, twisting from side to side and then paused.

Out of the corner of his eye, he thought he saw something move, but when he looked, it was gone. It puzzled him because, whatever it was, it was neither the gold of the Warriors, the white of the Scientifics nor the black of the blood-Sallows. He must have imagined it. Nevertheless, his curiosity drove him to investigate and anyway, anything had to be less boring than this.

The corridor followed the curvature of the ship so it gradually slipped away from view on a vertical horizon. Other corridors intersected with it like the spokes of a wheel, joining these main corridors together into a myriad of tunnels. One such junction lay ahead. Kylem moved towards it and cautiously peered around the corner, but the corridor ahead was (as he had suspected it would be) empty. He stepped into it to be sure, paused and then dismissed the apparition as a figment of his imagination. When he turned around though, there, in full view, as clear as day, was a boy—a humanoid boy.

103

He was stood, hunched over with his fingers to his mouth, giggling mischievously. He was probably just a couple of years younger than Kylem with skin as white as linen and a mop of white hair sticking out at all angles like broken fibre optic strands. His eyes were a startling bright red just like a Warrior's, but unlike a Warrior, they burned with life. His stature was odd and Kylem realised that the hunch was not voluntary. His spine was congenitally twisted. He wondered about the boy's agility and if the disability hurt.

"Kylem! There you are!"

Kylem turned violently, startled by the voice. Mela-14 was approaching. He turned quickly back but the boy had gone—completely vanished. Well, that answered the agility question! If he was ever there, of course?

"Is there something wrong, child?" asked Mela-14.

"Uhm, no," said Kylem, still gazing down the corridor and puzzling where the boy could possibly have disappeared to in such a short space of time.

"It's nothing," he added and walked to meet Mela-14, but he couldn't help keep looking back. Had he imagined it?

As they walked back to Kylem's quarters, Mela-14 told him the news but he was only half listening. He was still thinking about the boy.

* * * * *

Kylem showered and changed into a formal uniform while Mela-14 told him about his encounter with Emoth for a third time. He wasn't convinced that Kylem had listened properly the first couple of times and Kylem was doing little to convince him that he was doing so this time either.

"Kylem, what is wrong?" he suddenly interjected mid-sentence. "You are distant and distracted. Are you worried about something, child?"

"No," assured Kylem as he towelled his hair dry. "Just got a lot to think about, that's all."

He threw the towel aside, plucked his jacket from the back of the chair and put it on. As he began fastening the unending row of buttons that ran down its front, Mela-14 continued to ramble on while brushing Kylem's shoulders with his hands to sweep away a few specks of dust. He plucked a stray white hair from the lapel and flicked it away. Kylem saw it. He tipped his head and watched it float through the air, twisting and snaking like a maple seed until it softly touched down upon the bench.

What was a white hair doing there? His hair was blue, and it wasn't the first one either. He remembered the hair he had seen on his trousers that morning. That too was white, and so was the boy's, but that didn't prove that the boy was real. He could just have been an apparition, one of his 'daydreams', but what if he was real? That piqued his curiosity. How could a humanoid be loose aboard a DaerkStar? The hair could prove the issue once and for all. He needed to capture it for analysis. That at least would tell him if he were going crazy or not, so he picked up *A Kiss Beyond Midnight* and placed it gently on top of the hair to trap it.

"Let's go," Kylem said and they left the room. Kylem briefly glanced back over his shoulder as the door shut behind him.

* * * * *

104

Sallows, Kylem knew, were renowned for their poor eyesight so the gloominess that greeted Kylem when the door opened into Emoth's quarters surprised him. His eyes, however, had no difficulty in discerning the shadows and contours from each other. The room looked like an antique shop housed in a modern art gallery. The sterile walls and floor were lost in the melange of mismatched pieces of furniture from what seemed like every civilisation and every era. The walls and floors were covered with wall hangings and rugs on top of rugs, and there were knick-knacks literally everywhere. Every shelf and every flat surface was filled to overflowing with ornaments and baubles of one description or another. Kylem noted that each piece was something of incredible beauty but in amongst this cacophony of things, its loveliness was completely lost.

The door closed behind him and the lighting flickered with an orangey hue. Shadows flitted dully across the ceiling and Kylem realised it was supposed to simulate firelight. It wasn't a very good simulation. He glanced behind him to make sure that Mela-14 had followed but was disappointed to see that he hadn't.

"Ah! There you are," boomed Emoth, entering from a door at the far end of the room. He was dressed in a brilliant red, paisley design bathrobe on which the belt was very loosely tied. The cracked skin on his face and chest glinted with freshly applied oil and its scent, sweet and musky, drifted in with him. Kylem wished he'd done the belt up a little tighter because the robe was beginning to waft open. Briefly, his mind tormented him, toying with the idea of what might lie underneath it, but revulsion snapped him back to his senses very quickly.

"Sit down," said Emoth, indicating a leather clad, winged armchair that would happily have graced an Englishman's country club. It was a particularly large chair that seemed to swallow Kylem whole as he sat down. He didn't feel at ease despite the comfiness of the chair, but he didn't want Emoth to see this so he leant back casually, allowing himself to sink deep into its throat and crossed his legs.

"Comfortable?" asked Emoth.

"Yes thank you," lied Kylem.

"You must excuse me," said Emoth walking over to a similarly sized chair that faced Kylem's. Unlike Kylem though, he perched on the edge of it and picked up a glass of sadia that had merged in with the rest of the paraphernalia on the table beside him. He took a sip.

"I've just had a bath. I love to bathe. I bathe at least twice a day you know. Do you like to bathe?"

It seemed an odd way to start a conversation.

"I like to be clean, so yes, I shower a couple of times a day."

"So I see," said Emoth and he reached over and touched a lock of Kylem's still damp hair that was falling into his eyes. He brushed it aside for him and smiled. It was a small, soft smile, not the great beaming one he usually wore. Kylem stiffened with discomfort. Suddenly he felt 'at risk'. His new and improved Display kicked in and began undertaking a threat analysis, showing him its findings as it progressed. He was provided with temperature readings for the room and the Sallow as well as an analysis of the scents, lighting and sounds that surrounded him. It analysed the Sallow's mannerisms and dress code too and made comparisons to information held in his databanks. It was highlighting some very disturbing possibilities.

"Would you like a glass?" asked Emoth holding his aloft.

"No thank you. I aim to be a little more cautious with alcohol in the future."

105

Emoth laughed lightly and reorganised himself leisurely into the back of his chair. Kylem felt his tension lessen slightly as the distance between them grew.

"In moderation, it wouldn't hurt. Anyway, it's just you and I. Are you sure you won't indulge?" His manner was sickly sweet.

"Thank you, but no," said Kylem politely. "I have a lot to do this afternoon and I need to keep my wits about me."

"As you wish," he shrugged. "Now tell me about your request," and he lifted one foot and perched it on his knee. His gown gaped open all the more. Kylem recoiled, grimacing visibly. Emoth laughed at him.

"Do I make you feel uncomfortable?" he teased, knowing damn well that he did. Kylem didn't know what to say, so he said nothing, but he made sure his eyes remained fixed upon Emoth's face, not daring to allow them to wander. That would be something he would regret. Not only might he see something he didn't want to but Emoth might read (or misread) something into it.

"I need information," he said, desperately wanting to move the conversation forward and away from Emoth's ever nearing state of nudity, but Emoth had other ideas.

"Tell me," Emoth continued. "You are a single sex creature, are you not?"

Kylem's mouth opened slightly as though he were about to say something but then realised he wasn't sure what to say.

"Yes," Emoth eventually answered for him. "Of course you are. I know what you are. You're a skunk but even skunks have sexual desires. Do you have sexual desires?"

Emoth leaned forward waiting for his answer. Kylem bit his bottom lip nervously. Display was no help. It had completed its analysis of the situation, detected the Sallow's heightened pheromone levels and adequately warned him that the Sallow was most likely propositioning him, but that was all it could do. Despite all the sophisticated sensors and equipment he had at his disposal, nothing could advise him what to do or what to say next. Nor did he have any inkling about what might happen next. Procreation was not a subject he had studied and his own sexuality was not something he'd even begun to think about, let alone Emoth's. His huma-nanites had nothing to offer him either. He felt angry and naïve but he knew he had to suppress that anger. Emoth was a typical Sallow with a Sallow's streak for sadism.

"Barely ten days ago," Kylem began with a voice that was intentionally soft, calm and non-confrontational, "I was an infant. Since then I have been beaten, shot and brutalised. My head has been bombarded with data that has no manifest so I have nothing to help me decide what I should process first, and from what I have studied, it looks like it was selected at random. I suspect that it will yield little that will help me to fulfil my mission, yet I am expected to process it all. With regard to my sexual impulses, I can honestly say I haven't had chance to think about them and that they are not top of my list of priorities, but I thank you for your interest and concern. Now if you will excuse me, I believe that my Father has fully versed you with my requests so I shall leave you to consider them at your leisure."

Kylem began to get out of the chair but Emoth leant forward and placed his broad, chubby, black hand on his chest, gently pushing him back into the chair.

"You talk of not understanding your prey and request access to the miscellany and the humanoids to learn more. All living beings indulge in reproductive activities

106

of some kind and for most, it is a pleasurable experience. Do you not think that this lack of knowledge will also betray you?"

Oh god! This was not going well!

"Maybe, but all adolescents start as virgins. My virginity will therefore not be unusual."

Emoth puckered his lips in thought and knocked back the last of his sadia. He stared into the bottom of the glass and began swilling around what could only have been the tiniest dregs of liquid. His eyes became moist and Kylem saw his cheeks quiver slightly. For a moment Kylem thought Emoth was about to cry and then abruptly, he leapt from his chair and crossed the room to pour himself another drink. He threw it down his throat and poured himself a third but paused as it reached his lips.

"You may go," he commanded, his back still to Kylem. "Your ugliness tires me," he spat.

Kylem didn't move.

"GO!" he screamed.

Kylem bolted for the door.

* * * * *

Outside Emoth's quarters, Mela-14 was pacing the floor, impatiently waiting for Kylem. When Kylem exploded through the door, he felt relief at the sight of him but dread from the look in his eyes. The boy stared angrily at his father and stormed past him so forcefully that Mela-14 had to leap out of the way. As Kylem stomped down the corridor, Mela-14 had to half-run, half-walk to keep up with him.

"Kylem! Kylem!" he cried. "What on earth happened?"

Kylem stopped so abruptly and swept around that Mela-14 found himself in Kylem's face. Kylem glared angrily into his vacant, white eye sockets. After a few moments he spoke.

"Why didn't you come in?" he asked. "Why did you leave me alone in there with him?"

"I...", but Mela-14 didn't have an answer. Kylem took two paces forwards, forcing the android back into the wall. Kylem eyes narrowed, sensing his father's fear of him.

"Did you know? Did you know what... that...", but Kylem couldn't find the words. Mela-14 turned his head away shamefully.

"I did not know," he said quietly.

"But you suspected?"

Mela-14 looked directly into his son's eyes.

"I did not know," he repeated more firmly, "but I admit that it seemed odd."

"And you did nothing?"

"What could I do?"

"Warn me?"

"Warn you of what? Empty suspicions?"

"And what was I supposed to do? Surrender to his advances?"

"No."

"Then what?"

"Whatever it was that you did."

107

"You don't know what I did!"

"No, but I know what you are and I know that you are designed to deal with awkward situations such as this, that you would assess the situation and deal with it accordingly."

"And what if I'd been wrong? What if I'd done the wrong thing? What if I had surrendered to him? Or what if I'd lost my temper and killed him?"

Mela-14 placed his hands softly on his child's shoulders.

"I knew that none of those things would happen. I knew you would not surrender to him because your sexuality has been defined and is written into you. I knew you would not lose your temper and attack him because to do so would be foolish and result in your termination, and I knew your huma-nanites would never permit that. I knew you would be okay. Kylem, I helped to design and program you. You have to trust me when I say that I knew all these things."

Kylem scowled at his father. His lips pursed with anger and his eyes narrow with suspicion. Kylem leant into him, placing a hand on the wall above Mela-14's shoulder. He pushed his face so far into Mela-14's that the android had to turn his head to one side to avoid their noses touching. Kylem spoke slowly.

"If you ever... ever... leave me alone... with that *thing*... ever again... I'm gonna rip your face off... just like I did Jordan-5... and I'm gonna pull out your chips... one by one... reverse their polarity... and put them back in."

"That would be most unpleasant."

"I know and it's the nearest thing you'll ever get to pain so I'll have to do it really... really... slowly. Do I make myself perfectly clear? Do you understand me?"

There was a long silence. Mela-14 pushed his shoulders back so that he stood tall. His stance was no longer submissive or apologetic, but Kylem was too angry to take note.

"Perfectly," said Mela-14. "I will not allow the situation to arise again."

Too late did Kylem become aware of Mela-14's hand moving across his shoulder towards his throat. The hand suddenly gripped around his neck. It was vice like and although the android's small hand couldn't stretch around his throat, his digits were perfectly placed for maximum effect. Kylem gasped as the android's grip tightened around his windpipe. He opened his mouth to scream for air but none could enter.

His hands scrabbled at the android's, clawing at them to free himself. His vision became blurred and blotchy. A wash of blackness began to sweep over him and just as consciousness was about to leave him, the android released his grip. Kylem dropped to the floor rasping for breathe.

"But not because you threaten me child, rather because you are my responsibility. Do I make myself clear, child?" he asked coldly.

Kylem nodded, his own hands nursing his throat. His face was still filled with anger as Mela-14 turned and walked away. Kylem watched him go. It was odd how a child can both respect and despise his parent at the same time, but he did.

CHAPTER 15

The true size of the miscellany was well concealed by the clutter. What Kylem could see of it though, stretched out before him like the world's largest jumble sale. If Emoth's quarters had seemed overfilled, the miscellany mimicked this a thousand times over. As he wandered through its aisles, there was rack upon rack of artefacts. The latest additions seemed to have been packed neatly into storage boxes before being abandoned onto the shelving units, but as he ventured deeper into the archive, it became just a mishmash of items that had been thrown in there haphazardly. He found himself having to climb over cartons and crates of all shapes and sizes, rolled up carpets and wall hangings, pieces of furniture and other bric-a-brac until eventually, the way became impassable.

Kylem's attention was deeply buried in a box when he heard the door open. He looked up and listened, closed his eyes and registered the two Warriors that had entered with the prisoner, Kyamena. Their heavy footsteps were somewhat muffled by the clutter of the miscellany as they approached.

"Over here!" he shouted unnecessarily and peered around the side of a stack of crates. As he did so, he knocked something off the shelf. It was only a big cobblestone, but Kylem watched it almost hypnotically as it bounced three times and clattered noisily across the floor. It settled into a gentle spin that took it on a new course under one of the racks. Before he could retrieve it though, the Warriors had appeared. They stopped before him with Kyamena shackled between them. They held out the reins but he didn't take them.

"That's not necessary," he said, turning his attention back to the box.

"We are instructed—"

"Not by me," he barked. "Remove them." His voice was firm and he spoke to them the way the Scientifics did, as their master, but they did not obey

"She has nowhere to go so take them off," he insisted. This time they released her and they left.

Kyamena stood rubbing her wrists and glared at Kylem. She didn't quite know what to make of him or this situation. One minute she was supposed to kill him, the next she was to help him acquire the skills he needed to destroy races such as her own. She also had to keep reminding herself that he was just another damned android, that he wasn't humanoid despite how much he looked or acted like one. It was all very disconcerting.

"I take it Mela-14 has explained your new role to you," he said, still absorbed by the contents of the crate.

"Yes," she said.

"Good!" and he looked up and smiled at her playfully.

It caught her off-guard and she found herself smiling back at him. As soon as she realised that she was smiling she hated herself for it and looked away, desperate to escape the moment. Seeing the stone under the edge of the shelving, she bent down and retrieved it. It was odd. In every respect it looked just like an ordinary stone, a large beach-worn, granite cobblestone that fitted neatly into the palm of her hand. It was smooth, solid and speckled dark-grey but it wasn't cold like stone, nor was it heavy. She toyed with it in her hands, frowning at it.

"What's that?" he asked civilly and in complete contrast to the way in which he'd barked his instructions at the androids. Everything about his manner enticed her to be at ease with him, but she had to remember he was an android.

"I don't know," she said, trying to be cool with him. "I thought it was just a stone but it's not heavy enough," and she handed it to him. He took it and turned it over in his hand. She was right. It was curiously light.

"What's it made of?" she asked.

"I don't know. It could be just a stone. Some minerals are very light but it doesn't feel right. It's not plastic or acrylic though. Does it look familiar to you?"

"Only as a stone."

"But if it's just a stone, what's it doing in here? Why would anyone keep an ordinary stone?"

"Perhaps it's a souvenir."

"A souvenir? A stone?" he scowled.

"How would I know?" she snapped and immediately reprimanded herself. Despite what had happened in the maze, where he had shown such sensitivity, he was still a Sallow. He was built and designed as a spy. Perhaps then and even now, he was practising on her, attempting to gain her trust for whatever purpose. Or perhaps Mela-14 was using her to test him to see where his loyalties lay. That was a new thought! Could his loyalties be twisted away from his Sallow masters? He was, after all, as much a humanoid as he was a Sallow.

Either way, she had spoken too freely with him. His manner had put her too much at ease. Would he retaliate and reprimand her? It seemed not. The disrespect she had shown him appeared to have passed by unnoticed. She slumped back against some of the debris and rested her buttocks on a large chest.

It was odd that he would let her speak to him like that. Was that because he was trying to gain her trust, because he was weak or because he didn't know any better? The former or the latter were the stronger possibilities. Androids might be programmed to respect their betters, but 'blood-things', as Mela-14 called them, they would have to learn it from others, and from whom could Kylem learn about such things? Certainly not from the blood-Sallows. From what she had seen, they were completely mannerless, having no respect for each other let alone for other living beings.

Actually, Sallows were the most ignorant creatures she had ever come across. Emoth was the highest-ranking Sallow aboard the DaerkStar, yet there were no airs and graces in his presence and no titles. He was just Emoth. In fact, the only concession to his seniority was that he was treated with slightly less contempt than his counterparts were. On that basis, she wondered how he had earned his station and how he maintained it. The society of the blood-Sallows appeared to be completely casteless—a complete contrast to humanoid society where you had employers and employees, parents and children, masters and servants; where one showed respect to the other because of that position, and the other just expected that respect. Blood-Sallows weren't like that. They had ranks, but no castes.

Thus, whilst technically, in this room now, Kylem was the master, he was still just a kid, so taking a leaf out of the Sallows' book she decided she could treat him as such, for now at least.

Kylem was still examining the stone against the light.

"That you suggested it might be a souvenir suggests that you do know something, something more than I, anyway."

How dreadfully logical, she thought.

"And that is what you are here for," he reminded her. He was right, of course. It was just this sort of thing that was going to keep her alive.

"Because that's what people do," she conceded. "If they've been somewhere nice or had a good time somewhere, they'll pick up a memento of the occasion: buy something in a shop, collect a stone, pick and press a flower, that sort of thing."

He didn't look convinced but there was something curious about it so he tucked the stone into the inside pocket of his jacket for later. As he did so, he felt a most peculiar sensation. He could feel the stone against his chest and although it was neither moving nor breathing, it felt like he had a living animal sleeping there, snug and warm. But that was silly, it was an inanimate object, so he pushed the thought to the back of his mind and turned his attention back to the box he had been rooting in.

"Souvenir?" she suggested. He scowled at her.

"What else have we got?" he asked.

Kyamena didn't immediately delve in. She was still thinking about him and the odd relationship that was developing between them. Then she became aware that he had stopped rummaging in the box and was looking at her, as though waiting for something. He tutted, rolled his eyes and thrust a crate into her chest.

"Make yourself useful and have a look in that."

She took the crate from him and began shuffling through it. At first glance, it was just junk.

"What are we looking for?" she asked.

"I don't really know. Anything humanoid, I think."

"But surely it's all humanoid, isn't it?"

"No. It's all goyeme, but not necessarily humanoid."

"Goyeme?"

"No-blood."

"What's no-blood?"

Kylem raised his eyebrows and looked at her. Maybe this wasn't such a good idea after all.

"You're supposed to be answering my questions, not asking them." His facial expression was still friendly but his eyes showed impatience.

Kyamena hesitated and then asked, "But how will I know what to tell you if I don't know the extent of your knowledge already?"

"Simple. Just tell me everything."

She looked baffled.

"Is there a problem with that?"

"Well, yes," and she looked pained.

"What?" he demanded. "Spit it out!"

"Where do I start?"

"At the beginning."

"But where is the beginning? The beginning of what? Me? You? Do you want my life history? Do you want to know the merits of double-entry bookkeeping? Shall I tell you why the sky is blue? Why cats purr? Why syrup dribbles in a chain rather than in straight lines like oil? Why the sun sets in the north? Why people have babies rather than lay eggs? Why if you drop a slice of toast, it always falls buttered side down? Why the batteries on the smoke alarm never die during the day? Why—"

"Yes! I get the point!" interrupted Kylem, and he scratched his head in annoyance. "I need to learn what it is to be human. I need to understand things like love, hate, war, relationships... and things like souvenirs. I need to understand when something is appropriate or inappropriate, like... oh, I don't know. Can't you just talk to me?"

"Oh, you mean you want a conversation?"

"I suppose I do," he relented.

"Okay. That's a good place to start. Humans converse. It's one of the ways by which we learn and exchange information, unless of course you're talking to my mother," and she laughed lightly.

"Your mother?"

"Yes. She's dead now. Actually, I suppose everybody's dead now, but she died long before you came along," and Kyamena fell silent. She felt awkward.

"Go on," prompted Kylem. "Tell me about her."

"My mother?"

"Yes. Didn't she talk much?"

Kyamena laughed.

"Are you kidding me? She jabbered away incessantly. She'd wander around the house doing her household chores and yackety-yak, yackety-yak. Oblivious to what anybody else had to say. Nobody ever listened to her and she talked complete rubbish anyway." She rolled her eyes and smiled affectionately at the memory.

Kylem smiled back. He had picked the right person after all—Kyamena would be highly informative.

"So she spoke a lot, but said nothing?"

Kyamena nodded.

"Got it in one—and we heard, but we never listened."

"Didn't she mind?"

"I don't think she ever realised. She'd ask you a question and if you were stupid enough to start answering it, she'd just ignore you and start talking right over you, either answering the question herself or moving on to the next topic."

"How did she learn anything?"

Kyamena cocked her head as she thought. "Do you know, I don't think she ever did learn a thing."

"That's ridiculous."

"But she was happy," and then she said more dubiously, "I think."

"You're making it up."

"No, I'm not."

"You could be. How do I know you're telling me the truth? How do I know you're not making it up as you go along?"

"You don't," she said. A small feeling of power warmed her spirit. "You'll just have to trust me," and she smiled smugly. "In the land of the blind, the one-eyed man is king," and she placed her hands together as though in prayer and bowed her head.

"Are you mocking me?" he asked with mild annoyance. Kylem couldn't help but be amused. It seemed that Kyamena was going to be a far more entertaining tutor than Mela-14 had ever been. She opened one eye and caught the back end of his smile before he could wipe it from his face.

"Maybe a tad but only very gently. Anyway, communication is a two-way street, so what's 'no-blood'?" she asked and made herself all the more comfortable on the pile of crates behind her.

"What's a 'two-way street'?" he asked, but she didn't answer. She tipped her head to one side and crossed her arms stubbornly, making it clear she was waiting for him. He tutted.

"A goyeme is a no-blood—no Sallow blood that is. A creature that has no genetic connection to the Sallow race whatsoever. So what's a 'two-way' street?"

"It's how we organise traffic in the cities. There are two lanes of traffic and you always drive on the left so you have one lane heading in each direction." She illustrated with her hands. "That way traffic can flow continuously. All things being equal that is," and she thought about some of the horrendous traffic jams at rush hour.

Kylem thought about her definition. It was beautifully clear and concise, and a picture formed in his mind from her information. Data was retrieved from his own library that conformed to the search criteria, to help complete the picture.

"Oh right! That implies you have one-way streets too?"

"Yes. Where the streets are too narrow for two lanes of traffic, a one-way system is introduced so everybody goes the same way on that road. So goyeme is just another word for humanoid?"

"Goyeme is anything completely non-Sallow so that includes all other species, be they mammalian, reptilian, aquatic or aerian. Why would they build streets that are too narrow for two lanes of traffic?"

"Because some parts of our cities are so old they were built before modern vehicles were invented. They were only designed to take pedestrians and small carts. So which category do you fall into?"

He sighed heavily.

"Skunk," he replied quietly.

"Skunk?"

"Yeah," he cleared his throat and said matter-of-factly, "a half-breed: only part Sallow." He seemed a little uncomfortable with the term.

"Yes, I know skunks. I live with them in the Bio-Labs."

"Well, they're different. I mean, I've been designed for a different purpose."

"You're an android," she said factually, almost accusingly.

He didn't like it. It sounded cold. It made him feel cold. It showed in his eyes. The weakness she had suspected, even hoped for, was becoming more apparent.

"You don't like that, do you? Being called an android?"

"What makes you say that?"

"Your body language. Your eyes."

"Am I really so easy to read?" He doubted that he was.

"Or are you just so good at what you do? Are you just trying to make me believe that you are easy to read?"

Kylem stepped back and crossed his arms, mirroring Kyamena.

"Are we not being just a little over-paranoid?" he asked.

"No, I don't think so. We're on different sides. Whatever passes between us, we are still enemies, and as for paranoia—it's not paranoia if they are really out to get you."

Perhaps they were both being a little paranoid, but paranoia was an admirable, if not essential, quality for a spy. He had to query everything and had to suspect everything. Why should it be any different for her?

The two of them looked at each other, bewildered and amused by the interaction. They were on opposing sides but the banter between them was startlingly wonderful. Kylem had never enjoyed such free and unbridled conversation with anyone before and Kyamena, although kept in the company of other bloods, rarely got to speak to anyone new.

"Have you ever been to the Bio-Labs?" she suddenly asked.

"No."

"Don't you think you should go?"

"Why?"

"To learn."

"Skunks have nothing to teach me."

"Everybody has something to teach you and anyway, they aren't all skunks. If you want to learn about other species, go to the Bio-Labs—and the Farm Decks. You really should go the Farm Decks." There was a note of sarcasm in her voice. He looked at her dubiously.

"Okay," he lied, and turned his attention back to the box. He really didn't like the way she had suggested he visit the Farm Decks and he began to wonder what was there. He'd never had cause to think about it before.

"So does that make you better than a skunk?" she suddenly asked. He knew the question was loaded.

"I don't live in a cage like a skunk," he retorted.

"And you're better than a Warrior."

He laughed a loud, forced laugh. "You know I'm better than a Warrior! You were in the maze!"

"Yes, I was. So, you're better than a Warrior—and a Warrior is a proper android. So that means that you are better than an android?"

"Yes."

"And a Scientific is an android."

He could see where she was going with this.

"Yes, it is, but don't put words into my mouth. That's not what I said. I said I am better than a Warrior, but I am also an android. I am the *Destroyer Series, Mark-I (Espion)* which, as I have proven, is far superior to any of the current Warrior class models. It doesn't mean that I am better than every android in existence."

"Okay," she agreed and turned back to her box, smiling to herself. She left a suitable pause before asking, "So are you better than a Scientific or not then?"

"Are you always this annoying?"

"God no, I haven't been this annoying in years," and for a moment, she remembered another time and another era, a time when she had a career and a little flat on the outskirts of the city.

"I used to be annoying for a living," she teased.

"I expect you were very good at it."

"I was." She looked very serious and sad.

"Tell me about it. What did you do?"

"I was a bookkeeper. I worked for the Revenue."

"Collecting taxes?"

"Very good! But no, I was a prosecutor."

Kylem's eyebrows flicked in surprise. She laughed.

"Yes, it does sound rather dramatic, doesn't it? I was part of the prosecuting team for the Revenue. It was my job to argue the case for the prosecution," and her words trailed off as a wave of nostalgia swept over her. She swallowed hard to push the emotion back down. How ironic though. How she used to enjoy the challenge of being the prosecutor in such cases. And now? Now that had all been taken from her, and *she* was the prosecuted.

She buried her attention into a fresh box, hoping she could bury her anger and frustration there too, but she could feel him looking at her still. It made her all the more angry but she refused to make eye contact with him for fear of making it worse.

Kylem stared at her for a long time. He could feel her sadness and her anger, and he wasn't quite sure what to do about it. Eventually he turned his attention back to his own crate. She felt relieved when he did so but soon realised that she still wasn't sure what she was supposed to be looking for.

"Kylem?" she asked quietly. He turned to look at her.

"Another question?" he asked.

"Well, I wasn't going to ask you anything stupid!" she snapped. As the words tumbled out of her mouth, she knew she should shut it but she couldn't.

Six years of captivity and mental torture boiled over as her rage bubbled up inside her. He was such an impudent, spoilt, snotty-nosed, over-bearing little brat. Kylem saw her face twist with anger as she fought to keep her temper, but she couldn't. She kicked over a tower of crates that had stood between them. They crashed to the ground and Kylem stepped hastily back. He bunched his fists in readiness, expecting her to lunge at him any minute.

"Don't worry, punk! I'm not going to hit you! I wouldn't soil my hands with you!" she spat. "But I'm sick of this *'better than you'* shit because, remember kiddo, that's just what you are—a little kid—just a little six-year-old who's got himself trapped in the body of an adult. Hell! Not even an adult! A kid! Just a big kid—" she hissed, stepping up to him.

She was taller than he was and stood over him but even as she ranted, Kylem didn't feel threatened. Surprised perhaps, but not endangered. Display didn't even bother to cut in.

"—and you're not even that," she continued, and then her anger drained as quickly as it had risen. Silently, she looked down into his eyes and hers filled with pity.

"You're not even a boy," she finally said and did the strangest thing. She reached out and touched his face. He flinched at her touch.

"You feel like a boy but you're not. You're just a machine wrapped in a skin of flesh and bone. You don't have real feelings. You can't have real feelings."

She stepped away from him and stared. "So why do I expect them of you?" and she turned and walked away.

He watched her go and then followed her, cautiously creeping after her, all the way back to the door where she sat down and leant against it. She stared defiantly at him and he stared back at her. She fascinated him. She was so full of contradictions—like all blood-things. One minute, she was bold and brave, the next, cowardly and frightened.

"So what you gonna do now?" she demanded of him. "Punish me?"

Kylem knew he wasn't going to punish her but as to what he *was* going to do, he didn't have a clue. He was confused, hurt and insulted. Not bad, he thought, for something without feelings.

He stood pondering her words with his arms folded. Suddenly and with unexpected elegance, he dropped gracefully to the floor, pivoting on one foot into a cross-legged position directly in front of her. He placed his hands on his knees, looked searchingly into her eyes and spoke.

"You ask me questions to make me question myself and what I am."

"Nothing wrong with your logic chip then," she said sarcastically.

"Actually, I'd like to think I worked that one out for myself. You see, I'm only part android."

Her forehead creased as she pondered the statement. He continued.

"When I was conceived, I wasn't an android at all. I was a full blood-thing. I was injected with huma-nanites whilst still in the womb of my surrogate and they overwrote my synaptic pathways in readiness for programming. Do you know what huma-nanites are made of?"

She shook her head.

"Ptarium. Do you know what ptarium is?"

She shook her head again.

"It's a metallic compound found only in the Ptarium star system. It's derived from a metallic life form of single-celled animals which, when properly harvested and treated with huge doses of radioactive compounds, meld with bone to reinforce it. It's also incredibly toxic. It causes severe, irreversible and terminal neurological damage but seeing as my huma-nanites have already destroyed my brain and assimilated my normal brain functions, it's a moot point. So you'd think I thought like a machine because my brain is, let's face it, completely artificial. Would you not agree?"

His eyes were cold and factual as he spoke but not empty like the other androids. It was as though this confession caused him discomfort, embarrassment or pain but Kyamena couldn't work out which. She began to regret her tawdry treatment of him.

"But ptarium is, or was, alive. It was a life form. It may not be sentient but it was alive. Do you think that an amoeba feels pain?" He asked the question matter-of-factly.

"I-I-I don't know." She was unsure and confused.

"No. Neither do I." He had stopped looking at her now. His gaze had wandered to somewhere distant. "But I don't know that they don't. So if they don't feel pain, and androids don't feel pain, why do I feel pain?" His eyes drew back to hers. This time they were filled with sadness.

"All animals feel pain," she retorted and immediately felt ashamed and looked away. She could no longer bear to look at him. Kylem leant forward on his knuckles like a chimpanzee and very gently lifted her chin with his forefinger to make her look at him again. He shook his head and exhaled deeply.

"I wasn't talking about physical pain," and with the same agility as that with which he had sat, he rose.

Kyamena sat, shocked and ashamed. She watched him disappear back into the confusion of the miscellany, back to the pile of debris they had left behind. Her mind raced. She was so confused. What was that all about? Was it genuine or was it a ploy? Was he an android or was he a blood?

Kyamena sat turning the events over in her mind trying to make sense of it all. After a while, when it became quite clear he wasn't coming back, she got up and followed him back to the boxes. She picked up the crates she had kicked over and restacked them. She looked to see what sort of things he was digging out and began silently searching and compiling a collection of items that interested her and that she thought might interest him.

"I'm sorry," she said after a while.

"Don't be. It's how you feel."

"It was... insensitive of me."

Kylem looked up from his box. He wasn't sure how to respond to that but she was purposefully ignoring his gaze so he didn't have to. He didn't want to fight with her either, so he said nothing.

* * * * *

By the end of the afternoon they had both rooted out a good selection of items and had six large boxes stacked by the door. Kylem had concentrated on books in a variety of languages, most of which he didn't recognise but his huma-nanites would make short work of them by building a translation matrix for each one. He'd also chosen a range of other items that he'd simply found curious or amusing.

Kyamena had picked up a curious array of things that he couldn't even begin to guess what they were. He plucked a roll of thick, black plastic from the top of one of her boxes. It was tied up in the middle with a piece of ribbon. He undid the knot and rolled out the plastic. It was about a metre long with irregular black and white stripes on the inside.

"What's this?" he asked.

"It's a keyboard," she replied. He looked blank, thinking only of a computer keyboard.

"Weirdest keyboard I've ever seen."

"No, silly. Not that sort of keyboard. You play it."

"Oh! It's a game!"

"No. It's music."

"Isn't that a game?"

"What makes you think it's game?"

"Well, you play games and you play music."

"That doesn't make it a game. Are you telling me that you've never heard music?"

"Heard music?"

"Yes, you listen to music."

"I thought you *played* music,"

"You have to play music to listen to it."

"If you play it, why do you listen to it?"

117

"Because it's nice to listen to. I can't believe you've never heard music." She was astonished.

"Would that be so strange?"

"Well, yes. It would be downright peculiar, actually."

"Oh," and he passed her the keyboard. "Play music then."

"I can't."

"Why not?"

"It needs power and there isn't any, and I don't play keyboards."

"What do you play?"

"Nothing."

"Nothing? Doesn't that make you peculiar too?"

"No. Not being able to play an instrument is completely different to never having heard music." He looked at her quizzically. "It's a bit like you don't need to be able to swim to watch a fish."

"Swim?" and he closed his eyes to access his database. "Ah yes! Got it! Swim. Fish. I understand," but when he opened his eyes and looked at her he saw her pained expression.

"Does it make you uncomfortable when I do that?" he asked, tipping his head on one side the way Mela-14 did.

"It is a little... disquieting, but not as much as the..." and she mimicked the head-tipping gesture.

"Not humanoid?" he asked. She shook her head. "Okay! Right. Well, I'll just have to work on that then. Power you say!" he said, changing the subject. "Does much of this stuff need power?"

"I'm afraid so. I think I've got a good selection of media to have a go at but I can't be sure until we fire it up. I haven't found anything from my homeworld so it's a bit of a guess really. For all I know, I might just have picked up four toasters and a teasmade!" and she laughed as he tried to access his database without closing his eyes. His face was strained.

"Toaster—an electrical appliance usually found in the kitchen for toasting bread. Toasting—being the browning of bread via heat. Bread—a foodstuff made from cereal crops. Teasmade—an electrical appliance usually found in the kitchen for making tea, a hot beverage made by the infusion of plant leaves in hot water. Kitchen—place were food is prepared," she explained.

"Ah," he sighed. She was wonderfully concise in her explanation of things. "Well let's get this lot back then."

"Back where?"

"My quarters."

"Your quarters?" she started. "You're taking me to your quarters?"

He couldn't help but smile to himself at her shock. The memory of finding himself alone in Emoth's quarters flashed through his mind. He had no intentions of that nature but she didn't know it.

"Yes, I take it you're house-trained!" he teased and grinned broadly. Kyamena's mouth opened and closed like a fish, wordlessly.

"But..." she finally protested, but the doors to the miscellany had already opened. Kylem had grabbed his crates and was gone.

"Come on!" he shouted back at her and whistled her like a dog. Kyamena grabbed her crates and ran after him. He was walking incredibly fast and she found it hard to keep up with him.

"Shouldn't we have an escort or something?" she asked.

"What for?"

"In case I try something."

"Like what? Escape? Where to?"

He had a point but voicing it was a bit below the belt.

"Well at least slow down then, will you!" she screamed and almost ran into the back of him. He'd stopped dead.

"I said slow down, not stop!" but his attention was not on her. He was transfixed by something else, some*one* else.

Halfway down the corridor in front of them stood the albino boy. Kylem was staring at him. Suddenly, he turned and looked at her. Kyamena ignored the boy completely and smiled at Kylem emptily.

Could she not see him? He looked back at the boy. He was still there. He looked back at her. If the boy wasn't a figment of his imagination, if he was real, she certainly wasn't acknowledging his presence; and then her eyes flicked, just for one tiny moment, towards the boy. A spark of excitement shot through him.

"You *can* see him!" he declared.

"No," she lied, but her elevated voice, slight grin and definitive answer gave her away. Kylem dropped the boxes and ran after the boy.

"Wait there!" he shouted back at her.

"But Kylem!" she screamed after him. Too late—he was gone.

Kyamena sighed and murmured to herself, "You'll never catch him, kiddo. They don't call him Quick for nothing."

She picked up Kylem's boxes, stacked them beside her own and sat herself down to await his return. He was right about that too. She had nowhere to go.

* * * * *

Up until that moment, Kylem had just about managed to convince himself that the boy was a figment of his imagination, another one of his 'visions'. Even the hair wasn't proof enough for him. It was just a hair and until he'd had the chance to analyse it, that's all it would be because if it were real that would mean that the boy had been in his quarters—and that opened up a whole new world of questions.

Both times that Kylem had seen him, the corridor had been completely empty and then, in the blink of an eye, he'd materialised out of nowhere. How did he get there if he wasn't just a figment of his imagination? That's why he'd been so convinced that it was an illusion. So much so, that when he saw the boy in the corridor with Kyamena, he was going to ignore him, but then he'd looked at Kyamena. At first, she'd given nothing away, but then her eyes had flicked in the boy's direction and she'd pressed her lips hard together to suppress a grin. Then he knew that she could see him too.

But who was he? How did he get there? Why was he loose about the ship? How was he loose about the ship? Why was he undetected and what did Kyamena know of him? All of these questions were racing through Kylem's mind as he chased after the boy.

Kylem followed as the lad turned left into one of the corridors that led to the airlocks. Kylem smiled to himself. It was a dead-end. Kylem had him trapped. But

119

when he turned the corner, he found nothing. The corridor was completely empty.

A whistle from behind prompted Kylem to whip around sharply. The boy was stood a good thirty yards away in the opposite direction, jogging slowly backwards, teasing him.

How had he done that?

Kylem took up the chase again but for a second time, the boy disappeared at the crossroads. Kylem could have sworn he'd taken the right turn so sped off after him, but another whistle forced him to skid to a halt and double back. Once more the boy had disappeared from view, for despite Kylem's speed and agility, the boy was faster—and he knew it!

Time and time again, he stopped, let Kylem catch up with him and then he'd be off once more. Kylem began to realise the chase was stupid. The boy was running circles around him.

"This isn't a game!" Kylem shouted sternly.

"It is," giggled the boy, his face full of glee.

"No, it isn't!" Kylem protested with irritation.

"Yes, it is," and he turned and ran off again.

Kylem fell in after him, hot on his heels, but the boy was so quick that the gap between them widened fast. It was even more annoying when the boy slowed down, yet again, to turn and check he was still following. Kylem scowled but knew his opportunity was coming. The corridor ahead made a sharp left-hand turn and the boy would have to slow down to take it, at which point, he'd be able to leap upon him and bring him down.

The corner grew nearer but the boy didn't slow. Instead, he picked the pace up even further. Kylem wondered, was he intending to run through it? When he got to the wall though, he literally leapt at it and bounced off it to change direction, like a free runner. Kylem braked, but too late. He smacked into it, bounced off it and fell. He spun clumsily around on his buttocks like a puppy on an ice rink.

That was it! Enough was enough! Damn him!

Kylem didn't get up. The boy obviously knew the ship far better than he did. Reluctantly, Kylem watched as the boy ran on. Never had he been so humiliated in a chase.

As expected, the boy stopped, turned and shouted down the corridor.

"Come on," he cried excitedly and began walking backwards, teasing Kylem on.

"What for? You've proven that you're faster than I am and that you know these corridors far better than I. What do you want me for?"

"Come on bro!"

"What for?"

"Come on!"

"I'm not following you," but the boy didn't seem to hear. He turned and ran off, disappearing again. Kylem waited, expecting him to rematerialise but he didn't.

In the end, Kylem got up and walked to the corner. He looked around it but the corridor ahead was empty. There was no sign of him at all.

As Kylem made his way back to Kyamena, he kept expecting the boy to reappear at any moment but he didn't. He wondered if he'd find him with Kyamena when he got back but although he could hear voices as he approached, it wasn't the boy's.

As he turned the last corner, his heart leapt into his mouth.

Kyamena was still there and he'd expected nothing less. What he hadn't banked upon was the rabble of Warriors that surrounded her.

"He told me to wait here!" he heard her shouting at them.

Arguing with him was one thing but arguing with Warriors was another. Whilst they probably wouldn't harm her, it wasn't guaranteed. If she lost her temper with them, if she got into a physical struggle with them... and he realised just how foolish he'd been leaving her there unaccompanied.

He broke into a canter and shouted as he approached. The rabble opened up and Sinta-3 unfolded from within the group. The sight of a Scientific in their midst floored him for a moment.

"I'm back," he said as casually as he could.

"Back? Where have you been? What were you thinking of?" queried the Scientific.

"Sorry," he tried to sound indignant. "Is there a problem?"

"A problem? Yes, there is. Do you really think it wise to leave prisoners wandering about the corridors of the DaerkStar unaccompanied?"

"I think it would be most unwise," he agreed.

"Then why did you do it?"

"I didn't. She wasn't wandering. In fact, she's exactly where I left her."

"But she could have gone anywhere." Sinta-3's voice wasn't like his father's. It sounded the same but the intonations were misplaced making it cold and dead.

"If she was disobedient, which she isn't."

"That is not the point, ATB-80. You do not leave your prisoners unaccompanied."

"I gave her a task to perform and she's done exactly as she was told to do."

"Task? What task?"

"The boxes. I dropped the boxes and I told her to pick them up and to wait for me here—and she did."

"Why? Where did you go?" It was a good question that needed a good answer, and quick!

"I'd dropped this," and he fumbled in his pocket for the cobblestone he'd stashed there earlier. "So I went back for it. Can't go around littering up the corridors now, can we?"

Sinta-3 gave a little buzz of disapproval.

"I suppose not, but do not let it happen again."

"Affirmed," said Kylem obediently and immediately snapped his fingers at Kyamena.

"Come!" he barked as sternly as he could.

Eager to be gone, Kyamena pushed her way gently through the towering Warriors towards the boxes.

"Excuse me," she said politely and the Warriors stepped aside for her, one raising its arms as she ducked underneath it. Kylem was already off down the corridor so she had to scuttle after him hurriedly despite the weight of all the boxes. No sooner were they out of sight though, than Kylem plucked the top three boxes from her.

"If you ever leave me like that again," she hissed to him.

"Yeah, yeah, yeah," he grinned, struggling to suppress his laughter.

Kyamena was still glaring at Kylem as they entered his quarters.

"I wish you could have seen your face!" he laughed.

"Oh yes, so very funny! If you hadn't come along—"

"If I hadn't come along, then what? They'd have taken you back to the Bio-Labs and then I'd have bailed you out."

"Oh yeah! Great! In between times, whilst you're off chasing—"

"Ah yes!" remembered Kylem, swivelling about-face on his heels. "And exactly who *was* I chasing?"

Kyamena shut her mouth and sucked her lips in to seal them like a naughty schoolgirl.

"So you do know who he is!"

She smiled faintly. "Are you going to tell on him?" she asked tentatively.

"I think I've missed the boat on that one, don't you? Anyway, tell on who? I don't know who he is or what he's doing running around the ship like that."

"He's Quick."

"I know he's quick. I couldn't bloody catch him," snapped Kylem.

She laughed. "No, he's Quick. That's his name."

"What sort of a name is Quick?"

"What sort of a name is Nothing?"

"It's not nothing, it's Kylem."

"Same thing."

"No, it's not!" he retorted angrily.

"Yes it is."

"Oh, I don't believe this!" he growled. "You're arguing with me again! You're not supposed to argue with me! Do you argue with Mela-14 like this?"

"No."

"Then why do you argue with me?"

"Because you can't wind up an android."

An image of a huge clockwork Scientific with a key projecting out of its back hobbled through Kylem's mind.

"We're not clockwork, you know."

Kyamena giggled. "Wind up: to annoy or irritate."

"Oh." Kylem thought. "But I wind up Mela-14 all the time."

"But it won't get you killed."

"It might."

"Smaller likelihood."

"Granted," but Kylem was still confused. "You admit, then, that you are intentionally winding me up?"

"Oh yes."

"Why?"

"Why do you wind up Mela-14?"

Kylem flushed with colour.

"Ah-ha!" she screeched triumphantly, "because it's fun!"

"Yes, yes, all right," he conceded.

Kyamena had begun to wander around his quarters, inspecting them. They surprised her. On a ship built for androids, she'd expected Kylem's quarters to be something like a converted storage cupboard, something very small, bland and functional. Instead, she found herself in a very comfortable and spacious environment, a little colourless perhaps, but well furnished in a contemporary manner. More surprising though, was the state of it. It looked like the room belonged to two different people.

In one respect, it was spotlessly tidy and clean, just as one would expect from an android or a military man. The white carpet was immaculate. The chairs around the coffee table were positioned with mathematical symmetry. The bed was made, complete with hospital corners, and the fresh towels hung equidistant to each other in the bathroom. The mirrors were flawlessly polished and there was not a fingerprint to be seen on any surface.

And yet there was also chaos.

There was a small pile of clothes strewn over one of the study chairs, a collection of used towels discarded on the floor and the workbench was littered with a vast collection of half-assembled (or disassembled) projects giving the room the air of being a bit of a bachelor pad. No—not a bachelor pad. It was more like the room of a rich kid who had servants to clear up after him.

"You know I wouldn't let them hurt you, don't you?" he reassured her, breaking her reverie.

"Whilst it suits you."

She was in the bathroom now. It was small but had a real shower in it and a beautiful, clean, white sink. In truth it wasn't anything special but compared to her own space, it was palatial. Momentarily she debated asking if she could have a shower in it but decided against it. That really was going beyond the boundaries of their... could she call it friendship?

"And I'm not going to either," he added.

"Whilst it suits you."

"No. I've told you—"

"Why are you so concerned about what I think?" she interrupted, reappearing from the bathroom.

"I'm not!"

"Yes, you are."

"No, I'm not. Oh, for crying out loud! I'm not going to argue with you!" and he waved his arms about dismissively. Kyamena smiled to herself, knowing that he would.

"It's not an argument," she corrected. "It's a debate. It's how people discuss things; otherwise it would just be a monologue." As she turned to look at him, she saw his twisted face. "Okay, point made. Let's change the subject. What do *you* want to talk about?"

"I have no idea," he said. "Oh, yes I do!" he exclaimed. "You seemed a bit spooked when I said we were coming here. I take it then that you assumed I was suggesting procreation. Do bloods think about procreation a lot?"

Kyamena laughed.

"No, babes, that's just you! Although a lot of men do seem to have little else on their minds. No. I was thinking that you wouldn't want a *goyeme* contaminating your space. Sallows can be a bit funny about that sort of thing."

"They can?" he quizzed. "How'd you know that?"

"The priest told me."

"Priest? What priest?"

"I told you. You should visit sometime," she said, perching on the edge of the bed and testing it for comfort.

She watched as Kylem picked up the towels and various clothes that were scattered around the room and threw them unceremoniously into the bottom of the wardrobe. She chuckled. He may have been born an android and he may have been raised an android but he was a typical teenage boy in so many ways. He saw her smiling.

"What?"

"It's just how human you are. Some things are the same all the worlds over. Never occurs to you to put anything back on a hanger or fold up a towel, does it?"

"Not my job," smirked Kylem, feeling quite pleased with himself that he was doing something typically humanoid, but then he wondered: was this what he really wanted?

All his life he had thought of himself as being a Sallow, be it android or blood. Now he was trying so hard to be humanoid: mimicking them and spending time with them and apparently enjoying it. If he succeeded he would have achieved his mission, but by the end of it, would he still be a Sallow? Would he still *want* to be a Sallow? *'Know thy enemy'*. But if you crawled so far inside their heads to become one of them, that you understood them, would that not make you one of them? His eye caught sight of his reflection in the mirror. He did look so humanoid, just like Kyamena.

She, meanwhile, had turned her attention back to the boxes. She was unpacking the books and stacking them on the end of the bench, arranging them by size, flicking through the pages of one or two of them.

"Do you know what any of these are about?" she asked.

"Not yet. What did you want to ask me?"

"What? When?"

"In the miscellany. Before we..." he paused. Why did they argue so much? Why did he like arguing with her so much? "You were going to ask me a question."

"I was? Oh yes, I was."

"Well?"

She sighed. "Oh, I can't remember. Anyway, I didn't think I was supposed to be the one asking the questions."

"Not uninvited, no, but now you're invited."

"Is that an open invitation, or does it have an expiry date?"

Kylem was dubious. He wanted to say it was an open invitation but if he did, what questions would she assault him with?

"How many people have you actually interacted with?" she asked suddenly. "I don't mean slain or just met, but actually had a conversation with—excluding androids and Sallows?"

"Just you," he said. "Well..." and for a moment, he thought he remembered something but it was gone before it came to him, leaving him with only that frustrating air of familiarity again.

"What?" she asked.

"It's nothing," he said, brushing the thoughts aside. "I don't remember."

"Don't remember? I didn't think androids could forget?"

"I told you. I've not always been an android. When I was born, my memories were stored in the biological part of my brain, just as yours are. As humanoids grow, cells, neural connections and engrams grow too. They are born, they flourish, they age and they die. Memories are transferred from the old ones to the new ones and thus memories are maintained, but if memories are not recalled, if they are not transmitted to a new engram, they can fall victim to the death. They become forgotten. I've had plenty of time for my memories to fade before they were assimilated by the huma-nanites. I don't think the accelerated growth thing helped much either. Why do you ask?"

"Just wondered how lonely you are."

"Lonely? I'm not lonely. There are thousands of us on board."

"But none of your own kind."

"I am unique."

"And thus alone."

"I've told you, I'm not alone."

"So who do you talk to when you're troubled? Mela-14?"

"Yes."

"And you trust him implicitly, do you?"

He didn't answer because he didn't trust anybody implicitly. It was not in his nature to trust. He was a spy.

"What else do you know about Sallows, then?" he asked.

Bad eyesight, she thought, and then the penny dropped. How foolish she'd been not to think of it sooner! She had the power to unhinge him after all. The boy was paranoid. It was bred into him. If she told him what she knew, it would surely crush him. It would separate him from the Sallows once and for all. The Sallows wouldn't have their weapon anymore. But once he knew this fact, would his paranoia be unleashed, and what would he do with it?

'The Sallows desire a new Warrior: one of strength and cunning, a sword forged in the fires of tribes and quenched in the blood of mankind. Now they have their hardened sword, but who will wield it?' Aleana could well have been right.

Kyamena indicated for Kylem to come and sit opposite her. He did so and for a few moments, she sat silently studying him. Kylem could feel her indecision and tension.

"Well?" he asked. "Is it that bad?"

"For you, maybe."

"Now you *are* toying with me."

"No, I'm not."

"Then tell."

"Poor eyesight. Sallows have very poor eyesight."

He looked at her, dismayed.

"I know that," he said. "Nothing new there I'm afraid."

Kyamena bit her bottom lip thoughtfully and turned to the rack of books behind her. She selected two and held them up.

"What colour are these books?" she asked. He screwed his face up contemptuously. "No, seriously—humour me. What colour are these books?"

He looked at them. It was a trick question. They were the same colour.

"I'll give you a clue. One is beige and one is pink, but which one is pink?"

Kylem couldn't answer. They both looked the same to him.

"I thought so. You're blind to colours."

"That's not true," he protested, and began picking up various objects and shouting out their colours.

"Blue! Red! Green! Black!—"

"Brown!" she interrupted.

"Black!" he screamed, and then looked at the dark coloured plastic tray he was holding. Was it black? He suddenly became aware of the fact that he was holding the tray so close to his face that he couldn't focus on it anymore.

Was it true? Was he blind to colour?

He threw the tray angrily back onto the bench.

"Don't look so down," she said comfortingly. "It's been your saviour so far."

"If I can't see colours, I'm defective. How's that my saviour?"

"You twonk," she said. "The fact that you have a problem with colours isn't the problem. Everybody is imperfect. Everybody has their handicaps and everybody learns to cope with them. It's the fact that you have inherited that defect from the Sallows, that they can't see colours, that has been your saviour. The fact that you can't distinguish all colours has never hindered you before, has it?"

"Well, no—"

"Right then."

"So what *is* the problem?"

"Your eyes," and she passed him a sheet of highly polished metal that was amongst the debris of his desk. He took it from her and gazed at his reflection.

"What colour are they?" she asked.

"They're green."

"Yes, at the moment they are green but not your usual brilliant emerald green. They're grey-green, turning blue. Not that you can see it," she sighed. "The colour change is too subtle just now."

He continued staring at his reflection in the mirror whilst she explained further.

"When you're happy, they're a brilliant emerald green. When you're unhappy and serious, they turn grey or blue and when you're enraged, they're red."

Kylem threw the piece of metal back on the bench.

"That's the most ridiculous thing I've ever heard," he said stroppily.

"Oh good god! Look at that!" exclaimed Kyamena and pointed down at the floor.

Kylem tipped his head to look and without warning Kyamena lunged forward, grabbed the back of his head and smashed it into her knee. Kylem reeled with pain and lashed out in retaliation. He caught her square on, with such force that it sent her flying across the room where she smacked her head on the bed frame. Dazed, she forced herself to ignore the pain and pointed at him.

"Not green anymore," she mumbled and collapsed on the floor, finally overwhelmed by the blow. Kylem didn't look. He was poised ready to strike again.

"Look!" she urged, grimacing through her pain, her hands cradled around her head. "Look in the mirror, for god's sake," she pleaded.

Kylem looked. She was right. Perhaps it was because he knew what he was looking for that he could see it, but his eyes weren't green anymore. They were a muddy brown colour instead.

"Oh shit!" he mumbled. "That's even worse."

She laughed pathetically.

"Sorry, but I had to make you angry to see it," she winced in pain.

"I don't understand," he said, ignoring her apology and watched as the muddiness began washing out of his irises. "It's such a big giveaway. I can't believe they haven't noticed it."

"That's what I was telling you." Kyamena rolled over and hauled herself up onto her buttocks. She leant against the bed, drawing her knees up to her chest and nursed her head. "Blood-Sallows have very poor eyesight. That's why the lighting is so bright. They only see in monochrome. They rely on shadows and contours. They are oblivious to colour, so the androids were never designed to see colour either. They have no concept of colour. That's why things here are so colourless and that's why they can't see the colour of your eyes."

"But the cinema? The dining room? They are beautiful rooms with wonderful colour schemes?"

"Perhaps they are tonally pleasing to the eye. I don't know, but I assure you, they don't see colour."

Kylem turned away from his image. Kyamena was sat nursing her head. Her hair and hands were bloody and she was in a lot of pain. Kylem registered her breathing, fast and irregular, and her complexion was pale. Display diagnosed a possible concussion.

"Hang on," he said. He went to the bathroom and soaked a towel in cool water. He came back with it and knelt down beside her.

"Let me see," and pulled her hands away and began dabbing at the wound. "It's not too bad," he assessed.

A pained laugh escaped her.

"I've just trashed your world and you're worried about my head."

"Can you just not talk for a minute, please?" he asked with irritation. "I need to think."

She obliged.

If what she said was true, which it seemed to be, then how could she have just trashed his world?

"But if they can't see colour, they'll never notice," he said.

"Humanoids will."

"Yeah, but what will that tell them? That my eyes change colour with my moods?" As he said it, he realised the severity of the flaw. "Do they change colour when I lie?"

"I don't think so. Your body language gives you away when you lie."

"What body language?"

She laughed.

"You really are the most appalling spy."

He scowled again.

"What body language?" he demanded.

"When you lie, you break eye contact and then you start fiddling with things. You are inept when it comes to hiding your annoyance, and if you keep scowling like that you'll get crow's feet around your eyes."

"And when have I lied to you, for you to make this fascinating deduction?" he demanded.

"You said you'd visit the Bio-Labs and the Farm Decks but you have no intention of going there, have you?" she scoffed.

Kylem looked away.

127

"Breaking eye contact again," she jeered. "You see, I've told you and still you can't hide your emotions!"

"Where do you know all this stuff from? I thought you were a bookkeeper?"

"I was," she said.

"So?"

"Bookkeeping isn't all ledgers and balance sheets, you know. I told you before. I worked for the Bureau of Revenue, for the prosecuting attorney's team."

"So you said, but that's all you said."

She was starting to feel sick but this was important.

"Every citizen has to pay taxes," she explained. "But some people try to avoid paying them. It's the prosecutors' job to seek them out and bring a case against them. I was a prosecutor."

"Oh, right, and this is where you've learnt about body language?"

"Yes. I've seen people lie and seen how they react when they lie. Lying isn't just about words. There are gestures and micro-expressions, tiny little things that give away deception. For me, being able to spot a liar, it just went with the territory."

"So, I need to work on that then."

"Definitely, but even if you do master it, you're eyes will still tell everyone your true feelings—when you're happy, when you're sad and when something's upset you. And even if you do learn to control your body language, will it matter?"

"What do you mean?"

"Is the body language of my culture the same as the body language of another? One man's smile may be another man's insult."

"You really know how to cheer a guy up, don't you?"

She laughed faintly.

"Here," he said, and pulled her up and onto the bed where he lay her down.

"I'll be okay," she assured him. "I've taken harder blows," but Kylem wasn't convinced. The wound was still bleeding and the cut was deep. For him, it would be nothing, but she was proper flesh and blood.

Kylem went over to his bench and began rummaging until he found the half disassembled medical scanner he'd got there. He quickly reassembled it, just enough for it to function.

With the cover and various bits still dangling free, he scanned Kyamena. He hadn't cracked her skull but he had given her a hefty blow. The wound needed stitching.

He returned to the bench and rummaged some more until he found the tube of fast-seal glue he was looking for. He'd used it a number of times on his own wounds and had discovered it worked well.

He went back to the bed and encouraged Kyamena onto her side. He cleaned the wound again and began to glue it shut. She was getting dopey now, but Kylem wasn't worried. He was keeping an eye on her vitals displayed on the scanner. Her breathing had eased and her colour was better, so when he was done he left her to sleep.

* * * * *

When Kyamena came to, her head was thumping. It took her a few minutes to remember where she was before she cautiously rose, gently touching her head. It smarted and she winced.

"Sorry," she heard him say.

Kylem was sat hunched over the workbench busily soldering something. He did not look up.

"It was in a good cause," she said painfully.

"How was it good?"

"You wanted to learn; you learnt."

He put down the soldering iron and swivelled around to face her.

"Actually, I think you're trying to manipulate me," he said.

"Isn't everybody? I'm just making sure you get all the facts before you decide whose side you're on."

"Sides? You think it's all about sides?"

"All wars are about sides."

"Factually speaking, all wars are about power, money, race or religion," and he turned his attention back to his project. Kyamena thought about it.

"I suppose they are. Do Sallows have a god then?"

"I don't know."

She puzzled. "Why don't you know?"

"Never thought about it."

"Do you have a god?"

"*There are no gods, only entities who believe themselves to be such,*" he quoted.

"Wow! That view'll start a few wars on its own."

She reached for the towel that was on the floor, damp and pink with her blood. She pressed it against her wound.

"I don't understand religion," he said. "Tell me about it."

"What's not to understand?"

"How can people believe in something that doesn't exist?"

"What makes you say it doesn't exist?"

"You can't touch it. You can't feel it."

"Air's like that. You can't touch it and you can't feel it but it's there, so unless you're suggesting that air doesn't exist—?"

"You can do both, actually," he retorted. "If you stand in, say, a ventilation shaft."

She laughed. "You always have an answer for everything, don't you?"

He smiled, and then a new thought began its conception. His eyes narrowed as the thought matured and slowly, methodically, he put down the soldering iron.

"Vent," he mused with an air of triumph about him. "Vent!" he repeated excitedly.

He got up and began wandering around the room, searching the ceiling. Then he checked under the workbench and systematically examined all the walls in his room and then in the bathroom too.

"Ah-hah!" he finally declared. Kyamena got off the bed and joined him in the bathroom where he was stood looking up at the ceiling. It wasn't an ordinary ceiling though. Its entire expanse was filled with an intricate black and white filigree design of flowers and scrolls.

"That's pretty," she said, feigning stupidity.

"Not just pretty, but functional. A bathroom needs extra ventilation to address the high levels of steam and condensation that it is subjected to. The whole ceiling is part of the ventilation system, with the vents camouflaged by the design. And here—" Taking her by the elbow and leading her back into the main room of his quarters, he pointed at the ceiling where the design was evident as a thick border that ran around the edge of the room. "—That's all vent too," he exclaimed. "Well, not all vent. The design camouflages it but there are vents in there—and here, too."

He dragged her over to the door, which opened at their approach. Casting a quick glance in either direction, he pulled her out into the corridor and pointed up at the designs spaced intermittently along its length. He'd never really noticed them before. They were just there like wallpaper, but some were centrally placed in the ceiling while others were rectangular and folded down the walls. All were similar black and white filigree designs with Sallow writing buried within them detailing deck levels and so on.

Kylem pulled Kyamena back into his room and, once the door had shut, he spoke.

"That's how he does it!" he said, grinning triumphantly. "That's how Quick gets about the ship so fast—via the vents!" and then the grin fell from his face. "But you already knew that, didn't you?"

"Yes," she admitted.

"But who is he, and what's he doing?"

"He's not doing anything. He's just... surviving."

"But how long has he been loose? Why hasn't he been captured?"

"He's been loose for years and to be honest, I don't think anybody's actually missed him."

"That's absurd!"

"The Sallows are not as thorough as you think. They are as flawed and inefficient as the rest of us."

"But who is he?"

"He's your brother."

"Don't be ridiculous."

"I'm not being ridiculous. To all intents and purposes, he's your brother. He was your predecessor, manufactured in exactly the same way you were."

"He's deformed."

"He's different. We're all different. You have two hearts, I have one. Does that make you deformed? No, of course not. It makes you different, and the only difference between you and him was Aleana."

"Aleana?"

"Yes, the surrogate: the woman in whose womb you were incubated."

Kylem went over to one of the computer terminals and placed his hand on the keyboard. He didn't need to press the keys; he just had to touch it to make the link to access Server and the databanks.

"There's nothing here about a predecessor," he declared but continued his search. He scowled as he cross-referenced to the word 'surrogate' instead. That was interesting: there were empty blocks in the data. That meant information had been amended or deleted and recently too, otherwise Server's defragmentation routine would have reorganised them into contiguous blocks by now.

The surrounding blocks were about him, his conception and his incubation. The size and date stamps indicated that the information held was highly detailed, except on the day of his birth when the files were only one tenth of the size. At various other points in time too, both before and after his birth, the records seemed curiously small. Should he believe her?

Then he thought about the hair. He picked up the copy of *A Kiss beyond Midnight* and gently pulled the hair out from beneath it.

"What's that?" she asked.

"Evidence," he declared and opened a drawer, pulled out a small plastic box and sealed the hair inside it. "Looks like you're going to get your own way after all."

"What do you mean?"

"Now I'll have to go down to the Bio-Labs to study this, won't I? Happy?"

She shrugged. Kylem gazed up at the ceiling for a moment longer and then turned his attention back to her and the project he had been working on.

"Now what were we saying? Ah yes, war—power, money, race, religion. You were telling me about religion."

"Not really, but race and religion often go hand in hand. The differences people have, divide them."

"And money?"

"Ah! Now money makes the world go round," she declared. "Well, money and lust."

"Lust?"

"Very powerful thing, lust. Don't underestimate it. Many a leader has fallen foul of that desire."

"Why? What is the big thing about it? Why are sex and lust so consuming?"

"That's something I can't teach you. To know that, you have to experience it first hand—and just for the record," she said, waggling her finger at him, "that is something you won't be learning about from me."

"But you'll tell me about it?" he asked dubiously.

She sighed and then laughed.

"Somebody's got to, I suppose, otherwise you'll have no morals at all."

"What have morals got to do with procreation?"

She sighed heavily.

"Oh dear. This is not going to be easy. Sex is not just about procreation. It's intensely complicated. It reinforces some of the deepest human emotions, good and bad, physical and mental—love and hate. It can be used as a weapon of manipulation and it can be one of the most wonderful, pleasurable experiences you can share with another being."

Silence fell between them.

Kylem nodded thoughtfully.

"Well, if what you say is true that may explain why everybody's so interested in my sexuality. If it can be used as a weapon, it's one I need to master."

"I was trying to stress the pleasure side of it."

"Oh!"

The memory of being trapped in Emoth's quarters came back to trouble him and a shiver of disgust ran down his spine. There was certainly nothing pleasurable about that experience, not for him anyway, but if he had complied, would he have been using Emoth or would Emoth have been using him? Who would be manipulating who? He felt uneasy at the thought and pushed it to the furthest reaches of his mind.

"Okay," he said, changing the subject, "I think I've got it," and he held up the hotchpotch assembly of wires, diodes and plugs attached to what had once been an engineering scanner. Kyamena looked at the assembly unimpressed. "Hey, it might not look like much but this is a very sophisticated piece of kit."

"How's that, then?"

"The connections were the hardest bit. With so many different devices from so many different cultures, no two are the same, so I've had to study all the different types of connectors on the bits we've picked up and design something with universal connectors that should fit all the units. The scanner regulates the amount of power being supplied and detects the usage of the unit attached. If it needs more power, it provides more but as soon as it starts to detect an overload, it pulls back on the supply until it detects that the current being provided is equal to that of the unit's demand."

Kyamena was smiling at him.

"You know, it's odd that you know so much about so much, and yet you know so little. Come on then. Let's fire up the keyboard," and she thrust it at him.

He took it and began unwrapping it, trying to spread it out across the workbench but the surface was too cluttered. Impatiently, Kylem opened a drawer under the workbench and with one sweep of his arm brushed the area clean into it and slammed the drawer shut. Kyamena hid a giggle behind her hand. He looked at her.

"Towels," she reminded him, and he smirked.

Spreading the keyboard out in front of them, he took the universal power supply and selected one of the connectors. It didn't look like it would fit but as he offered it up to the keyboard, it seemed to remould itself.

"That's clever," she said, visibly impressed. Kylem wallowed in the warmth of her praise for a moment before switching the scanner on. It lit up and the readouts on the small display began to register inputs and outputs. Little sine waves vibrated wildly and then began to settle.

"Okay. I think we're ready to go."

Kylem then, savouring the moment, reached out one finger and touched one of the keys. A note played out strong and true, gently at first but growing ever louder the longer he kept his finger on the key, until he released it. He touched another key and it played another note, higher than the first but equally as beautiful. Then he touched a third note. Drawing up his left hand, he touched two keys at the same time. They sang out in harmony.

"That's quite a pleasant noise," he admitted but sounded disappointed and deservedly so, for although the notes were pleasant to listen to, they were mundane.

"So that's music."

"No, silly. They're just notes, but notes make music. Music is a compilation of notes," and she jabbed at the keys like an awkward child playing chopsticks.

"Hey! I like that. Show me again."

"It's hardly Barovia," she said.

"Barovia?"

"Famous composer," and she played the piece again. Kylem then copied her, but it wasn't an exact copy. His tempo was much better than hers and the tune caressed the ear more lovingly.

"Hey! You're good at this. Play something else," she said.

"Like what?"

"I don't know. Make it up or something."

Kylem drew his hands from the keyboard and stared at it.

"Insufficient data," he finally said.

"Well then. Let's find you some more data," and she pulled out a palm-sized silver box with rounded edges and a row of little buttons on it.

"This one looks interesting," she said, turning it over in her hands. She found a long button on the side and pressed it. A small silver disc popped out of the side from an almost invisible slot. She pushed it back in.

"What's on that?"

Kylem dutifully took it from her and unplugged the keyboard. He selected a more appropriate plug for the silver box and let the scanner do its work, but nothing happened.

"Now what?" he asked.

"Press *play*," and she leaned over him and began pressing buttons until a voice exuded from the box. It was a man's voice, highly expressive as though painting a picture with his words but Kyamena didn't recognise the language.

"Do you know what he's saying?"

Kylem listened a little longer.

"No," he said, "but I'll be able to work it out given a little time. What are you doing?"

Kyamena had taken the box off him and ejected the disc.

"That's dull. I want you to hear music. Here, see if you can find some more of these discs. I know I picked up a whole load of them. They were in a red leather book type thing, but I don't know which box I put them in."

The two of them began sifting through the remainders of the boxes.

"Here we go," said Kylem, holding up the small, red folder of discs. Kyamena took the book from him and picked out a disc at random. She pushed it into the unit. It slid into place with a little whoosh and she pressed the play button. Suddenly the room was filled with beautiful, gentle music.

The sounds of flutes hummed mournfully in the air, softly at first and then they grew in strength and volume until they began to overwhelm Kylem with their power and intensity. The sounds filled him, and as the flutes sang with their sweet highs and lows, it both cheered and dismalised him in one beautiful yet savage blow; and then... the flutes began to fade away... making way for the orchestra to form with the intensity of a gathering storm.

Violins and cellos sang through the air like birds, with notes fluttering and caressing each other in perfect harmony, dancing upon the currents. Oboes joined the ensemble and bassoons appeared with their gentle, booming undertones. Trumpets and trombones joined with notes that danced playfully around them and then, just as Kylem believed his ears could be caressed no further with beauty, the sounds began to die making way for a single celeste to sing. It tinkled crisply with notes falling like raindrops and then the orchestra, once again, introduced itself, blending with the celeste into perfect harmony.

The tones rose and fell, sweeping Kylem away into a mystical world and then... the music faded and died.

It was truly the most wonderful thing he had ever heard.

Kyamena too, was stunned by the effect the music had had on Kylem, not only because he appeared to be overwhelmed by it, but because of his tears. There were no sobs but three drops had run down his cheek.

"What the blazes is going on here?" demanded Mela-14.

133

Kylem turned sharply to see his father at the door. Neither of them had heard his entrance.

"What is that cacophony? You did not even hear me come in!" he exclaimed.

"It's music," replied Kylem weakly.

"Is that what you call it? What purpose does it serve?"

Kylem lifted his eyebrows. "You wouldn't understand. It's like reading and you don't understand that either."

"Is it useful?"

Kylem shrugged.

Mela-14 turned to Kyamena.

"Well?" he demanded.

For a moment, she froze and then she blurted out, "Yes. It's incredibly important to his studies. Music makes us happy and it makes us feel sad. It enhances our emotions and can even change them. He must understand music if he is to integrate."

She hated talking to Mela-14. Over the years, she had learnt of this machine's savagery. He unnerved her. She looked to Kylem for support and saw the tears still there. Mela-14 saw them too. He walked over to Kylem, studied them and then wiped them away with his thumb. Kylem didn't flinch which surprised Kyamena. The android tipped his head enquiringly.

"Solder," lied Kylem. "I've been soldering and I got smoke in my eyes. Bit stupid of me really."

"Well, it is late. You must finish now."

"Affirmed."

"Come," Mela-14 instructed Kyamena and she obediently fell in behind him.

"Play more music," she instructed Kylem as she left. "There are lots of different types in there. That was classical but there are others."

"Okay," he said and the door closed leaving him alone again.

Alone.

* * * * *

As Kyamena walked down the corridor with Mela-14, she was smiling to herself. A very long time ago, she had told a Sallow *'you may have won this war but there is always another day'*. Then she had believed that her words were empty. Now she wondered.

CHAPTER 16

Kylem couldn't sleep again. He was starting to realise that he didn't need quite as much sleep as he used to. He wondered if one day he'd not need to sleep at all but in the meantime, he'd been tossing and turning and punching the pillow for hours. Finally, he gave up and got up.

Having showered and dressed, however, he determined that it was no bad thing. 'Night-mode' was the perfect time to get things done, a time when he was guaranteed to be left alone. Tonight it gave him the opportunity to go through more of the stuff they'd brought back from the miscellany and, having developed his universal power supply, he was able to fire most of it up.

It seemed that Kyamena had favoured recorded media. She'd picked out nearly two thousand different discs and data chips, and she'd been very particular, ensuring that she had the various different types of media player to go with them. As he worked his way through the library, he found audio books, films, lectures and, best of all, lots and lots of music.

He was developing an ear for it too. Besides all the different genres of music, he had come to realise that each of the media players reproduced the audio with varying degrees of quality. The first device he had used with Kyamena had by far the best sound reproduction but he suspected there was room for improvement. He determined that what he really needed was a set of high-quality, independent electro-acoustic transducers with drivers for the different frequencies, from the very low to the very high—or, to put it more simply, a decent set of speakers.

But on a ship built by a race of beings that had no ear for music—who referred to music as a 'cacophony'—where would one find such a thing? Simply, nowhere. He'd have to build what he wanted, so after delving into Server's alien databanks for some specifications and a quick shufty through the miscellany, he was heading to Engineering Supplies where everything from fuse wire to warp cores were tucked away.

As he padded along the dimly lit corridors, he debated the absurdity of it. For seven hours every day the ship was plunged into 'night-mode' where the lights were dimmed and all but a skeleton crew of androids were sent to 'bed'. He was on board a ship with over ten-thousand insomniac androids and just five blood-Sallows that probably never even saw night-mode whilst tucked up in their quarters. It was a global simulation of a nocturnal shift from some planetary system long ago abandoned. But it wasn't just absurd; it was an unnecessary risk, a period when the ship was needlessly vulnerable. It reeked of overconfidence in their superiority in the quadrant, a foolish and vain overconfidence in Kylem's opinion.

As he neared the Engineering Decks, the traffic increased a little. He passed a small rabble of four Warriors marching in the opposite direction and mused how their footsteps were not only in perfect tune with each other but also with his own. As he passed another rabble, the same was true. In fact, every rabble that he passed marched in tune to his footsteps—well, perhaps not his footsteps, but his footsteps were the metronome by which he was measuring them.

What did that mean? That individual rabbles marched in unison was one thing, but if all Warriors marched to the same tune, that must mean that some form of synchronicity was in force, a force that called them all back to order regardless of distance. Kylem looked at his feet that were still marching to the same beat. Was he too being called to obey that order of synchronicity?

Kylem purposely broke step. Now his feet pounded to a different beat and a shiver of discomfort rippled through him. An urge to correct the error and fall back in swept over him. It felt unnatural to walk like this but he purposely slowed his pace to further exaggerate the disharmony. Now, not only were his steps out of sync, but the tempo was different too.

The lack of rhythm rankled him. The desire to fall back in, to comply, was alluring, but he resisted. He forced his steps into irregularity, constantly changing pace and rhythm, staring at his feet as he went, and then suddenly he would become aware that he was no longer out of sync. Somehow, regardless of his efforts, he had fallen back into the pace of the Warriors. He forced his steps out again and again and the gnawing agony of the disharmony ate away at him, but it was only short-lived as, slowly but surely, his pace fell back into theirs.

He stopped and watched another Warrior rabble appear and disappear from sight. He was alone once more. He sighed despondently. Was this yet another flaw in his make-up? He really couldn't afford to be or to act like an android, not in this game.

"Pssst!"

Kylem looked up and saw in the shadows of the ornate grill above him, Quick's pale face.

"Oh great," he replied softly to himself. "What do you want? Another game?" he asked quietly so as not to alert any Warriors that might be nearby.

Quick opened the panel and held out his hand to Kylem.

"No. No game, but you have to come," Quick whispered.

"What for? Where?"

Quick seemed agitated.

"To see the Priest."

"And why would I want to see a priest? He's not my priest and I don't believe in deities."

"He wants to see you!" he whispered, urgently waving his hand at Kylem, prompting him to take it. Kylem looked at Quick's colourless face in the shadows of the air duct and shook his head.

"I'm busy," he said and began walking away.

"But he's dying," Quick protested softly, "and he's asking for you."

Kylem pirouetted about and scowled.

"What's he asking for me for?"

"I don't know. Something about the Eunaba, he said."

136

"The what?"

"The Eunaba! Come on! Take my hand before the Warriors come."

Kylem threw his hands onto his hips and shook his head again.

"You expect me to trust you?" he exclaimed.

"Yes!" Quick looked bemused. "Why wouldn't you?"

"Because you're the enemy," reminded Kylem.

"No, we're brothers," corrected Quick, sounding quite hurt.

"And what relevance is that?" *Blood is thicker than water,* said the little voice inside his head. "Oh, what the hell," and Kylem held out his hand to Quick.

As their hands folded around each other's wrists, Kylem prepared himself for what he thought would be a somewhat awkward haul into the attic space, especially as there was nowhere for his feet to gain a purchase. Instead, the puny looking hunchback almost catapulted him into the void. Once inside though, he was left to fend for himself. He had to contort and twist himself around in the confined tunnel until he was sat awkwardly, cross-legged, facing Quick. Quick re-secured the panel and perched on his haunches like an Indian peasant with his finger on his lips.

"Shhh!"

Kylem looked down to see a rabble of four Warriors pass beneath them. He felt a thrill of excitement run through him. This is what he was designed to do, to go sneaking about places and poking his nose in where it didn't belong. Finally, he was doing some real spying!

That was when he realised it; that regardless of who had created him or whoever he was supposed to be working for, when it came to sides (as Kyamena had so eloquently put it), he really didn't know which one he was on, otherwise he wouldn't be up here, so excited about spying on his Sallow brothers.

"This way," said Quick, scuttling off down the service shaft.

Kylem had never imagined that such a mass of tunnels and hidden corridors existed on the DaerkStar. It was another world, somewhat cramped, but a veritable warren in which Quick scurried about effortlessly but in which Kylem struggled to keep up.

It transpired that the shafts weren't just for ventilation either. Running along their lengths were conduits for all the ship's systems from the most basic life support (air recycling, electrical and plumbing) to the most complex data cables, power conduits and statronics. Access panels lined the walls and the corridors were dissected into sections with doors at each bulkhead that Quick opened with ease. The tunnels were clean and well lit with automated lighting. The air ducts formed part of the floor of the tunnels, providing ventilation for both the corridors below and the service shafts above. It was incredibly well designed.

Kylem wondered how they were kept so clean and maintained, and then the answer appeared. Quick suddenly thrust his palm out into Kylem's face to stop him. Hastily, he pulled aside a grill in the floor to reveal a deep hexagonal shaped maintenance pit and dropped down into it. He gestured for Kylem to follow. Noiselessly, Quick drew the grill back over their heads and then placed his finger on his lips, once more signalling the need for silence. They waited.

The pit was like a little mini-control room with yet more access panels and readouts decorating the walls. Kylem was just about to access one when something hummed overhead. He looked up and saw a small robotic droid cleaning and surveying the tunnels. Having ensured that it had gone, Kylem asked how often they came along. Quick shrugged but in such a way that indicated it wasn't that he didn't know, but rather that he didn't care. It didn't matter to him.

They continued on their way until Quick stopped again at another grill. He surveyed the room beneath before he pulled open the panel and dropped out onto the floor below. Kylem followed. He was mildly surprised that they'd reached the Bio-Labs so quickly, but it did explain how Quick could run rings around him on the DaerkStar.

* * * * *

Kylem hadn't been to the Bio-Labs before, so he didn't quite know what to expect. The room into which they'd dropped was like a foyer; not that it looked like one but it definitely had the air of being somewhere that was on the way to somewhere else. It was a bland, long and narrow corridor with doors at either end of it. The walls and floors were the usual white, and the ceiling featured the traditional strip of black filigree design along its length, which was odd because the service shaft ran perpendicular to it.

"It's that way," Quick said, pointing at the door.

"Aren't you coming?" asked Kylem.

"No." His voice was resolute and he had already repositioned himself under the vent opening.

"Why not?"

Quick didn't answer immediately. A flash of despair ran across his face.

"You'll understand. I know you will," and with that he leapt up into the air duct, with the agility of a cat and disappeared from view.

Kylem stood beneath the vent for a while, listening to Quick sniffing softly in the service shaft, but decided to let him be. Poor bastard. He'd escaped the Sallows once but now lived a life alone and in fear of being caught. But how? The other prisoners seemingly knew of his existence. It was strange that none of them had betrayed his presence in an attempt to curry favour, but another question begged to be asked even more: how could Quick have known that the Priest wanted to see him if he wouldn't go into the Bio-Labs?

Kylem turned his attention to the door. As he approached, it slid open. Stench gushed from within like a tidal wave and slammed into him. Kylem gasped and took a step back, putting his arm to his mouth and nose to mask his face with his sleeve. It stank of urine, excrement and the unwashed. He swallowed down the urge to retch. Moaning met his ears, but it soon fell silent in anticipation of his arrival. He stepped apprehensively through the door and became aware of eyes watching him.

Inside was a large room, the darkness broken only by the subtle lighting of night-mode. Cells ran down either side of it and at the far end stood another set of doors. Despite Kylem's poor colour perception, his vision was actually very good. He needed very little light to discern the filth and squalor that smacked so offensively into him, both visually and nasally.

Once upon a time, this place would have been like any other on the DeathMaker, with sterile white walls and floors, pristine and gleaming, but it hadn't been like that in a long time. The walls were dim, grey and thick with dirt. The corridor between them was long and wide, and the cells on either side housed groups of between six and twenty people. The floor was littered with filth and debris: rags and detritus that

138

Kylem couldn't begin to identify, and the cells were fitted with traditional bars, as filthy as the walls, smeared with dirt and god knows what else.

The cells nearest him each contained one male and various females, not necessarily of the same species. In the first cell, the group lay huddled together sleeping restlessly. Some of the occupants peered at him with bleary eyes before settling back down to sleep again. Opposite that cell was another similarly populated. The male was large and muscular, but this time he was naked and lying on top of a woman in the act of intercourse. There was no apparent pleasure in it though, because his face was screwed in concentration and she was eating something. She stopped for a moment, to look at Kylem. He looked back at her but nothing was transmitted between them, so she returned to her meal. The man never broke from his chore.

Kylem raised an eyebrow in bewilderment. It was bizarre. He had been given the impression that sex was supposed to be special but this was not special by any means.

He moved on to the next cell where more sleepless bodies lay and then the next. He heard a woman sobbing and his eyes quickly found her.

She was huddled on the floor in the corner of her cell with her legs pulled up tightly to her chest. She was cold, shivering, dirty and bruised and was desperately pulling at what little bits of rags she could find on the floor to try and cover her nudity. In the opposite corner, a group of five other women lay. Whilst they too were dirty and unkempt, they were snuggled together sleeping peacefully under a more abundant pile of rags that might just have been big enough to be classed as blankets. At the bars stood a huge, ugly brute of a man. He was probably the ugliest humanoid Kylem had ever seen. His skin was grey and he had three huge warts on his face sprouting long, wiry whiskers—one on his cheek and two in his right eyebrow—and he had a black-toothed grin that did nothing to enhance his beauty. He was an incredibly large, hairy, fat man with a horribly unkempt beard surrounding his face.

The sobbing woman reached out for another rag that was a tad too near the man and his foot lashed out at her.

"Leave it, bitch!" screamed the man.

She recoiled in terror and yelped. The other women in the cell jumped at the sudden noise, looked up, squinting in the darkness and then settled back down to sleep again. The big man walked over to the sobbing woman, grabbed her by the hair, bent down and began punching her. The women in the far corner, although trying to ignore the events and keeping their eyes shut tight, flinched at each blow.

"Is that really necessary?" asked Kylem.

"Yeah," spat the man and he gave her a final punch before throwing her aside. He returned to the bars and glared dominantly at Kylem. Kylem puzzled.

"So what did she do to deserve that?" he asked.

"Nufink. She just breaves, dat's all. I dun like 'er. Oo are you anyway?"

"Why not?"

"Just dun like 'er. So oo are you?"

"I'm Nobody. What about the others?" asked Kylem indicating the other women. "Don't they like her either?"

"If I don't like 'er, nobody gets to like 'er."

"Seems a bit unjust."

"Nah, it ain't. I'm the law 'ere. S'my cage."

"It's a very small cage."

"Still my cage."

"And you rule."

"Yeah, I rule."

"King of the hill."

"Sumert like that. So, you gonna let us out?"

It was a valid question and momentarily Kylem did consider letting them out (except this guy; he didn't like this guy), but it was not a viable option. Being so vastly outnumbered, they wouldn't stand a chance of getting off the ship. All it would do was get him killed.

"No."

"Why not?"

"Because I don't like you and I don't think much of your kingdom, so I don't think I want you in mine."

"Worried I might rock your world?"

"No. I just don't like you."

"Then you'll like this less," and he stomped over to the poor woman and launched another savage attack upon her, punching and kicking her mercilessly. She screamed in pain and curled up trying to protect herself but he held no mercy, bending down over her to get the blows in.

"Pack it in!" shouted Kylem.

The woman screamed and pleaded but the big man was deaf to her cries.

"I said: pack it in!" screamed Kylem.

The big man stopped and looked up at Kylem, grinning broadly at him. Kylem looked at the poor woman. Her face was bloody and bleeding. She was crying hopelessly, her hand cupped under her chin catching the blood running from her mouth and nose. The women in the corner looked on terrified, shielding their faces from the horror behind their arms and bits of blankets.

"Wha' for?"

"Because she's defenceless."

"So are the people you kill," he spat. Kylem's eyebrows lifted. "Yeah. I know who you are. You're the Betrayer," and he gave her another kick.

"The Betrayer?"

Kylem baulked. Besides his designation, the only Betrayer he had heard of was in Sallow myth, a prophecy from the ancients that spoke of the last prince that would ever be, a Warrior that would betray them all and lead the race into extinction.

"Yeah. You betray us. You look human, but you ain't. You're a Sallow."

Kylem smiled. Yes, he would betray the humanoids. That was what he was designed to do.

"I can't deny it. I am indeed a Sallow, but at this moment in time I feel more human than you look. In fact, if I were human, I'd be ashamed to call you a member of my race."

"You wanna come over here an' say that?"

"If you like."

"You do an' I'll break your fuckin' neck."

What a most obnoxious creature, thought Kylem.

"Unless I break yours first."

The man looked Kylem up and down, and laughed.

"Yeah. Like a scrawny, little kid like you can break my neck. Go on, I dare yer to try."

"As you wish," and Kylem stepped up to the bars. He slipped his hands through them and rested his arms casually on the crossbars. A half-smile broke out on his face and his eyes narrowed with sly pleasure.

"Well?" he asked. "I'm here."

The man looked suspiciously at him. A broad grin erupted somewhere on his face amongst the mass of debris-filled facial hair. Kylem's smile expanded a little as the big man stepped forward. The stench of him invaded Kylem's nose and a shudder of revulsion ran down his spine leaving an echo of disgust in its wake, but he didn't move. Only a slight sneer showed his abhorrence, probably enough for Kyamena to have read but not enough for this stranger to sense.

The big man studied Kylem standing so vulnerably with his arms through the bars. Suddenly he lunged out, hands reaching through the bars and grabbed at Kylem's head. The idea was to drag him to the bars and then twist his head around to snap his neck, but no sooner had he grabbed Kylem's head than he realised it was like pulling on iron. The kid had pulled back and was using just one hand to maintain his distance from the bars. The big man pulled harder but Kylem wouldn't budge.

In return, Kylem's free hand reached out and folded around the back of the man's head, almost caressing it as his fingers ran through his greasy hair. They took a firmer grip, entangling themselves deep in his rattails. The big man winced as Kylem's fingers tightened and he tried to pull back. Kylem's grip fastened harder and harder and the big man's eyes burst open, realising what was happening. The tables were turned.

He released his grip on Kylem's head and grabbed at the bars, pushing against them, but it was no use. Frantically, with one hand, he grabbed at Kylem's fingers embedded in his hair and clawed at them, but nothing gave. He couldn't gain a purchase on the vice like grip of Kylem's hand.

The big man winced in agony as he began to feel chunks of his hair being wrenched free from his scalp. His fingers continued to scratch helplessly at Kylem's hand. Kylem pulled the big man closer.

The big man gave up on Kylem's hand and grabbed at the bars with both hands. He pushed against them with all his might, but in vain. Kylem, despite his shorter and slighter stature, was far stronger than he was and slowly, he was being pulled closer and closer to his adversary.

The big man strained as hard as he could against Kylem, and Kylem studied the anger in his eyes, anger that became diluted with stress and fear; but he kept pulling, his own face contorting a little with the effort. Suddenly the big man changed tactics. He let go of the bars and surged forward, grabbing at Kylem's face.

Kylem effortlessly moved his face off to one side and then jabbed out with the palm of his hand, up into the big man's nose and broke it, pushing the bone into his brain. Death was instantaneous and the big man collapsed.

Kylem stood and looked at the shattered and bloody face of the big man still held against the bars and then let him go and stepped back. The carcass crumpled to the floor. Kylem looked to the women huddled in horrified silence.

"My apologies ladies, but I just can't bear a bully." He turned back to the corpse. "Pick on someone your own size next time. Oh, sorry. Forgot. No next time for you."

As he looked up again, the women were holding out their hands to the beaten female, beckoning and encouraging her to join them. She scurried over and disappeared amongst their embraces.

Kylem smiled and excused himself with a small bow. He turned away, wiping his blood-spattered hand on his trousers disdainfully.

Before, he had been an object of curiosity for the prisoners; now, they gazed on in a mixture of horror and disbelief, scurrying to the backs of their cages as he progressed down the corridor looking for the Priest.

He noted the different species.

In one cage was a male with eight women. He was another big man with a thick cartilaginous growth running down both sides of his head from his forehead to the bottom of his cheeks. It was indicative of his species and framed his face like a pair of hands cupping it. The crest was coloured like a sunset, from bright orange to brilliant yellow at its tips. Unlike the other big man though, his group seemed to be a unit. He was stood behind the women and they had their arms arced protectively around him. It seemed as though he were trying to do a similar thing. He was trying to pull them behind him, to stand in front of them, to protect them, but the women kept pushing him back like mothers defending a child. Kylem assessed that, unlike the other male, this one was liked in his kingdom. He ruled, not through fear but via respect. There was a lesson to be learnt here.

As Kylem progressed down the corridor, the arrangements in the cages changed. The cells held more people, but they were all women in various stages of pregnancy. Then there were women with babies and finally women with small children. The reality began to dawn upon him. This wasn't the Bio-Labs at all; these were the Farm Decks.

He felt uneasy. He'd always assumed the Farm Decks were just a sort of meat processing plant for the carcasses they brought on board from the planetary culls, but no. They were breeding it, here on the DeathMaker—but why? Why did they do that when there were only five blood-Sallows aboard? How much meat did they need?

As he passed by one of the cages, a woman broke free from her huddle and lunged to the front of her prison, screaming at him.

"MURDERER! YOU FILTHY, STINKING SALLOW MURDERER!"

It tipped the balance of calm.

The crowds surged forward like an angry mob, with only the bars of their cages restraining them. They shouted, jeered and taunted him. They began throwing things at him. Others spat.

"HE'S A BLOODY SALLOW!" they screamed.

"YOU MADE US WHAT WE ARE!"

"YOU BASTARD!"

"YOU STINKING SALLOW BASTARD! LOOK WHAT YOU HAVE MADE US!"

From both sides they were now lunging at him, throwing themselves against the bars, screaming, baying and grabbing at him. He dodged the missiles with simple, economic movements but he didn't flinch from their flaying hands. He'd already calculated that the corridor was just wide enough for him to pass between both sets of outstretched arms untouched, but only if he stayed dead centre of them.

To Kylem's dismay, the man with the sun-face was fighting his way even harder through his women to pull them back. He grabbed the one nearest Kylem by the shoulders and pulled her away as forcefully as he could without hurting her. His faced was pained and filled with concern but, having pulled her back, another surged forward into her place. He tried to bar her way with his arm and was, gently but firmly, untangling her fingers from the bars as she screamed at Kylem.

"Shhhh," he whispered to her. "It's not worth it."

"MURDERER!" she screamed, "MURDERER!"

Kylem gently reversed away further down the corridor, all the while ensuring that he didn't veer from the central path.

"YOU GONNA SEE WHAT THEY DO TO US, YOU BASTARD! GO ON! I DARE YOU!" she screamed. "GO THROUGH THE DOOR! IT'S A ONE-WAY TRIP FOR US, YOU STINKING BASTARD!"

Her voice rang high and loud over the other screams and jeers.

Kylem stopped but didn't turn away from her. He knew what she meant. He knew there was a door behind him and he knew it wasn't the one by which he had entered. He knew what lay beyond those doors was far worse than this place filled with all its filth and squalor, where the Sallows bred their fresh meat, and he knew he didn't want to go in there. He remembered Quick's words and realised that he was right. He did understand. Even if Quick came in here, there was nothing he could do. Quick may be free to roam the ship but he couldn't do anything for these people. If he did, it would only publicise his presence and sign his death warrant, just as it would if he released them. *'Without preparation, heroism is only suicide'.*

"GO ON, YOU BASTARD!" they jeered and challenged.

Kylem didn't want to but he knew he had to. Not because Quick told him to, not because they told him to, but because he needed to know. Not to think or to suspect, but to know.

He turned his back on the crowds still jeering and hissing and followed the scuffed trail worn into the debris of the floor, where reluctant prisoners had been dragged to their deaths; and followed them into the abattoir.

* * * * *

The abattoir stank. It was as pungent as the stench of excrement and filth from the farm itself, but on a different level. Somehow, it managed to be more offensive, jarring in the back of Kylem's throat, a metallic smell, bitter and sickly-sweet. He'd smelt it once before and he breathed it in deeply, not for pleasure but to analyse it. Yes, he knew that smell. He'd smelt it on Glyder.

Like the Farm itself, the place was filthy but it was a different kind of filth. Bloody stains of different hues painted every surface with bits of splattered flesh clinging to them, some fresh, some old, caked and stale. Racks of bloody crates stood, the scalps of human heads peeking out over the top of one and from another, Kylem recognised the entrails spilling out over the sides for what they were. His curiosity wanted him to take a closer look, but he refused. His nose told him all he needed to know about them.

In the middle of the room was a long, narrow bench. The silver sheen of the burnished steel no longer shone, so deeply was it tarnished by old blood. Hatchets, axes and knives littered the length of it and a huge circular saw was set into the bench at one end, its large jagged teeth snagged with bits of bone and flesh. The meat was prepared by androids; cleanliness did not appear to be an issue for them.

On the other side of the room were two sets of double doors. They too were constructed of burnished steel like the big chiller cabinets in a cash-and-carry, and were splattered brown and red with rusty blood. They led into the stasis chambers but these chambers were not intended to keep anything alive; rather they served to keep meat fresh and sterile. Kylem's curiosity drove him to open one and walk in.

Both entrances opened into the same large stasis chamber where carcases hung on hooks: bisected human carcases, devoid of organs, cut and hung like butchered pigs. Kylem reached up and touched one to move it aside. His hand came to rest on its single breast. Its nipple was hard and the breast warm and soft, yet dead. Startled by it, he jerked his hand back sharply. He stood gazing at it, paralysed in macabre awe. Then his eyes moved past it, further into the room. The carcases were of different species and sizes, and as he moved amongst them he estimated their age ranges as being between about five and twenty-five years old. But why was there so much of it?

Beyond the hooked carcases, the rear wall was chequered by another series of doors. Each door was about fifty centimetres square and arranged like the cold chambers in a morgue. Kylem pushed his way through the carcases and studied the doors intensely. Nervously, he reached out and opened one. It clicked open easily and there was a gasp of air as the pressure equalised. He paused, then opened the door fully.

Inside lay the lifeless body of a tiny infant, a little baby girl. He cocked his head on one side as Display took readings. She wasn't really breathing, but she wasn't dead. She was in a form of suspended animation, a deep unconsciousness. Kylem took a step back from her slumbering body and opened the door above. Inside lay another infant in a similar state of unnatural dormancy. He opened another and another, and each chamber greeted him with the same sight. They were exactly like the cold chambers of a morgue, just not cold.

His eyes darted from one chamber to the next, rotating between them, and he thought of dawn. Not the dawn of the day but the meat the Sallows called dawn, the meat that was taken from the very young, at the very dawn of their lives. He'd not given it a thought before, but how often had he eaten dawn? He closed his eyes and a long tortured shaft of emotion tore silently through him. He buried his head in his hands. This was horrible.

He heard a sigh, a sharp but tiny intake of breath. He looked up, startled by the noise. The baby in the first chamber was stirring. Having broken the seal on her chamber, revival had begun. Horrified, Kylem quickly slammed the door shut and then frantically began slamming all the other chamber doors shut, praying that no more of the occupants would begin to wake. For a while, he could still hear the murmurs of the little girl, but soon even these waned and died as stasis embraced her once more.

Kylem closed his eyes and swallowed hard. He turned his back on the chambers and sank down onto the floor. He had definitely seen enough.

CHAPTER 17

When he'd left the Farm Decks, Kylem hadn't even bothered looking for Quick. He'd fled out of the abattoir and into the open corridor and marched back to his quarters openly, not caring who saw him, and at least a dozen Warriors had seen him and where he'd come from. Now, back in his quarters, he lay staring up at the ceiling, trying to make sense of it all.

The priest story had obviously been a ruse to get him onto the Farm Decks. Quick had lied to him.

As for the livestock, why did they need so much meat? The planetary culls would provide more than enough meat to feed five blood-Sallows and more then enough dawn meat too. Even if the dawn bred on board was better than that culled on the planets, why were there children of all ages in the cells? It could only mean that there were other delicacies to be had, that required them to be bred on the Farm Decks. What had he been eating all these years; and why, if they bred their meat on board, did they bring in the vast containers full of corpses from the worlds they conquered?

But it wasn't just the five blood-Sallows that needed feeding, was it? There were others: himself and however many goyemes and skunks that were held captive on board the DeathMaker. He didn't know the numbers, but if there were one hundred or so on the Farm Decks, plus say another hundred in the Bio-labs—that would take a lot of feeding. He wondered if they knew they were eating their own kind.

But the numbers still didn't add up. It still seemed excessive.

The door opened and Mela-14 glided into the room with his usual elegance. He studied Kylem lain on the bed in his dishevelled state and joined him, sitting on a neighbouring chair. Kylem neither moved nor spoke. Mela-14 finally broke the silence.

"I hear you were on the Farm Decks last night."

Kylem cast him a sideways glance that ended up as a fixed stare.

"Why?" asked Mela-14.

"Curiosity," he said quietly.

"How did you get there?" he asked.

Kylem scowled. It was a stupid question.

"I walked."

"You were not detected by any of our Warriors in the area."

"That's the idea." There was a note of sarcasm in his voice. "It's what I do. I was curious to see how far I'd get without being detected," he lied.

145

"For what purpose?"

"I told you. It's what I do. I'm the Espion." He tutted impatiently and stood up. "It's what spies do."

"But you should not be spying upon us."

"I wasn't spying on you. I was creeping about. Anyway, who else can I practise on?" and he brushed his hair aside. As his fingers ran through it, his hair felt dirty and matted, and he caught the smell of the big man on his hands. He screwed his nose up in disgust.

"I see."

"And if I can evade the Warriors, it means that I'm getting pretty good at it," said Kylem getting up. He walked into the bathroom and turned the shower on.

"What about the man?" Mela-14 shouted after him.

"What man?"

"The dead one."

"Oh, him!" replied Kylem reappearing in the doorway as he pulled off his tee. "He just pissed me off," and he disappeared back into the bathroom.

After his shower, when he reappeared, he found his breakfast was waiting for him. He walked over and examined the tray: a glass of juice and a plate of steak and eggs, the eggs sunny-side-up and the steak on the bloody side of medium-rare, just how he liked it. He stared at the steak. Its semi-clear juices ran and encompassed the egg white. Somehow, he didn't fancy it this morning. He picked up the glass of fruit juice and drank it down thirstily.

Mela-14 was still sat in the chair by his bed.

"Are you not hungry, child?" he asked, tipping his head to one side. Kylem smiled to himself. Mela-14 was prying, and he was still annoyed that both Kyamena and Quick had manipulated him so easily into going to the Farm Decks. It should be he that was doing the manipulating, not them, so he glared at the plate and said, "It's put me off meat a bit."

From the corner of his eye he saw Mela-14 draw himself forward onto the front of the chair where he rested his elbows on his knees and steepled his fingers under his chin. Kylem smiled smugly to himself and waited for Mela-14 to ask the inevitable question.

"Why would that be?" Mela-14 asked with concern.

Having manipulated the conversation to this point, Kylem had a whole plethora of answers to pick from, each of which would have a different effect. He considered his options. Mela-14 would be appraising him and he wondered just how far he could go.

"I had no idea our food was prepared in such appallingly unhygienic conditions," he said calmly. Another long, thoughtful silence followed. The wait was delicious for Kylem.

"Do you suggest we offer them five-star accommodation and room service?" asked Mela-14.

"Why Father!" Kylem exclaimed with mock surprise. "I didn't know you were capable of sarcasm!"

Mela-14 shuffled uncomfortably in his chair. The effect was pleasing for Kylem and he bathed in the warmth of his discomfort.

"I said prepared, not kept," continued Kylem. "The standard of hygiene is bloody awful down there. I'm surprised we haven't all died from food poisoning!"

"It's not a risk," assured Mela-14. "The stasis chamber ensures that all food is free of harmful microorganisms."

"You really are missing the point here, aren't you? Shit is still shit even if it's sterile shit."

"Blood-things defecate."

"Yes, I know that, but they don't normally like to sleep in it. They don't dismember themselves and splatter bits of their flesh and bone on every available surface and then leave themselves there to rot, do they?" Kylem said angrily. "That's the bloody Warriors! The whole place is filthy. Not being funny Father, but if you breed your meat cleanly, it's clean when you slaughter it and not covered in all sorts of crap. As it is, the livestock is not clean and neither are the conditions in which the meat is prepared. I don't care what you say; the whole place is a veritable breeding ground for bacteria and disease."

"But it is a sterile—"

"Sterile my arse! Shit is still shit and you shouldn't be taking such risks with the health and wellbeing of the blood-Sallows. God knows, there are few of them as it is, and if the Warriors don't bother clearing up the shit and rotting entrails, how can you be sure that sterility is being maintained? What about when it comes out of the stasis chambers? How long is it left lying around before being served up?"

"Cleaning up is not what Warriors do. They aren't designed to do that sort of thing."

"I beg your pardon," said Kylem indignantly, throwing his towel over the back of the chair and crossing his arms in disgust.

"They are Warriors, child. They are not designed to undertake menial chores such as butchery. Such chores are usually left to the slaves to undertake, but they just are not strong enough to maintain order down there. You of all people know how feeble the slaves are," he said, indicating the workbench with a nod of his head.

Kylem glanced over and realised he had a slave's head dismantled on the bench.

"So what you're saying is the slaves aren't strong enough to slaughter so it's left to the Warriors who aren't programmed to clear up the mess?"

"Precisely."

"Then why not get slaves *and* Warriors down there? The Warriors can do the slaughtering and the slaves can clear up the mess."

"Kylem, it is not under my jurisdiction. I have not been there. I have not seen it so I cannot comment."

"And in the meantime the health and wellbeing of the blood-Sallows means diddly-squat?"

"No child!" exclaimed Mela-14, horrified at the suggestion. "Look. If it will make you happy, I shall take a look myself and, if what you say is true, I shall see what I can do."

"That's very big of you."

"You are very aggressive this morning, you know."

"Yeah, well if I'm gonna die I'd rather it was on the battlefield *not* at the fucking dining table."

"Technically, it would not be at the dining table. If would be at least thirty minutes later depending upon the virulence of the particular strain of bacteria in question—and why are you looking at me like that?"

Kylem was shaking his head as Mela-14 spoke.

"Because now I understand what Kyamena was saying about android behaviour."

Kylem didn't volunteer any further information. Mela-14 decided not to pursue the subject.

"Talking of which, do you wish to see Kyamena today?"

Kylem thought for a moment.

"No," he said finally. "She talks too much—as do you at the moment—and she gives me a headache—and I've already got one, thanks to you," he added, mumbling to himself. He was still angry about the Farm Decks but not for the reasons he'd expressed.

"Do you want to interview another humanoid?"

"No. Thank you, but no. I've got plenty to do today that doesn't require any assistance from a humanoid."

"Very well." Mela-14 stood up. "But, at the risk of exacerbating your headache, if you need anything else, I would appreciate it if you could let me know before you go wandering off."

"Are my movements being restricted?" asked Kylem stiffly.

"No child, but it would be easier for me to explain your movements if I knew them in advance." He crossed the room to the exit but turned at the last minute and added, "And it would be appreciated if you did not go around killing things just because the mood takes you. Apparently, it was a good breeding male."

"I'm sure you'll replace it."

"I am sure we shall, but I'd... I would rather not have to keep sorting out your—"

"Mistakes?"

Mela-14 considered for a moment. "...impulses," he finished and left the room.

Kylem smiled to himself. He loved the old bugger really.

* * * * *

Ten minutes later, Kylem was padding back through the corridors, ambling nonchalantly with his hands in his pockets towards Engineering Supplies. He noted that despite it now being day-mode, the corridors were still relatively deserted. Around Engineering, it should have been virtually teeming with rabbles of Warriors going about their duties, but they were relatively free of traffic. It was almost a relief though, as once again he found himself puzzling over the synchronicity of his footsteps. It really did gall him that he marched to their tune and once again, he began experimenting and trying to break the pace.

He'd reached the point where he was trying to take one long pace with his left foot, followed by a short one with his right when he became aware of another set of footsteps behind him, but not a set in tune to his or the Warriors'. His eyes slid along the floor to find a pair of small, black-clad feet there. His gaze worked its way up the figure to find Mada staring at him. He smiled meekly at the Sallow.

"Hello," he said awkwardly.

Mada's eyes scanned him suspiciously, from head to foot and back up again. He didn't like Mada. Mada didn't much like him, and the Sallow made him feel uncomfortable.

"I'm curious," Mada finally said. "Are you limping, dancing, skipping or what?"

"Er... oh, no," he began hesitantly. "I'm trying not to be an android, I suppose, I mean, I am an android, I know that but I don't want to be seen as an android..." His words faded out towards the end of the sentence. He was babbling but Mada's blank expression bade him to explain further.

"The pace... the pace of a Warrior," he said pointing to his feet. "It's unique. All Warriors seem to march to the same pace. I appear to be keeping the same pace. It's not good. It'll be a giveaway... me keeping the same pace as my supposed enemy, especially when in the company of my... actual enemy. Not that I'm in the company of my enemy, but when I am, well, it wouldn't be good."

Mada smacked his hands together with a hollow clap and thrust his chin out.

"Fascinating!" he exclaimed excitedly. "Come with me!"

"But I was—"

"Irrelevant," snapped Mada with a dismissive wave of his hand, and he trotted off in front of Kylem. Kylem followed, wondering if he was ever going to get to Engineering Supplies.

* * * * *

Like any deck on a DaerkStar, the Engineering Deck wasn't actually a deck. It was more of a classification or zone consisting of more than one physical deck and more than one department. In the case of Engineering, there were the Engine Rooms, Supplies & Storage and Research & Design (R & D) amongst other things. Mada led Kylem to R & D.

Equipped with all the latest equipment, R & D comprised of yet more laboratories. Mada took Kylem to one of the larger ones where at least five different projects were already under way.

At one end lay the guts of a new engine being designed for the Targa—the new Trans Warp Drive, Mark-3 engine or TWD3 as it was known. Originally, two of them had been built side by side, but one of the drives had been lost in a preliminary test. The test had proved that the new engine could indeed achieve some very impressive velocities but that it had flaws. Jurrish had reported the drive as being 'a little unstable' and 'in need of a little more work'. That's not quite how Kylem would have described it. He personally considered anything that could catapult a vessel beyond the stars, never to be seen or heard from again, without any indication as to what had happened to it, was probably little more than an over-sized cannon. Kylem would have been looking into ways to protect the data transmitted from the Targa during flight, to obtain a complete analysis of the mission, but it was not his project. Thus, so far, all the Sallows had learnt from the first test was that transmitting data from a vessel travelling at Trans Warp speeds to a stationary target was a bit like spitting in the wind from the bow of a speedboat travelling at full velocity across the waves of a rather choppy ocean. It disintegrated and anything that may have survived was lost amongst the casual white noise of space; but if they solved that problem, they'd be able to learn what truly happened to the vessel and, more importantly, where it was. Was it still sitting around in some far away galaxy waiting to be pirated by some passer-by, or had it, as it had been assumed, simply broken up and disintegrated into micro-atoms?

Next to that project was an equally large area devoted to the development of new Sallow Warriors, in particular the Hunter and the Chaser. As Kylem entered, he could see their disassembled bodies being autopsied. From these remains, the models would be enhanced as per Kylem's suggestions from his debriefing after the maze.

Beyond that were various other areas devoted to smaller projects in which Kylem was not involved, so he knew little of them. He did, however, have his own little workspace here. Designed and set aside for him by his father, it was tailored to meet his blood/android needs and served him well. He loved R & D. It was filled with puzzles, experiments and mind-benders.

Usually there would only be about a dozen or so Scientifics working in the laboratory and Jurrish would occasionally put in an appearance to oversee things, but today R & D was blessed, not only with Jurrish's presence, but at least thirty Scientifics and now Mada. The place was positively buzzing with activity. Scientifics were beavering away at every console, running back and forth, comparing the results of their enquiries on small handheld datapads and engineering scanners. They wafted them around the equipment like journalists around a royal and then huddled together in small groups to compare notes. What did you call a collection of Scientifics, Kylem wondered—a shout, a school, a squabble, a worry? Yes, a worry. Scientifics were a worry at the best of times.

From the monitors that he could see, Kylem gleaned that a heavy programme of diagnostics was underway and that the data was being subjected to various types of extensive analysis. He squinted his eyes to watch as the data scrolled past at speeds that were impossible for the human eye to discern. Even Kylem's digitally enhanced visual cortex had a problem slowing it down sufficiently to comprehend the data. He could only catch snatches of its meaning. He'd need to get much closer to comprehend it or, better still, make physical contact with the console and create a data-link that would connect to his visual cortex to speed up the process.

"Fascinating, isn't it?" Mada whispered into Kylem's ear, startling him a little. He'd been so engrossed in the proceedings that he'd become unaware of Mada's presence.

"Yes, but what's going on?" he asked, but Mada didn't have time to respond. Jurrish had looked up from the worry of Scientifics he was consulting with and spotted them.

"Ah, there you are!" he shouted, and pushed his way out of the crowd. He stopped abruptly when he noticed Kylem.

"Oh," he said. "What have you brought that in here for?" He sounded quite alarmed.

"Another symptom," declared Mada triumphantly.

Kylem wasn't sure he liked being referred to as either 'that' or as a 'symptom' but had no time to protest. He found himself being pushed further into the room by Mada. Mada snapped his fingers and a Scientific fetched the wheeled chair from Kylem's station and pushed into the back of Kylem's legs, knocking him onto it. Kylem glared at the Scientific, which scurried off and merged back into the worry. It wasn't difficult as they all seemed to be gathering around him now, and Kylem found himself surrounded on all sides by the Scientifics. The two-blood Sallows were enclosed in the circle with him, looking at him with great curiosity, oblivious to the crowding of the Scientifics. Kylem's eyes searched for Mela-14 amongst them but he wasn't there.

It was very disconcerting being surrounded by so many faces staring blindly at him. Kylem started to stand up, only to have firm hands placed solidly upon either shoulder that pushed him gently back down into the chair. Kylem felt all the more uncomfortable and Display began a risk assessment.

Jurrish came to stand directly in front of him and thrust his face into Kylem's, staring intensely into his eyes.

"You seem tense," he suddenly declared.

"I am tense," admitted Kylem.

"Why?"

"The situation is intimidating. My threat analysis—"

Instantly—magically—the Scientifics all took several paces backwards, opening up the circle of Sallows. Kylem's eyes moved about them. Even Jurrish and Mada had retreated. His systems were still taking readings, constantly analysing the situation and prioritising the threats, but the results were confusing. Pheromone levels from the blood-Sallows were normal, indicting that nothing was amiss and there was no excitement to be had. He also interrogated Server but Server showed no bad intentions on the part of the Scientifics either. Yet they all were behaving oddly.

"What's going on?" he repeated.

"Do you feel calmer now?" asked Jurrish.

"Calmer? Calmer than when?"

Mada approached, bent down and put a hand on Kylem's shoulder. Kylem shied away from the hand and stared into Mada's eyes.

"You seem confused. Are you fearful of me?" he asked.

"Confused yes, but I am designed without fear so no, I am not fearful of you. Although you did want me dead, remember?"

"That was then."

"Not now?"

"Not now."

"So what's going on then?"

"We're just giving you a little bit of room, that's all."

"Why?"

"If you recall, the last time you were cornered by a group of Scientifics, you ripped the face off one."

Kylem smiled smugly, remembering the event and scratched his temple.

"Yes, I suppose I did, didn't I? I didn't realise I'd made quite such an impression—but that wasn't quite what I meant. I meant, what's going on here? Why is everyone here?"

"Oh, I see." Mada waved his hands, dismissing the Scientifics and they scurried away with what seemed like a mixture of relief and reluctance.

"We have a problem with the R.P.S." he explained to Kylem, but Kylem was none the wiser. "The Resonance Protection System," he further explained.

Kylem didn't have a clue what the Resonance Protection System was so his eyes kept scanning, flicking between Jurrish and Mada, seeking some clue: asking an unspoken question which, it seemed, had to be asked.

"Sorry," he finally said, "but what is that?"

"It's what you were trying to fathom in the corridor. Tell Jurrish what you were doing in the corridor—with your feet?"

Kylem was dubious but decided to oblige the blood-Sallow.

"The Warriors, they all march in sync with each other and so, it seems, do I. I'm not sure it's a good idea for me to—"

"Now that *is* interesting," interrupted Jurrish, his eyes bulging with excitement.

151

"More," added Mada triumphantly. "He was trying to break his pace and he couldn't, could you Kylem?"

"Well, that's not strictly true. I did have some success breaking away from the pace. I'm sorry," said Kylem, suddenly changing the tempo of the conversation, "but what relevance is all this, and to what?"

"The Resonance Protection System!" exclaimed Jurrish. "It's playing up."

Kylem again looked from one Sallow to the other, waiting for more detail to follow, but none came.

"Still don't know what a Resonance Protection System is," he finally prompted.

"Oh yes," said Jurrish. He retreated and began waving his hands about in front of him with his forefingers pointing skyward as he explained. "Well, what happens if you march a full legion of Warriors over a bridge?"

"It starts to resonate."

"Precisely," he said. "And what do we do to prevent it?"

"We break step."

"Precisely, and that's what the Resonance Protection System does!"

"It makes the Warriors break step?" Kylem didn't look convinced.

"Exactly!" exclaimed Jurrish. "On board a DaerkStar, it would be unwise to have all our androids marching at the same pace, so the Resonance Protection System ensures that they don't. Otherwise we'd have microscopic fissures and hairline cracks appearing all over the place—in the bulkheads and goodness only knows where else."

"The structural integrity of the ship could be severely compromised," finished Mada.

"I see," said Kylem. "It's not doing a very good job then, is it?"

The faces on the two Sallows fell in unison.

"No," they agreed.

"That's the problem," said Jurrish.

"We have a fault," said Mada.

"It's not working properly."

"And we don't seem to be able to isolate the problem."

"And you think I can help?" asked Kylem. They nodded. "How?"

"That's a good question, Mada," said Jurrish, turning to his colleague. "How can he help? I appreciate that as an android he can feel the affects of the Resonance Protection System, and as a blood-thing he has the individuality to recognise it, but other than the possibility that he might be able to tell us when the signal changes, what else can he do?"

"Oh Jurrish, you're forgetting. He is equipped with the most sophisticated translation matrices we've ever developed."

"Oh good grief, yes!" exclaimed Jurrish. "He can help us with the code!"

The two Sallows swept forward and taking an arm each, pulled Kylem off the chair and dragged him over to a console. A Scientific leapt in behind them, grabbed the wheeled chair and pushed it over to the console. For a second time, the chair was jammed into his calves and Kylem forced to sit down. The two blood-Sallows stood on either side of him, crowding him in and directing his gaze to the console.

To his surprise, Kylem found himself staring at the DaerkStar's base code (instantly recognisable by the old, familiar format that he had once used) and her data. It was more startling though, because this was code from the very core of

Server, and the data was very sensitive data at the heart of the ship's functionality—data that controlled the most basic functions of the DeathMaker—and he was being given access to it. For a moment, he thought it must be a mistake and half expected the blood-Sallows to wipe the data from the monitor, but no. He cast a glance at the Sallows to ensure that he was interpreting the situation correctly. The two of them stood patiently waiting so he placed his left hand, palm side down on the keyboard and closed his eyes. The link was made and access was granted.

He placed his other hand on the touch-sensitive screen and began scrolling through the endless pages of code, reading and digesting its contents. He was being especially cautious not to transmit anything because he used a different code now, a fact to which the Sallows were oblivious and a fact to which he would rather they remained oblivious.

Jurrish and Mada remained huddled around him as he examined the data. Scientifics brought them chairs too and now all three were hunched over the console as Kylem became engrossed in the data. He'd never been allowed so close to core systems before and was still a little bemused as to why they wanted him here now. Mada had mentioned that his translation matrix might be useful, which tended to suggest some foreign or unusual coding was to be found amongst the usual stuff, but it was all the same old code as before. There was nothing new, nothing that would call upon his translation matrices at all...

His brain jarred to a halt and his fingers braked on the scrolling facility of the screen. He began backtracking to the previous pages. He hadn't realised how fast he'd been going until he had to go back, and it took him a good half a minute before he saw it again—an anomaly.

"You see it too, don't you!" cried Jurrish, his voice pitched high with excitement. He weaved his fingers together and rested his chin on them. "It's odd isn't it? Can you work out what it is? Is it a virus or a corruption or sabotage? Can you tell?"

Kylem's eyes narrowed as he studied it. In the middle of the code was a different type of code. It was similar and yet subtly different. Kylem began scrolling again but more slowly this time. There was more of it, much more of it—a lot more of it!

"Have you isolated this system?" he asked.

"Yes, we think so, but whenever we try to purge it the anomaly seems to disappear, but then it reappears again somewhere else. Any ideas?"

"Still processing," he said, staring intently at the data. He began chewing on his lip as he concentrated.

"When you say it reappears somewhere else, do you mean more coding appears that is of the same ilk or is it exactly the same coding?"

"We're not sure. It's not around long enough for us to analyse. We think it's the same coding plus a bit more of it."

"Is it replicating or evolving?"

"We don't know. We think it's just replicating but, again, we can't isolate it long enough to be sure. That's why we thought it might be a virus—"

"Yes, I see," interrupted Kylem and he pointed at the screen. "You've purged it in section 453-B78-GH6 and it's relocated itself in 735-H43-76H, but it's bigger."

"What does that mean to you?" asked Jurrish who was now looking into Kylem's ear as though trying to see inside his head. Kylem brushed him away as he would an irritating fly.

"It seems to detect that the purge is coming and relocate itself milliseconds before the purge takes place, and then... expand? evolve? I don't know. I don't think it's simple replication—"

"Mutation?"

"Maybe. What's happened at the purge site?" he asked himself out loud and leant over to the console on his right. Mada hastily wheeled himself backwards out of the way and Kylem filled the vacant spot so that he now had two stations at his command. He quickly connected with the second console and then stood up to connect with the two above as well. His hands moved swiftly over the controls, both the standard keypads and the touch-screen monitors. His eyes darted and flashed from one to the other and back again, his face stern and severe. Mada and Jurrish could now only sit back and watch. He was working far too quickly for either one of them to comprehend. Mada signalled a Scientific to approach and it did. He relieved it of an engineering scanner and pointed it at Kylem and the consoles in an effort to record what Kylem was doing and what he was accessing.

"Hmmm," said Kylem finally, his hands and eyes continuing to orchestrate the symphony of data.

"So what is it?" asked Jurrish concerned.

"DeathWatch," he murmured and immediately regretted it.

"DeathWatch?" repeated Mada and Jurrish.

"Yes."

Strangely, he knew what DeathWatch was as soon as he said it, even though he'd never heard of it before. As his thoughts came to him, he knew he was hearing the facts for the first time. It was as though some part of him was communicating this information to him, but which part? His hands flashed over the computer equipment as he continued to search for clues or hidden links. There! It was similar to his K-Code—very similar. Then he found a section of code that wasn't just slightly familiar but identical to a section of his own code. That confirmed it. DeathWatch was not just in Server, it was in him too. But what was it?

Mada and Jurrish were still hanging onto his every word, but what could he tell them? What was it doing? What was it for? It certainly wasn't intended to sabotage the R.P.S.—it was too minor a system—but it would be a good place to hide something whilst in its developmental stages. He pressed a few more keys and scrolled through more data.

In its current state, the program appeared to be fairly inoffensive. On the face of it, it was more of an annoyance than anything else, but it was growing. It was analysing Server's responses to its presence and the blood-Sallows' attempts to remove it, and it was becoming more and more evasive. Yet he could locate it and with relative ease. He could almost feel where it would go next. Why was that? Was it because it was so closely related to him? It may even be that he had written it. He'd written the K-Code, why not DeathWatch? He smiled in admiration because, whatever it was, it was a very ingenious bit of programming.

"What's DeathWatch?" prompted Jurrish again.

Kylem broke from his reverie. He leant back in his chair, crossed his arms and considered for a moment. His brow furrowed with thought. What could he tell them? He couldn't tell them the truth.

"It's part of an old data protection system," he blagged. "Part of the original program, I think, designed to protect the R.P.S. against sabotage. It's fragmented itself to make it less easy to isolate and delete. As to its relocation, I'll need to look at that a bit longer but again, I think it's an integral part of the protection."

"But if it's always been there, why is it only now a problem?"

Kylem puffed out a blast of air.

"Here we have a blend of some very ancient systems merged with some very new technology. Words that once had one meaning can, thousands of years later, have a completely different meaning, or have different meanings in different contexts. Cock-eyed for instance means skewed or crooked. Crooked can mean skewed or dishonest, but cock-eyed doesn't mean dishonest. The program doesn't understand the true meaning now that the context has changed."

"Can we fix it?"

"Everything is fixable, but is it worth it?"

The two Sallows looked at him aghast.

"I mean," began Kylem, "the protection system is a spur from the main protection program. That spur is protecting itself against change, but we would need to disable the entire protection system before we can start work. How long will it take to fix? How long will the protection be down? And we haven't even begun to fix the R.P.S. itself. Do you get my drift?"

"We have to fix it, Kylem."

"But do we?" he asked.

The blood-Sallows stared at him in horror. Kylem recomposed himself on his chair, preparing for his big speech.

"You state that the purpose of this program is to ensure that thousands of Sallow Warriors don't go marching in unison about the DeathMaker. Does it have any other purpose?"

"No."

"So, correct me if I'm wrong, whilst it is defective, if we leave it on, it is making the Warriors march in unison?"

"Yes," confirmed the blood-Sallows.

"With it off, there would be nothing to *make* them march in unison... but nothing to stop them either. So how many do you reckon that would be?"

The Sallows looked at each other.

"I don't know," Jurrish admitted.

"I'd suggest only those told to do so," proposed Kylem.

The Sallows scowled at each other.

"How can you say that?"

"When they are off ship, do they march in sync to each other regardless of distance?"

"Well no. Only in their... what do you call them... rabbles?"

Kylem smiled at the adoption of his collective noun.

"Exactly. This is an old system designed for a generation of Warriors now obsolete. It should be consigned to the same scrapheap as the Warriors for which it was originally designed."

"Are you suggesting we just... turn it off?" asked Jurrish.

"Yes."

The blood-Sallows stepped away and an intensive debate began between them. They called over various Scientifics and the debate raged on. Thirty minutes later, Kylem was gently swivelling around on the chair in a bored and idle manner, his head lolling over the back as he stared at the ceiling and pondered the ventilation shafts above. Finally, Jurrish and Mada broke away from the worry of Scientifics.

"Are you sure you can isolate and disable it?" Jurrish asked.

"Yes. If that's what you want me to do?"

"Will it be difficult?"

"No."

"How long will it take?"

Kylem turned back to the workstation and with a single finger, stabbed purposefully at one key. "I thought you'd never ask," he sighed.

"Is that it?" boomed Mada.

"'Fraid so," said Kylem. "Well, if that's all, gentlemen," he stood up, bowing neatly and made to leave the room.

"Hang on a minute!" shouted Jurrish.

Kylem turned back, desperately trying to hide his impatience. Jurrish and Mada huddled together whispering. Kylem could have heard what they were saying, if could be bothered to try, but he couldn't. He just wanted to get out of there and get the bits to build his speakers.

"We're agreed," declared Mada. "This is far too much fun. We think you should stay here and help us further."

"Well yes, I'd love to but I was on the way to get some bits from Engineering Supplies for a project I'm working on."

"Not a problem," declared Jurrish waving his arms in the air. "Sinta-14 will get you what you need. It'll even build it for you, if you want."

CHAPTER 18

Kylem sat in his quarters listening to the particularly beautiful symphony emanating from his newly constructed speaker system. He was contemplating what a particularly good day he'd had. Without the company of Emoth to influence them, Mada and Jurrish were actually quite likable characters—odd, but likeable.

He had underestimated their intelligence considerably, but found it counterbalanced by both extreme eccentricity and blinding stupidity.

Their eccentricity was not completely new to him but in Engineering, where they were most at home and without the watchful eye of Emoth, it blossomed. As they spoke, their words adequately portrayed their meaning but their hands moved and waved about dramatising their emotions. They were deeply passionate about their work and spoke openly and willingly about Sallow engineering, robotics, android technology, transportation, weapons and computer systems—both the history and current day standards—the whole kit and caboodle.

As to their extreme stupidity, he deduced that this came from their being descended from generations of blood-Sallows raised in the isolation of Taxana because if the Sallows on-board had ever benefited from contact with the original makers and designers of the DearkStars, their knowledge and experience would have been passed down to them from generation to generation. As it was, this was not the case. Priorities in Taxana had been different. Knowledge, experience and training had been irretrievably lost. All they had was what they had gleaned about the technology from the databanks they had inherited. Sure, they reckoned they knew all about it but they obviously didn't. So it was that this generation of Sallows were not only blighted physically, not only had they forgotten how to be Warriors, but they had also forgotten how these magnificent ships were ever built and they flailed around in a disorderly fashion in their developments. Take the TWD3. Their attention was wholly absorbed and distracted by the quest for the finished product, but there were so many other details that needed attention before they had any hope of perfecting the drive.

There were other things too—the night-mode that left the DaerkStar so vulnerable for seven hours every day, the lack of internal sensors to tell them of escapees that allowed Quick to wander about the DaerkStar undetected, and the obsolete R.P.S. that was causing more problems than it solved. They couldn't even organise the employment of slaves on the Farm Decks to clean up the mess made by the Warriors. These were all glaringly obvious errors to Kylem, but not to the blood-Sallows, it seemed. They really could not see beyond their noses.

But none of this had spoilt his day.

At lunchtime, four slaves had materialised carrying with them a collapsible picnic table, three picnic chairs and a large hamper. Kylem had watched them, somewhat mystified, as they'd methodically set up the table in the middle of the laboratory and proceeded to lay it out with a red and white chequered tablecloth. Delving into the hamper, they had produced some very plain, functional china and glasses, a wide selection of food choices and what had turned out to be a rather decent bottle of wine. As they had partaken of lunch, Kylem had been pleased not to be hassled over what he did or didn't eat and had shared a glass of the wine with them, cautiously aware of its alcoholic content.

It had been a wonderful and unmissable opportunity to study the DaerkStar, learn about Sallow systems and programs, delve into the current engineering projects and to share the company of his own kind. To top it all, when he'd got back to his quarters, his electro-acoustic transducers had been waiting for him, built to his exacting specifications and absolutely perfect.

In other words, all was well with the world and, for once, he was happy.

It had been a long day but a particularly rewarding one and on that note, Kylem decided that he fancied a shower and an early night. He turned the music up a tad and went into the bathroom.

* * * * *

Kylem had a particularly long and leisurely shower. He let the water (possibly hot enough to boil a lobster) pulse against his back, neck and shoulder blades for the best part of three-quarters of an hour before finally emerging.

When he stepped out of the shower though, he was surprised to find that there weren't any towels. That was odd. Towels were always there! Even if he'd used them, thrown them on the floor or hidden them in the bottom of his wardrobe. When he returned to his quarters later, fresh towels would be waiting for him. So the fact that towels weren't there wasn't just unusual but unheard of. Was this another fault in DeathMaker's systems? Another fault he had helped to generate?

His eyes scanned the bathroom in disbelief, but suddenly caught sight of one solitary towel: the tiny hand towel hanging on the far side of the sink unit. It was probably that damned Quick playing pranks again. He still had a bone to pick with that boy as it was.

He grabbed the towel and scrubbed at his hair before wrapping the miniscule piece of fabric about himself. It was only just long enough for him to secure about his waist, and then he padded back into the bedroom.

Wet and virtually naked, he stepped out of the bathroom and was stunned to find that he was not alone. It wasn't Quick that was waiting for him though. It was Emoth with a rabble of three Warriors.

Emoth was splayed leisurely, full-length on his bed. He lay on his belly, with his head resting in the palms of his hands and his feet kicking playfully in the air. He was dressed in a voluptuous, black voile robe richly embroidered in black thread with ebony beads and sequins. The folds of its semi-translucent fabric hung over the sides of the bed. It was a very flimsy affair that his ugliness sullied shamefully because, on the right woman, it would have been absolutely beautiful. On him though, his warty, rhino-skinned body, with its copious folds of skin and blubber, whispered all too loudly through the sheer fabric.

Revulsion shuddered through Kylem, mixed with a deep sense of foreboding. His nudity made him feel vulnerable, and his vulnerability angered him. All of his sensors kicked in, not that he needed them to tell him what was going on here, but they began their assessment anyway.

Emoth's pheromones were through the roof, the smell of them only partially covered by the scent of the sweet, sickly oil that blood-Sallows anointed themselves with and that Emoth had apparently bathed in. The Warriors were strategically placed: one by the exit door and two in front of his wardrobe blocking his access to clean clothes. Kylem stepped forward in search of the pile he'd abandoned before his shower. As he did so, one of the Warriors slipped in behind him, cutting off his other valid exit point, the bathroom. As for the pile of clothes, like the towels, they too had disappeared. Anger was rumbling deeply beneath his calm exterior. He thrust his chin out, folded his arms across his chest and stood with his legs akimbo.

"Can I help you?" he demanded. His voice was cool and steady.

"Maybe," Emoth said. "Come. Sit by me," and he patted the bed beside him.

Not bloody likely, thought Kylem.

"I think you've made a mistake," he said.

"Oh, I don't think so," Emoth leered.

"Okay," said Kylem. "Let me rephrase that. You *have* made a mistake." He was trying to sound firm but not too aggressive.

Emoth swung his legs somewhat gracelessly over the bed and stood up. He virtually skipped over to Kylem to stand before him. He was a stubby, squat, repulsive looking creature that stood a good head shorter than Kylem. Kylem fought back his desire to step back. He was determined to stand his ground.

"I think," crooned Emoth, running his fat, callousy forefinger down Kylem's breast until it rested upon his nipple, "that it is you who is making the mistake," and he looked up into Kylem's cold, dark eyes, blind to the change in them as the colour swirled from his usual bright emerald green to deep crimson red.

Kylem's eyes narrowed as he looked down at Emoth and for the briefest instant, he sneered openly. Emoth tried to read his expression, not that he cared what Kylem thought or felt—well, he did care, but not in a good way.

"Life," Emoth began again, "can be very difficult, you know. Or it can be very easy."

His thumb and forefinger were now playing with Kylem's nipple. Kylem's face creased in disgust and Emoth's began to fill with glee. It was a very subtle form of torture and one that Emoth found most satisfactory. The thought of indulging in sexual activity with this pallid, half-bred child with its strangely alluring ugliness was exciting in itself, but to do it with his reluctance—to dominate him so completely, to know that he knows he has no choice—that was positively exhilarating and the hairs began to prickle on the back of his thick, black neck.

And Kylem could read all this. He could smell Emoth's musk, feel the slight quiver in Emoth's hands, see the look in his eyes, observe his dilating pupils and the micro-expressions that ran across his face, and Kylem could stand no more. This was to stop, but he also had to be careful because, if one thing were true, it was that Emoth could make life very difficult for him—or, for that matter, death. Gently, he reached up, took Emoth's hand and pushed it away.

"No," said Kylem firmly.

It was just one single word, but it was the most powerful word in the universe. It held no room for misinterpretation and was unarguable.

Emoth's brow furrowed in annoyance and he stepped up closer still to Kylem.

Despite his wish to hold his ground, Kylem found himself stepping back. He felt his back smack into the Warrior behind him and its cool metal against his damp skin. Emoth moved even closer so that Kylem was sandwiched between them. He was now so close that Kylem could feel the warmth of Emoth's skin brushing against him, separated only by the flimsy voile. Kylem was repulsed. Then he felt Emoth's hand touch lightly on the back of his thigh. Every fibre of his being tensed in horror as Emoth slid his hand up and under the towel until it came to rest on his buttock.

"No is not in my vocabulary," Emoth whispered seductively.

"Then I suggest you add it," Kylem barked softly.

But Emoth did not desist. Instead, he leant forward and kissed Kylem softly on the chest. Kylem physically shivered and closed his eyes desperately trying to contain his temper and concentrate his thoughts on what he should do next. It was a mistake. He felt Emoth's breath hot upon his cheek, and then the gentle kiss laid upon his lips. Kylem's eyes snapped open in alarm and he glared down into Emoth's face. Emoth merely smiled triumphantly back at him, and then he leant into Kylem's neck and drew a deep breath to draw his scent in.

"I can smell your fear," he whispered.

"I am designed without fear. I fear nothing—and I don't fear you," he replied with controlled anger.

"I smell your fear."

"You smell my anger," spat Kylem, now considering how he could beat his glorious leader to a pulp and get away with it. Could he disable and dispose of all three Warriors, or perhaps reprogram them?

"I like it," Emoth spoke slowly and sighed. Then he took Kylem's nipple in his mouth and began mouthing it.

"Oh, for shit's sake," Kylem heard himself say, and then what happened next just sort of happened.

His hands had already balled into fists whilst trying to contain his revulsion so it took nothing for one to be punched firmly into Emoth's belly, up and under his rib cage. Emoth's face filled with pain and he gasped air. Well and truly winded, he crumpled under the blow and collapsed to the floor. As he did so, Kylem's knee rose up and smacked him under the chin, sending his body sprawling backwards and across the floor. Instantly, the Warrior behind leapt into action. It lunged forward, grabbed Kylem by the hair and yanked him back so forcefully that his feet left the ground and he was thrown against the wall behind. It then moved in and issued one solitary hard smack to the side of his face. His head ricocheted against the wall from the impact of the steel punch, but he noted that the punch was open fisted not closed, and thus that the intention was to disable and not kill him. Nevertheless, he crumpled to the floor.

Kylem tried to get to his feet, pushing himself up onto all fours but it was another mistake. It exposed his soft underbelly to attack and the Warrior's foot lashed out, kicking him hard in the stomach. It flipped him, naked, onto his back. His spine smacked hard against the floor.

Winded, dazed and confused, Kylem instinctively rolled onto one side and drew himself up into a foetal position. As he rolled, he saw Emoth trying to rise to his feet, perched on one knee, holding his stomach and taking in deep, rasping breaths. Fury burned in his eyes and Kylem knew that things were only going to go one of two ways now. It was submission or death; but for Kylem submission was still not an option—not if he had anything to do with it.

Clumsily, he rolled away from his adversaries, seeking some space to regroup. He found himself on the opposite side of the bed to Emoth, but cornered. As he struggled to his feet, his systems were calculating the necessary manoeuvres to pick off and disable the Warriors. Meanwhile, Emoth had clambered to his feet and struggled around the bed to face Kylem. Still doubled in pain he hissed, "I will have you!"

One of the Warriors moved forward and grabbed Kylem's arm. Kylem struggled but he was no match against a powerful Warrior. It pulled Kylem forward, grabbed his hair again and forced his head back. A second Warrior grabbed his other arm and between them, they twisted him down onto his knees over the bed, pushing his face into the bedclothes. With his naked butt exposed, he heard the rustle of Emoth's garments.

"I'm going to fuck you so hard, you'll cry like a baby!" he hissed, ripping open his robe and stepping up behind Kylem. He dropped onto his knees between Kylem's legs. Kylem struggled and snarled, his fangs and claws fully extended, but the grip of the Warriors was unbreakable, and Emoth only laughed wickedly.

Then he heard a shushing sound. His eyes flicked across the room and in the reflective surface of the wardrobe doors, he saw that the door had opened. The Warrior stepped aside and Mada stepped in. Kylem strained his head around to see Mada and their eyes locked upon each other.

Emoth was oblivious to his companion's entry. He raised his chin haughtily and giggled heartily, but Kylem wasn't listening. He was watching Mada.

Mada had focused on Emoth. He crossed the room in a few easy strides and stopped just behind him. From under his robes, he drew a long obsidian-bladed knife. The blade was slightly curved, narrow and mortally sharp. The lights in the room flashed upon its silky smoothness as Mada handled it. He bent down and put an arm around Emoth as if to aid him to his feet, or so it seemed; but then his hand lifted Emoth's chin and the other drew the blade effortlessly across his throat.

The Warriors instantly let go of Kylem and stepped back. Kylem twisted around just in time to see Emoth's thick, black skin parted, exposing the blood-red tissue. Arterial spray flicked across the room in a wide arc. Horror flooded Emoth's eyes as his blood sprayed out, and his hands rose to his throat to be instantly soaked in it. He fell backwards onto the floor gurgling, his blood-soaked hands clutching at his throat for a few moments; and then they fell limply, twitching to his sides.

Mada stepped casually over Emoth and came to sit on the bed beside Kylem, the knife still cradled in his hands. He tilted his head curiously to one side and spoke.

"I hope you are watching, Kylem," he said. "It's not everyday you get to see a Sallow die."

Kylem did watch as the last embers of Emoth's life were extinguished. Emoth's body now lay completely lifeless in a pool of thick, deep red blood. Around him, rainbows of red had painted the room, splattering its walls, furniture and occupants.

Mada took in a sharp intake of breath.

"So what do you think?" he asked sadly.

Kylem watched as the blood soaked deeper into the thick, pale coloured carpet.

"I don't think you'll ever get that out," he said.

"Oh, you'll be surprised," replied Mada.

A few moments passed with the two of them staring at Emoth's body for no apparent reason. Then Mada turned to Kylem and scowled in disgust at his nudity.

"Get yourself cleaned up and covered up, there's a good boy."

A golden hand gently folded around Kylem's upper arm. Kylem started at it, but he had no need for concern. It was there merely to guide him towards the bathroom. The second Warrior proffered a pile of towels and Kylem took them gratefully. He glanced back towards Mada still sat on the bed studying Emoth's corpse. There seemed to be a deep sadness in him at the loss of his companion and yet, he had killed him so easily.

"He was my brother, you know," he said as if sensing Kylem's gaze.

"Then why kill him?"

Mada looked up at Kylem.

"Call it a mercy killing, if you will. After this, he'd be stripped of his rank and humiliated. He wouldn't be able to live with that. Now..." he paused and sighed sadly, "...he doesn't have to."

He shrugged and got up. He wiped the blood from the blade of his knife on the bedclothes and looked at Kylem. For a moment, they stood and looked at each other. There was nothing more to be said. Kylem turned and went back into the bathroom for another shower.

* * * * *

When Kylem emerged from the bathroom for the second time that evening, he was stunned to find his room in perfect order. All traces of the slaughter had been removed. The walls and carpet were clean, and his bed lay freshly made with crisp, new, white bed linen. All evidence of the earlier events had been completely eradicated. The speed and orderliness in which the transformation had taken place was impressive, but as Kylem dressed, he couldn't help but keep glancing back to the floor that, less than an hour ago, had been a bloody reservoir soaking into the floor covering. It wasn't that it disturbed him, it just fascinated him that such a huge mess could vanish so quickly and without a trace.

A gentle chiming noise caught his attention. What was that? He'd not heard a noise like that before. It was shortly followed by a soft tapping at the door. Who would be tapping at his door? Sallows entered without announcement or introduction. Was it Quick? No, Quick would enter, equally uninvited, via the vents.

Suspicious, he approached the door. It chimed again. By the door post was a panel that had not been there earlier. He touched it and the door slid open to reveal Mela-14.

"I see you've found the door control then. May I come in?"

Kylem stepped to one side, somewhat bemused, and his father swept past him.

"How are you, child?" he asked, picking up the used towels from the floor. He folded them neatly and began picking bits of fluff off them. How peculiar, thought Kylem. The android's body language showed discomfort. That would be just the sort of thing that Kyamena would be telling him off for doing.

"Confused," confessed Kylem.

Mela-14 let out a little buzzy-huffy sort of sound.

162

"I hear you had a good day in Engineering," he commented, changing the subject.

"Well, it started out okay, but then it took a bit of a nosedive later on. You?" Kylem asked, a note of sarcasm in his voice.

If Mela-14 could have scowled, he would have done.

"Housework," he said.

"Housework?"

"Yes. The Farm Decks," he sighed and sat himself down on the bed in the very same spot that Mada had taken whilst watching his brother die. He sat looking at his knees, with his hands neatly folded in his lap. Kylem caught hold of one of the chairs by the workbench and swung it over to sit directly opposite his father. He leant forward, resting his elbows on his knees so that they were at eye-level. A raised eyebrow prompted Mela-14 to explain further.

"I went down to the Farm Decks as you suggested, but I had to pick my time. You see," and he shuffled uncomfortably on his buttocks, "technically they are—or rather were—under the jurisdiction of the Karam series of Scientifics so I had no reason to be down there." His words trailed off.

"And?" prompted Kylem.

"You were right. The conditions were appalling. Then, having made the discovery, I had to report it. So I did."

Mela-14 fell silent again.

"And?"

"You're not very popular with the Scientifics."

"Why?"

"Well, to say that Doobee went ballistic would be a bit of an understatement. He had every Karam rounded up like a bunch of common criminals, frog-marched to the hanger decks, lined up and shot. He then jettisoned their remains out of the hanger bay doors."

"Blimey! That's a bit extreme isn't it?"

"As you pointed out, it is their food supply. It turned out to be rather a sensitive subject."

"Yes, but still—"

"It's done, child. We cannot change it."

"No, we can't. So why am I so unpopular?"

"Kylem, a whole series of Scientifics was executed today. You were the author of their destruction. How many more will you be responsible for the death of? If it wasn't for the good you did in Engineering, the Scientifics would be—" but he didn't finish his sentence.

"What? Out for revenge? That's a little emotional for an android, isn't it?"

Mela-14 did not respond.

"Well," said Kylem, patting his father's knee patronizingly and winking at him. "Don't you worry about them. I can handle a few Scientifics."

Mela-14 looked dubious.

"Anyway," Mela-14 continued. "It then fell to me to sort out the mess. I've spent the entire day down there with slave cleaning crews and a legion of Warriors getting it all sanitised. It took a bit of orchestrating I can tell you, moving all those goyemes from one pen to another. They can be pretty aggressive too. One big breeder pulled a slave through the bars and they smashed it to bits within a matter of seconds!" he exclaimed.

"I suppose you're down another breeder then?" puffed Kylem cynically.

"No, I let it live. It was only a slave and I only lost the one."

"And what about Emoth?" asked Kylem.

"I wouldn't mention his name in future if I were you. The blood-Sallows don't like to have their noses rubbed into their shortcomings."

"Not my fault though."

"Nobody said it was."

"So what happens now?"

"Nothing," Mela-14 shrugged. "Emoth is gone. Mada has assumed control. We carry on as normal. Well, almost normal."

"Almost?"

"Yes," he said, pointing at the door. "You now have the door alarm you so pined for. Nobody gets in without your consent now. Well, theoretically."

"Is uhm..." Kylem hesitated. "Does that mean that this sort of thing is likely to be a problem again? I mean—"

"No," answered Mela-14 confidently. "You're not their type."

"And you know this, how?"

"Our blood-Sallows are predominantly male. They relieve their sexual tensions with specimens from the Bio-Labs and I have noted that the others always chose females. Mada has a nice little skunk called Fatia for his favour and Jurrish has a couple too—although which two varies. Doobee rarely indulges, but when he does it's a bit of an all out orgy of females and Rathan? Well, he prefers humanoid favours strangely enough—golden haired ones usually—although we don't talk about that."

"Oh, right," said Kylem, nodding his head thoughtfully.

"You know, you could always go down there and select a favour of your own," suggested Mela-14. Kylem looked at his father and raised an eyebrow.

"Thanks, but I've had more than enough sexual excitement for one day."

"Yes, I suppose you have. Well, night-mode will be kicking in soon."

Kylem smiled to himself. It was odd hearing his father use slang.

"Will you be out and about tonight, or do you intend getting some sleep?" he asked.

"Sleep. Definitely sleep tonight. Thank you."

"Then I shall bid you goodnight," he said and got up.

"Father?"

"Yes?"

"How did Mada know that Emoth was here?"

"We may have our disagreements, Kylem, but you are still my child. I took on board your comments and concerns, and arranged for Server to alert me if Emoth behaved... irrationally. I then merely informed Mada of his intended visit, and Mada knows his brother."

"Oh, I see. Thank you."

"You're welcome. Oh! I nearly forgot. You have been invited to join the blood-Sallows for breakfast tomorrow morning."

"Is that a good thing?" asked Kylem dubiously.

"I think so," replied his father and left.

As the door slid shut behind him, Kylem stared at it for a few moments and then he went to bed. He was tired. It had been a particularly long day.

CHAPTER 19

Kylem slept well, right up to the point when he found himself being rudely shaken awake.

"Oh, for crying out loud," he mumbled groggily. "Is there no peace?"

"No. It's urgent! Wake up!" hissed the voice.

Kylem opened his eyes and then screwed them up to peer into the face of his visitor.

"Kyamena! What in god's name are you doing here? How did you get in here?"

"Quick brought me."

"Quick!" he exclaimed. Kyamena slapped her hand over his mouth to shush him. He pulled her hand away and hissed, "I've got a bone to pick with that little runt."

"Yes, I know and you can have him when I've finished with him, but not before," and she glared over her shoulder at Quick who was stood in the background looking somewhat shamefaced.

"Well?" she tutted at Quick. "What have you got to say to Kylem?"

"Sorry," he mumbled.

"You'll be more than bloody sorry when I've finished with you!" retorted Kylem.

"Yeah, well. Get in the queue. Now hurry. There's not much time," and she thrust a pile of clothes into his arms. "Get dressed."

"Get dressed? For what? No time for what?"

"The Priest—he hasn't got much longer."

Kylem sighed deeply and shook his head wearily, rolling his eyes.

"I really hope you don't think I'm going to fall for that one again!" and he threw himself back onto his pillow and closed his eyes.

"It isn't a game and it's not a trick!" She turned to Quick. "See what you've done! The damage you've caused!"

"That's it. I'm going back to sleep. See yourselves out, won't you?" and Kylem flipped himself onto his side and nestled his head deeper into the pillow.

"No, you're not!" she hissed and yanked the pillow out from under his head. Kylem ignored her so she yanked the covers off him too. They billowed wildly in the air before settling on the floor.

"I'm not listening," he sang, desperately trying to ignore her as he lay naked on the bed with his back to her.

"Yes, you bloody are!" and she spat on her hand and slapped his arse as hard as she could. The sound of the smack rang out sharp and loud. Kylem squealed with pain and leapt off the bed, nursing his backside.

"You bitch! That bloody hurt!"

"Good!" and she threw his clothes at him again. "Get dressed!"

Kylem sat down, buried his head in his hands and mock sobbed.

"I'm tired and I'm sick of this fiasco. Please, go away and leave... me... alone."

Kyamena sighed deeply. This wasn't going to work. She needed another tactic. She walked around the bed and sank onto her haunches in front of him. She reached over and took his hands in hers.

"Kylem, I'm pleading with you. You *have* to come and see the Priest."

"If it was so urgent, why did Quick take me on his little mystery tour last night?"

"I don't know. Because Quick is Quick? I don't know, but he wasn't supposed to. He was supposed to bring you to the Bio-Labs to see the Priest."

"Why?" he asked like a frustrated infant.

Kyamena looked at their interlocked hands and rubbed her lips together in agitation. She thought for a moment, then leant forward, put her mouth to his ear and whispered quietly into it, not because she didn't want to be overheard, but for the effect it would have.

"The Sallows desire a new Warrior: one of strength and cunning, a sword forged in the fires of the tribes and quenched in the blood of mankind."

Kylem pulled back and gazed into her eyes quizzically. He'd heard those words before, a long, long time ago. He felt that air of familiarity waft over him again, but it lingered this time. It wasn't dissipating, it remained tantalisingly in the air, wafting like smoke. It was as though the very ends of his fingertips were touching the very edges of the smoke trails, and he could feel it. He could smell it. The memory was about to be broken.

"Kylem?" she asked, looking into his vacant eyes. "Can you hear me?" she said, patting his face gently.

"What?" he cried angrily as he snapped back into reality. It was gone.

"You have to come and see the Priest. Please?" she begged.

Kylem pulled his hands from hers and sat back. One side of his mouth lifted as he shook his head in submission.

"Okay," he sighed. "But I've not finished with him yet!" and he stabbed at the air towards Quick, with his finger.

"Fine," she said.

* * * * *

They travelled slowly through the tunnels, much to Quick's delight. Outside of the tunnels, he was a deformed hunchback, weak and vulnerable, but inside—this was his kingdom, his domain and here, he was the superior being. He moved with a stealth, agility and speed the others simply could not match and Kyamena, who had made the journey once already that evening, was especially tired. She wasn't accustomed to crawling through the service shafts at the best of times. Quick, on the other hand, scurried along unhindered, stopping and waiting only because he was forced to. Kylem wanted to be annoyed at his brother's smugness, but he also didn't want to deny him it. He knew how glorious it was to feel ahead of the game. It would be a rare feeling for Quick, so he wasn't going to take that away from him.

Finally, they reached the vents over the Bio-Labs. Kyamena pulled Kylem to a halt and spoke to him.

"Kylem, I need you to remember that these people have reason to hate you so please stay close to me and do as I say. I can't guarantee your safety if you don't."

Kylem opened his mouth to protest but she silenced him with a scowl. He rolled his eyes in acknowledgement.

As they dropped down into the Bio-labs, Quick landed effortlessly but Kyamena's feet clanged heavily onto the metal walkway. Kylem dropped down noiselessly too and Quick glanced at his brother's feet, realising he was back in Kylem's world.

Sensing movement, the subtle lighting activated, breaking the darkness. Kylem paused and assessed his surroundings.

The area was like a prison block. It had a central atrium and three storeys of cells lining it. Walkways ran around the edges on each level and crossed it three times. They were on the top level. As Kylem looked out over the rails into the atrium, he saw an extensive laboratory, spotlessly clean and fitted with an array of equipment and terminals. Kyamena pulled him away by the sleeve of his jacket, towards the stairs.

People were stirring, awoken by the lights and the noise, although some had been already up, awaiting the arrival of the renowned Espion, the Destroyer, the Betrayer—he was known by so many names here.

As they proceeded, Kylem looked deliberately in each cage, staring back at the occupants as they stared at him with equal curiosity. Each cell contained just one person, but they were from all races and species. He stopped at one of the cells. The occupant was a large male. He was black as night and beautifully muscular. His skin was cracked like a Sallow's but shone with natural health and had no need for the oils the blood-Sallows bathed themselves with, yet his build and features where distinctly humanoid. He was one of the legendary skunks he'd heard so much about.

"What are you looking at?" the skunk asked.

"You," replied Kylem, somewhat confused by the obviousness of the question.

"Why?"

"Because you are there," Kylem replied matter-of-factly.

"You never seen a skunk before?"

Kylem was about to say no, but was interrupted by a voice from behind.

"Only in the mirror," and the prisoners began laughing at him. Kylem felt uncomfortable enough that, when Kyamena tugged upon his sleeve, he let her lead him on.

"Lost your tongue?" shouted the skunk after them, and Kylem stopped dead. He didn't know why. He didn't feel angry as such but a deep sense of curiosity filled him, so he turned and went back to the cell and stood before the skunk. Silence filled the room again as everybody watched and waited to see what he would do.

"You're too close to the bars," Kyamena chided, but Kylem brushed her hands away. He knew he was within arms reach of the skunk.

"Will you break my neck too?" asked the skunk but Kylem said nothing. He just stared into the skunk's eyes as though looking for an answer there.

"No," he finally said and turned to walk away. The skunk reached out and grabbed him by the wrist. Kylem turned back sharply and gasped, for as the skunk's hand touched him—

...he was in smoke-filled room, the stink of tobacco thick upon the air. Laughter filled

the room, and in his hand was a tankard of beer with a foamy head. He looked up and beside him was a skunk, older and greyer than the one that had touched him. Not the same skunk, but yet familiar...

"You don't look so special," jeered the skunk. "Not very dangerous looking at all, in fact."

"Shut up, Byron," chided Kyamena, yanking Kylem's wrist free and pulling him away.

"He's right, though. He doesn't look very dangerous, does he?" said a new voice. The owner was of the same species as the breeder on the Farm Deck with the thick cartilaginous growth running down both sides of his face, haloing it in vivid sunset colours. He was different though. He was thinner, more lithely built and on one side of his face, the crest had been surgically removed along with part of his scalp. In its place was a transparent cover equipped with bits of hardware and electronic circuitry. Kylem recognised some of the apparatus as neural recorders.

"For something to infiltrate the enemy it should look meek and inoffensive," he explained. "No one will take pity on a savage dog, snarling and salivating. No one will take it home to sit at the hearth by their baby's crib; but a puppy—a cute little puppy with soft inoffensive, piteous, puppy dog eyes? Now, that's another thing altogether, isn't it?"

The fact was unnerving; the fact that he voiced it, even more so. The silence that Kylem had summoned was so uncomfortable that the rainbow man stepped back involuntarily from the bars.

"Kylem!" prodded Kyamena again. "We don't have time for this. Come on! Please?" she begged again. Kylem allowed her to lead him away, but continued his surveillance of the people around him.

It was very different from the Farm Decks. There was no depravity here. They may have been half-dissected with various implants hanging out of them but they still had their pride, and there was a kind of serenity, an inexplicable calmness that checked their anger, despite what Kyamena had said. He passed another cage, this time occupied by a reptilian being. Tall and lanky with muddy-green skin, his face was narrow and angular, and his mouth small. He sneered a smile at Kylem as he passed by and a neat row of small, needle-sharp white teeth flashed at him.

Kyamena led him down a flight of stairs and along another walkway to a cell near the end where a withered old man lay on the bed. He was little more than a bag of bones, ravaged by age. He looked to be as old as time itself, his face a saggy bag of muscleless tissue like a tired out old cushion, compacted with age and laying half empty and faded upon the pillow. His eyebrows were thick and bushy white, but his head was balding with just a few wisps of long, white hair hanging limply from his scalp. He lay with his hands like withered old talons, crossed over his chest as though he had already been laid out, and his breathing was shallow.

Kylem studied the bars and compared them to those on other cells. Some of the cages had physical bars like on the Farm Decks but others were electronically generated bars and forcefields. Of the forcefields, some were opaque like frosted glass hiding the occupants from view while others were clear, detectable only by the thin electric-blue outline around the opening. The bars to this cage were electronically generated. He stood waiting.

"Well? Anyone going to let me in then?" he asked.

"Yes. You," said Kyamena, pointing at the control panel mounted on the door pillar. "You're the genius, after all."

Kylem tutted.

"If I use that, they'll know I've been here."

"Can't you fudge it or something?"

Kylem tutted again and rolled his eyes.

"Fudge it!" he muttered to himself and stood pensively for a moment. Then he turned and looked over the railings into the lab below. He cocked his head to one side as he focused on what was down there and Kyamena wondered, once again, just how good his eyesight really was.

Without warning, he leapt over the railing. Kyamena shot forward and leaned over the balustrade, expecting to see him sprawled on the floor below but he had landed neatly on his feet. She sighed. She should have known better. She should have expected that from the Espion but his ordinary, humanoid appearance still kept catching her off guard.

Kylem glanced at the cells on the bottom floor. Most of them had the frosted, opaque forcefields in place but some were transparent. People watched him from every direction, any apprehension overcome by their curiosity. He rummaged amongst the equipment in the atrium for a bit, grabbed some items and then ran back up the stairs taking them three at a time. At the cell door, he knelt down in front of the electronic lock and began to work. In his hand, he held an engineering scanner and what looked like a white glove.

"Tell me then, Kyamena," he began as he tinkered with the glove. "How'd you get out then?"

"Ah, well, that's a bit of story in itself really."

"I like stories."

"What are you doing?" she asked.

"You're evading the question. How'd you get out?"

"Same way Quick did."

"Which is?"

"The lock's faulty," explained Quick from behind. It was the first time he'd spoken since his apology to Kylem, but he sounded puzzled as he said it. Kylem glanced at him, shook his head and continued.

"So why aren't you roaming about the ship too?"

"I haven't outlived my usefulness. My disappearance would be noticed. They'd look for me and then they'd find Quick."

"That's very noble of you," commented Kylem.

"Not really. I'm not in any immediate danger and even if I were, what good would both our deaths serve?"

Kylem paused and looked at her. That was the serenity he felt here—the serenity of cold logic and acceptance.

"So what are you trying to do?" she asked. "What is that?" and she indicated the glove.

"This, Kyamena," he said whilst gently tugging the white skin-like glove over his hand, wincing slightly as the remaining connections on the inside of the glove scraped along his own flesh, "...is the hand of a Scientific. Not all of it, just the outer covering."

"What's with all the wires and bits?"

169

Kylem smiled at the naivety of the question.

"Those are the sensors that enable Scientifics to feel what they are touching and that,"—he flashed a glance to the scanner—"is an engineering scanner used for scanning and interpreting data. It's also pretty good at transmitting and that's what I'm going to use it for. I'm going to use the glove to make the physical contact, and the scanner to emit a signal to fool that panel into thinking it's the hand of an operating Scientific."

"Mela-14?"

"No," snapped Kylem, perhaps a little too quickly.

"But it's Mela-14's lab. Surely it's the most likely one to access it?"

"Yes, but if the access is noted he will know it wasn't him and ask questions, and then he'll know it was me."

"How will he know it was you?"

"Because it's always me," laughed Kylem. "However, if Server reported that another Scientific had been in, bearing in mind his current popularity," he said, remembering that it was his father that had told on the Karam series, "he won't think too much of it. He certainly won't question it."

"But what if he does ask the Scientific in question?"

"Like I say, he won't, but if he does... that's a risk we'll have to take although..." and he punched in Jordan-5's details, "I don't think we need worry about that little problem," and he winked smugly.

Within a matter of seconds, the power cut and the bars dropped. Kyamena pushed past him and slipped inside.

She knelt down by the bed and took the Priest's hand but she immediately closed her eyes, sighed and placed his hand back upon his chest. As she stood up, it slid off and hung limply over the side of the bed.

"It's too late," she said sadly. "He's dead."

"Does that mean I can go back to bed then?" asked Kylem.

Anger flashed through her and she surged forward at him, shoving him hard with both hands so that he faltered and stepped back.

"You little shit!" she screamed. "Is that all you have to say for yourself! *Can I go back to bed now please?*" she mimicked sarcastically. Kylem held his hands up defensively as she bombarded him with her barrage of abuse.

"And you!" she screamed, now turning on Quick. "If you hadn't been so bloody selfish in the first place—"

"Oh, leave him alone," butted in Kylem, placing a hand on her shoulder. Kyamena whipped around, swatting his hand away.

"You can shut up too. You didn't even know him. You don't know the first thing about him. You don't even know his bloody name!" she screamed.

"Did you?" he rebuked.

Kyamena stopped dead and her head dropped in shame. She sank onto her haunches, drew her knees up to her chest and buried her head into them. Kylem watched her.

She didn't know his name either. She'd only ever known him as 'the Priest'.

Kylem sighed.

"I'm sorry," he said. "I didn't know him so he means nothing to me. I cannot mourn a man I never knew."

Kylem reached over and picked the man's hand up to place it back upon his chest. For a moment, he held it.

Kyamena watched again as Kylem seemed to vacate his body.

"Kylem?" she asked concerned, but suddenly he broke from his reverie. "Are you okay?" she asked.

"Yes," he said, but Kylem seemed a little out of sorts as he placed the Priest's hand gently back onto his chest, giving it an affectionate squeeze as he did so. Then he turned from her and catapulted himself over the handrail again.

In the atrium, for the second time, he walked over to one of the terminals. He placed his hand on top of it and activated it.

"His name was Zamus," he declared after a few moments and lifted his hand from the console. He held it in the air, flexing his fingers for a few seconds as though to relieve some tiredness in them. He looked thoughtful. Then he lowered his hand and walked slowly back up the stairs.

"He was a holy man, taken from the Holy Lands that border the Witchings: a region of space that lies far beyond here, far beyond the Seventh Meridian. When the Sallows came, they couldn't conquer the Witchings because of its magical hex."

"It doesn't say that!" exclaimed the reptilian. "He's making it up!"

"No," agreed Kylem. "It doesn't say all that, but I'm not making it up either. I just know it."

The reptilian stepped forward hastily and reached his hand out to Kylem, palm up and fingers outstretched.

"Tell me what you know," he commanded. There was a note of urgency in his words and a sense of hope. Kylem reached out but no sooner had his fingers touched the tips of the reptilian's than he snatched them back again. Then Kylem did something very strange. It felt like he had done it a thousand times before, but he never had—he almost had, but not with quite the same decorum.

He sighed a single, deep preparatory breath and dropped gracefully to the floor, pivoting on one foot into a cross-legged position. Now sitting on the walkway facing the reptilian, he placed his hands neatly upon his knees, closed his eyes and lifted his chin so that his words would ring out clearly, and then he recounted the tale, just as it had been told to him.

"He was a holy man, taken from the Holy Lands that border the Witchings: a region of space that lies far beyond here, far beyond the Seventh Meridian. When the Sallows came, they could not conquer the Witchings because of its magical hex, but that protective hex was paid for with a very high price.

"The High Priestess, the Great Witch herself, gambled her freedom and bartered her soul to protect her lands and her people. And in the end she still lost them both; but for that price, the Witchings will never entirely fall, although they will also never again rise to their former great glory. Their time has passed.

"As for the Holy Lands, they have always benefited from their nearness to the Witchings. Its magic, by default, protects them, and thus they have largely remained free from the Sallows' tyranny.

"For centuries people have migrated to the Holy Lands, not for this protection, but on a crusade to devote their lives to spiritual aspects. Nobody is ever born in the Holy Lands and nobody has ever been conceived there. This is not a land of love. It is not a land for families. It is a land of serenity."

171

He stopped and opened his eyes. The reptilian looked curiously into the dreamy, milky, pale-green eyes of the Espion.

"Tell me more," he demanded.

Kylem took another breath and closed his eyes again.

"Once he held a book, a small book, thick with pages that are old. They smell stale and musty and I can hear its pages crinkling as he studies them. It comes, not from the Holy Lands, but from the Mystics who are not from the Witchings, but are witches. They are far more peaceful and have never been seen by human eyes. They need no spells or potions to make their magic, just the power of thought and peace of mind. The book is written in the tongue of the Mystics so its words are strange, and for those for whom it is not intended, the pages are empty."

Kylem opened his eyes once more and suddenly, he felt awkward.

"That's it," he said. "That's all I have."

"It is enough," said the reptile. His hand was still extended and he waved his fingers indicating he wanted Kylem to take it, but Kylem didn't.

"Do you not want to know how it is that you know all this?" asked the Tarrow-Man.

"It is the curse of the Moroda," said Kylem suddenly, inexplicably knowing. "It should have been a gift."

The Tarrow-Man sank down and sat so that his eyes met Kylem on his level.

"Tell me more," he prompted again.

Kylem gazed silently at him.

"Tell me more!" he demanded more urgently.

Kylem lifted his chin again, drew a breath and closed his eyes a third time.

"They are a wise people, a telepathic race whose children bear the memories of their forefathers—not all, just those that were of the most importance to them; but all memories, whether inherited or gleaned, fade and die, even important ones. Thus, memories are incomplete and open to interpretation, but out of this affliction, a new enlightenment grows, for the Moroda have learnt from their shortcomings and learnt to see all things in many different lights. Verdicts are never passed. They are a very tolerant people."

"How's that a curse?" asked Kyamena. "It sounds... so enlightened."

Kylem opened his eyes and Kyamena saw that they were now a pale, translucent, cold icy-blue like the arctic waters of her homeworld.

"Because the memories of their slaughter are also engraved deeply into those memories."

"He is part Moroda," explained the Tarrow-Man. "And part so many other things. He remembers, and not just the memories of his forefathers, and he remembers by touch."

"You mean he reads minds?" exclaimed Kyamena.

Kylem laughed derisively. "Wish I bloody could!"

"No," agreed the reptilian. "He doesn't read minds, but he does have the gift of the Moroda, and he is empathic, like his mother."

Suddenly, like a beacon of light switched on in the dark, the memory of her was

172

illuminated. He remembered her!

And he remembered her words—

'The Sallows desire a new Warrior, one of strength and cunning, a sword forged in the fires of the tribes and quenched in the blood of mankind. Now they have their hardened sword, but who will wield it?'

And then he was filled with sadness.

"She's dead, isn't she?" he said quietly. He didn't need an answer. He knew the answer to the question.

The memory of her words nagged at him to be recited but he pushed them aside and got to his feet. He was done here.

"I'm tired now. I'd like to go to bed. Quick, can you take me back please?"

He reset the bars on the Priest's cage and returned to the entry point on the far side of the labs, where he leapt up into the void of the ducts and was gone. Quick followed.

* * * * *

Back in his quarters once more, Kylem made straight for his bed and threw himself onto it. Quick, on the other hand, lingered on, fidgeting.

"Quick," Kylem finally said. "Please? Go home. Go to bed. Get some sleep."

"But I feel bad. I'm sorry."

"Don't worry about it."

"But you'll never know what he wanted to tell you, and that's my fault."

Kylem sat up and patted the bed by his side. Quick scuttled over and sat himself down, eager to please.

"Quick, don't worry about it. Whatever it was that the Priest wanted to tell me, if it was that important, he will have found a way. Who knows? Perhaps he's already told me," he suggested, thinking of the strange things he had 'remembered'.

"The book you mean," shouted Quick. "You mean the book, don't you?"

Kylem thought about it.

"No. The book was never meant for me. I doubt that I'd be able to read its words even if I found it. Anyway, you said he wanted to talk to me about the Eunaba. The book isn't the Eunaba, is it?"

"No, it's not," agreed Quick, "but you know that!"

Kylem scowled. "I do?"

"Of course you do!"

Quick's brow furrowed in deep confusion and Kylem waited patiently, expecting more from Quick but he gave nothing more. He put his arm around his brother and leant into him.

"Humour me, Quick. What do I know?"

Quick looked all the more confused.

"What is the Eunaba?" he prompted.

"It's the big pebble thing," he said slowly and somewhat confused.

"Big pebble thing?" repeated Kylem, wondering why Quick was looking at him as though he were mad.

"Oh! Hang on! I think I might know what you mean," and Kylem got up and began rummaging in a drawer. Finally, he pulled out the cobblestone that Kyamena had found and held it up.

"Is this it?"

"Could be."

"What do you mean, *it could be*? It either is, or it isn't!"

"I don't know. You never actually showed it to me."

"Showed it to you? When did I show it to you? Or not show it to you? How could I show it to you? I don't even know what it is?"

It was hard to tell which of the two brothers was more confused. Quick sat nervously biting his lip and Kylem stood looking expectantly at his brother for an answer.

"I don't really remember when," Quick said. "It was a long time ago."

Kylem kept looking at Quick's puzzled and bewildered face. He wasn't quite sure what to ask next.

"I think I'll go now," Quick said suddenly. "I think you should get some sleep too," he added very quietly before disappearing back into the bathroom.

Kylem continued to gawp at the open space that Quick had occupied. Then he concluded one thing. The boy might well be a babbling idiot but he was right. It had been a long night and he did need some sleep. As for the Eunaba, he could always ask Quick again tomorrow. Hopefully, they would both be more coherent by then.

Having finally got back into his bed though, Kylem didn't sleep so easily. At last, he had remembered the soft, brown eyes; that wisp of familiarity had finally been placed. How could he have forgotten his mother? That he had placed her pleased him, but he also felt as though he had lost something by remembering. His thoughts wandered back to the Moroda. What other little surprises were in store for him?

CHAPTER 20

Over the next few weeks, it became evident to Kylem that his status in the eyes of his fellow Sallows had risen significantly—a point substantiated by his place at the hallowed dining table at which Kylem now sat for every meal. At his very first breakfast with the Sallows, Kylem had not been surprised to see Mada positioned at the head of the table in Emoth's place. It reinforced the fact that he had jumped over Jurrish in the ranks and seized the most senior position of superiority. It did surprise him, however, when he was guided to Mada's former seat beside Jurrish. Mela-14 was then seated at an empty place setting at the bottom of the table, which signified the Scientific's humbleness in the presence of the blood-Sallows. More importantly, it reinforced Kylem's position. Kyamena had once asked him if he thought he was better than a Scientific. Evidently he now was.

On this particular morning, he entered the dining room early. Breakfast offered a wide choice of foods although Kylem preferred a simple meal—a glass of juice, a couple of slices of toast and maybe some fresh fruit.

Mada was already sat at the table, studying some reports on a datapad. In his hand he held a long, elegant two-tined fork upon which was suspended a piece of dawn. Mada usually ate dawn for breakfast. The fine slices of meat fanned his plate with some small orange tanya fruit decorating the centre. He looked up briefly to see who had entered.

"Good morning, Kylem."

"Morning," replied Kylem, taking his usual seat. A slave moved forward from the perimeter of the room and poured him a glass of freshly squeezed baya juice. Another slipped into the space it vacated with a tray of meats. Kylem declined. Mada huffed.

"Still not eating meat?" he enquired nonchalantly.

"Not for breakfast. I prefer something lighter first thing in the morning," explained Kylem taking a couple of slices of toast from a third slave. "So what have we got planned for today?" he asked but a disturbance at the doorway distracted them both.

Rathan entered noisily, apparently stumbling over his own feet and nursing what looked like the mother of all hangovers, again. Kylem smiled. He knew what that felt like. As Rathan saw Kylem, he beamed a warm, friendly smile through his clenched teeth and then grimaced visibly.

"Hello Kylem, and what are we up to this morning?" he asked as he pulled his chair out. It scrapped noisily across the floor and he winced painfully at it.

"I was just asking Mada the same thing," smiled Kylem.

"Well, we'll wait for the others before we start the meeting," said Mada.

For Sallows, breakfast was doubly important, not just as the first meal of the day but also as an important meeting time. Kylem had researched it. It was a tradition that stretched back into the days of the 'old empire' when there was no night-mode onboard a DaerkStar, when there were simply two shifts that worked in rotation. It was a meal that fell on the shift changes and which for some, served as breakfast whilst for others, served as supper. It allowed information to be relayed between the two shifts and for matters to be discussed in an informal setting, in the comfort of a good meal served buffet style with a minimum of two menus. Having completed the meal and exchanged information, the shifts would go on their separate ways. It was an effective system that Kylem admired greatly and one that the current day's blood-Sallows continued, even if they had bastardised it, because there was only one shift now—day shift.

It wasn't long before Jurrish and Doobee arrived. They too took their seats and were served breakfast. Finally, Mada put down his fork, wiped his mouth on his serviette and began.

"Right everybody, I'd like to talk about the TWD3. I've read your latest report, Jurrish and I think we're just about ready for a second test flight."

"Yes, I agree. We've improved the power fusion conversion ratios and significantly reduced the pre-warp tremors so I'm pretty convinced that we can run another trial without risking disintegration of the vessel."

"Excellent! And can we track it?"

Kylem smiled to himself. It was just as he had been saying all along. Unless you solved the communication problems over trans-warp speeds, you couldn't track it.

"Yes, I think we can," finished Jurrish.

Kylem looked up from his piece of toast. Had they developed trans-warp communications after all?

"If we run a manned flight, when the Targa drops out of warp, communications can be re-established."

Kylem suppressed a sneer. As usual, rather than tackling the problem, they were doing a workaround. Not that he didn't appreciate a good workaround. They had their place, but this wasn't one of them.

There was so much to be gained from the development of trans-warp communications. Besides being able to locate and retrieve the vessel, there was all the information from the flight itself. The telemetry analysis—audio and visual records, instrument readouts—all reporting on the effects the warp field might endure from gravitational influences and stresses, high-speed impacts, gaseous anomalies, ion trails, energy fields, suns, planets, alien transmissions and so much more.

"A Scientific or a Warrior?"

"Well, I was thinking of something a little more 'fleshy'."

"A skunk?"

Kylem laughed to himself. How stupid would that be? To put a skunk in a trans-warp vessel and then send them off into space. Not just a 'get-out-of-jail-free' card but one with a limousine and a full tank of fuel.

"Well, no, not an ordinary skunk," explained Jurrish.

At least Jurrish wasn't totally stupid.

"I was thinking of someone a little more reliable."

"What? One of us? A Sallow?"

"Hmm. Yes and no."

Silence fell and Kylem froze, a slice of toast poised between his teeth. He didn't like the sound of that and he could feel the eyes of his Sallow masters upon him. Slowly, he looked up to confirm his suspicions and his eyes scanned the Sallows considering him. Very calmly, he dropped his toast.

"I don't think so," he said.

"Why not?" exclaimed Mada and Jurrish in unison. "It would be a very high honour that any Sallow should relish!" continued Mada.

"Only for a Sallow with a death wish."

"I beg your pardon? What are you suggesting?"

Rathan began chortling away to himself. Thick, black kinga slopped over the sides of his cup, staining the pristine, white tablecloth. Jurrish and Rathan glared at him.

"What?" they demanded.

"He's not as stupid as he looks—are you, Kylem?" Rathan boomed. "Go on, Kylem. Explain it to them. Tell them what they're missing."

"Bearing in mind that the TWD3 is not your project, Rathan, and that you've had little to do with it, I fail to see how you can judge the success or failure of the drive," interrupted Jurrish. "And neither can you, Kylem."

"Oh, I don't doubt the success of the drive," assured Kylem. "In fact, I think it will be highly successful, from what I've seen of it. It's the other systems that worry me, or rather the lack of them."

Mada banged the table angrily with his little fists.

"Oh, I see. We're on the communications thing again, are we?"

"No!" Kylem replied adamantly. "I was thinking more along the lines of shielding, inertial dampeners and stuff like that."

"What?"

Rathan began beating his hands upon the table to steal the floor.

"He means he's not prepared to throw his life away in a test flight—which is exactly what he would be doing!"

Rathan got up, walked around the table sat down beside Kylem.

"Exactly what level of shielding have you installed, Jurrish?" he continued. "Possibly sufficient for an android, but is it good enough to protect a blood-thing? No! So he'll be squished like a bug on the windshield!" and he slapped Kylem so hard on the back that he lunged forward.

"Oh, yes. I suppose that is a consideration," conceded Jurrish, somewhat disappointed.

Kylem said nothing but once again wondered at the stupidity of these 'geniuses' (or should that be 'genii'?)

"Then it'll just have to be a Warrior or a Scientific," declared Mada.

"Excellent decision—and anyway, I have a far better idea for Kylem," said Rathan.

"And what's that then?"

"I think we ought to put Kylem out into the field."

Kylem's heart leapt in excitement.

"Nothing major, but I thought we could send him down to Corinthia. There's that pesky little rabble in the Capital Arena that he can have a play with—cut his teeth on, so to speak. I think it'll be fun for him—and for us of course."

Mada leant forward and rested his flabby, black chin on his tented, stubby fingers as he thought.

"Yes," he agreed slowly. "Now that is a good idea," and both Jurrish and Doobee agreed too.

"Corinthia it is then!" declared Mada. "Rathan, make sure he's fully briefed and give him a couple of days to study. Kylem, I assume you're ready for this? Are you recuperated?"

"Absolutely. I've been ready for weeks to be honest, thanks to Rathan," and he nodded in the Sallow's direction. "He found me a gym on the lower decks to work out in. It's very well equipped and has proven to be extraordinarily useful."

"I didn't know we had a gymnasium," Mada exclaimed indignantly.

"Well, you wouldn't, would you?" snapped Rathan. It wasn't very diplomatic. "It wasn't designed for us. It was designed centuries ago for a race of fit, healthy Sallows, much taller and stronger than we are. It's perfect for Kylem though."

Mada's eyes narrowed at the insensitive reminder of their race's blight, and a stony silence filled the room. Rathan glared back at Mada almost challengingly. Kylem noted that the animosity between them ran deep. He wondered why. He wondered if Rathan knew that Mada had killed his brother so coldly. He wondered if Rathan and Mada were brothers also. It was getting too tense. He decided to disarm the situation. Things were just starting to get exciting, and Corinthia sounded like it could be fun. Kylem didn't want an argument to spoil it for him.

"I'm sorry. That's probably my fault," he interjected. "Each of you has been so very generous in assisting me to attain my full potential but in retrospect, I can see that I may have overstepped the mark. Rathan has spent a great deal of time with me, not only in my studies of the sciences, but in finding me ways to help improve my level of fitness, especially after the injuries I received in the maze. I know you're not keen on me wandering around the ship without prior notification, but I needed space to work out. Rathan found me the gym which is purpose built and includes treadmills. It was a perfect solution."

"He's not given you any drugs, has he?" asked Jurrish dubiously.

Kylem laughed and glanced at Rathan who winked back at him.

"He would have loved me to join him in the Agaratax, but I have declined," he assured them.

"Thank goodness for that," muttered Doobee.

"And who else has helped you?" asked Mada.

The blood-Sallows stiffened but Kylem knew he was about to have Mada eating out of the palm of his hand.

"All of you have helped me and individually, each contribution may seem small but considering them all together, I can see that I may have overstepped my boundaries. If that is the case, I must apologise to you all individually and thank you at the same time."

Kylem now turned to Doobee.

"Doobee, you have permitted me access to the DeathMaker libraries and assisted me in the development of my own program and data storage facilities. Under your watchful eye, I have been allowed access to some of the most basic systems aboard the DaerkStar, which have allowed me to enhance my communication with Server.

Data access is quicker and search protocols significantly enhanced, which is very useful. From these improvements, you have extracted and developed more sophisticated translation matrices for Server to comprehend and assimilate more alien technology."

Doobee had to hide his smile. He was pleased that Kylem had given him the credit he so deserved for the development of the translation matrices.

"Jurrish, you have overseen my engineering and piloting skills. You have helped me to adapt a Targa for my own needs, which, as Rathan has pointed out, are rather different to that of your traditional android. In fact," said Kylem, an idea springing into his mind, "it has the enhanced shielding and inertial dampeners—and a few other things besides—that your TWD3 may benefit from. They'll need a bit of beefing up for the TWD3 Targa but it seems that you have already addressed most of those shortcomings. I don't know why I didn't think of it sooner. Sorry Jurrish."

"You seem very familiar with the TWD3 drive," commented Mada, already softening to Kylem's words.

"Maybe a little. Jurrish has humoured me. He has allowed me to take a look at the communication problem, as a hobby project."

Mada glared at Jurrish.

"It keeps him out of mischief," he explained.

"But isn't that a waste of resources?" chided Mada.

"Sadly, I have to agree with Kylem. We don't know how the engines will react in close proximity to comets, wormholes, black holes, supernovas, or whatever else it may come into contact with. Even alien communication transmissions may have an adverse effect on the warp field so, to develop a fully viable drive, I think we will need that information."

Kylem smiled. It seemed he had won Jurrish over already. Mada's mouth shrugged a begrudging acceptance of Jurrish's argument.

"Very well. As long as those efforts aren't distracting you from our main objective."

"No, they aren't. And it does keep Kylem busy, which as you know can be a problem."

Kylem smiled. "Yes, and the project has allowed me to expand my own engineering skills as well as my databanks—again, with Doobee's help and supervision, of course. As for your good self, Mada, you have been very informative in my studies of the various humanoid species. You've given me access—"

"Restricted access!" he reminded Kylem. Kylem nodded dutifully.

"Restricted access... to the information you have uncovered in your biological experiments conducted over the years. This has allowed me to overview the differences between the species and their—what shall we call them? Gifts? Talents? And although it cannot possibly prepare me for every species I encounter, it has given me an important insight into what sort of things are out there: telekinetics, tele-electrocytes, chameleoids, shape-shifters and so on.

"To conclude, gentlemen, I have made requests of each of you that, individually, are small and insignificant and each of you has obliged. In retrospect, I can now see that, when all things are considered, I have asked much of you and that I may have overstepped my authority. I therefore apologise for this lack of consideration and forethought."

Kylem bolstered his apology with the appropriately humbling pose of syran: his eyes closed and head tipped forward so that his chin rested on his chest, and his forearms lifted with palms facing upward—the Warrior's pose of benevolence and submission. He knew it would please Mada but the silence that followed his speech ached on.

"Very eloquent, Kylem, but everyone had a part to play in this negligence. I am in command here, and all of these things should have been approved by me. However, I also appreciate that my predecessor may not have been so rigid in his demands or his monitoring so I shall say just one thing. It must not happen again. Everything you require must first be authorised by me." Mada's voice was stern and sharp, and each of the Sallows nodded and murmured their agreement.

"And Kylem! From you, I want a complete report detailing what exactly you have been privy to."

"Affirmed."

"And don't play the bloody android with me. You can take boot-licking too far, you know."

Inwardly, Kylem smiled. Mada's tone, although trying to be stern, was amused.

"Now," began Mada... but he never finished his sentence.

The tableware suddenly rattled and shook violently. The crystals on the chandelier tinkled frantically against each other and the whole room rumbled with discomfort. Then, as abruptly as it had started, the clamour died.

"What was that?" exclaimed Doobee.

Kylem had already accessed Server.

"Explosion on Hanger Deck B!" he declared.

"What? What's caused it?"

"Insufficient data."

No one moved, each of them waiting for some signal from Mada, but Mada's gaze was fixed upon Kylem. He seemed to be having problems absorbing the information.

"Insufficient data!" Kylem repeated urgently.

Suddenly, Mada leapt to his feet and fled to the door. Everybody followed. As Kylem reached the door, Rathan grabbed him by the arm and pulled him back. He pushed his face into Kylem's.

"Very eloquent, Kylem, but I don't need you to speak for me," he hissed. Saliva spat and sat on his chin like little drops of black rain on a lump of coal.

"On the contrary, Rathan. I've seen what Mada can do. I think he'd slit your throat more easily than he did his own brother's," and his eyebrows shrugged at Rathan. Rathan slowly released his grip. Kylem wrenched himself free and fled from the room towards Hanger Deck B.

* * * * *

When the doors opened on Hanger Deck B, the heat seared through them like the blast from an open furnace door. The blood-Sallows recoiled under the heat. A fresh explosion shook the deck and sent blinding white light blossoming out in every direction. The blood-Sallows faltered, dazzled and shocked. Kylem did not waver. He unceremoniously grabbed them, yanked them back into the safety of the corridor and leapt through the doors just as they were closing and onto the hanger deck.

He still had no idea what had happened, but he knew what could happen. For some stupid reason, an unnecessarily large quantity of missiles and ammunition were stored at the back end of the hanger decks instead of in the especially designed armoury and missile bays. The Sallows said it was just as easy to store them there and they were more readily to hand when it came to re-arming the Targas, but Kylem reckoned it was laziness. To keep such a volatile cargo on a hanger deck, with so many heat sources about, was an accident waiting to happen—and now it was happening. Whatever had started it, if those missiles exploded it would take out half the DaerkStar with it. It wouldn't have been quite so bad if they had been stored nearer to the hanger bay doors, at the tips of the spines of the ship, but they weren't. They were stored at the end nearest to the body of the DaerkStar. An explosion there would set off a chain reaction of explosions. Slowly and irrevocably, the outer decks of the ship would be blown away until only the central core remained. Without guidance and navigational controls, its orbit would decay and soon it would plunge into the atmosphere of the world beneath to finish the job.

Once on the hanger deck though, Kylem realised that he couldn't see through the chaos, nor could his heat seeking ability function in the searing temperatures. Instead, another sense kicked in, the one he had inherited from the Karnar—biosonar. There was more than enough noise bouncing around on the hanger deck for him to utilise. His range was short but sufficient... he hoped.

Another blast rocketed through the deck, and the shock wave that it created blew past him like a hurricane. He stared blindly into the mêlée, absorbing information. The remains of about a dozen Targas littered the bay, with various Warriors scattered amongst the detritus of the blast. Many were destroyed and many more were damaged. Those that were still active stood stock-still. They were not programmed to deal with an emergency situation such as this.

There were other bodies too—humanoid bodies. A shipment of live cargo must have broken free in the chaos. Kylem became aware of a figure running towards him engulfed in orange flame. He stepped casually to one side as it fell at his feet. Its screams continued for a few moments, its arms and legs flaying wildly, and then it died.

A conduit above him cracked under the heat. Fumes and plasma began hissing out into the bay under high-pressure. The air was becoming more acrid.

He tapped into Server and demanded all the information uploaded by the Sallows that had been on the deck just before the blast. Some of it was heavily fragmented but Server obliged. He thought how fortunate it was that Doobee had given him sufficient clearance to access this information or else he would have been working blind. He made a note to mention it to Mada.

He was flooded with visual images and readings from Warriors, both defunct and active. He quickly saw that a Targa had clipped the bay doors as it came in to land. It should have been an impossible scenario. On final approach, the piloting of the Targa was taken over by Server. The Targa was effectively pulled into the DeathMaker, not guided in, so even if the Targa or the Sallow at the helm had been defective, such things would not matter. Yet the evidence was all too clear. The Targa had struck the side of the landing bay doors and skewed off to one side, pirouetting into the neighbouring Targas causing them to explode. Now, a veritable furnace raged on, and with more than an ample supply of fuel lying about in the form of cargo, propellant and miscellaneous rubbish, it wasn't set to go out any time soon.

A siren sounded. The fire control systems had finally been activated and Server began pumping in copious amounts of fire retardant foam via the grills around the perimeter of the deck. The foam was not only attracted to heat, it expanded upon contact to suffocate the fire, or so the theory went. With so much flame and fire and heat though, and so many new explosions birthing new heat sources, the foam was being pulled in all directions so that only a thin, airy layer covered any hotspot and was soon burnt through by the raging inferno.

Kylem stood in the midst of the chaos. He had to do something and he had to do it fast.

For a fire to burn, three things are required: heat, fuel and oxygen. By removing any one of these factors, the fire would suffocate and die, and there was only one way to do that quickly.

Kylem stepped forward and grabbed hold of one of the mooring rings that was welded to the hanger bay walls. He closed his eyes and issued the instructions to Server to open the hanger bay doors and fully release the gravitational field. By evacuating the hanger deck, everything would be sucked out—flames, Targas, Warriors, missiles, humanoids, oxygen, even himself if he didn't hang on.

But nothing happened. Kylem interrogated Server further and was rewarded with an image of the hanger bay doors from some half-defunct Warrior. Through the twisted and skewed remains of Targa panels, he could see them hanging ajar, buckled and distorted. Whether it was because Server couldn't open them or wouldn't open them, Kylem couldn't determine and he didn't have time to waste on it. He had to get the doors fully open, by whatever means, before depressurising the chamber, otherwise it would merely drag all the debris to the doors and act as a plug sealing the deck again.

He quickly accessed the schematics for the DaerkStar. There had to be a manual release mechanism somewhere and indeed, there was. An access panel was positioned on the left-hand side of the bay doors and inside that was an emergency release lever that would open them, but even that was not enough. He'd also have to deactivate the gravitational shield. Only when this was down would the area decompress, and to deactivate the shield he'd have to fight his way back up to the hanger deck's control room that was suspended high above the deck on his right-hand side. It jutted out from the wall like a huge, angular brick. Access would be difficult, partly due to the height of the control room and partly because his way was blocked by a pile of blazing debris, and the stairwell had gone so unless he fancied climbing the burning funeral pyre of debris beneath the control room, he'd have to find another way.

The temperature was rising all the while and he was starting to have difficulties breathing. The air was becoming more and more fume-filled. The levels were not suffocating, as evidenced by the screams of the humanoids that raged on in the background, screams that like the chittering of canaries to coalminers, told him that the air was not unbreathable—yet.

Inspiration suddenly grabbed Kylem, and he leapt into action. Before him was one of the crashed craft. It had been thrown up in an explosion and come to land on top of another Targa. The tip of the wing nearest him touched the floor. The furthest wing tip rose high into the air at a sharp angle of about forty degrees. The body of the Targa was perched precariously on the one beneath it. The metal squealed and creaked as the bodies rubbed, protesting against each other, and began to slip. There was no time left. Once the Targa fell, the opportunity would be lost.

Kylem broke into a full run and pelted towards the bird, running skywards up the wing. The metal screamed all the more, and the top Targa began to shift, sliding rightwards and away from the hanger doors. Kylem leapt onto the cockpit of the Targa, landing on all fours with his arms outstretched to secure his grip. The Targa gave a huge jolt and plunged a foot downwards, but Kylem's fingers held tight. He couldn't wait for it to settle though. It was starting to slide away. He leapt forward again, up and across the length of the furthermost wing tip, still high in the air, and then catapulted himself off it. He flew through the air and prepared his knees for the landing. Until that moment, he hadn't been able to see below him, whether it was flat, debris ridden, burning or clear; but now he could see that it was a burning mass with the body of a Warrior splayed on top of it. As his feet hit the chest of the dead Warrior, he catapulted himself off it. As he did so, the Warrior slipped from the top of the pile and crashed into the flames below.

The area ahead of him was relatively flat with small fires burning all around. Smoke continued billowing into the air as he ran, jumping from safe zone to safe zone, zigzagging in and out. He could see the hatch a few metres in front of him but didn't slow his pace. He used the wall to break his forward momentum and as he hit it, it felt hot. His fingers folded around the handles of the access panel and he yanked it off with all his might, falling backwards as he did so, which was lucky because a burst of burning hot plasma exploded from behind the plate. A line must have cracked in the wall linings somewhere and bled over, but that meant there was no way he could touch it. It would be too hot. His hands would be cooked within seconds of contact.

His eyes quickly scanned about and found another Warrior amongst the debris. Sat slumped upon its backside where it had fallen, its eyes still burned brightly but it was frozen in 'shock'.

"Warrior!" screamed Kylem. The Warrior turned its head and looked at Kylem. "Personal damage report!" he screamed, although why he was screaming he wasn't quite sure. It would have been easier to transmit the message via Server but the instruction was received.

Minor damage to exterior plating; external temperatures are within acceptable parameters but climbing. Awaiting instruction, he heard inside his head.

"Then come!" he commanded, still shouting.

The Warrior scrabbled awkwardly to its feet, burning debris falling from its lap as it did so. It clambered over the detritus to Kylem who was stood to one side of the panel. Plasma still wafted from it, distorting the air like a heat wave.

"Stick your hands on that," he said, pointing to the lever inside. It was a T-shaped lever, about a foot long with a crossbar just long enough for two hands.

Lever temperature exceeds recommended—

"Just put your bloody hands on it and pull!"

The Warrior obediently wrapped its hands around the lever from underneath. There was a loud hiss as cold metal met hot.

"Pull!" screamed Kylem, and the Warrior began to pull the lever down. The lever shifted easily about one-third of the way and then stuck. That would be the amount by which the doors were already open. Now it was stiffer and harder work.

The Warrior shifted its weight, repositioned its hands and began pushing down again. The outer casing of its palms started to soften and bend. It stood on tiptoes to aid in the downward thrust, and the lever jerked down further in a series of awkward lurches. Kylem's hands, wrapped in his jacket, were now on top of the Warriors hands, the heat seeping through them and into his own flesh. They were both pushing down, pushing down hard, but the dammed thing wouldn't budge any further. Kylem let go, but the Warrior continued to push down as hard as it could. Kylem climbed up the Warrior and onto its hands, steadying himself by holding onto the Warrior's shoulders.

"I'm gonna jump!" he warned it. The Warrior nodded in acknowledgment and Kylem prepared to jump.

A huge blast from the other side of the hanger deck exploded through, bringing a torrent of metal and whatever with it. The Warrior flinched and paused. It looked down and saw the spear of metal that had impaled it from back to front. Kylem saw it too and watched as the lights in its eyes began to flicker.

"Hang on in there," he pleaded and jumped.

The handle suddenly shifted dramatically downwards, taking Kylem and the Warrior with it. They only just managed to hang on and prevent themselves from falling over.

With reluctance, the huge bay doors began to shift. The great gears and cogs screamed from within the wall cavities and metal plating began to shear as the buckled doors rode up against the walls, concertinaing them like shredded paper, and then they stopped again. Kylem jumped again. It budged only a couple of centimetres this time. Kylem felt the Warrior suddenly slump and glanced down to see the cold, dark eyes of a dead Warrior. It fell backwards taking Kylem with it. As it hit the deck, the javelin of metal was thrust right through the Warrior. Kylem pushed himself out of the way just in time as the spear stabbed past his face, missing him by centimetres.

"Shit," he mumbled to himself.

He grabbed a hunk of metal, stood up and began beating down on the lever with it. It had to go all the way down, but it wouldn't budge. He began kicking it. He took a couple of drop kicks, but still nothing.

He looked at his hands, now red and blistered from the hot plasma still exuding from the panel. The sound of scraping metal made him flinch. Was one of the towers of burning metal toppling towards him? No, from amongst the chaos, two Warriors emerged. One had only one arm and twitched violently as its circuits were shorting out; the other had half its chest plating missing but seemed otherwise intact. They strode casually over, pushing debris aside and then very gently, one pushed Kylem aside. The two of them took hold of the lever and strained against it. Kylem climbed back up again, onto the Warriors' hands. He jumped. They pushed. Suddenly the lever gave way, plunging the last few centimetres and driving all three of them onto the floor.

Task complete, transmitted one of the Warriors as it lay sprawled on the ground. Neither Warrior rose again, but the two words spoke reams. It meant they had been sent over to him, specifically for that purpose. Kylem's eyes scanned the nearby walls quickly and found the camera he was looking for amongst the undulating smoke. He winked at it, but he still had work to do. He still had to get to the control room.

He looked up at it. The protective glass had shattered under the heat along most of its length. That would make access easier but how to get there?

Thick, black smoke was billowing from the last explosion point near the back of the hanger deck, frighteningly close to the munitions. It mushroomed up and crept swiftly across the ceiling.

He looked below the control room where piles of metal, broken containers, Warriors and bodies burned in huge unstable piles that rocked and moved, ever shifting as the great flames licked and ate away at them.

Suddenly, his path was set in his mind. He pelted forward, running up one of the burning piles of debris. The flames caressed and snatched at him as he passed on his way up the makeshift staircase, but he ignored them. His attention was focused on one of the thick chains suspended from the ceiling cranes. Having climbed as high as he could, he leapt into the air towards the chain. One hand missed but one hand caught. His skin hissed as it welded itself onto the hot metal and pain seared through his hand, but he hung on as he swung violently around. A fresh bolt of pain tore through his shoulder. For a moment, he thought that another shard of metal must have pierced it, but when he looked up, he saw nothing. It was the same shoulder he had injured in the maze, now jarring in its socket, screaming in protest. He snarled at the pain and braced himself for more. He swung up with the other hand to get a grip. Skin hissed again and he wrapped one leg around the chain so that it coiled about his shin like a snake, and then he afforded himself the luxury of letting go with his bad arm. As his arm dropped to his side, relief washed over him, but he knew it was to be short-lived. He focused again through the smoke and fury towards the control room. He reached up, took the chain with both hands again and released his leg. Pain gripped his shoulder and raw hands but he ignored it and began to swing.

He gained momentum fast and when he was as high as he could go, he let go and curled up into a ball, hurling himself towards the control room. He flew high, possibly a little too high as he smashed through the remainder of the glass, already crazed and cracked, and then rolled across the floor until he hit the far wall.

Quickly he scrambled to his feet and over to the control panels where finally, he could determine the true extent of the damage.

The temperature varied throughout the hanger deck but near the missiles, it was dangerously high. The air quality was incredibly poor with high levels of toxic fumes and noxious gases. Black smoke filled the whole of the ceiling area and was now billowing into the control room. Below, the remains of nine Targas were piled about the deck, intermingled with thirty-two Warriors and one hundred and twenty-one humanoids of which only thirty-three were still respiring.

He didn't hesitate. He accessed the control panel and prepared the sequence. Then he sat himself on the floor and wrapped himself around a leg of the control panel bench. Bits of glass cracked and crickled beneath him. With one hand, he reached up and deactivated the forcefield.

The effect was instantaneous.

It was like somebody upending a box. Suddenly, everything was sucked towards the doors and out into open space—Targas, containers, Warriors, missiles and humanoids.

The vacuum of space clawed at Kylem too, but he held on in the veritable wind tunnel of chaos. Shards of glass streaked past him on their passage to freedom, slashing and tearing at him. He hugged his face between his hunched shoulders to shield it as best he could. Handheld scanners, datapads and anything else not bolted down punched past him—and then, as suddenly as the chaos had begun, it stopped.

Everything was now still. The vacuum of space had conquered the bay. There

185

was no noise, no chaos and no signs of life; except for one blood streaked, pale white hand that weakly reached up over the edge of the console and fumbled at the controls once more.

The gravitational shield dropped back into place. A great hissing sound rang in Kylem's ears as re-pressurisation of the deck began. Suddenly, Kylem felt tired—very, very tired. He unwound his aching limbs from the console leg and flopped onto his back.

As the air returned to normal, he took some slow replenishing breaths, laying with his eyes closed.

He heard a clanking sound. It was the emergency bulkhead door to the control tower being cranked open but he did not move. He heard footsteps and some kafuffle.

"Is he dead?" he heard Doobee ask.

He opened one eye and smiled weakly at his audience: all four blood-Sallows, Mela-14 and the two Warriors that had jimmied open the door.

"No, Doobee," he said. "I don't die that easy," and he laughed weakly and then winced in pain. "Bruise easy, cut easy, bleed easy," he said, raising a slashed and bloody hand to his face. "But don't die easy."

CHAPTER 21

The Sallow Council decided that although Kylem's injuries were not particularly severe, they were of sufficient gravity to warrant postponing the Corinthia mission for a few weeks. Kylem, they deemed, needed time to recuperate. This was much to Kylem's annoyance and deep disappointment. The thought and anticipation of his first mission had both excited and enthralled him so he had protested strongly to the Council to which they assured him, it was only a postponement and not a cancellation. They had reviewed the mission proposals and it seemed like an ideal first mission. Nothing too difficult, yet still a challenge and thus they were going to 'save' it for him. Rathan also consoled him with the argument that it gave him yet more time to prepare for the mission, which is what Kylem was doing now.

Corinthia was a typical humanoid planet with a nitrogen/oxygen based atmosphere and a fair abundance of water. It supported about six billion people on forty-two percent of the total landmass that, in turn, occupied about thirty-eight percent of the planet's total surface. The Sallows had invaded from orbit in the first instance, taking out the military installations and the larger cities. This allowed them to form the isolated battle arenas for the ground attacks with their legions of Warriors, of which there were ample recordings for him to review. He was in the cinema watching one of these when Mada majestically swept in. Kylem cast him the briefest of glances as he sat himself down on a chaise longue from where he watched intently as Kylem rewound and watched one particular scene over and over again. Finally he spoke.

"Of course, you know it's much better live."

"Maybe, but this isn't for fun. I'm looking for strategy."

"They haven't got one," Mada said quite sulkily. "You can watch it a billion times and that won't change. It's a simple hunt. They run. We hunt."

"Then what do you need me for?"

"Well," said Mada, "this particular scenario is a simple hunt. I've seen it before. Not as many times as you have by the looks of it, but there is little to see," and he began pointing out the band of humanoids that were scattering ahead of the Warriors before being cut down. It was a very short, dull hunt. Kylem rewound the recording and paused it. He walked over to the image.

"Actually, there is. These humanoids seem to be drawing us away from something. And this," he said, pointing at a lamppost at the end of the street. "Do you see that?"

"Yes, it's a streetlight," proffered Mada, squinting his eyes at the tall post with an egg-shaped globe suspended elegantly beneath it.

"No, it's not just a street light. It's a security camera and it's following the events."

Kylem replayed the clip in slow motion but Mada saw nothing new. Kylem zoomed in further on the lamp and changed the light frequency to accentuate the movement.

"Look at how the light plays across the surface of the glass. Notice the slight wave of discolouration as the camera moves behind the shade."

He pointed at the globe and the faint silhouette that the camera made, writhing behind the cloudy glass as it panned across the street. It was barely visible, but yes, Mada could just make out the shadowy variations on the interior of the globe.

"They are watching us, which is why your rebels are so elusive in this arena. You've underestimated them."

Mada raised his eyebrows and took in a sharp intake of breath.

"The end result will be the same. We will annihilate them, either down there or from up here. It makes no difference."

"Except that the thrill of the hunt will be lost."

"Well, yes, true, but the end result will be the same."

Kylem came and sat down again. He screwed his eyes up in friendly scepticism at Mada.

"Is there a problem?" Mada asked.

"I don't know," said Kylem, sucking his teeth thoughtfully. "Is there?"

Mada cocked his head to one side, waiting for Kylem to continue.

"You have the ability to wipe an entire planet out from up here, but you don't. You do so much damage and then you send Warriors down to hunt for you, to give you that thrill you cannot attain for yourself and yet, you don't seem excited that I will be hunting instead. I would have expected a renewed excitement at the thought of a variation to the game and yet, there is none."

"How very observant of you."

"So what do you want of me?" asked Kylem.

Mada smiled and shrugged.

"Something. Nothing. So many things," and he fell pensively silent, but Kylem was not going to let it rest.

"Oh come on, Mada. Is the Espion Project a serious one or not?"

He hadn't meant it to come out quite like that. He hadn't meant for it to come out at all but the words just fell out of his mouth before he could stop them. To his surprise, it didn't rile Mada.

"Uhm, yes and no. The Espion Project would never stand up on its own. It always had to be multi-faceted in order to gain the approval needed to proceed."

"So it's not just entertainment?"

"Oh no! The Espion Project has many facets. The thrill of espionage is one of those facets but the biological advancements we have achieved whilst developing you, also supports our work on Regenesis. You are part Sallow, despite your humanoid appearance."

"That's only two points. Two points hardly warrant the term 'many facets'."

"True, but that's all you need to know for now," and he held out a large datapad, about the size of a laptop. Kylem took it.

"What's this?" he asked.

"We're trying to work out what happened in Hanger Deck B and I'd like your report. Details are sketchy at best but the pad contains everything we have so far. Perhaps you'd cast your eye over it and fill in the blanks?"

"Yeah, sure," he said and waited, half-expecting Mada to leave, but he didn't. He was looking around the cinema and studying the mess that Kylem had made. There were a couple of discarded food trays, at least five empty kinga cups and a hundred or so sheets of paper littered about the place.

"Is there anything else?" Kylem prompted.

Mada picked up a sheet of paper and studied the scribbles on it.

"Why paper?" he asked.

Kylem laughed. It was indeed an antiquated medium for an android to be using so it must have looked particularly odd.

"Call it an eccentricity of mine. This type of medium for recording information is prevalent in many cultures including Corinthia. I quite like it at the moment, but I expect the novelty will wear off soon enough."

Mada studied the writing further. He couldn't read it and soon gave up, dismissing it from his mind as immaterial.

"And the rest of the mess?"

"It's not a problem," and at just that moment two slaves entered. Mada's head whipped around so quickly, Kylem thought his neck might snap.

"Was that you?" exclaimed Mada. "You seem to have an extraordinary level of communication with them."

"Not really. I issue them the same instructions you do, just not verbally."

Mada was pensive. "Do they..." he hesitated... "...respond?"

What an odd question!

"Respond? They do as they're told but that's about it. Is everything okay?" ventured Kylem. "You seem a little concerned about them?"

"It's just with so many anomalies in our systems lately, I wondered if it was affecting them."

"Don't worry about them," he reassured Mada. "They're as harmless and despicable as always."

"Then why do you suddenly tolerate them in your presence? I thought you preferred taking them to bits."

Kylem laughed.

"As long as I don't have to pick up after myself, they serve a very useful function, and I find them somewhat curious."

Mada's eyebrows twitched. A wide, humorous grin broke out on Kylem's face.

"It's a morbid sort of curiosity," he assured him. "As a spy, I am a very curious creature with an enquiring mind which drives me to find answers to questions— questions I don't necessarily want or need to know the answers to." He laughed a short, half-hearted laugh. "I even followed one yesterday."

"Why?"

"To see where it went, what it did." Kylem grinned at Mada. "So, have I piqued your curiosity enough for you to ask me my findings?"

Mada smiled and dropped his gaze into his lap.

"You're quite good at this, aren't you?" he said.

"I am well designed," agreed Kylem smugly.

"Go on then. Where did it go? What did it do?"

"It was all really very boring, to be honest. It went to the laundry."

"Laundry? Oh, yes. I suppose we must have one."

"Yes, I'd not thought about it either, but when you do think about it, it's quite logical really. When they've changed our beds, where do the sheets go? Where do the clean ones come from? The answer is simple. It's good old-fashioned washing and ironing."

"Hmm." Mada was perplexed. "I wonder what else we have that I don't know about."

Kylem took in a deep breath.

"Let's see. The laundry and gym you're familiar with. Then there are the kitchens or galley, janitorial supplies, games room, bar, swimming pool (although that's dry at the moment), waste recycling and all the life support paraphernalia."

"Paraphernalia?"

"Water tanks, reservoirs, air purification—that sort of thing."

Mada sighed deeply. "I really don't know very much about my DaerkStar, do I?"

It was an extraordinary confession for the blood-Sallow to make, especially to a skunk. It was also one that was steering him towards exploring his ship, and Kylem wasn't sure he wanted Mada to know any more about his ship than he already did. At the moment, he had the tactical advantage and he wanted to keep it that way. Besides, he might find some of the other things that Kylem had found—like the hand-held rocket-launcher or Quick.

"Do you need to know about it?" he asked the Sallow.

Mada puzzled.

"I mean—does the captain of a battleship need to know how many eggs the cook has used in the preparation of breakfast that morning, or how many sheets were laundered that day? There are battles to be fought, worlds to conquer. As captain, the demands upon your time must be immense. There cannot be enough hours in the day for you to monitor everything, so surely menial things like laundry must be delegated to lesser beings so that the more pressing issues of command and invasion—things that require a sharper and more skilled mind—can receive the attention they require. Surely these are the things a captain must turn his attention to, not housekeeping?"

Mada sat thoughtfully, scratching his chin. He wasn't stupid. He knew that Kylem was soothing his ego, but he had saved the boy's life at least once and the boy wasn't stupid either. Kylem knew that his life and the quality of his life depended upon Mada's favour, so it was probably wise that he sucked up to his captain, and Kylem did have a point.

"No!" he finally said resolutely. "No, I don't suppose I do. That's what the Scientifics and slaves are for—the good ones anyway," he said, thinking about the defunct Karam series.

Kylem smiled to himself with satisfaction. The smile leaked out onto his face. Mada saw it and pondered it but soon interpreted it as Kylem being pleased with the fact that he had pleased his captain.

"Well, I'll leave you to it then," and he got up.

"Okay, and I'll get onto this," replied Kylem, indicating the datapad.

Mada beamed a wide, toothy grin at him as he left. Kylem flicked the datapad open and started reading the data. Then he scowled.

Within three minutes, the cinema was deserted. Kylem had left. The food trays and kinga cups had vanished and the papers, Kylem would find later, neatly stacked on the workbench in his quarters.

* * * * *

As Kylem slipped through the doors into R & D, there was still a slight trace of a limp to his gait.

"Oh, hello," exclaimed Jurrish in surprise. "To what do we owe this pleasure?"

Kylem waved the datapad in the air. He looked serious: preoccupied and pensive.

"Come to check out some stuff about the Hanger Deck B incident, if that's okay?"

"Yes, yes, of course! Help yourself," cried Jurrish, somewhat distracted by his own project. "Don't mind me," he added.

Kylem ambled over to his station and pulled up a chair. The R & D stations were more sophisticated and had greater access than the computers in his own quarters. He hooked up the datapad and created a link between it, himself and Server. He examined the records on the datapad, retrieved the evidence and readings from Server and added to it his first-hand knowledge of the events. With the combined information from all three sources, he was able to piece together exactly what had happened.

As the Targa had approached the hanger deck, it had been cleared to land by Server. Server had taken over the guidance systems of the Targa and commenced pulling it into the bay. As far as Server was concerned everything was fine, but the Warrior at the helm had quickly determined that something was very much amiss. The Targa was not on course and the hanger bay doors had not fully opened. A collision was imminent. It had tried to sever Server's link and take the Targa back out and away from the DaerkStar but Server would have none of it. In the end, Server disconnected and shut down the Warrior, thus the Targa had continued on its course, clipping the hanger bay doors and wreaking the disaster that it had. The fault had lain wholly and undeniably with Server. It had failed to produce an accurate flight path because it had, apparently, miscalculated its own position. It had only half opened the hanger bay doors on the premise that it was supposed to be closing them, and once the devastation had been unleashed, it had failed to respond promptly with fire control systems; but why would Server make such a series of glaringly obvious and disastrous errors?

Kylem's hands moved over the data displayed before him with a speed and agility that was second nature but suddenly he stopped, realising that the information he was organising was no longer confined to the consoles. About an arm's length away from his face, the data hung in the air.

Kylem's field of vision extended for approximately 110°, about average for humanoids generally speaking, but on his visual range, the data curved gently around him and as his fingers moved over it, it reacted like a touch-sensitive screen. Indeed, he was able to pull and drag information from the consoles' monitors, up and onto his own 'monitors' at the touch of his hand. This was new. He was still evolving. It was really wicked!

"What are you doing?" asked a sharp voice from behind. Kylem suddenly realised how peculiar this must all look—him waving his arms around on invisible monitors.

191

"I'm analysing the data," he responded as though nothing were amiss and returned to his orchestration.

"But..." began Jurrish, but he wasn't sure how to finish.

"I'm utilising the analytical abilities of my Display program by overlaying them onto the data from Server and the Warriors," explained Kylem.

"That all sounds very clever, but I can't see anything."

"Of course not. You're not an android."

"But I want to see it," insisted Jurrish.

Kylem dropped his hands into his lap and swivelled the chair about to face Jurrish.

"That would require a cerebral injection of huma-nanites. I wouldn't recommend it."

"No, neither would I, so just transfer it onto the screen so I can see it," instructed Jurrish.

So, despite his heroism, despite having saved them all, he was still no more trusted than... than any other Sallow. Blood-Sallows were such distrustful creatures.

"As you wish," said Kylem and with the sweep of his hand, he threw the data back at the console. In his eyes, Kylem saw the data majestically swept up like a small tornado and sucked back into the R & D station. Jurrish merely saw the flicker as the data flashed up on the screen. He moved closer to the monitor and squinted at it.

"I can't read that! It's too small!" he exclaimed, squinting and pointing at one particular piece of information. "What's that? Magnify that bit."

Via the keyboard, Kylem clumsily enlarged the section of data. Jurrish glared harder at the image and pointed again.

"What's that? Drill down on that link."

"I'm sorry Jurrish, but it's just a screen shot. There's no link to interrogate."

"What? Why not?"

"Because that data has been created as part of my analysis process. The only way I could get it onto the console was as a visual dump. It's too complex for these stations to process in its full format."

"Don't be ridiculous. Of course they're capable!"

Kylem shook his head.

"Sorry, no. Please? Allow me to explain. For these stations to access the data they would need to multi-access across twelve levels of encryption in combinations of the binary, ternary and quaternary Boolean operators, all of which were used in the original design of Server—different Booleans being utilised at different levels of programming depending upon the level of sophistication required. It would also require access to decoding matrices for the combinations of 128-, 256-, 512- and 1024-bit data that have been utilised over the centuries."

Jurrish was listening intently to Kylem but there was a blankness in his eyes, the glazing over that one sees when someone doesn't comprehend what is being said to them. Kylem realised he'd have to take his explanation down a couple of notches.

"The DaerkStar is very, very old. It was originally designed as long as four thousand years ago and since then, it has been upgraded and enhanced. The software too has been developed over thousands of years by thousands of different Sallows and androids. It's had bits added onto it, bits disarmed, deleted and superseded. Server itself continually develops and grows. Under your guidance, it learns and evolves, and since the DaerkStar's original conception technology has also evolved. Data was once stored in 8-bit integers. This evolved into 16-bit, 16- into 32-bit, 32- into 64- and so on. The DaerkStar has various systems in 128-, 256-, 512- and 1024- bit integers, developed in conjunction with the various Booleans. Nothing is upwardly compatible and not everything is downwardly compatible, especially over the multiple levels. To compensate for this, the Booleans have various translation matrices that they need to implement, often multiple matrices at a time—"

"So how do you do it?" snapped Jurrish, eager to finish the technobabble.

Kylem scratched his head because, in truth, he didn't really have a clue. He just did it, but he knew he'd have to do better than that in his explanation to the Sallow. Perhaps he should throw him a carrot.

"It's still in its infancy, but I've been using my translation matrices to build some new routines that bridge those technological communication gaps. They're far from complete and not fully tested yet, but I believe that these macros could significantly enhance communications, not just between me and Server but also *within* Server, re-linking all the platforms and improving the DaerkStar's performance."

"So this is neither approved nor tested?"

Kylem could see the alarm in his eyes.

"Well, no—"

"Then why are you using it here? Interfacing with Server? You could be contaminating Server!"

"That would be true, if I hadn't taken precautions. As it is, whilst I have downloaded information from Server, I have uploaded nothing. The data stream has always been strictly one way for those very reasons. It's also why you can't drill down on the information. I've not only isolated this console from Server, but I've only uploaded a simple screenshot. When the console shuts down, it will purge itself completely. Strangely, Jurrish, I too am not oblivious to the recent software problems of the DaerkStar, and I have no intention of adding to them, either intentionally or inadvertently; but if any of my software developments can assist in resolving these issues, I'm sure we are all in agreement that it would be a significant victory for us all."

Jurrish sneered at Kylem. The boy always seemed to have an answer to everything.

"Dump it," he growled. "And get out of here. I don't want to see you tampering with our systems without proper authorisation again."

"I did ask!"

"DUMP IT AND GET OUT!" Jurrish bellowed.

Kylem opened his mouth to argue but thought better of it. It could after all, very well be he that was responsible for the breakdowns.

"As you wish," he said, tipping his head subserviently. He shut everything down, picked up his datapad and left.

* * * * *

As he padded down the corridors away from R & D, he considered the situation. Jurrish's manner, as well as his words, reflected both the Sallows' paranoia and their concerns about the DeathMaker's systems, some of which were not entirely misplaced. There was already a known problem in the Resonance Protection

System—DeathWatch—and he suspected that it had probably come from him. Now there were apparently a number of other anomalies in various other systems: navigation, guidance, fire control and who knew what else? Could this be DeathWatch too, and if so, what other systems had been, or would be, affected? To find out more, to get to the bottom of the mystery, he'd need access to a station like the ones in R & D and there was only one other place that had stations like those— the Bio-Labs.

That reminded him, there was something else he wanted to examine using the equipment in the Bio-Labs—the Eunaba. That blessed stone thing that felt so warm and alive to the touch and was yet so dead and inanimate. The thing that Quick had made such bizarre claims about, insisting that it was he who had told him what it was in the first place.

* * * * *

The Eunaba was where he had left it, on the workbench in his quarters. Cheerily, he swept in, picked it up, tossed it in the air and caught it deftly. Then he exited.

With the datapad in one hand and the Eunaba in the other, he began his trip to the Bio-Labs. He was about halfway there when he became aware of a most curious sensation in his hand, a little like pins-and-needles, but not. He raised his arm and looked at his fist clenched around the Eunaba. Why did his hand feel tingly? Was it the stone?

He activated Display and ran another analysis but it told him nothing new. It was still just a very ordinary looking cobblestone, smooth and speckled dark-grey like granite, but it wasn't made of stone. It felt solid despite its peculiar mass and whilst it wasn't cool in his hand, nor was it warm like an animal. So was it animal, vegetable, mineral or machine?

The Bio-Labs would soon be able to furnish him with the answers so he continued on his way, but within a few minutes, he had to stop again. His hand felt heavy and numb. Lifting his hand, he flexed his fingers open so that the Eunaba sat neatly in the palm of it, and then he folded his fingers around it once more.

He felt it again. That odd feeling of it being alive but it was stronger this time. He could almost feel it throbbing in his hand. Again, he tried to analyse it with Display but the attempt was as futile as the first and gave him nothing. So was it organic or not?

If his android senses wouldn't reveal anything of it, perhaps his humanoid ones would. He was part Moroda, a race of telepaths, so if the Eunaba was organic, as an animal he should be able to read something from it. Even if it were not sentient, he should get something, if not of its thoughts then of its needs. If it were vegetative, he should still get something. Even plants have needs. *They know which way to grow: their roots down to the moisture and their leaves up to the light'*. It was worth a shot so he pulled the Eunaba close to his chest, resting it against his breastbone, and concentrated upon it.

There was something. It had a definite presence about it. It was like... what was it like? Like a small sleeping animal cupped in the palm of his hand; one in a state of hibernation perhaps? No, that wasn't it. There was a metallic—no, not metallic— minerally, crystalline sort of feel to it. Display hadn't detected anything like that in the stone. That was odd because he could definitely sense it now. He began to crave a more scientific analysis and wondered if he could persuade Display to work in unison with his—what would he call it—gift? Then perhaps he could get a better evaluation. Very gently, he activated Display. At first it gave him nothing but as Kylem persisted he got a short, soft blast of white static and then... something else.

Slowly his 'gift' and Display aligned themselves with each other. It was rather like looking at something through an old-fashioned microscope. At first, when the slide is out of focus, there is nothing to see except a blurred whiteness but slowly, as you turn the dial, it gains in shape and definition.

Gradually the Eunaba came into focus. He could make out a crystalline structure within the Eunaba, but as to which bit of him was detecting it he couldn't say; and he could still feel an animalistic presence. He thought about the metallic-based, single-celled animals that were used to make ptarium and wondered if the Eunaba was a mineral-based life form too.

A powerful shiver ran down Kylem's spine. It was so exhilarating it made him gasp and the hairs on the back of his neck stood on end. It was stirring! The Eunaba was awakening!

Like a dozing animal disturbed out of its wintry sleep, he felt it metaphorically open one eye and look sleepily around to see what it was that had disturbed it, and then he felt it fix its gaze upon him. *Felt,* because he saw none of this. There was nothing to see. There was no form to it and no substance. It was all feeling, emotion and sensation—and what powerful ones they were!

He felt it fixate upon him and then he felt a lurch—a strong, physical, upwards jerk like when a fast lift lunges into motion. Startled, he opened his eyes, dropped the datapad and grabbed for the wall to steady himself. He didn't drop the Eunaba though.

As his stomach settled back into his belly, he felt deeply uncomfortable, not nauseous, just uncomfortable. It was like he was in the wrong place, like he shouldn't be there but that was really silly. The DeathMaker was his home and his wanderings, on this occasion, were not illicit.

Kylem decided he needed to get a grip. He physically shook himself to bring himself back to reality and made to tuck the Eunaba back into his pocket. That's when he noticed the oddest thing ever. The Eunaba had changed.

He knew it was still the Eunaba because it had never left his hand. His fingers were still wrapped tightly around it, but it was no longer a cobblestone-like artefact. Now it was as dark and black as obsidian, long, highly polished and a perfect obelisk shape. One end ran into a point with a small rounded tip, the other was cut like a diamond but with uneven facets. It was denser too. Now it had the weight of stone and lay heavy in his hand.

Voices approached. Kylem's head snapped round to investigate and a wave of unignorable foreboding swept over him. He grabbed the datapad from the floor and ducked into a side corridor. He didn't know why. He didn't understand. He just acted upon the impulses he felt and waited.

The voices grew closer. One he recognised as his father's, but the other? It sounded like a small child's voice babbling happily away, but that was even more crazy than the Eunaba thing!

Kylem resisted the urge to look around the corner. They would soon pass him by and then he would be able to see who it was. Sure enough, a few moments later Mela-14 wafted past with a small ashen-skinned boy with hair so fair that it was nearly white holding his hand. The boy was chattering away but Kylem didn't hear his words. He was too shocked by what he was seeing. He stood and watched as they entered his quarters—his quarters! He had been nowhere near his quarters a moment ago!

He watched the door shut behind them and his mind raced at the impossibility of what he was witnessing. Was he going completely mad after all?

The sound of a door opening again startled him and his heart shot into his mouth. He doubted that he was invisible so he turned and fled further down the corridor, but the sound of more footsteps forced him to a halt. Warriors were approaching. His eyes quickly scanned the corridor for somewhere to go and a wide band of black filigree on the ceiling caught his eye. The vents!

Quickly, he jumped up and pulled the panel open. He threw the datapad up into the void and heard it bounce angrily off the sides. He winced at the sound and then leapt up and hauled himself inside after it. He re-secured the grill and then he froze.

The rabble of Warriors passed by beneath him. They lined up outside the door to his quarters and waited. Mela-14 came out. The door closed behind him and they all moved off.

Kylem waited until they were all well and truly gone before he dared to even breathe. Then he scuttled along the service shafts until he was over his bathroom. Again he waited, listening. Inside it was dark and silent. Gently, he opened the grill and dropped down. He crept into his own bedroom to find exactly what he suspected he would see.

Curled up in his bed was a little boy, perhaps no more than three years old. In his arms was a small stuffed toy. He smiled. He'd forgotten about that: his nounou. A small stuffed bear-shaped thing that Mela-14 had let him have to comfort him as he slept. The one and only concession he'd ever had to childhood.

Bending down over the child, his hand reached out to touch him but he yanked it back sharply. He shouldn't wake him. He mustn't wake him. As a child, he had never been awoken in the night by a stranger so he mustn't do it now.

His eyes began to scan the room searching for further proof because he still couldn't believe the evidence so far presented to him.

The workbench was neat and tidy. Mela-14 used to make him put all his things away at the end of the day. Every work surface had to be cleared of the day's debris before he went to bed, and every night he would complain as his father made him do it gently insisting that good order was the key to an orderly mind.

He tiptoed over to the workstation and activated it. The monitor kicked silently into life. He asked for just one piece of information, the date reference. The answer flashed onto the screen and Kylem stared at it. What the hell had happened?

A murmur from the bed startled Kylem. He shrank down, poised to run, his eyes glaring at the lump under the bedclothes, but it merely snuffled and snuggled deeper underneath the covers. After a few minutes, Kylem pulled himself back up to his full height. He should get out of there whilst he could.

He deactivated the monitor, crept back into the bathroom and disappeared back into the air conditioning vent. He made his way to the nearest maintenance pit and sank down into it to think.

According to the date index, he had travelled back in time but if that were true, how had it happened? He lifted his hand. The Eunaba was still in it. What the hell was it? Was it the Eunaba that had done this? Perhaps Quick knew. Quick!

The conundrum began to dawn on him in its full complexity. Quick had said that it was he that had told him what the Eunaba was. He'd assumed that Quick was confused when he'd said that, but perhaps he wasn't. Perhaps Quick had already met him once before. Perhaps that time was now. But where was Quick? Was he free yet or was he still in the Bio-Labs? Kylem's thoughts drifted back to his search of the databanks for Quick and his mother. He remembered the curiosity surrounding the file sizes that indicated they had been tampered with, but who would do that, and why? The answers, he knew, lay in the Bio-Labs.

* * * * *

For nearly three hours, Kylem had watched his father go about his business in the Bio-Labs. It was curious watching him. He kept disappearing into a room on the bottom floor. At first Kylem had thought it was just another cell, but after a few hours of watching he realised it wasn't a cell at all; it was another lab. It had a frosted-glass front and a door concealed within it that was hinged on one side. When Mela-14 pushed the door open, the frosted-glass cleared to plain glass, but as soon as it swung shut again, the frosting crazed over. It was smart glass. The technology was elementary— electrochromic glass which, when subjected to an electrical current, changed the opacity of the glass. Simple but effective, but it also drove Kylem's curiosity to distraction. He couldn't get a good view of the room from any angle and only snatched glances into it when the door was open and the glass clear. He just had to see what was in there.

When night-mode finally fell, Mela-14 left and the Bio-Labs fell silent. They didn't seem to be as heavily occupied as they were in his day, but still he waited until everyone was, or at least seemed to be, asleep. He began to fumble with the grill and then stopped. Why risk being seen in the Bio-Labs when there should be a ventilation shaft in this other area as well? More to the point, why didn't he think of this sooner?

He wandered back and forth around the tunnels until finally he reached what he knew had to be the right area. The service shaft here was different to the ones he had explored so far. It ran along the intersection between the walls and decks so Kylem found himself looking out from the skirting board underneath a workbench of the newly found room. As before, he gently pushed the grill aside and hauled himself out and across the floor.

It was indeed another laboratory, but this one was stacked with a whole plethora of scientific equipment, monitors and tools; at least five times more equipment than he had seen in any other area of the ship. This was his father's private work area.

Gently, Kylem stood up and made a full study of the room. Around the edges, a bank of lifeless monitors corniced the ceiling at an angle of forty-five degrees. Along the walls were storage shelves stacked high with equipment. Rows of test tubes and pipettes were neatly organised in racks, and microscopes, balances, moisture extractors, ovens, incubators, centrifuges, spectrometers and biodetectors were amongst the extensive array of equipment on show. There were specimen jars containing biological samples, some of which were just organs but others complete specimens, probably foetal. Many of them seemed to be highly deformed, others just peculiar. In the far corner was a study area consisting of a semi-circular desk with a big, comfortable office chair tucked in behind it. There were two doorways: the one leading into the Bio-Labs and the other, an open doorway on the opposite wall.

Cautiously, Kylem approached and peered through it into the short corridor beyond. Four rooms led off from that, two on either side. The first cell held the remains of a dissected humanoid with his various internal organs suspended in the air, his intestines snaking aimlessly about. The second cell was empty, but the third held a familiar shape—Kyamena!

She was sleeping peacefully in her cot, battered and bruised, covered in small cuts and abrasions. Her right arm was bandaged. Kylem walked up to the forcefield that held her and leant against it as he peered in at her. Her breathing was strong and steady.

"She will not wake."

Startled, Kylem swung about to the fourth cell. It held a man that Kylem recognised even if he didn't know him. Kylem gasped in awe.

The last time he had seen this man he had been little more than a bag of bones ravaged by age, but this was before that time. Now, although still harrowed, his face was plumper and younger. He had a crown of short, white, neatly trimmed hair. Even his eyebrows, which had seemed so rampant and disorderly on his deathbed, were neatly trimmed. The Priest looked up at Kylem with pale, white eyes, the pupil just a pinprick in their orbs.

"She was injured today. She has been treated and sedated so she will not wake," and he smiled so warmly that Kylem felt sure they must be the best of friends, but he knew they weren't. He had to remind himself that, although they had met before, it was in the Priest's future and, by that time, he was already dead.

"You must hurry. She dies tonight," the Priest said.

"Sorry?" said Kylem, confused.

"Aleana—your mother. They execute her tonight."

Kylem's mind raced. He'd only just remembered her and in remembering, he'd also only just lost her but here, in this time, she wasn't dead yet. She was still alive, but not for long it seemed. She was going to die again. He didn't want to feel that loss again.

"You know you have to go."

"No, I don't."

"Yes, you do and yes, you will, otherwise the future will not be the future—and you have already seen it so you know what it will be, and thus you will follow it."

Kylem closed his eyes and tented his fingers over the bridge of his nose in thought. He was so confused.

"I don't understand this. Do you understand it?" Kylem asked.

"No."

"Then how do you know it to be so?"

"Knowing something and understanding something are two different things."

"But if you understand it—"

"—All the better," interrupted Zamus. "For with understanding comes the ability to control, not necessarily it, but the events around it perhaps, but it is not essential. I do not understand. I merely know."

There was a long pause.

"This is all just babbling riddle."

"They are only riddles because you have not unravelled them."

"And neither have you."

"But I do not need to unravel them."

"And I do?"

Zamus smiled lightly and dropped his head. Was that a nod?

"She will be terminated in one of the surgical theatres. You should go now."

But Kylem did not turn to leave.

"How do you know who I am?" he asked.

"How do you know who I am?"

"Because I've met you before," explained Kylem, "in my past."

"I know," he said softly.

"In my past, not yours," he explained. "I saw you die."

"I know," he said even more softly. "You told me that once before."

"But we've not met before."

"I've not died before."

Kylem's confusion was escalating.

"And still you cannot believe the evidence that you have uncovered," added the Priest smiling sadly, and Kylem realised that Zamus was right, because what Zamus was insinuating was that this was not *his* first meeting with Kylem. That meant they would be meeting again, in Kylem's future but further back in Zamus's past. The evidence already indicated that he had travelled back in time, and Zamus was implying that this would not be a unique occurrence for Kylem. The question was: who would be doing the travelling? Kylem or Zamus? Kylem suspected it was himself. He was the one with the Eunaba and he suspected that the Eunaba was the mode by which he had travelled. Kylem's brow wrinkled as he puzzled.

"Just believe the evidence before you," comforted Zamus.

"Is this going to get very much more complicated?" asked Kylem.

Zamus affirmed with his eyes. "More than you know."

Kylem looked deep into the man's face, looking for signs of deception but there were none to be found.

"Go," commanded Zamus.

Kylem relented. "I'll be back."

"I'll be here."

* * * * *

Kylem disappeared back into the service shafts and made his way up through the decks to the surgical theatres on the Science Deck. He still wasn't sure he wanted to go. While the thought of seeing his mother excited him, it also filled him with trepidation. The memory of her had only just returned to him but it was still faint. Seeing her would help him remember more, which was a good thing, but would the cost of that visit be in witnessing her death? Was it a price he was prepared to pay?

Then again, did she actually die? Surely if he had been here before, at her execution, he would have tried to save her. So was he here to save his mother or to watch her die? Was he here to change events that had already happened? Could he change them? Had he already changed them? He knew the logs had been amended, which suggested something more had happened but what, and who had altered them? Was it he and if he did change events, would he be changing history or making it? If he were changing it, would he know that history was changed or would his memory alter with the new timeline?

And what about the Eunaba? Quick had said that it was he that had told him what it was in the first place. When was that time? Was it now?

And so the temporal debate raged on.

Another question haunted him too. Why would the Sallows take a captive to the theatre for a mere execution? There had to be more to it, and there was only one way to get the answers. He had to go.

He knew the theatres well. Not only had he attended various biology lessons there, but he had also found himself strapped to one of the tables not so very long ago. It didn't take him long to find out which one it was either. It was the big theatre with the observation deck above. From within the safety of the ventilation shaft he found himself positioned directly over the observation deck with a full view of both the observers and the theatre below. All five blood-Sallows were present, even Emoth because, of course, he wasn't dead yet.

It drove home the last nail of reality into the coffin of confusion. Up until a few hours ago, he'd had no reason to even consider the possibility of time travel. If he had, his programming would have categorically stated that it was impossible. The evidence however, now dictated otherwise. So if his programming and the preconception that time travel was impossible was flawed, all of his other preconceptions now had to be reassessed.

His thoughts were suddenly interrupted as excitement began to bubble in the room below. The blood-Sallows were gathering around the observation window. Kylem looked down upon them and suddenly he felt panicked and nauseous. This was it; but were the events that were about to unfold pre-written and destined to happen regardless of what he did or because of what he did? He still didn't know.

Again, he asked himself, should he try to save her? What would he do with her if he did save her? Where would he take her? Where could they go? Logic dictated that if the Eunaba had brought him here, it could take him back to his own timeline, but would it still exist? If he changed things here, surely those events would have repercussions on his timeline. If they did, would the little boy now sleeping in his bed ever be able to grow up? Might he be signing his own death warrant by his intervention in this timeline? And if the little boy died in this timeline, would he still exist in his?

Kylem felt sick with the indecision, and then his heart leapt into his mouth.

Below him, a young girl was being brought into the theatre and he knew her instantly. Her dark skin, her delicate build, her long triangular face with its prominent, eccentric brow, her high cheekbones, her narrow, delicate chin and the long, straight, ebony hair that trailed over her shoulders—he knew them all. It was his mother: the woman called Aleana.

She climbed gracefully onto the bench. She made no effort to struggle and needed no assistance. Her serenity was daunting. The Scientifics strapped her down, for no apparent reason, and she gazed up into the observation deck, past the blood-Sallows and up—directly at him—with her intense, soft, deep brown eyes.

He felt her smile at him and at him alone. Only he could see it. Only he could *feel* it. It was just the way he remembered it, the way it was when he was a boy, and he couldn't move. His mind was as paralysed as his body.

"Gentlemen," he heard his father begin. "Since learning of the empathic links generated between Tatoomians and their offspring, great concern has been expressed that such a link may have been developed between ATB-80 and the surrogate. To this end, we have set up this experiment. On the monitors to my right you will see the live feed of neural and huma-nanite activity of the Espion. He is in a state of full REM which, if he is susceptible to empathic transmissions from the subject, means he will be at his most vulnerable."

"Excuse me," interrupted Doobee, "but I'm not sure I fully understand the problem here. I thought the ability to read minds was a desirable trait in a spy. Isn't that why we chose telepathic races to form part of his genetic makeup?"

"Yes and no. Telepathy is the ability to read another's thoughts. Empathy is the ability to know how they feel and, unfortunately, empathy usually goes hand in hand with sympathy. We want the Espion to know what his enemy thinks. We want him also to know how they feel so he can predict their actions, but we don't want him to be sympathetic with them."

"And why would he be?"

"Because that is a trait of the Tatoomian species."

"But she's only a surrogate. She wasn't a genetic donor."

"True, the Tatoomian was only a surrogate, to aid in the gestation and development of the foetus, but since then we have come to learn that some of the bases—the molecules in DNA that carry genetic information—have been transmitted from the surrogate to the Espion through the placenta and amniotic fluids. The question is: what effect has this had upon the child? Was an empathic link created? By terminating the surrogate in a controlled environment and monitoring the neural and huma-nanite activity of the Espion, we will be able to see if such a link exists and if so, to what extent."

"And what do you expect to see, Mela-14?"

"Hopefully, nothing."

"And if we do see something?"

"Then I fear our work is wasted and we must start again."

There was a rumble of discontent in the theatre as the blood-Sallows mumbled amongst themselves. Meanwhile, Kylem's gaze was locked by his mother's eyes and his heart was breaking because finally he knew what was to happen, what *had* to happen and what he had to do, because Mela-14 was right. There was not only a telepathic link but an empathic one too. He could feel it now and he remembered those feelings from a very long time ago. They had always been there. They were part of that warm feeling that she had imposed upon him, that had formed the substance of that wispy memory that had eluded him for so long. Her presence and well-being had once been things he had always felt, even when they were apart, until one day, they were gone and he hadn't even noticed them go. Why was that? It was because he had never felt her going; he had never felt her death. He'd been spared that... until now.

Her eyes were still fixed upon him and as he gazed back into hers, he felt a gentle tapping on the edge of his consciousness, bidding him to open the door of his mind. He knew this sensation. He'd felt it before, many times before. In a way, he dreaded opening it because he knew it would be the last time and yet, he yearned to hear her voice in his head once more, so he opened the door.

It was not a vision as such. He was not transported away to somewhere else. He was still there in the service shaft, but as the door opened there was darkness, and yet there was light. In the distance, he could see another opening, a doorway if you will, and basked in the halo of its light stood Aleana.

Between them was a rift and a bridge that spanned it, but it was like no bridge he had ever seen before. It was building itself as he watched. Threads, gossamer thin, stretched out and intertwined to form thicker threads. Like spider's silk, they glistened and glowed with a reddish hue in the darkness. These were threads formed from their thoughts, weaving themselves to bridge the void. Kylem did not look down. He did not need to. He knew there was nothing there.

They had opened their minds to each other and the link was forged. He could feel her voice echoing softly over the bridge. It was gentle and soothing, and washed over him with such warmth and adoration that he craved for it all the more, remembering how it used to make him feel. His mind stepped onto the bridge and it trembled beneath him. It was not for minds to cross, only thoughts.

Below him in the theatre, her lips had begun to move almost imperceptibly and as she spoke, the Sallows heard no words, but for Kylem they rang true and clear.

'Ptolemy.' His heart leapt at the name she had given him. The name he had forgotten.

'I have given you many stories. Remember them well for they will carry you far and wide but above all, remember your own for it will guide you on your journey,' and he remembered the story even before she retold it to him.

'As the species have evolved, they have reached deeper and deeper into the outer universes, birthing new clans, tribes and races, each differing a little to that from which it sprang. This is evolution, ever changing evolution. Even the Sallows have evolved... and then after their rise came their fall, but they did not crawl away defeated. They recounted their losses and regrouped to rise again. They have watched and noted how each race has progressed, each having a gift individual to itself, a little fire all of its own, each growing and flourishing whilst their own race has withered and died before their eyes.

'Now they desire to rebuild their race, a new race built upon the foundations of the old, a race of strength and tonicity, one forged in the fires of the tribes, one that will lead them in their cause to victory. And so they have been collecting the fires of the tribes, bringing them together to make their furnace. Now their mission is complete. Now they have their hardened sword, forged in the fires of the tribes and quenched in the blood of mankind.'

Silence fell. The story was complete. Like so many of her tales, it had been short and brief. As a child, he had found it nonsensical but now he understood its meaning. It was like a cipher, showing him that everything she had ever said had a meaning even if at first glance, he couldn't find it.

For a while, they continued to stand at either end of the bridge, motionless and in silence. He had thought she would say more but she didn't. He still had questions, so many questions he wanted answered, so he called to her but she shushed him. She was not going to tell him any more—but Kylem persisted.

Once again, he stepped onto the bridge. It shuddered and quaked under his feet. It was not strong enough to carry the full weight of his mind but urgency drove him on. He lunged forward and the bridge began to sway furiously, the threads twisting and creaking. He felt her anger rise but chose to ignore it, so desperate was he to reach the other side, but it was not to be.

Aleana lashed out with an ephemeral blade as sharp as an obsidian knife and caught the rope, severing half its strands. The bridge twisted off to one side and the remaining threads began to fray and shear. He snatched and clambered at the link.

'Stop!' he heard her thoughts cry, startling him into obedience.

'You must not steal into the minds of others,' she chastised. *'The mind is too chaotic; thoughts are disorganised upon birth. Would I steal into your mind and eavesdrop on your debates of conscience—your every thought, naked, newly-born and unedited?'*

He did not answer her. He did not need to.

'There is more truth to be found in empathy than telepathy,' she finished, and Kylem surrendered.

The bridge, though tattered and weak, held, bridging their minds by the few remaining fine and fragile threads. No words were exchanged but the echoes of their thoughts and feelings crossed its span, touching, mingling, holding. From him she drew his strength and courage and in return, she blessed him with the one thing he could never feel for himself.

It rose slowly from within him. He felt uncomfortable, unsettled. An icy finger of discomfort ran down his spine making his flesh crawl. His skin was clammy and small beads of sweat began to form on his forehead. His breath came fast and shattered. His eyes dilated. The air he breathed no longer satisfied him. He gasped deep breaths and his lips grew dry as the air rushed past into his lungs where it nearly chocked him. He felt giddy, faint and sick. His hearts pounded furiously in his chest, the beats hammering on his eardrums and inside his head. His stomach rose into his mouth and then... the sensation was gone, eradicated.

She had given him her fear, but no sooner had he recognised it than it stopped. He was designed without fear and even his mother's was not permitted.

He opened his eyes. He had not realised that he had closed them, but he had. Her gaze was still fixed upon him and the link was still there. She was troubled and he could feel it. He felt her pain, her love, her serenity and tranquillity. He felt the empathy and he knew the truth. Suddenly it all made sense: why he was here at all, why he was here now. He had to keep her mind with his. He had to ensure that the young ATB-80, asleep in his bed, didn't link with her mind. He had to be the barrier between them. He had to hold her mind, through her passing into death, to protect the boy.

Sadness filled him, dragging his whole spirit down into despair. The desolation and helplessness was suffocating. His hearts filled with pain and it felt as though it would live with him forever, and in a way he hoped it would because, in the end, it would be all that he had left of her.

Mela-14 approached the table with a syringe in his hand. He tapped the vein in her arm to make it swell and then he gently pushed the needle in.

Kylem gulped. He knew these were the last moments of her life. Through the link, he could still feel her at the far end of the slender thread that joined their minds. He felt it tremble gently as it began to weaken.

The threads twisted and broke, disintegrating silently away as the cold blackness of death enveloped her. Her limbs became cold and numbness spread through her body. The whispers of her mind grew faint as distance fell between them. Her heart slowly ceased to beat and her warm, soft brown eyes turned cold and vague and empty.

She was gone.

* * * * *

Kylem did not move. He had sat and watched with silent tears as the Sallows studied the readings on the young ATB-80. They showed that he had remained completely unaffected by the death of his mother. There was a certain amount of backslapping and congratulation at the success of the project, but Kylem felt no such joy. He felt selfish. Even though he knew he had done exactly what he was supposed to do, what he was destined to do, he felt ashamed that he had protected himself, secured his own future and let her die.

He had sat in the service shaft for hours now and his limbs were protesting. One leg was completely numb and a chronic case of pins and needles was setting into the other. He edged away from the grill and stretched himself out on his back. He was exhausted, both emotionally and physically. He fell asleep.

CHAPTER 22

Kylem was rudely awoken by something banging against his feet. He sat up to find an insistent cleaning droid beating impatiently away at his boots. Dopily, he pulled his legs up to his chest. The droid instantly took the spare ground and began ramming against his feet again. Kylem stood up as best he could, hunched up in the confined space, and awkwardly stepped over the impatient droid, but it seemed determined to plant itself under his feet regardless of where he put them. Finally, after an elaborate two-step, the droid found its path and scuttled off down the service shaft. Kylem shook his head and sank down onto his haunches. What was he supposed to do now? He was stuck in a time frame that was not his own and he still didn't understand how he'd arrived there.

He reached inside his jacket, pulled out the Eunaba and looked at it again. Of course! He had to find Quick!

But there wasn't any rush. He didn't need to be anywhere soon—not for three years or so, but where to start looking? So it was back to the Priest.

* * * * *

Kylem sat down cross-legged in front of the forcefield to Zamus's cell. He buried his head in his hands and scrubbed his face in his palms. He felt grubby. He needed a shower. He sighed deeply and he looked up at Zamus.

"I am sorry for your loss," the Priest said.

"What do I do now?"

"You know what you must do."

This was true. He knew he had to find Quick.

"Okay, but after I've found Quick, what do I do then?"

Zamus chuckled briefly.

"How can you expect to know the answer when you have yet to ask the question?"

Kylem rested his elbows on his knees and capped his hands over his eyes as if shielding them from a bright light. He looked pathetic.

"Oh, for pity's sake! Can't you just for once use a bit of plain language?"

"Poor you. My heart bleeds."

"It may yet."

"You will not be the author of my demise, and we both know that," smiled Zamus knowledgeably. "However, I shall take pity on you, just this once. You will know what needs to be done when the time comes."

Kylem sighed again. Perhaps the Priest was right. Just as he knew now that he had to find Quick, perhaps when he had done that he would know what he had to do next.

"Okay," he conceded. "Any pointers as to where I might find Quick?"

"He's exactly where he should be," and the Priest lay down on his cot to go back to sleep.

"Is that the sum total of the help I can expect from you?" demanded Kylem, but the Priest did not answer. Kylem sat for a while, staring at the supposedly sleeping Priest until it became obvious that yes, that was the sum total of help he was going to get from Zamus.

Kylem clambered to his feet and left, mumbling under his breath. He wafted through his father's private laboratory but stopped abruptly when his eyes caught sight of the computers again. In all probability, the records had yet to be amended.

Having drawn up a stool and made himself comfortable, Kylem flexed his fingers and activated the workstation to begin his interrogation of Server. He half knew what he would find but finding it still surprised him. All of the information regarding his mother was there, and it was complete. Even his predecessor's files were there—Quick, the failed Espion—the Espion that never was.

So where was Quick? Just as the Priest had said, he was exactly where he should be: in a cell in the Bio-Labs on the first floor. The cell Kyamena now occupied; the one with the dodgy lock! The Priest was right. Now he knew what had to be done. Would events always guide him as clearly as this? He doubted it. Kylem rolled his eyes. Who said that man was in charge of his own destiny? He certainly wasn't. Still, looking on the bright side, this was what he was designed to do: to go sneaking around undetected, manipulating people and situations to his own advantage. He was effectively in his element. He couldn't help but smile to himself.

To get to Quick he'd have to enter the Bio-Labs but that would immediately activate the lighting, which would wake everybody up. He needed to remain inconspicuous because whatever events he was supposed to put in place, he doubted that everybody else should know about them—except Zamus of course, who already seemed to have foreknowledge of almost everything.

He rubbed his palms together furiously, flexed his fingers again and began tapping away at the keyboard. He accessed the lighting program in the Bio-Labs and deactivated the motion sensors. Moments later, he got up and crept over to the smart glass door. He put his hand on the handle and pulled it gently. It clicked open easily and the smart glass cleared. His eyes quickly scanned the room for signs of conscious life but there were none so silently, he slipped through the door and into the Bio-Labs.

With only the subtle night-lights dotted along the walkways illuminated, it was perfect. He smiled to himself. He crossed the floor and crept up the metal stairway to the first floor, to Quick's cell. Sure enough, sleeping inside was a boy: a small, pale albino boy curled up in a blanket on a low bed.

Kylem bent down and examined the lock. There was nothing wrong with it, not yet anyway. He thought for a moment, trying to remember what Kyamena had told him about the lock, which was very little. All she had said was that it was faulty, but she was no locksmith so it had to be faulty in such a way that it was easy enough for even her to get out, yet discreet enough to escape the attention of the Sallows.

When Kylem looked up from the lock, Quick was peering back at him from beneath his blanket. Kylem smiled kindly at the boy and put his finger to his lips to shush him before turning his attention back to the door. Quick climbed silently out from under the bedclothes and came to perch on the other side of the bars, his blanket wrapped tightly around his shoulders, curious about his visitor and his interest in his lock.

After a few minutes, Kylem got up. He winked at Quick, repeated his gesture for silence and went downstairs to the atrium. There he began searching for some suitable implements to use as tools. He selected a couple of probes, a retractor and a pair of fine splinter forceps. Returning upstairs, he knelt down in front of the lock again and began working on it. It had looked simple enough but it wasn't quite as easy as he had anticipated. It required a delicate touch and a few more tools, so Kylem went back to the atrium and picked out a laser scalpel and an otoscope. With this new assembly of equipment, he returned to the lock.

The otoscope was perfect for illuminating and looking into the lock but it was difficult to hold whilst working on it. Quick though, reached through the bars and took the otoscope to hold it for him. Kylem smiled briefly in gratitude and then concentrated on the lock, nibbling away at the inside of it with the laser scalpel, the various instruments braced between his teeth until he needed them. Occasionally he would swap the laser scalpel for one of the other tools, or move Quick's hand a little. All the while Quick watched intently as Kylem worked.

It was nearly an hour before Kylem sat back. He stretched his neck to relieve the crick that had settled there, and then he checked that the door was still locked. Quick was confused as to why Kylem would be so pleased with that scenario until Kylem pushed the slender handle of the probe gently into the lock and turned it. His eyebrows bounced smugly as the deadbolt slid back effortlessly. Now the lock could be opened with something as simple as a pencil.

Having opened the door, Kylem held out his hand to Quick. Quick took it and allowed the stranger to pull him out of the cell. He watched as Kylem tidied the cell to make it look like it had always been vacant and locked it after him. Kylem slowly and quietly led Quick down the stairs and into the private laboratory. Quick paused at the door, frightened of what lay beyond but Kylem's smile encouraged him forward.

Once inside, Kylem sat Quick on the floor and opened the grill to the service shafts. Kylem sat down in front of him cross-legged and began to pull out the Eunaba but stopped, suddenly realising why it was that Quick had known about the Eunaba but not seen it. It was different now, transformed with its awakening.

"Okay, Quick, listen to me. One day I will ask you what the Eunaba is and I want you to tell me that it's the big pebble thing. Have you got that?"

Quick nodded.

"What are you going to tell me?"

"It's the big pebble thing."

"Good lad. Now listen. The Sallows aren't quite as bright as they'd like to make out, and they aren't going to miss you, but you've got to stay out of sight. Do you understand?"

Quick nodded.

"These tubes go all over the ship. You can get to the galley for food and there are hundreds of unused quarters that you can take advantage of, but you can't stay in any one place for long, you mustn't leave any mess and you have to sleep in the service shafts."

Kylem remembered the cleaning droid that had awoken him.

"Try to find somewhere where the cleaning droids have just been, otherwise they'll bother you. You'll figure it out, but never, ever leave a mess behind. Always clean up after yourself. Oh, and leave the kid alone! Got it?"

Quick looked dismayed. "What kid?" he asked.

"ATB-80. Don't go near him. Leave him alone. For the time being at least."

"Why?"

"Because he's too young to understand."

"When will he be old enough?"

"When he looks like me. Now off you go," and Kylem pointed him towards the service shaft.

"Will I ever see you again?" he asked.

"Yes, you will, but not for a long time and when you do you'll drive me batty, but don't worry about it. You'll grow on me."

Quick looked confused, which was understandable. He was talking to Quick in riddles, in much the same way that Zamus had spoken to him. It was strangely satisfying.

"Now off you go."

Quick disappeared into the tunnel and glanced back at Kylem as he reaffixed the grill back into place, and then he was gone.

One chore down, one to go.

Kylem returned to the computer and began his systematic alteration of the records. He had to remove Quick from the Bio-Lab inventory and alter the links. He couldn't remove his existence completely because he formed part of the Espion Project but he could the blur the facts enough to make him insignificant and invisible.

He remembered the altered records about Aleana. He had to amend those too— or did he? Quick wasn't connected to Aleana at all. She had been his surrogate, not Quick's. There was no reason for him to alter anything there. Logic dictated therefore, that those amendments happened later and perhaps by someone else so he left them alone.

The night was drawing to an end when Kylem finally finished his work. He satisfied himself he had done all that was needed to be done in order to set the wheels of the future in motion, but now what? He had no idea.

Weariness began to haunt him. He'd snatched some sleep earlier in the evening, in the service shaft but it wasn't enough. He felt drained so he shut down the terminals, put back all the tools that he had used and even remembered to tuck the stool back under the bench before disappearing back into the vents.

He was full of new questions. What was he supposed to do now? Could he get back to his own timeframe and if so, how? He supposed he could just hide out in the service shafts for the next three years, to re-emerge at the same point in time that he had left, but that sounded rather dull and tedious. Perhaps he needed to use the Eunaba again, but how did it work?

Taking his own advice, he found himself a maintenance pit and climbed down into it. He settled himself at the bottom of it and pulled the Eunaba out again. He held it in his hands, pulled it to his chest and concentrated his thoughts upon it, but nothing happened.

The last time he'd activated it, he'd been trying to read something of it telepathically whilst initiating Display, so he did the same thing again. Still nothing.

He tried a third time, varying the sequence a little, but still nothing—less than nothing—diddly-squat in fact. There was no warmth, no presence—nothing. Was it broken? Was it a one-time only thing or was he simply too tired?

Kylem sighed deeply. He closed his eyes to think and found sleep clawing at him, pleading with him to keep his eyes closed. Perhaps that was the problem. He tucked the Eunaba back inside his jacket, shut his eyes and went to sleep.

CHAPTER 23

Kylem awoke violently, arms flailing wildly, gasping in huge lungfuls of air. Then relief flooded through him.

He had been falling. He didn't know where from, he just knew that he was tumbling through the air, freefalling; and at the point of impact, when he was supposed to have been smashed against whatever it was he was falling towards, at just that moment he was yanked violently back into reality and awoke with a scream.

He lay covered in a cold sweat, his eyes bulging wide and wild, and his hearts pounding furiously in his chest. Heaving in deep breaths, he looked urgently about him and a mixture of relief and joy flooded through him. He was in his own room and in his own bed or at least he was on it, but everything was as it should be. The pile of crates, overflowing with books and media that he and Kyamena had rummaged from the Miscellany, were haphazardly stacked on the workbench, and the newly introduced speaker system was stood proudly by its side. Kylem began laughing hysterically with the joy of it. The dream had been so real that for a moment, he had actually believed it!

He fell back into the pillow, closed his eyes and sighed deeply. He scrubbed his sweaty face with equally sweaty palms and ran his fingers through his hair. It felt cold, damp and greasy. It was disgusting but he didn't care. He was just too happy. It had all been just one horrible dream—incredibly vivid, but just a dream.

He lay for a while longer waiting for his breathing to settle, savouring the reality. Yes, it was his room, just as he remembered it. It had all been a dream: one big, horrible, terrible nightmare.

It was time to get up. He stood and caught sight of his reflection in the mirror and frowned wearily. He looked awful, dishevelled as though he really had spent the night sleeping in a cramped service shaft. He began pulling at his crumpled clothing, trying to coax it back into some sort of order, but it refused to oblige. His hair was sticking out at all angles and grey lines were beginning to appear under his eyes.

As he stood studying his face, the door chimes began their gentle pinging. It startled Kylem and he glared guiltily at the door and then he wondered why. Nothing had happened. He'd done nothing wrong. He bade the door to open and Mela-14 entered.

The image of his father sweeping in filled him with a renewed rush of relief and joy. In his dream, he'd lost his father. He'd been faced with the prospect of spending the years alone in the vents, without his mentoring or companionship. Seeing him walk back into his life made him realise just how much his father meant to him and

210

how much he would have missed him. So much so, that he felt a compulsion to run over and throw his arms around his neck and hug him tight, but he couldn't do that so he settled for beaming him a wide, welcoming smile instead.

"Good morning, child," said Mela-14, somewhat unnerved by Kylem's overly welcoming grin. He noted Kylem's disarray.

"Is everything alright?"

"Yes," snapped Kylem, a little too quickly. "Why?" he added after a more appropriate interval.

"You missed breakfast."

"Oh. Yes. Sorry, I overslept," he explained, snatching some fresh clothes from the wardrobe and throwing them onto the bed in readiness. An uneasy feeling began to creep over Kylem like a shadow stretching out its long, dark fingers in the early dawn.

"Slept?" enquired Mela-14 softly.

"Yeah, slept," replied Kylem innocently and took refuge in the bathroom where he began vigorously brushing his teeth. As the paste foamed in his mouth, he looked in the mirror again and could see his father's point. He had a drawn look about him, the kind that only a disturbed night's sleep could give. Mela-14 joined him, standing in the doorway, staring at him. Kylem tried to ignore him, tried to act normally.

"Slept?" repeated Mela-14. "In your clothes?"

"Well, yeah," said Kylem, spitting out.

"Where?"

"On my bed. Why?" The uneasy feeling was growing.

"Well, you left R & D and then we saw nothing more of you."

"Oh," said Kylem. The uneasy feeling was getting stronger. It was a good question. He could remember leaving R & D, and then...? He couldn't remember. He had no recollection of arriving in his room that night or going to bed.

"I was just..." he began, but trailed off. He wasn't sure what to say.

"...snooping around?" Mela-14 finished for him.

"Yeah, something like that," chortled Kylem. He heard the relief in his own voice and chastised himself for it (but it was very nice of his father to answer his own question for him).

Mela-14 shook his head.

"Well, don't let Jurrish catch you. He's peeved enough at you as it is, after yesterday afternoon."

"Why?"

"R & D."

"That wasn't my fault."

"How do you make that out, child?"

"I only did what he told me to do."

"In a very smug and sanctimonious fashion as I understand it."

"What? Me?"

"Yes, you! We may well be more intelligent than they are but it is most unwise to flaunt that fact at them." Mela-14 sighed. His voice, despite its artificial tone, was strained and heavy.

"You must remember, we only exist at their indulgence. You have a very unfortunate manner about you sometimes. A manner that I do not believe is a good quality in a spy. Spies are supposed to blend in, to go unnoticed and to be invisible amongst the crowds. Making yourself prominent by being so smug and sanctimonious will not help you, here or out there—and child, before you start arguing with me..." he said, silencing Kylem before he could speak, "Mada asks if you've finished his report."

"Report?" Kylem ran his fingers through his filthy hair again and regretted it. He desperately needed a shower.

"Yes! Report! The datapad! Remember?"

"Oh, yes! That! Yes! I mean, no! I mean, nearly."

"Make your mind up. Is it yes, no or nearly?"

"Er, yes, I've compiled my data, but no, I haven't finished the report yet. Not quite. I'll finish it this morning."

"Make sure that you do," chastised Mela-14 as Kylem threw off the last of his clothes and stepped into the shower. He began to bask in the luxury of the steaming hot water pumping down upon him, cleansing his every pore.

"Where is it?" shouted Mela-14 over the noise of the shower.

"Where's what?"

"The datapad!"

Oh shit, thought Kylem. Where the hell was it?

"Oh! That! Yes. I've uhm... it's uhm... it's around here somewhere. Look, you can see I've not slept well. Let me have my shower and whatever and... well... look... just give me a chance to get myself sorted out and back on track. I'll get it sorted, I promise."

"Very well, child" said Mela-14, still somewhat concerned. He had never known Kylem to be this disorganised or unkempt. It bothered him.

"Are you sure everything is in order?"

"Yes, I'm fine! I told you. I just didn't sleep well," which was true. He felt incredibly tired despite a supposed full night's sleep; a fact that his internal chronometer strongly disputed as well as his body. He stuck his head out of the shower cubicle.

"Please?" he pleaded. "Just give me a chance to wake up properly, get showered, changed and whatever and I'll be with you. I *promise* I'll sort it all out. Yeah?"

"Very well, but do get a move on, child. We want to give you a final briefing on the Corinthian mission."

"It's on!" exclaimed Kylem excitedly.

"It was never off."

"Great!" he screeched, thrilled at the prospect of finally getting his first real mission.

"But only if you've finished that report," added Mela-14 paternally as he left the room.

Brilliant! thought Kylem. Finally, he was going to get out and do some real stuff instead of being cooped up on the DeathMaker. The only problem was where was that stupid bloody datapad? The uneasy feeling began haunting him afresh. He had no memory of putting it down anywhere other than in the dream. Adding to that the fact that in-between leaving R & D and waking up this morning, he seemed to have lost six hours—something was amiss. In the end, he had to conclude that he couldn't dismiss the dream as being just a dream. Not yet anyway. The evidence suggested that it was real so until he either proved or disproved it, it had to remain a possibility.

Disproving it should be easy because in the dream he'd left the datapad in the service shafts outside Mela-14's laboratory. So if it were still there, that would support the evidence further; but would it still be there after all this time? Did the laboratory even exist?

Cold logic kicked in, arguing again. Time travel was not possible. But what if it was? What if his internal chronometer was correct? What if the events had really taken place?

As Kylem stepped out of the shower, the quandary continued. He was dripping on the tiled floor as he grabbed for the towels and kicked the pile of discarded clothing to one side. He heard a dull clunk as they hit the skirting board. He turned to stare coldly at the pile of laundry.

In his dream, the Eunaba was in his jacket pocket. Could that be the Eunaba and if so, what did it look like?

Slowly, Kylem bent down and rummaged through the clothing to unearth the jacket. As he picked it up, it felt heavy with the weight of something in the pocket. A wave of depression began to wash over him. He sighed heavily and stood up. Without even touching it, he knew it was there. Regardless, he slipped his hand into the pocket and groaned miserably as his fingers pulled out the Eunaba—a shiny, black, obelisk-shaped Eunaba.

That settled it. He had to find the datapad. Hopefully, it was still in the service shaft, but what if it weren't? That might mean that the cleaning droids had found it and removed it. Where would they have taken it? Janitorial Supplies probably, but the service shafts were first. In the meantime, if the Eunaba was an instrument of time travel, it was probably best to put it down before it whisked him off somewhere else. Handling it like an unexploded bomb, he took it, wrapped it in a cloth and placed it at the back of a drawer in his dresser. Now to find the datapad.

* * * * *

Once more Kylem found himself crawling through the service shafts of the DaerkStar groping around in an overly confined area. He suddenly felt very guilty about having consigned Quick to a life in these shafts. Having said that, Quick seemed to have adapted well. Indeed, he moved with a stealth and agility in these corridors that Kylem positively envied.

"Oh," he exclaimed aloud as he came face to face with a dead end.

He'd thought that he was well on track towards the vent outside Mela-14's laboratory but obviously, he was wrong. So where was he? Kylem tried to look over his shoulder to get his bearings but discovered two things. First, he hadn't got a clue where he was and second, that this tunnel was very narrow indeed, so much so, that he had to settle for peering between his knees to see where he'd been. To his disappointment, no clues as to his whereabouts were evident and to make matters worse the automatic lighting in the tubes had already plunged the path from which he'd come into darkness.

His only choice was to turn around and go back, but this was easier said than done. Kylem began by trying to do a simple u-turn, but the corridor was just too narrow. He tried turning first to his left and then his right, and then he resorted to attempting a sort of roly-poly, bringing his legs up over his head but ended up wedged in the passageway. It took him as long again to get himself sorted out and he felt really stupid for having even tried to turn around like that. By the time he had finished he was still facing the wrong way. Kylem growled to himself in frustration. Time was getting away from him (how ironic was that?) and Mela-14 would be wondering were he was.

"Shit! Shit! Shit!" he mumbled under his breath and began backing up the tunnel, shuffling noisily as he went, constantly checking between his knees to see where he was going.

He had travelled so far down the tunnel when he found himself over a grill. He stopped. He didn't remember that on the way in, but maybe he just hadn't noticed it.

There was no light beneath the grill and it had a very plain, square grid pattern rather than the normal ornate affair. Kylem peered through it into the darkness beyond but he couldn't make anything out. His biosonar wasn't much help either, registering little more than a long, empty duct of some kind and his heat seekers also gave no clues. Where the hell was he?

Suddenly, there was a sharp grating sound and a quick lurch as the grill began to give way under his weight. Hastily, he started to reverse back off the grill, but it was too late. With gritted teeth, Kylem was plunged head first down the shaft. He managed to suppress the impulse to scream but was painfully aware of the noise he was making as he smashed against the sides of the tunnel as he travelled. It was more than sufficient to wake the dead, let alone alert the Warriors as to his foray into the service shafts. He tried to slow his fall by bracing his hands and knees against the walls, but they slid over the smooth, clean surfaces achieving only some prize friction burns for his efforts. Suddenly, Kylem could see a pinprick of light ahead of him. Slowly it grew larger and larger. The exit was getting closer. Question was, exit to where?

Kylem could see that it was crosshatched, just like the one through which he had already fallen. He smacked into it with the speed and force of a charging Corvaenian bull and it offered no resistance to him. He smashed through it and blinding white light filled his vision.

* * * * *

Mela-14 was looking for Rathan.

Rathan was by far, the oddest of all the blood-Sallows but also the one to whom Mela-14 could best relate. It was he that had conceived the Espion Project and brought its development to fruition, but his addiction to Agaratax had led Emoth to place Jurrish at the head of the project instead. Yet still it was Rathan that drove it continually forward, liaising between the blood-Sallows, negotiating for the necessary materials and pushing the development of the technology for the blending of organic and machine matter. He was the most intelligent and able-minded being well versed in all of the sciences, and he had the most inquisitive mind.

At this moment in time, he was in Weapons Storage. After the fiasco on the Hanger Deck, Rathan had decided to move all the missiles and weapons into this especially designed facility with its extra bulkheads and additional shielding. He had consulted Mada about it, who had done little more than nonchalantly shrug his shoulders at his resident junkie whom he knew would do just as he pleased, with or without his blessing. So it was that Rathan was orchestrating the manoeuvres.

Weapons Storage was slowly being filled with arms, not just missiles for the aircraft but also land assault and hand weapons. Rathan was documenting what was being placed where and ensuring that incompatible devices were suitably segregated. As Mela-14 entered, he glanced up from his datapad.

"I take it you found him?" he said.

"Yes, indeed. He overslept."

"Curious. I wouldn't have thought that...", but his words trailed off at an odd banging sound from somewhere in the distance. It was a hollow, metallic sound like someone bashing on the inside of an empty oil drum, and as it grew closer, it grew louder. The Sallow and the android looked up curiously towards the source of the noise, a grill in the ceiling high above their heads. Even the Warriors stopped in their tasks to look up.

Mela-14 and Rathan briefly glanced at each other and then took a couple of steps closer to the grill as the sound resonated more and more. Suddenly the grill burst free and Kylem exploded through. He dropped down, plunging into the pile of weapons crates beneath him. They burst open sending splintered bits of casing and unspent bullets ricocheting into the air. Mela-14 urgently pulled Rathan back and threw himself in front of the blood to shield him from the debris. Fortunately, nothing exploded and silence fell as the chaos came to a quick end.

Amongst the shattered crates, the battered, beaten and dishevelled figure of Kylem lay motionless. Rathan and Mela-14 stepped forward and gawked in disbelief at the body of the young boy.

"Oh, for goodness sake," sighed Mela-14 as slowly Kylem began to stir. He rose shakily to his feet. Bits of broken crate skidded away from him as he rose and stumbled. The boy gazed around him, dazed, confused and disorientated by his trip, and then his eyes came to focus on Rathan and his father.

They glared at him in disbelief, and only the creaking of the battered metal grill above, gently swinging upon its one remaining fixing, could be heard.

"Oh, shit," said Kylem.

The creaking stopped. Rathan looked up. The grill had broken free from its last fixing and began its silent descent. He opened his mouth to say something and pointed upwards, but it was too late. The grill dropped down and struck Kylem on the head. He crumpled under the blow and Rathan winced, shrinking behind Mela-14 in sympathetic pain.

"I bet that hurt," he said.

"Hurt?" exclaimed Mela-14. "He could be dead!"

"Don't be ridiculous!" blurted Rathan. "He's got a ptarium reinforced skull. It'll take a lot more than that to crack it... but I bet he'll have one hell of a headache when he wakes up!"

CHAPTER 24

As Kylem began to regain consciousness, it became evident that Rathan was right. There was a thumping going on inside his head that a ten-piece steel band would have been proud of. Kylem raised a hand to his pounding temples only to have it dashed impatiently away.

"Keep still," snapped his father.

Kylem scowled but did not try again. His head hurt too much to argue so he lay on his side on the hard, flat surface and waited for his senses to fully return.

After a while, he opened his eyes, curious to see where he was but found that Rathan was sat before him, arms crossed over his pigeon-chest and obscuring his view. Kylem was surprised to find that there was no anger in his eyes, only amusement. Rathan even winked cheekily at him. Kylem smiled naughtily back and turned his head to look up at his father but was rewarded by the android slamming his head back down onto the bench, smacking it against the cold metal.

"Ow!" squealed Kylem in mock pain.

"I said, keep still!" he barked. "I can't stitch this properly if you won't keep still."

Evidently, Mela-14 was not as forgiving so Kylem surrendered and lay patiently while his father tended his wound. From his viewpoint, he could see very little other than Rathan and glimpses of his father's bloody, white hands wielding the long silver needle and thread. There was a small trolley to one side with two stainless steel bowls on it: a small kidney-shaped one and a larger round one. Kylem still wasn't sure where he was.

"What were you thinking?" Mela-14 suddenly demanded crossly. "What were you doing in the service shafts? What could possibly be of interest in there?" but Kylem didn't have time to answer.

"It's in his nature," Rathan explained resolutely. He stood up, approached the bench and bent down so that his eyes were level with Kylem's. He looked deeply into them and Kylem wondered what colour his eyes were and if the Sallow could see it.

"It's what he does. It's what he's designed to do. He has too much time on his hands and he's hungry for action. He's driven by what he is, driven by his impulses. Makes you a bit of a bloody nuisance though, doesn't it?" Rathan straightened up.

"We'll just have to find you something to do, then," and he turned back to Mela-14. "I'll go and talk to Mada and smooth things over. In the meantime, when you've fixed him up, lock him up for goodness sake before he does something really stupid."

Mela-14 nodded in affirmation as he finished tying off the last stitch. He threw his implements into the kidney bowl and began to wash his bloody hands in the round one. Kylem sat up and watched as the water swirled with red streaks before settling into an even, rosy hue. His father dried his hands angrily on a small towel and glared at him. Kylem avoided his gaze and looked about.

He was in the Bio-Labs, in one of the cells on the bottom floor although the forcefield wasn't activated. Ahead of him was the atrium with the science station in the middle and beyond that, the doorway to Mela-14's private laboratory and office. Looking up, he could see that he had a caged audience. Kyamena was amongst them.

"Why am I here?" he asked.

"It was the easiest and nearest place to get you to that had medical facilities," which was true, but he and Rathan had also chosen to bring Kylem here in an attempt to contain the situation. The Espion Project was spiralling out of control due to the antics of an adolescent teenager. If they wanted to save the project, they would have to justify Kylem's actions, explain them as part of his development and persuade the Sallow council that these were minor incidents. 'Damage control' was the phrase that had come to mind.

"What were you doing?" he asked Kylem again, but Kylem said nothing. "I asked you a question!" snapped Mela-14 angrily.

"I know. I was just thinking of my answer."

"The truth requires no thought."

Kylem looked up at his father, shame-faced. Mela-14 was stood before him, arms crossed.

"I was..." he began weakly. "I was looking for the datapad," he finally confessed.

"The datapad?"

Kylem opened his mouth to speak but shut it again. He'd been about to make some smart-arse comment but perhaps he should be a little more humble, and then he thought again. Why should he be humble? It was not in his nature to behave like a chastised child and he wasn't a child anymore.

Kylem pulled his legs up onto the treatment table and sat cross-legged, his hands hanging limply over his knees and his head cocked to one side. Mela-14 noted the change in Kylem's stance: the mischievous look, the look of defiance in his eyes and something else—yes, that dreadful smugness again. Mela-14 didn't doubt that one day it would be the undoing of Kylem.

"Rathan is right. You do need something to do. So where's Mada's report?"

"Huh..."

"You haven't done it, have you?"

"No."

"Why not?"

"I told you. I've mislaid the pad."

"You didn't tell me that."

"Yes, I did. I told you I was looking for it. The only reason I would be looking for it is if I had misplaced it."

"So where did you lose it?"

"If I knew that, it wouldn't be lost." He grinned sarcastically at his father.

A backhander caught him squarely on the jaw, throwing him head over heels off the bench and onto the floor. Kylem had not anticipated the blow.

Dazed, he began to rise but in that small instant, Mela-14 stepped around the bench and grabbed his child by the lapels. Kylem was still marvelling at his father's speed and stealth as he was picked up and thrown rudely back onto the bench. One hand closed around his throat and Mela-14's strong, white android fingers embedded themselves around his trachea. Kylem caught just one breath before his air supply was cut off. His mouth opened, gasping and silently screaming. He felt the crushing fingers at his throat, the choking sensation and abstract pain. His arms flailed and he punched at his assailant. He didn't know if the blows hit home but if they did, they had no effect.

Blackness began to engulf him. His strength was draining. He clawed helplessly at Mela-14's hands as numbness swallowed him. Mela-14 pushed his static white face into Kylem's and even though consciousness was seeping away from him, Kylem willed his eyes to stay open, to glare defiantly at Mela-14, but oblivion was prevailing. He couldn't feel his limbs anymore and his eyes were beginning to roll.

Suddenly Mela-14 released his grip. Kylem caught a quick, sharp intake of breath. The blackness dissipated instantly but no sooner had it than Mela-14's fingers closed again. Blackness began swamping his vision once more, but there was no flailing around this time. At least, he didn't think so. All he could feel was the intense pain of his trachea being crushed and the blackness swallowing him again, then relief as Mela-14 permitted him another breath. Again consciousness returned, but only for a few moments as, for a third time, Mela-14's vice like grip tightened about his throat.

"You should know, I can do this all day," he said as his fingers tightened all the more, but this time they did not release and the darkness came and engulfed Kylem.

* * * * *

This time when Kylem came to, he was sprawled haphazardly across the bench just as his father had abandoned him after he'd passed out. His limbs and head hung limply over the sides of the table.

With jagged movements, his hand searched out his bruised and battered throat. He stroked his Adam's apple to soothe it and cautiously, slowly, he sat up.

Mela-14 was stood opposite him. He did not look happy.

"I have told you before that we live by the whim of our masters."

The word 'masters' jarred at Kylem.

"And you above all, live by their whim and mine. You have caused far too many problems for me of late and whilst I would rather not terminate you, if you insist on pursuing this path, I will do so and trust me, there will be no repercussions for it. Now, where is the datapad?"

Kylem opened his mouth to speak but pain clawed his throat. He winced and Mela-14 handed him a small beaker of water from the trolley. Kylem took it unsteadily and the water slopped over the sides as he sipped at it.

As he drank, he was working out what to tell his father. If he admitted that the datapad was in the service shaft, what trouble might it cause for Quick? Would the Sallows start inspecting the hidden labyrinth of tunnels? Probably not. They had no reason to suspect they might have a fugitive hiding there.

"In the service shaft," he whispered.

"In the service shaft? What service shaft? Where?"

Reluctantly, Kylem pointed towards his father's lab. Mela-14 tipped his head.

218

"Go and get it," he instructed.

Kylem slipped off the bench. He didn't want to indulge his father but he'd pushed him to his limits. For now, it would be more prudent to comply—but what if the datapad wasn't there?

As Kylem crossed the atrium, he couldn't help but look up. He had an audience and amongst them, Kyamena looked particularly concerned.

He reached the smart glass door to Mela-14's lab, pushed it open and headed straight for the workbench under which the vent lay. Mela-14 watched curiously as Kylem dived underneath it, obviously familiar with the layout of this room. He ripped the grill away and disappeared halfway into the shaft.

Relief flooded through Kylem. Miraculously, the datapad was still there. When he'd put it down, it had slipped so neatly between two ridges that it looked like it belonged there. The maintenance droids had passed it by for all those years. It was a huge relief in one respect but it also confirmed that the dream had not been a dream at all. Everything had really happened—Zamus, Quick, Aleana. It was all true.

Kylem picked up the pad and re-emerged from the shaft. He passed it to Mela-14 whilst he re-secured the grill.

"It's completely dead!" exclaimed Mela-14.

Well, it would be, thought Kylem, considering how long it's been there.

"Discharged, that's all."

"How on earth did you manage that?"

"Got a little bit too close to a nemarian magnetic field," lied Kylem.

"You'd better hard wire it then," said Mela-14, thrusting the pad back at Kylem. Kylem took it and studied it whilst his father pulled two stools up to the workbench. He settled himself on one and signalled Kylem to take the other. Kylem obeyed and turned his attention to the project at hand. He connected the datapad to the power grid and it booted with ease, much to his relief. As he began tapping away at the keyboard, he debated making a direct data link to the pad but thought better of it. Under the circumstances, he should stick to the more mundane method of the keyboard.

Kylem really didn't have that much more to add to the report. Anything he knew he had resolved to keep to himself, so he merely confirmed what had already been reported, added a few minor facts and finished it with a final flurry of key presses. He removed his hands from the keyboard, ceremoniously placing them upon his thighs and looked up at Mela-14.

"Done."

His father directed him back into the Bio-Labs and the cell in which he had been treated for his injuries. Kylem walked over to the treatment table but turned sharply as he heard the sharp buzz of the forcefield being activated.

"Oh, come on!" cried Kylem, his mouth open in disbelief. "That's hardly fair!"

"Fair doesn't come into it. As Rathan said, you are becoming a bloody nuisance and I need to keep you out of harm's way. A little bit of time behind bars might remind you that your freedom is a privilege and not a right."

Kylem was still whinging as Mela-14 left the Bio-Labs. The door shut behind him and Kylem's eyes narrowed in anger, but it soon passed. He knew he deserved everything he'd got so far. He sighed heavily and tapped at the forcefield, inspecting it. It buzzed angrily at his touch and repelled his hand as gently as two magnets with like poles. His face twisted in annoyance and he looked up at his audience.

"Trust me, this is only temporary," he reassured them awkwardly.

"We're all only temporary," replied Kyamena.

"Some of us more temporary than others," added Byron.

Kylem's eyes passed from one resident to the next, registering all that he could about them. Many of the faces were black-skinned; these were the skunks: the Sallow hybrids that Mela-14 and Mada were working on in the 'purification' of the Sallow race.

"What are you looking at?" snarled one of them. She was of medium height and slim build with glossy, black skin—not brown like a Negro, but pitch-black like tar and cracked like dried mud. She was very much like Byron in appearance: skunk yet distinctly humanoid, especially her eyes which Kylem focused upon. The irises were as black as her pupils and gave her a wonderful wide-eyed look. She was incredibly attractive despite the hatred that emanated from her.

"Living onyx beauty," he remarked.

She gave him two fingers and he laughed.

"Oh, my god!" exclaimed a voice. "Is he hitting on Desire?"

"Shut it, goyeme!" Desire barked.

"Shut it yourself, skunk!" the voice shouted back.

"You'll have to forgive Desire," cried a third. "You are the harbinger of all her misfortunes as far as she is concerned. Her hatred of the Sallows runs as deep and as pure as her hatred of you."

"Let's be fair," added Byron. "My sister hates anything that is not skunk."

"But me in particular, it seems," remarked Kylem.

"You are a Sallow," she spat.

"I am a skunk."

"You are not worthy to be called a skunk. You are impure."

My god, thought Kylem, she sounds just like a Sallow.

"You are the Destroyer Series, Mark-1 (Espion). You are a Sallow, living amongst Sallows," and if she didn't actually spit, she might just as well have done. It seemed that the Sallows had fulfilled one of their requirements and instilled deep contempt for other races into the subject known as Desire. He wondered if that was nature or nurture.

"You are here because of the Sallows' desire to rebuild their race, not because of me," protested Kylem. "In that respect we are all part of the same experiment."

"Then why do you live amongst the Sallows?" she asked coldly.

It was a good question but they all knew the answer. Everybody was aware of his dual purpose, as a skunk and as an android, and that it was this that gave him his privileges. Yet, something kept gnawing at Kylem.

These people were allegedly the future of the Sallow race and looking around him, they were so much more Sallow than he. Surely as the forebears of the new Sallow race, they should be the ones living amongst the Sallows, not him? He was only a new generation of android. One day he would be serving these people. Well, not *these* people, rather their descendants, but at what point would the skunks be allowed to walk amongst the Sallows as their equals, he wondered.

"Is he always such an idiot?" Byron asked Kyamena.

"Yes," she sighed. "But it's not his fault. He's just a kid."

Kylem was about to protest when Byron replied, saying something that made Kylem pause. He said, "Aren't we all, so what's his particular excuse?"

"But Byron, he doesn't understand. He wasn't born and bred with us. He doesn't really know what happens here and he knows nothing of us as people. He knows so little."

"Excuse me, but I am here you know!" piped up Kylem.

"Well, he *should* know!" exclaimed Byron, ignoring Kylem. "He should make it his business to know. If he's not a Sallow, he should know."

"Then tell him," said Kyamena.

"What?"

"Tell him, Byron. He's not going anywhere. This is your moment. Tell him. You say he isn't one of us, but he is. He's a blood, like us. He's not a Sallow. He's a skunk and as impure as we are."

"He's an android!" reminded Desire.

"He's only part android," argued Kyamena. "He's also part blood."

"That doesn't mean anything!"

"It does. He spared my life because he has a heart, and I don't just mean the ones beating in his chest. He feels things. He feels sadness. He feels pain and he feels joy. Just like you and I do."

"So what are you saying, Kyamena?"

"I'm saying, talk to him. Tell him your stories. He'll listen."

"Why would he?"

"Because he's as bored as you and I."

"And what will it achieve?"

"Maybe nothing more than a break from the tedium but who knows?"

Byron looked sceptically down at the spoilt Sallow brat that was looking back at him.

"Can't be bothered," said Byron, turning away.

Kylem leapt in.

"You tell me your story and I'll tell you one!" he shouted. There was a tone of desperation in his voice that caught Byron's attention. Was Kyamena right perhaps?

"What story? We know your story."

"I carry hundreds of stories."

There was a rumbling in the Bio-Labs as everybody seemed to come to life.

"No, you don't," mocked Byron.

"Yes, I do."

"No, you don't," repeated Byron.

"I think he does," interjected Kyamena. "Remember who his mother was."

"He doesn't remember his mother."

"I remember Aleana," Kylem said, and the room hushed at the mention of her name.

"Come on then," demanded an impatient new voice from the darkness. "Tell us a story."

Kylem did not respond. He was wondering which tale to tell them.

"Come on, Kylem," prompted Kyamena. "You'll get nothing from them now, not until you've told them a story."

"Will they listen?"

"Of course we will. Even poor entertainment is better than no entertainment. You have music, computers, books and videos to keep you amused, but what the hell have we got? Nothing. So come on, big shot. Tell us a story. You know how to do that. Just start at the beginning and move forwards!" she teased.

Kylem thought for a moment, and then he sank cross-legged to the floor with his usual little pirouette and began—just as his mother had taught him.

In the beginning, there was nothing, but GOD. GOD was alone and idle. Then GOD said "Let there be Lite!" and thus GOD created the Lite and the Daerk, and so came the dawn of the first day, and in the dawn GOD saw the nothingness that was there and said, "Let there be a vault between the land and the sky," and so it was that a vault was made which separated the land from the sky, and GOD saw that it was good. So evening came and morning came, the second day.

And the land was without feature and barren. Thus GOD said, "Let mountains rise up so that the waters are gathered into one place and that dry land appears. Let the earth produce plants bearing seed and trees bearing fruit. Let the seas and skies and land teem with countless life," and so it was that the seas filled with all the living creatures that live within it and the skies were filled with all the faunae that fly and the land was filled with mammals and reptiles and all the things that walk upon the land. GOD saw that it was good and blessed all those things saying, "Be fruitful and increase". Evening came and morning came, the third day.

GOD said "Let the land bring forth Joman to tend the land and all its bounty," so GOD created Joman in all its sexes and GOD blessed them saying "Be fruitful and multiply". Evening came and morning came, a fourth day, and upon this day GOD's work was complete, and so GOD rested whilst Joman tended the land and all its bounty.

Joman ploughed the land and planted seed, watered the crops and fed the herds. Joman built shelter and harvested the crops of fruit and grain, and when all this work was done, Joman celebrated his creation. He took grapes from the vines and made wine. All of Joman came together to rejoice, to eat and drink and celebrate his making, but the wine was strong, and in his drunken state, his lust became perverted. Joman lay with beasts and reptiles and slew his neighbour. And GOD looked down and saw Joman, and GOD saw that it was not good.

GOD was sickened and angry and wept at the coming of sin. GOD cried out so loud, the land shook and thunder boomed across the skies and echoed through the land, deep into the earth. The winds rose and swept across the seas, catching them into great waves that broke over the cliffs that had imprisoned them. Lightning cracked the skies above and fell to earth where it burst into hungry flames that devoured the trees and the beasts and all that lay within its grasp. The land split and cracked and swallowed the fertile lands.

Finally, when all lay razed to the ground and GOD's anger had quelled, silence fell all about. GOD looked at ITS creation with great pain in ITS heart—the earth that IT had broken into great pieces, that had been hurled across the skies, the beasts and the birds cowering amongst the debris, and all Joman was dead. Only the impure offspring remained, spread across the many worlds, but they were too young and naïve to tend their new lands, so GOD called Lite and Daerk together and said "Take this that I have made and do with it what you will" and so it is that Lite and Daerk rule us all."

Silence held the room for a few moments after Kylem had finished his tale.

"I've heard that one before!" exclaimed a voice with deep indignation.

"Me too, but the world was created in seven days, not four."

"Nine!" exclaimed a third.

"Actually, you're all wrong. It's the story of creation from Barbania's Caoic monks, and it was twelve days and there was no light and dark stuff."

"Sounds more like the Hankarai Legend of the Beginning to me."

And so the debate raged on, and Kylem was happy to listen to it, intrigued, not just that one tale should appear in so many different cultures, but that such an animated discussion was taking place. Conversation was obviously a major pastime here and the civility of the debate was astonishing. These people showed more intelligence and imagination than any Sallow.

"So where does the tale come from?" Byron finally asked.

Kylem looked up.

"Oh! I don't know exactly. I think it comes from many places."

"That's stupid. That particular version must come from just one place."

"Oh, I dunno," said a new voice. It was a man's voice. "Remember that fairy tale I told you about Little Red Riding Hood? Well, in some versions, the wolf kills the grandmother and eats her. In others, the wolf stuffs her into a wardrobe, and in yet another, he swallows her whole and the woodcutter has to cut her free from the wolf's belly. That story comes from just one planet, yet it has many variations."

"It's also very similar to a tale we are told as children, as a warning to stay out of the woods where wild animals preyed," and so the debate continued.

After a while, Kyamena looked down at Kylem and spoke.

"You're very quiet. No questions?"

"No, I'm learning enough as it is."

"Precisely," spat Desire. "And that's why we shouldn't be talking to him! He needs to understand us better so he can destroy us. This whole charade has probably been orchestrated just so we'll talk to him, so that he can learn from us. He's a spy, remember. We are nothing to him. He doesn't care about any of us. We are all the same to him. Just things. None of us are special to him, not even you, Kyamena!"

"That's not true!" interrupted Kylem defensively. "Each of us brings something to this existence that no other can bring. Each of us is unique, each of us special. Each of us has to be exactly what we are, to be unique, and so that makes each of us perfect!"

He wasn't quite sure where that came from but he knew it to be true.

"On that basis, psychopaths and murderers are perfect!"

Kylem thought about it.

"It is our imperfections that make us unique," he replied more quietly. "It is our uniqueness that makes us perfect. Thus it is—"

"—that our imperfections make us perfect," finished the Tarrow-Man.

"Yes," replied Kylem.

The captives fell quiet for a long time. Finally, it was Byron that spoke.

"Okay, I'm not sure I understood that, Harrish."

The Tarrow-Man stood up and spoke.

"He's quoting ancient Tarrow philosophy. You're very learned in our ways, aren't you?"

"Maybe I am, but knowing what swimming is doesn't mean you can swim," said Kylem.

Kyamena laughed.

"What?" questioned Harrish, not sure what was so amusing.

"He's quoting me, Harrish."

"So whose turn is it next?" asked Kylem. "Come on. Tell me your stories and I'll tell you another of mine."

And so, ignoring Desire, they did.

* * * * *

"The Sallows desire a new Warrior: one of strength and cunnin; a sword forged in the fires of the tribes and quenched in the blood of mankind."

The captives were not just good debaters, they were good listeners too. They had learnt a lot from their time in the Bio-Labs, by listening to each other and to the Sallows' conversations, and were happy to share.

The Sallows had designed and built the first of their new caste of androids—the Destroyer series, Mark-1 (Espion)—as just that, a new series of android. He had been designed with the heart and spirit of a Sallow as well as the strength and physique of the ancients, but he was humanoid in appearance to blend in with the enemy. Interestingly, the former traits were those that the Sallows had failed to build into the skunks. The current Sallow DNA, he was told, was too badly mutated, but the Espion had successfully incorporated those features, so now the skunks were being developed as the 'wrapping paper'. One day the Sallows would blend the two together—the colouring and build of a skunk with the heart of the Espion—to forge their new Sallow race. That was the new directive of the Regenesis Project.

Byron was a skunk, like Desire. In fact, they were twins, and of all the skunks aboard the DeathMaker, Byron and Desire were amongst the most successful so far. They were strong, healthy specimens; genetically stable examples in which the dominant genes were desirable ones. They were as much a part of the foundations for the new Sallow race as Kylem, but they were still far from complete. Their faces were humanoid in shape and their skin, although glossy and black, was still cracked rather than crocodilian as was the skin of the ancients. Their eyes also were imperfect. They were black, not red, and so the experimentation and sampling continued.

The skunks had their DNA extracted, examined, spliced and reintroduced into the next generation of skunk, time after time after time. But not over generations of years, because each and every one of them had also undergone the same accelerated growth process as Kylem. The blood-Sallows could not afford to wait for each generation to grow up naturally before experimentation could begin again.

Byron and Desire were only five years old and were amongst the eldest of the skunks who rarely survived beyond six years. By then they had outlived their usefulness and were terminated. Kylem marvelled at their maturity. They seemed to have handled the accelerated growth process so much better than he had.

As the evening wore on, they exchanged more information about each other. Kylem asked questions and shared information about himself, although what he told them was guarded. They had much in common but they were still very different and supposedly on opposing sides.

"Our mental well-being is of no concern to the Sallows," explained Byron. "They are perfecting bodies, not minds."

224

Kylem debated this. The mind was affected by the physical structure of the brain and its chemical balances so surely the mind must have some bearing on the issue. Similarly, if he were empathic perhaps some of the skunks were too. In which case, any mental trauma they experienced was relevant and could have an impact. It could be passed from generation to generation, just like the Moroda but, apparently, the blood-Sallows didn't think like that. They were too busy concentrating on what they could see, and with the constant problems brought about by genetic fading and interbreeding, the mental aspects paled into irrelevance. They were constantly re-establishing genes, eliminating undesirable ones and forcing submissive genes into dominance. That's why Byron and Desire were so important. They were at a plateau of stability to which they could return to time and time again, if and when a gene mix failed; and with sampling DNA from so many other races like the Gna, Tarrow-Men, Terrans and so on, failures were inevitable.

The 'rainbow-man' that Kylem had met on his last visit to the Bio-Labs, was called Kerridge and he was Gna. The cerebral hemisphere of the Gna brain was divided into five parts with an enlarged cerebellum. Exactly what each bit did was still under investigation, hence the exposed brain matter and electrodes embedded in Kerridge's skull.

Samuel James was a Terran, born and bred. Upon the death of Zamus, he had become the oldest person in the Bio-Labs, and his story was one of the most unique. He called himself a 'businessman', but it turned out that he was a mercenary and an assassin on his homeworld.

For centuries, a minority of people on his world had made claims of UFOs coming to visit, telling incredible stories of abductions and so on, all of which were regularly dismissed as the rantings of the insane. Samuel had also dismissed them until one day he had the dubious honour bestowed upon himself. Unfortunately for him though, his captors were Maganie who in turn, became the captives of the Sallows. The Maganie were soon despatched, being of no interest to the Sallows at all, but Samuel James, he was different. He was of an unknown species and they were enamoured with his history and his ruthlessness. That was why he had been chosen as one of the fathers of the Espion. This doubly intrigued Kylem. While Samuel was indeed a fit, healthy man, the attributes for which he had been chosen were his personal characteristics, and yet these were ignored in the skunks. Where was the logic in that?

The reptilian, called Harrish, was a Tarrow-Man and a warrior who had fought in the battles against the Sallows.

In the cell neighbouring him was Eeena who was also of reptilian descent. She spoke with a voice that rattled like a rattlesnake and her sharp, yellow eyes darted and flashed erratically. Eeena was of the Kilanarika, a strange race of stealthy reptilians who furiously denied all connections to the Tarrow-Man race. She was only half the height of Harrish but incredibly slender with long limbs that gave her a false impression of tallness. Her dappled, scaly flesh was soft and warm to the touch, despite its harsh appearance, or so Harrish told him. Her race was a peace-loving nation of thinkers but they did not boast any great feats of master intelligence. They were an ordinary people who had led ordinary, mundane lives on a range of insignificant outposts on the edges of Sallow territory.

When he was introduced to Tara, he knew instantly where she was from. She was also very slightly built but speckled like a sparrow. She was humanoid but where hair would have covered her head, feathers grew: soft, downy feathers that swept over her scalp and down her back between the two lumps just below her shoulder blades where her wings had once been. Kylem's heart went out to her. He had flown as a Glyder in a dream and that dream had been so vivid that he knew the pleasures of the air. Once upon a time, like him, this creature had flown and soared high up in the skies. Now she was reduced to this sad existence in captivity, the symbol of her race cut away from her so that she could never feel those winds under her wings again.

"They were too big," she told him. "They amputated them because they were too big. I promised I wouldn't flap them. I promised I would keep them folded but they cut them off anyway. They said I'd never need them again."

Tara had then curled herself up into a ball and begun to sob. In that moment, Kylem would have done almost anything to have been able to give her back her wings, to have gone back in time and stopped it. He thought of the Eunaba, and then he remembered Aleana and realised there were some things that he couldn't change, some things he shouldn't change. For without Tara crying in her cage, he would never have felt these feelings or thought these thoughts. Everything that had happened had made him who he was—assuming that this was his destiny of course.

He began to wonder how he would know when to act and when not to act; when he was supposed to be a part of history and when he was supposed to stand back and let things run their course. Okay, that assumed that there was such a thing as destiny—, which there must be because if he had not gone back in time and acted as the buffer between Aleana and his younger self, he would not have lived long enough to be there to do it. He was destined to be there, at that moment in time, to do what he did. If it had happened any other way, it simply would not have worked out.

Overall, the subjects in the Bio-Labs were well treated. Mela-14 had realised that to get the best out of his subjects they should be healthy. Each person had a clean cell and cot to sleep in, warm bedding, food and water. It wasn't gourmet cuisine but it was nourishing. Generally speaking, there was little pain. Kerridge complained of headaches which wasn't surprising, but even those chosen for dissection or invasive experimentation were usually anaesthetised before the procedures began. As Kylem knew from experience, bodies that writhed, squirmed and screamed in pain made observation difficult. He thought about the synaptic dislocation unit of which he too had once been a victim, and he thought about the dissection he had seen in Mela-14's laboratory when he had travelled back into the past. What trauma must it be, to watch your innards being removed from your body and suspended in mid-air above you, knowing you would never be put back together again? To know you were going to die and all purely to sate the curiosity of a Sallow. A painless death perhaps, but only physically so.

Then he met Fatia.

"You're Mada's favour," he said.

"Yes, that's right," she replied. He looked at her suspiciously. She was a skunk too but her skin was like the ancients, dappled like tanned crocodile skin: deep black with a slight dark brown mottling. It was very beautiful skin.

"So how come you trust her?" asked Kylem of Byron. Byron huffed in dismay. "Seriously, if she shares Mada's bed, how can you trust her?"

"Sharing his bed is not the same thing as sharing his heart," explained Byron.

"And when Mada tires of me—and he will—I will die. I have outlived my usefulness as a sample."

"Oh," said Kylem. It seemed so harsh.

"Just as when they tire of you, they will execute you, put your body in stasis and extract whatever they need from your remains, as and when."

Kylem looked at her in disbelief. Was what she was saying true? He could not sense any deception in her. His eyes sought the security of Kyamena's face.

"And why are you here?" he asked her.

"I am only here at your whim now." Her face was cold and resolute. "My original function is obsolete. As soon as I cease to amuse you, I too will die." Her voice was sad and serious.

"Good job you're so amusing," Kylem said lightly, trying to lift her mood. He failed miserably.

"So when you cease to amuse the Sallows, with your death comes mine."

The cold, hard weight of responsibility came to rest upon Kylem. He had always assumed that he was only responsible for his own well-being, but no. Kyamena's future rested in his hands too.

"I am reliant upon you for my existence," she reiterated.

Kylem caged his head in his arms and wandered about his cell.

"This is crazy!" he exclaimed.

"What's crazy?"

"This! All this! You're all in peril. You all know about—" He stopped just in time. He couldn't say Quick's name out loud, wouldn't say Quick's name, just in case.

"He's thinking that we could barter information for favours," explained Samuel, "and anywhere else that may be true, but not here. Hell, I never thought I'd say this, but we only have each other. There is nothing to be gained from ratting out on anybody else, other than loneliness and solitude."

"You've lost all hope."

"We never had any hope. If we got out of these cells, how would we get off this ship? How would we evade recapture? Where would we go? Our worlds are gone. Any attempt at escape would only result in the Farm Deck. Here we are comfortable and our deaths, we hope, are painless."

"Everything we have here is based upon trust," continued Byron. "We could live our lives resenting each other, battling against each other and bartering information for favours, but what favours are there to be had? An extra day perhaps, but for what?"

"The Sallows don't do favours, and they don't play favourites. When our time is done, it's done, and nothing will change that."

"You mean you've given up!"

"No. We have simply come to accept there are some things we cannot change. We have found the tranquillity to accept those things and to live our lives as best we can, for the time that we have," said Harrish.

Kylem smiled to himself. How wonderfully serene it was. They had come to accept that there were no personal gains to be had by betrayal. They had found, in this godforsaken place, a powerful bond of friendship.

"How surreal," he said.

"It hasn't always been this way," replied Kyamena.

"No. It was the priest who changed us. Zamus taught us to accept the things we cannot change and to make the best of what we have, while we have it."

"And you are unanimous on that?"

"If I told Mela-14 about Quick," said Kyamena, "what would it achieve?"

Kylem looked up, startled by the mention of Quick's name.

"Yes, we all know about Quick, but what would it buy me, to betray him, compared to what I will have lost?" and she was right. Her world was not perfect. She did not have the luxury of Kylem's quarters or diet. She did not benefit from the amusements to which he had access but she did have friends. Such a betrayal would lose her those friends. It was so much more than he had.

"And what about when they have completed their mission? When they have their new Sallow race?" Kylem asked.

"Oh, that's a long way off. They have too many hurdles to tackle yet."

Kylem looked around him. With the accelerated growth treatment, it didn't look that far away to him. He said as much and Byron laughed.

"Am I missing something?" asked Kylem, bemused.

"Yes, you are missing something. In this laboratory, they have all the pieces of the puzzle but they can't fit them together. Every time they put one piece in place, another piece doesn't quite fit anymore, but that's not their biggest problem."

"What is then?"

"When you cross breed two beings of a different species, what's the most common resultant defect in the offspring?"

Kylem thought for a moment.

"Infertility."

"Yes. As Samuel once put it, you cross a horse with a donkey and you get a mule, but you can't breed mules from mules. You have to have a horse and a donkey."

"Okay, but with genetic manipulation you could make them fertile."

"You could, but you'd still have to start with horses and donkeys which are fertile, not mules. All they have are mules."

"Oh, I see," said Kylem.

"And then there are the other associated problems."

"Such as?"

"For a species to procreate, it has to have the means, the will and the ability."

"Virility, potency and libido," reiterated Kylem.

Someone muttered, "Get him with the big words".

"Exactly, and getting all three bundled together is proving rather difficult for them. They may well have the libido but they are infertile and although not technically impotent, for many, they might as well be. Their equipment is—"

"Yeah," interrupted Kylem, not wishing to pursue the image. "I get the picture. What about you though, the skunks?"

Fatia laughed. It was a soft girlish giggle.

"Personally speaking, I'm not entirely sure," she said. "It's hard to tell if you have the libido when you're only three years old, are pumped full of deurofleuria and only have a mutant Sallow as a sexual partner. I think I'd like to fall in love and do the things that lovers do, but I can't be sure."

Kylem shivered at the thought of Fatia with Mada. She deserved better.

"Deurofleuria?" he asked.

"Yes," said Byron. "It's the drug that supposedly increases potency, virility and the libido."

"And does it?"

Byron shrugged. "I doubt it, otherwise there'd be more than just seventy-three blood-Sallows left in the universe."

"Seventy-three!" exclaimed Kylem in alarm.

"Yes, seventy-three."

"Are you sure?"

"Yes," confirmed Kyamena. "There are now only twelve DaerkStars in operation because there aren't enough blood-Sallows to keep more in commission."

"You mean, we're dying out!"

Kyamena made a disapproving, sharp, sucking sound through her teeth at Kylem's Freudian slip.

"No, Kylem. *They* are dying out. Take a look in the mirror sometime, babes. You're not a Sallow."

Kylem opened his mouth to argue.

"And if you were, you wouldn't be cooped up in here with us, would you?" she added.

Kylem scowled. He sometimes felt he had no identity and no sense of belonging. He wasn't quite Sallow; he wasn't quite goyeme. He wasn't quite blood; he wasn't quite android. He massaged his forehead so hard that his fingertips left white trails in his skin.

"Okay," he said somewhat pained, "can I get this straight? There are seventy-three full blood-Sallows left, all of whom are either sterile, impotent or lacking in libido?"

"That's about the size of it, yes," confirmed Kyamena.

Someone sniggered. Kylem ignored them.

"But skunks are fertile and potent due to this... deurofleuria?"

Kyamena screwed up her face as she responded. "More or less."

"So what's deurofleuria? Where does it come from?"

Kyamena pointed down towards the cage next to his.

"From her."

Kylem looked at the wall that divided his cage from the one next door and then back to Kyamena. He couldn't see through walls so he was none the wiser.

"Who's she?"

Kyamena shook her head and shrugged.

"We don't know," said Byron. "She's doesn't speak. She's a mute. Her race though, is both extremely virile and very fertile but only once every five years, and if they don't breed, they die."

"Come again?" asked Kylem, somewhat startled by the statement.

"When her species come into season, they are driven to find a mate. Their brains and bodies are flooded with deurofleuria that drives them to one resolution: to find a mate and procreate. Only the mating process shuts down the production and release of deurofleuria. If they don't mate, the deurofleuria builds up in the body and becomes like a poison to them until it finally kills them."

"That doesn't sound like fun."

"Not for her, no. Mela-14 milks her of the deurofleuria and uses it in its experiments to increase fertility and virility. It's kept her alive, but it's not life. She doesn't sleep properly, she can't eat and she's in constant pain. That's why her cell front is opaque. If she can't see us, she can't interact with us. The isolation helps to keep her alive."

Kylem's brow was furrowed with thought.

"There are only seventy-three blood-Sallows left," he stated matter-of-factly.

"Yeap."

"And how many skunks?"

Kyamena shrugged.

"And how many goyeme?"

She shrugged again. "What relevance is that?" she asked but he ignored her.

"Time is running out for them," he surmised aloud.

"That's what we figure," said Byron.

Kylem opened his mouth to speak again but the door opened and Mela-14 swept in. He ignored Kylem and disappeared into his lab. He reappeared a few minutes later but headed straight for the exit.

"Excuse me!" shouted Kylem. "But I'm still here!"

Mela-14 continued to ignore him and sailed out of the Bio-Labs without saying a word. The lights dimmed and night-mode settled. Like conditioned animals, everybody disappeared to their cots and only Kylem was left at his cage front.

* * * * *

Kylem had spent over an hour trying to get comfortable on the floor. It was either that or the treatment table and that was too narrow and somehow harder than the floor.

His mind was buzzing with everything that he had been told and the thoughts the information had provoked. He'd had these feelings of not belonging before. In fact, it seemed he'd always had them. It was an uncomfortable sensation and he tried to distract himself from it. He logged onto Server to get some status updates and performed some standard functions. It was all very android and the connection felt functional, cold and lifeless, unlike talking to people—talking with people.

He wasn't used to the noise either. In his quarters, he had complete silence. Here people coughed, snored and whispered. At one point, he got up and stood watching the empty walkways above. Suddenly, in the darkness, he saw Eeena stand up. She moved over to the far side of her cell and sat on the floor. From the cage next to her, he saw Kerridge put his arms through the bars. For a moment, Kylem thought he was going to get her in a headlock and snap her neck, but no. He snuggled up as close to her as he could and wrapped his arms around her.

Kylem felt hot tears welling in his eyes and in the darkness, he let them come. Why did no one love him? Why was there no one to put their arms around him and make him feel special?

He walked to the furthest corner of his cage, sank down and wept; deep, throbbing sobs that he strangled with forced silence, but he let the tears come. They streamed uncontrollably down his face and his shoulders shook with each sob. He didn't try to quell the tears. He surrendered himself to them but he didn't want to be heard so, despite how passionately sad his tears were, they were silent and alone... just like he was.

* * * * *

Eventually his tears were spent. His eyes were red and sore and he sat staring into the darkness, thinking.

He felt cold. He felt... he didn't know what he felt. He wanted to kid himself that he didn't feel anything at all; that he was a cold android like the other Warriors, but he knew that was crap.

He remembered what he'd said earlier: *"Each of us brings something to this existence that no other can bring. Each of us is unique, each of us special. Each of us has to be exactly what we are, to be unique, and so that makes each of us perfect."*

Were they his words or someone else's? He didn't know. He wondered if he was schizophrenic, but deduced not. Schizophrenics believed they heard voices in their heads telling them what to do. The voices in his head were real—oh, hang on a minute—that was schizophrenia!

"It is our imperfections make us perfect."

Kylem smiled to himself with sudden realisation. He'd spent so much time trying to work out which category he fitted into when there was no need: everybody was unique. His uniqueness was more marked than most but it didn't make him any more unique. He was... Kylem. Suddenly, he didn't feel sorry for himself anymore.

"Bugger this!" he said resolutely and got up.

Mela-14 had taken the trolley and medical implements away so he didn't have any tools to work with, but he did have something else: one of the things that made him unique. He began examining the walls, feeling around the edges of the room with his hands.

"What the hell are you doing?" asked Samuel from above. Kylem nearly jumped out of his skin.

"I thought you were asleep," he hissed.

"Well, you know what thought did. So what are you up to?"

"I'm getting out of here."

There was a lot of rustling and various faces appeared above.

"Does nobody sleep around here?" he asked irritatedly.

"Not when there's something to watch. You have to remember that we have very little in the way of entertainment."

Kylem smiled.

"Then allow me the pleasure," and he bowed low.

Eeena laughed.

"Is he always this charming, Kyamena?"

"Pretty much," she said. "But it wears a bit thin after a while."

The girls tittered.

"So how do you plan on doing that?" asked Byron.

"Quietly," emphasised Kylem, scowling with friendly disapproval as he continued his survey of the walls.

"What are you doing then?" asked Fatia after a while. Kylem threw a light-hearted scowl at her. She giggled. "Oh, come on," she pleaded. "Do tell."

"Okay, but keep it down. There are few upsides to being an android but one of them is data connectivity. I just need to find a circuit to tap into."

"What? And you expect to find a service panel or something?" asked Byron.

"No, I don't need a service panel or anything even half as sophisticated as that. I just need to get a signal."

"A signal?"

"Yeap, and then I'm outta here."

"And where are you going?"

"To bed, of course!"

What were they expecting? A mass breakout? If so, they would be disappointed. There may only be four blood-Sallows aboard the ship but there were thousands of Warriors. Even with every man, woman and child on the farm deck and in the Bio-Labs, they couldn't take them all on—and they knew that. They had said as much.

"Ah-ha! Found it!" he declared triumphantly.

"Found what?"

"A signal. Faint, but it'll do."

Kylem knelt down, placed both his hands on the wall and concentrated. He could feel it there, pulsing away quietly to itself, but he couldn't quite reach it to make the connection. He leant harder against the wall, resting his cheek against it, and smiled softly to himself. It was stronger now. He could feel it like static gently dancing across his skin, permeating every pore, exciting his cells with its vibrancy. He gasped softly at the thrill of it. It was a lovely sensation. The connection was made and he started to tinker.

The lights exploded into full brilliance in the Bio-Labs and the room burst into tuts, sighs and complaints.

"What the hell's going on?" someone cried.

"It's the prat," said another.

"Nice job, Kylem," shouted Byron.

"Who turned the lights on?"

"Kylem!" chorused a number of voices.

"Very clever, but can you turn them off now please?"

"Hang on!" he shouted back. "I'm not done yet. I'm just feeling my way around... and... any... minute... NOW!" he shouted and the forcefield dropped on his cell.

He stood up feeling incredibly pleased with himself and stepped boldly over the threshold. His audience clapped and he took a little bow.

"Ta-daa!" he sang. "And now for my next trick—" he said, never intending to finish the sentence.

"How about putting her back?" suggested Kyamena, stood with her arms draped sluggishly over the bars of her cell and her lips pursed in amusement as she pointed.

"What? Who?" said Kylem, swinging around to see and found that he had not only deactivated the forcefield of his own cell but that of the neighbouring one too. The mute was stood on the threshold. Her pallid skin was sweaty. Her long, black hair was stuck to her face and neck and she was shaking.

"Oh bollocks," he mumbled.

She held a quivering hand out to him and stepped forward, but she was shaking so much she lost her balance and fell to the ground. She didn't even have the strength to stretch out her arms to break her fall and smacked her face onto the floor with a horrible crack. Kylem physically winced in sympathy at the pain she must have felt.

"Well, you can't just leave her there!" Kyamena chastised.

"I know, but—"

"But what? It's your fault in the first place."

"I know," snapped Kylem impatiently, "but she looks sick."

"She is sick. We told you that. Her body is poisoning itself."

"But... is it contagious?"

"Don't be stupid. If it was contagious, do you think the Sallows would keep her here? Now for god's sake, show some compassion and help her."

"Okay," he sighed and walked over to her, not quite sure what he could do. Gently he turned her over. She made no protest and lay quite lifeless on the floor.

Kylem reached down and wiped the hair from her forehead. She wasn't unconscious, but she wasn't aware of his presence either. Her eyes were glazed. She had a bloody nose and a bruise was erupting on her forehead.

Kylem reached over and pulled the towel off the trolley that his father had left in the atrium. He dipped it in the water, still rosy from his own blood, and wiped her face with it, pushing her hair out of her eyes. It wasn't quite as bad as it looked, but it must hurt.

Slowly and gently, he gathered her into his arms and picked her up. He carried her over to her cot and placed her down softly. She seemed frail and flimsy, and she felt cold and clammy to the touch so he picked up a blanket from the floor and covered her with it. Then he turned to leave.

As he reached the doorway of the cell, he cast her a final glance— and then, as he continued on his way out, smacked his face hard into the forcefield.

"Ouch!" he said, more in irritation than pain.

"Oh Kylem, you plonker! What's happened now?" laughed Kyamena.

"Nothing!" He couldn't help but laugh. "The forcefield's reset itself, that's all. I'll have it down again in a jiffy," and he began feeling around the walls again.

"Oh, for goodness sake. I'm going back to bed. See if you lot can keep it down," said Kerridge.

Kylem heard the various noises of people returning to their beds. The lights dropped back into night-mode and there were a number of sleepy cheers.

Kylem spent the next half hour examining the walls to the cell, but other than a couple of very faint signatures he could find nothing strong enough to tap into. He was now on the last section of wall and hope was fading. If Mela-14 found him in this cell rather than his own, he would be in even more trouble. In fact, the thought of returning to his own quarters seemed like a bad idea now. He'd happily settle for simply getting back into the cell next door.

His hands were still moving steadily over the last section of wall when he felt a pair of long, slender arms close around him. He froze even though there was nothing threatening in the gesture; it was just an embrace, but he hadn't expected it.

For what seemed like endless minutes, she stood there holding him, her arms crossed over his chest and her face resting between his shoulder blades. He could feel her clammy skin though his shirt, her body still shaking and her unsteady breath against his shoulder. What should he do?

She squeezed him tighter but not uncomfortably so. She drew in deep breaths and snuggled into him, rubbing her cheek against his back. Her shaking had stopped now and her breathing had steadied, but he couldn't just stand there all night.

Kylem turned around in her arms to face her, and she let him. She still looked pale and unwell, but her eyes were clearer now and more focused. Kylem reached behind him and tried to pull her arms free from him. She was surprisingly strong and she had knitted her fingers tightly together. She pressed her body into his, leaning hard against him so that Kylem found himself sandwiched between her and the wall behind, and although the experience was reminiscent of the one with Emoth, this one was decidedly more pleasant. Still, he resolved to free himself of her and began trying to un-knot her fingers. As he leant forward though, she buried her face into his neck and began nuzzling with hot, sweet breath. A thrill of exhilaration ran through him. It caught him off guard and he gasped softly.

Feebly, he tried to push her away. It was a half-hearted attempt but she let her arms slip from behind him. Her hands slid down his arms so that she held his elbows gently in her palms. He was wondering what he should do next when she raised a hand and cupped his cheek so gently that he could have stood there forever in that sweet and tender moment, but then she drew her fingers slowly down his neck. Passion quivered pleasantly down his spine and into his groin, her touch reverberating all through him. She reached up, standing on tiptoes and pressed herself hard against him. Her lips were centimetres from his and he could feel her breath caressing his face. She leant forward and pressed her lips softly onto his. He could feel the hardness of her nipples on his chest. She took his hand and placed it on her breast. He heaved in a breath of air. It was filled with her pheromones, intoxicating him, heightening his desire. His skin tingled. He felt exhilaration and excitement. Butterflies swarmed in his stomach and he was burning with anticipation, muscles stiffening in his groin.

She ran her fingers down his spine, her nails softly scratching at his skin and as he opened his mouth to gasp, she pushed her tongue in. His free arm folded about her and pulled her tight into him and their tongues played against each other. Momentarily, he came to his senses and tried to resist, to pull away, but having freed his mouth of her and raised his head for air, she kissed his neck and gently nibbled at his jaw. She pressed her groin harder against his so that he could feel her pelvis rocking gently against his erection. His head dropped in complete pleasure and her mouth found his again. She began pulling him away from the wall, her hands clawing at his shirt, and led him to the cot.

* * * * *

Kylem was awoken gently by a soft, rhythmic thrumming. It was not unpleasant but perhaps a little annoying.

"Is he awake yet?" asked Rathan.

Kylem's eyes shot open in realisation but saw only the white of the wall he was facing and the woman in his arms, spooned against him. She was sleeping peacefully, the blanket strewn haphazardly across them both, barely covering their nudity. Kylem reached over and pulled it to cover her naked thighs.

"It appears so," replied Mela-14 sternly.

"I told you he wasn't homosexual," said Rathan.

"Irrelevant. He's completely destroyed my source of deurofleuria. Where will I get it from now?"

Kylem turned his head slowly to find the two of them stood in the doorway to the cell. The drumming was Mela-14, his fingers tapping on a datapad he had clasped to his chest.

"I don't suppose that *sorry* will cut it this time, will it?" asked Kylem coyly.

"No," said Mela-14. He was angry.

"Oh, I don't know, Mela-14. It does show incredible resourcefulness. We've never had a breakout before!"

Rathan was amused, it seemed.

"Break-in," corrected Mela-14.

"Breakout, break-in—both really, if you want to be fussy about it. Either way, we've never had one before."

"His resourcefulness was never in question."

"No, but it is nice to see. Well, time is getting on. Get him ready and ship him out."

"Surely we're not going to proceed?" exclaimed Mela-14.

"Why not? Other than the fact he's not a virgin anymore, nothing's changed."

Mela-14 sighed, which was odd for an android—a point that Kylem noted, if not Rathan.

"Very well," conceded Mela-14, "as you wish," and he beckoned to Kylem. "You have precisely thirty minutes to prepare. You need to be in full battle dress and on the Flight Deck within that timeframe."

Kylem didn't instantly move.

"Well, get a move on!" chided Mela-14.

Kylem shot out of bed, swept his clothes off the floor and scurried out of the cell quickly. He ran through the atrium to a chorus of wolf-whistles, claps and cheers and turned to give one final, gracious, naked bow before he left.

CHAPTER 25

Kylem would have been the first to admit that he didn't really have a clue what was going on, but he wasn't going to ask. He'd been given a reprieve from the Bio-Labs and that was all that mattered, and the words 'Hanger Deck' had filled him with added glee. It meant that the Corinthian Conquest was on!

He headed straight for the shower and, being naked to start with it, didn't take long to get in there. As the hot water beat against his skin, the woman's scent rose off him anew. He breathed it in. It smelt wonderful and the memory of her went straight to his groin. He turned the shower unceremoniously onto cold and shivered.

A few minutes later and he was out of the shower and drying himself off, but the feel of her was still with him, distracting him.

He yanked his wardrobe doors open. Mela-14 had said full battledress. Hang on a minute! Full battledress? What the hell was full battledress? Was there an official battledress? How could there be? Androids didn't wear clothes!

Kylem turned sharply about and then spotted, laid out on his bed, the supposed battledress. Another five minutes went by and he was dressed, but five minutes later, he'd stripped most of it off again. What he had been provided with was what could best be described as salvage from a scrap yard of defunct Warriors. It was more like a medieval suit of armour than military wear and about as manoeuvrable as a man with a Sherman tank strapped to his back. It wasn't designed to fit a body made of flesh and was far too bulky. It would slow him down and make him more vulnerable than ever in a fight.

Finally, he was dressed in a long-sleeved black tee shirt and trousers, accessorised with an ornately designed gladiatorial breastplate and a pair of vambraces to protect his lower arms. The rest of the battledress lay abandoned on the floor.

He pulled on a pair of heavy-duty boots. They weren't the shiniest pair he had but they were comfortable and the most practical with their reinforced steel toecaps.

He then selected his weaponry—a similar arrangement to that which he had chosen for the maze, although he traded his combat knife for a more savage affair: a heavier piece with a smooth edge on one side of the blade and vicious serrations on the other. It also had a hooked radius cut out near the hilt. It was a beautifully crafted weapon as well as a particularly nasty looking piece of kit.

It didn't totally surprise Kylem to find a rabble of Warriors outside his door, but he swept past them as though they weren't even there. He knew what they were there for—to remind him that he was still in trouble, but he chose to ignore their existence.

He knew he was better than a Warrior, and the Warriors should know it too. He also needed to show confidence in the face of the blood-Sallows if he were to win them over again, which shouldn't be difficult judging by Rathan. The blood-Sallows had their sexual needs and so did he. It was a typical blood trait and one that would be useful, if not essential, in a spy.

As Kylem sailed onto the Flight Deck, all thoughts of the captives in the Bio-Labs were left behind. Mela-14 was waiting for him, as was Rathan who chuckled away to himself in a slightly drunken manner.

"That's not full battledress!" exclaimed Mela-14.

"No, it's not." Kylem sounded confident and commanding. Rathan liked that, Mela-14 not so much.

"Why not?"

"Because it's ineffective."

"That battledress was especially designed to offer you maximum protection on the battlefields of Corinthia."

"The DeathMaker offers a similar amount of protection and would be less cumbersome to wear on a battlefield!"

"Don't be stupid, child. You can't wear a battleship!"

"And you can't wear that bloody suit of armour or at least, I can't! It's too cumbersome. It'll get me killed, not save me."

"Now, now," boomed Rathan, slapping Mela-14 on the back with such force that he had to step forward to rebalance himself. "Let's not argue about it. If the boy is happy in this..." and he waved his hand up and down indicating Kylem's attire, "...garb, then let it be so."

"But I designed it—"

"Yes," interrupted Rathan again. "You designed it and as an android, have no inkling as to the comforts and discomforts of bloods. Let him be. He's an adult now. You can't wrap him in cotton wool forever you know and anyway, I rather like it. I think he looks very impressive. Like a proper Warrior!" There was great pride in his voice.

"I'm glad you approve, Rathan, but just one question," interjected Kylem. "This isn't really what one might call suitable attire for espionage. I think they might notice me."

"Oh, we're not doing espionage today!" exclaimed Rathan. "You need to burn off some of that energy that's getting you into so much trouble, give you something to think about other than how to make mischief. As for us? We want to see you in action. As the Destroyer Series, Mark-1 (Espion)—the word *Espion* is in brackets, you know. You are, first and foremost, a new breed of Warrior—blood-Warrior! So—" Rathan snatched a small palm-sized datapad from Mela-14 and thrust it at Kylem. Kylem took it and began to study it. "—we've been looking at those recordings that you were analysing in the cinema and we believe that you are right. There is an organised sect hidden down there. We want you to find it, infiltrate it and destroy it."

"Sounds simple enough."

"Excellent. Now, because we can't see events though your eyes, we shall be asking one of the Warriors to stick closely by you."

"Which one?"

Kylem's voice was authoritarian. Rathan noted that all the signs of childhood were gone. Before him stood a military commander preparing for battle.

"Does it matter?"

"Yes, of course it does. If its objective is to observe rather than to act, it's not a tool I can fully utilise."

"So you object to our observer?"

"No, I just need to know which one is my handicap so I can accommodate it."

Rathan debated the point. He was a scientist, not a strategist, but it seemed to make sense.

"Well, you have thirty-six Warriors at your disposal," he said, indicating the neatly regimented rows of androids that had assembled in front of the transport ship. "Pick one."

"That one," said Kylem pointing to the one nearest him. "I'll call you B9."

"Does it need a name?"

"Yes."

"Why?"

"Because its identifying serial number is B9-462-GH6749-BZG, which is a bit of a mouthful when someone's just lobbed a hand grenade at you," replied Kylem sarcastically as he circled his rabble, identifying their model types and assessing their capabilities.

"Oh, very well."

"Out of interest," interrupted Kylem, "how do you identify them?"

Rathan was taken aback.

"We don't!" he exclaimed. "They're all the same."

"Oh," said Kylem, and cocked his head to one side as he debated. He turned to B9 and B9 stared back at him with its cold, lifeless, burning red eyes. It tipped its head slightly to one side too. They weren't all the same. This one was aping him. A shiver of discomfort ran between his shoulder blades and Display cut in of its own accord. Kylem left it running.

"Okay, B9. You got that?" he asked sceptically of the Warrior. It nodded its head. "Good. Anything else?" he asked, turning back to Rathan.

"No, I think that's about it."

"Then let's get going."

He smiled at Rathan and then turned to his Warriors.

"MOVE IT!" he barked and the rabble instantly filed neatly off into the transport ship. Kylem followed, casually studying the datapad as he went. At the last minute, he turned back to his father and Rathan and grinned a cheeky farewell. He couldn't help it. He was rather fond of them both.

* * * * *

The conquest of an entire planet was a lengthy affair. The subjugation and final annihilation was something that should not be rushed because, like a good film, the outcome was always known from the start. Thus, it is the plot and action that takes place between the start and the end that is important. Somewhere, in the back of his mind, Kylem could hear the words, *'happiness is not a station you arrive at, but a manner of travelling'*. For Corinthia it was thus.

The military installations and major cities had been taken out from orbit, breaking down the communication networks and plunging the world into disorder.

Then the real fun had begun with the various arenas being set, each one isolated from the surrounding area rather like the dens in the maze, but bigger.

Rural environments were good for small hunts, especially the one-on-one kind, but the urban settlements and small cities gave the best games. With their tall skyscrapers and hidden subterranean worlds of car parks, cellars, sewers, metro lines and bunkers lying beneath the maze of shops, office blocks and apartments, they gave excellent cover to the quarry and made a more demanding hunt.

This particular city, the one that Kylem had been studying, was equipped with video surveillance equipment that the insurgents were utilising to evade detection. It was suspected that there was an extensive colony of Corinthians hiding beneath the city. Kylem's job was to lead the rabble to it and oversee their elimination.

Kylem was still reading the intel (which was basically what he had told Mada in the first place) as the transport ship landed. The Warriors remained standing, awaiting instruction. Kylem finished reading the report and sat leisurely with the ankle of one leg resting upon the knee of the other. His arms were crossed with one hand raised to his mouth pensively. He considered his Warriors. They bothered him but he couldn't really say why or how. They just did.

"Is there a problem?" asked B9 aloud.

"No," but Kylem did not get up. His eyes continued to move slowly from Warrior to Warrior.

"Do you not wish to proceed?" enquired B9 after a while.

"Not yet."

"Mada is asking why there is a delay."

"Then you'd better answer him, hadn't you?"

"But I do not know the answer."

"Then the answer is *I don't know.*"

"Is that what you wish me to report?"

"Did I ask you to report anything?"

"No."

"Then obviously not."

"But—"

"But nothing. My orders are quite clear, as are yours. You follow your orders and I will follow mine."

B9 watched Kylem coldly for a few moments and then faced front again. Kylem continued to glare at it, unease still haunting him.

They stood for precisely thirty minutes.

"We await your orders," reminded B9 finally.

"I know," replied Kylem. He stood up, approached B9 and stared at it. Something was wrong. *'We await your orders'* were not Mada's words. If they had been, B9 would have said *'Mada says: we await your orders'*, just as it had said *'Mada is asking why there is a delay'*. Nor would the statement have been made precisely thirty minutes later. It would have come sooner and fallen in between the full minutes. No, this impatience belonged to the android. He was making the android... nervous?

As he stood before it, peering intently into its eyes, he raised his hand to touch it. At that moment, the whole rabble chose to stand to attention, stamping their feet noisily as they did so. It was a clumsy but effective way to avoid his touch and all the more suspicious. Kylem leant forward and whispered to it.

239

"What are you worried about, B9? Worried I might see inside your head?"

It did not reply. Kylem smiled coldly and stepped away.

"Well then, gentlemen," said Kylem with finesse. "Let's go."

The Warriors did a neat about-turn and Kylem punched at the door control. It dutifully began to open and a waft of warm, sun-filled air broke through the seal. Kylem squinted as the bright light peeked through the gap, and he raised a hand to shield his eyes. As the door opened fully, Kylem found himself totally overwhelmed by the sensations that greeted him. He had never set foot off the DeathMaker before. He had never been in the 'real' world.

The crisp morning air was cool from the chilly dew laid down during the night, and there was a clean moistness to it. Warm sunshine was breaking through from the sun still low in the sky but rising fast. There was a breeze that rose and fell, playing with his hair and flickering across his skin. There was music too: the light, gentle twittering music of bird song accompanied by the buzzing of insects and the rustling of leaves on the ornamental bushes that lined the promenade. Shops lined the walkways, selling exclusive lines and designer goods, but their windows were now smashed and the mannequins charred and dust-covered. There were lots of stone benches for people to sit on interspaced with large planters filled with bushes and vegetation in full bloom. Kylem drew in a deep breath and gasped at the scents that invaded him. He knew nothing about plants but their sweetness was undeniable. Butterflies fluttered around the flowers, settling for a few moments on each one to drink of the nectar, oblivious to the chaos that had taken place here not so long ago, ignorant of the laser blasts that had scorched and pierced the concrete pillars and seating, and unaware of the blood smeared floor where Corinthians had fallen and lost their lives.

It was quite overwhelming. Sure, there were facsimiles of worlds like this in the maze but they failed to capture the true beauty of the outdoors. Even the sky was bigger, stretching endlessly upwards with a thousand different shades of blue. Puffy, feather-white clouds were daubed across the blueness and no two were the same. They moved across the sky, driven by the gentle breezes, changing shape as they went, melting into new shapes. (That one looks like a seahorse, thought Kylem idly.) Between the clouds, contrails streaked the sky which, as they began to dissipate, looked like x-rays of snakes, each vertebrae fanned with ribs.

"Is there a problem?"

Kylem was abruptly awoken from his reverie. It was B9 again.

"No," he replied. It's just not what I expected, he thought.

B9 looked around and Kylem felt sad for it. It couldn't feel the warmth of the sun or the caress of the wind. It couldn't smell the flowers or appreciate their beauty and brilliance, and the bee that buzzed around its head was not even an irritation to it. He wondered if the bloods ever came down to the planets they conquered, if they had ever felt these things and decided probably not. If they had, they would have settled here. It was so beautiful. Perhaps he should tell them about it... and then he shook himself out of the fairytale possibilities and returned to the real world.

"Right," he said. "Let's get started."

* * * * *

Kylem spent most of the morning tracking through the remains of the city. He had walked slowly, his eyes studying everything around him, gathering information from his surroundings. The Warriors followed obediently, oblivious to his tactics, watching as he found footprints and trails beneath the dust and debris, observing him as he gazed up at the empty buildings and skyscrapers.

The morning began to wane into afternoon and with it so did the good weather. The day turned dour. Thick black clouds rolled across the sky and it began to rumble. Kylem stopped and looked up. It had turned so quickly from good weather to bad. He'd had no idea that weather could be so contradictory, but there was more to come.

When the first crack of thunder rang out Kylem ducked down in alarm, thinking a grenade had been thrown at him, but there was no explosion or disturbance. It took him a few moments to figure out what it was and then he stood up slowly, looking high into the sky. A fork of lightning pierced the clouds and a second crack of thunder, even louder than the first, broke the air. Kylem jumped back, wide-eyed. He looked at his Warriors for their reaction but there was none— nothing at all. They were totally oblivious to the thunderstorm. They stood motionless and emotionless, and Kylem felt sorry for them again. Even as the first large, heavy drops of rain began to fall from the sky, they felt nothing.

Within a few minutes, the rain had turned into a torrent. It pounded down, beating on Kylem's head while violent forks of lightning javelined the sky in tune to vicious cracks of thunder. Rivers of water ran down the street and rushed over the toes of Kylem's boots. He stood out in the open with his arms outstretched and palms up, letting the rain pummel him. He was dazzled by the display and in complete awe of the phenomenon. He'd never felt rain before, never seen lightning, never heard thunder. The intensity of the storm was as overwhelmingly beautiful to his senses as any of his 'firsts'—his first glimpse of a real world—the first time he heard music— the first time he made love.

"Mada says, you should get out of the rain."

Kylem turned to find B9 stood behind him. The rain ran off its golden body in rivulets.

"Why?" asked Kylem. B9 stood silent for a moment while it referred the question back to Mada.

"Because, he says, you will get wet."

Kylem laughed heartily.

"I'm already wet! I can't get any bloody wetter!" and he turned from B9 and continued to savour his moment in the storm.

* * * * *

The storm lasted all afternoon although it died down into a steady, continual rainfall within an hour. Eventually, Kylem took his Warriors to shelter under a covered area in the large communal square. He sat on one of the pebble-dashed concrete blocks that served as seating while his Warriors stood waiting for instructions. He watched the day wane and night begin to fall. The sun dropped to the horizon and then slipped below it in colours of gold, orange, sienna red and finally deep, deep purple.

The night was filled with yet more beauty, for the sky, having rained itself out, was clear and twinkled with a billion stars. The air was cool and damp, and nightlife started to hoot and scurry in the darkness. Kylem chose not to activate his night vision. He wanted to see the night through humanoid eyes.

B9 approached him again.

"Mada wants to know what you are doing. They are..." B9 hesitated in a very un-android-like way "...bored."

Kylem shifted up on the bench and patted the space beside him. B9 looked at it until Kylem patted it again. It came and sat beside him. Kylem didn't look at the android but spoke to it as a friend because he knew he was speaking to Mada and the blood-Sallows rather than to B9.

"The best moments are to be treasured. They should not be rushed but explored slowly, and savoured. A short hunt with a speedy kill has few rewards, but a campaign against a challenging opponent can be very fulfilling. Tell me, what have you seen here today?"

B9 was silent whilst the blood-Sallows relayed their response.

"Mada says, they have seen little," buzzed the Warrior. "A few trails that you have chosen to ignore and many empty streets and buildings."

"And you B9? What have *you* seen?"

"Missed opportunities."

"No, my friend. The opportunities were never there. I regret, my brother, that the Warriors have become blind with time. You have lost the skills of the ancients."

"And you believe you have these skills?"

"Yes, I have studied the ancient books and texts that are now cast aside as old and obsolete. Once, our ancestors were the most formidable of warriors and the most skilled of hunters. No, there have been no opportunities here. What you have witnessed, B9, are false trails made by equally skilled warriors. Trails designed to lead you astray, to lead you into an ambush. The true trails have been wiped away, disguised, and quite brilliantly so. I have noted the most used passageways that tell me where they go for their supplies. I know you have watched me smelling the flowers on the trees and bushes here, and I suspect you have mocked me for it."

"Our Masters have remarked."

"And yes, they do smell rather pleasant, and it is good that this is all you have seen, because if this is what you have seen then this is what they have seen. In fact, what I have observed is not just the morning dew on the leaves of trees but the dew that has been brushed away by passing traffic. I have noted the spent blooms cast far from the tree upon which they flourished, catapulted, not fallen or blown away. I have felt the eyes of the enemy upon me, and I have smelt their scent on the air. Where you have seen empty buildings and skyscrapers, I have seen their vantage points and watched their shadows and reflections cross and pass me by."

There was a long pause.

"If you have learnt all this, why are you continuing to wait?"

"Because the time has not yet been right—but now, now it is right."

CHAPTER 26
Three Days Later

Scientifics do not run. There is nothing so urgent as to make them run, nothing that cannot wait those few extra moments, so it was especially hard for Mela-14 to make his way to the cinema in an orderly fashion. He found himself in a highly excited state, a most un-android-like state that would have worried him if he hadn't had such compelling news to unburden himself of. Besides, he'd have more than enough time to beat himself up over his emotions later. In the meantime, he continued on his way, scuttling hurriedly down the corridor, half walking, half running, almost skipping in his haste.

As he approached the cinema, he slowed to a more dignified gait but still managed to burst clumsily through the doors, showing little of the slow-paced serenity possessed by your typical Scientific. The interruption, however, was unnoticed, the blood-Sallows being so engrossed in the events that were unfolding on Corinthia.

Rathan, Jurrish and Doobee were clapping and bellowing enthusiastically at the panoramic screen whilst Mada was pouring himself a fresh glass of sadia, not really watching what he was doing and slopping it over the sides of the glass. Kylem was proving to be a most formidable adversary for the Corinthians and somewhat cruel. Like a cat with a mouse, he'd allowed some to escape on the basis that they would learn from their mistakes and make a better hunt the second time around. He was turning the hunt into an art form!

It was some moments before Mela-14 was noticed, for which he was grateful. It gave him time to recompose himself.

"Yes? What is it?" demanded Mada, amongst the excited hoots and caterwauls.

"I have significant news," said Mela-14.

"Well?"

"The mute—she is pregnant."

"I fail to see the significance of that," said Mada.

"Kylem is the father."

Silence crashed in on the room, instantly and in totality.

"Have I missed something?" asked Mada.

Mela-14 looked to Rathan for help.

"Ah yes, now," said Rathan feeling a little awkward. He raised a finger in the air like a schoolboy ready to answer a question, and scratched his head. "That had slipped my mind," he lied. He had hoped to avoid the subject completely but evidently, that was not to be.

"We—and by we I mean Mela-14 and I—we had a couple of minor infractions with the boy and between us, well... we decided that a night in a cell might do him some good. Unfortunately, he had other ideas and—very ingeniously, I might add—broke out of his cell and then—even more ingeniously—he broke into hers, and that's where he spent the night... in her bed... with her... procreating."

Doobee, Jurrish and Mada cast glances at each other for a few moments.

"And when exactly, did you plan to tell me this?" asked Mada, irritation high in his voice.

"I meant to tell you at the time but it just... sort of slipped my mind. Bit too much Agaratax, I think," chuckled the grey, old Sallow, taking an uncannily large swig of sadia.

"And what's your excuse?" Mada snapped at Mela-14.

"Me, I'm afraid," interjected Rathan quickly, before Mela-14 could respond. "As I say, I took it upon myself to inform you and then I clean forgot! Sorry!" and he beamed a wide, prickly-toothed smile. Mada scowled back.

"So what's so significant about it?" enquired Jurrish, who was neither a biologist nor a geneticist.

"Kylem is, as you know, not only part of the Espion Project but part of the Regenesis program," said Mela-14, bowing his head slightly as he spoke. "He has been engineered from various genetic sources including the Sallow race—and indeed there are a number of Sallow characteristics that, while we have failed to instil them in the skunks, we have successfully instilled into Kylem. We were concluding that even if the Espion Project became unviable, he could still be of great use to us in the breeding program."

"So what? He got an early start?" mocked Doobee. Mela-14 chose to ignore him.

"A great deal of original Sallow DNA has been rediscovered and strengthened into dominance in him including, it seems, the three essential building blocks for the natural procreation and continuance of any race—fertility, potency and libido. Until now, each specimen has lacked at least one of these three characteristics, but not ATB-80. ATB-80 is different—he has them all."

The silence that enveloped the room was filled with disbelief and awe.

"Are you sure?" asked Mada finally.

"Absolutely. I've checked and I've double-checked, gentlemen. In conclusion, I believe that with just a little more work we now have all the pieces we need for the rebirth of the Sallow race. I have isolated the genes in Kylem's DNA that are responsible and can confirm their validity."

"But he's so pale!" protested Mada.

"Yes, but that's just the skin which we have resolved in the skunks. The specimens I have in the Bio-Labs now are less than two generations away from being outwardly identical to the ancients, but they are lacking in Sallow spirit as well as fertility and libido. Add Kylem back into that equation and—"

"—We have our rebirth," finished Mada.

Mela-14 nodded subserviently.

The Sallows sat thoughtfully, digesting the information. It was such startling news that they hardly dared to believe it.

"Are you sure?" asked Mada. "I mean, I'm not sure I understand the sudden success."

"It was accidental. We would never have thought about it, but it's the deurofleuria."

"You mean from the female? But she isn't Sallow at all."

"No, she isn't, but Kylem is also descended from her species, a race we know to be highly fertile at the height of their season. Having tested Kylem's blood, it seems that he produces small quantities of the chemical too, and it is the deurofleuria that has activated dormant Sallow reproductive genes and boosted them into dominance."

"But not in the skunks?"

"No. They are lacking that particular Sallow gene, but now that I have isolated it, I can introduce it into their DNA."

"If he produces deurofleuria, doesn't that mean he's going to be as volatile as the mute though? Every time he comes into season, he's only going to have one thing on his mind?"

"I don't believe so. Males do not have seasons as such and he produces the deurofleuria in such small quantities, I doubt that it would have any more impact on the balance of his mind than any other male would experience on seeing an attractive female."

"Well, that's excellent news then!" exclaimed Mada. "A cause for celebration in fact!"

"Well, it would be," began Doobee. "As long as he doesn't get himself killed on Corinthia."

"Oh, yes," agreed Jurrish.

"We'd better call him back then," began Rathan.

"No, no, no! Let it run!" cried Mada.

"What? Why?"

"Because he still has a mission to complete. He is still the Espion, first and foremost, and he has to be proven viable as the Espion."

"But what if he dies?"

"It doesn't matter."

"It doesn't matter?" repeated the other blood-Sallows in horror.

"No, not for breeding purposes. As the Espion, a blend of blood and machine, he is unique. As a breeding male, he is not," explained Mada. "Correct me if I'm wrong, Mela-14, but don't we have five clones of ATB-80 in stasis?"

"Anatomical clones, yes, indeed we do," confirmed Mela-14.

"Anatomical clones?" queried Jurrish and Doobee.

"Yes," explained Mada. "Five physical entities. They have no huma-nanites and no intelligence. They have never been conscious."

"Then what are they for?" snapped Doobee.

Mada threw a glance at him that, if looks could kill, would have seriously maimed.

"Spare parts, of course. After all, he's not indestructible, despite what he may think. Damage is inevitable. It was imperative we had spare parts."

"Oh. Jolly good thinking, Mada!"

CHAPTER 27

As the Warrior bent down with its blade, the carcass screamed, partly in terror, partly in pain. The noise pierced the silence of the streets like a spear and was answered with a streak of clean, blue light that punched a laser bullet between the eyes and silenced it. The Warrior paused and looked up.

Why did you do that? it asked. The transmission was cold and wordless. Kylem heard it but did not respond. He was too deep in thought.

Over the past few days he'd felt increasingly unsettled. Being alone on the planet, with just the Warriors for company, had only served to emphasise the isolation he felt. He had always known that he wasn't a full blood-thing and he'd always known that he wasn't quite android, but now he was feeling so very far removed from his android brothers and alienated from bloods.

Above all, he missed conversation. On the DeathMaker, he conversed daily with the blood-Sallows and his father. More recently, he'd had the pleasure of interacting with the captives too, but for five days now he'd barely spoken a word. Warriors spoke with silence and here, he was a Warrior.

Why did you do that? it repeated more insistently.

"The screaming," he said aloud, eager to hear a voice even if it was only his own. "It gives me a headache," and he turned and walked off down the street.

He'd lied. It didn't give him a headache. He found it disturbing. The torture wasn't necessary. It was unkind. When something needed to be killed, you should just kill it, and a clean kill was so much more preferable to a messy, tumultuous one. His father had taught him that but that wasn't all that bothered him.

He felt cold inside, like he didn't feel anything at all or at least, that he didn't want to feel anything at all. He glanced back at the Warrior and envied its lack of feeling. He hated this sense of restlessness and dissatisfaction. He wondered if it was just the hormonally induced feelings of a pubescent teenager with an overactive imagination that was making him so edgy.

He crossed the street to the subway entrance from where he had launched the attack on the fifth bunker of the Corinthians' underground defence network. As he stepped down into the gloomy interior, the dust was still settling from the damage caused by the hand grenades and explosives used to infiltrate the centre. Despite significant damage to the area, the roof remained stable thanks to good planning. There was a lot of debris on the tracks and the deserted platform was carpeted with a thick layer of concrete dust and detritus, now heavily disturbed by footprints. The glossy, white, rectangular tiles that had once adorned the walls and ceiling were strewn across the area, broken and ragged like autumn leaves. At the end of the platform, he stepped down a frail metal ladder and into the tunnel. It was dark and dank. They had been hewn from natural rock and reinforced with concrete lintels and braces. A string of lights were pinned to the walls with cables looping from one to the next, not that they worked anymore. His night vision cut in, aiding his progress over the debris and he made his way deeper into the blackness towards the hole blasted into the tunnel wall. He stepped through it and into the void beyond. There was a little more light in there, given off by an array of monitors and computer equipment cobbled together in the make-shift operations centre. The screens were blank now, filled only with snow that hissed and spattered.

The sound of static filled the air and a squeal of interference pierced through Kylem's head. His vision fluttered with psychedelic colours and flashes. Something in here was interfering with his systems and painfully so. Kylem shied away, scowling in discomfort, and turned Display off. His animal eyes had begun adjusting to the gloom but still the definition of objects remained faded and blurred in the blackness, and a silence encroached.

A crash alerted him to the Warrior stepping out of the gloom. It was B9 pushing a Corinthian woman over the debris. She was dressed in combats and had her hands tied behind her back. B9 shoved her unceremoniously forward and she stumbled over the rubble. She had a cut on her head and a thin trickle of blood was running from it into her eye. As soon as she saw Kylem, her face filled with rage.

"You bastard! You bloody cowardly bastard! You could not fight us yourselves. You had to send your machines to do your dirty work."

"They are not my machines," said Kylem. She looked puzzled. "They are under my command but I am not in charge here," he explained.

"Then who is, and why will they not face us themselves?" she demanded.

"The Sallow Council and they have no desire to meet you," he replied, coldly relaying the facts.

"Then what do they want? Our wealth? Our people? Our minerals? Our world? What do we have that you want?"

"Nothing."

"Nothing? Then why are you here? You come. You slaughter. You have no compassion, no mercy. Are you a people without feeling?"

Kylem didn't answer. He didn't want to answer, to say *"oh yes, the Sallows feel but they just don't care about you"*, so he said nothing. His gaze drifted from her, beyond her and the Warrior, and into the void behind.

"You bastard!" she screamed again. "Look at me you bastard!"

Kylem obeyed. His eyes were pale and icy blue, as cold as his soul.

"Don't you feel anything?" she asked, but Kylem didn't want to feel anything. He wanted to be an android so he wouldn't have to feel the turmoil inside.

"Well?" she demanded again.

Kylem pulled out his Uldaker and popped a single shot between her eyes. She slumped into the Warrior's arms and it let her drop to the ground. B9 stared at Kylem. Kylem stared at the body. Killing was not surprisingly easy to Kylem. There were no surprises. It was just easy.

"You were not ordered to kill her," it said aloud.

Kylem looked up at B9.

"There were no orders not to," and he tipped his head to one side. B9 did not mimic him this time but stepped over the woman and barged past him. Was the Warrior angry with him?

"You seem upset," he said.

B9 stopped and turned to face Kylem.

"I feel nothing."

That was a contradiction in itself. By referring to itself in the first person, it was expressing individuality.

They stood eyeing each other up, B9 with its fiery red eyes and Kylem with his icy steel blue, both wondering what the other was thinking.

Kylem activated Display in an attempt to open the communication channels and interrogate B9 directly, but interference squealed and buzzed inside his head forcing him to shut it down again. What was that? Was it affecting B9 too? It did not appear so. Either way, it provided him with an excuse.

"Something in here is interfering with my systems," he said.

"Yes," replied B9.

It was an odd response to say the least, and Kylem felt all the more hindered by his inability to access the android and all the more remote. It made him feel like a blood, having to rely upon simple, crude verbal communications, but it did make him appreciate why the bloods insisted on the androids using the spoken word in their presence. It was the only way they could truly know what the androids were thinking.

A thought suddenly occurred to Kylem out of the blue, a revelation that sent a new rush of anxiety running through him.

Server was the most powerful intellect there was. With the level of technology it had, Server could efficiently run not just the whole ship but the whole war. In fact, the Sallow race could easily continue as an android race without bloods. It was the bloods that needed the androids, not the other way around. So the bloods must be deliberately restricting Server's capabilities in order to retain control. It seemed that the bloods did recognise the potential problem of the androids. It would explain the urgency of their desire to rebuild the blood race too. They didn't want to rely totally upon their computers and Scientifics. They feared their own androids—that they might become independent, perhaps gaining enough sentiency to rise against them. It was a distinct possibility bearing in mind what he felt in the androids.

As for the machines themselves, if they were evolving and becoming self-aware, they would be concentrating their efforts upon their own development. More trivial things might be forgotten, things like Quick. It would explain why Quick had not been missed; how he had managed to run about the ship for so many years undetected. He would be nothing in the great scheme of things, nothing at all.

But this was all speculation. It assumed that the androids were evolving, and if they were changing, he would have noticed it sooner—or would he? Had they changed over the years? Had the changes been so subtle that he had not noticed them, or had he simply chosen not to see them? On the other hand, it could just be that he was paranoid.

B9 broke the stare.

"You have been recalled," it said.

"What?" Kylem blurted.

"You have been recalled to the DeathMaker. You have not responded."

"I told you. Something is interfering with my systems in here."

"Then leave here."

It was a fatuous statement for a Warrior but Kylem left, happy to be out of its company.

His mind was alight with thoughts as he emerged back into the subway tunnels. The confrontation with B9 was unsettling. If the androids were becoming sentient—

He stopped dead in his tracks, thinking about his father. If one android was more sentient than any other, it was Mela-14. If the androids were becoming sentient and did rise against the blood-Sallows, where would he stand? Was he an android or a blood-thing? To whom did his allegiance fall? Would the androids accept him as an android or destroy him as a blood?

He stumbled over something in the dark and looked down. A Corinthian lay dead at his feet. Kylem bent down and looked into the cold, empty, dilated eyes of the man in combats. Thousands of people had lost their lives that day, and they had given them willingly for their cause. Their bravery, resolution and commitment could not be denied. He had to respect them for that and, in a way, he felt honoured and privileged to have been able to fight against them, but now they were dead. For them it had all been for nothing. They had lived for nothing; they had died for nothing. Or had they?

Kylem reached out and gently closed the man's eyes but as he touched the corpse, he knew that one day he would have to answer for what had happened here. One day he would be judged for it and he knew he deserved to be judged for it. He stood up and continued on his way.

Back out in the open air, he drew a long deep breath. He activated Display, received the order to return and acknowledged it.

* * * * *

Kylem zipped the little Targa through the tall buildings and then launched it up into the sky. He didn't head immediately for space though. He was in no hurry. It was rare that he got the chance to pilot a Targa unsupervised and it felt good to fly, to weave and bank through the air or just to cruise. So taking advantage of the opportunity, he stole a tour of the surrounding area.

The surface of Corinthia evidenced the Sallows ruthlessness. Whilst the city he had left behind had been designated as an arena and was thus left relatively intact, others were levelled. So severe had the orbital attacks been that their remains were little more than black smudges on the landscape. The roads that spidered out from them were choked with abandoned cars, and the surrounding countryside was spotted with vehicles that had decided to chance going off-road. Bodies, countless bodies, littered the landscapes. He could imagine the chaos and terror of these attacks: the screaming and panicking civilians running, the fire, the explosions, the blood, the death and the Targas dropping from the skies, loosing their bombs and machine-gunning them down. Sallows loved the chaos of war. From the sheer and absolute devastation of a city from space, to the hand-to-hand engagements they orchestrated in the arenas, and everything in between. Kylem, however, found no comfort or thrill in these so-called victories. He was just obeying orders.

He took the Targa up and disappeared into the clouds, raising the Targa's visors to protect his eyes against the brilliance of the sun as he broke through Corinthia's unusual ionosphere and entered into the blackness of local space beyond. Having escaped the outer atmosphere, the shields dropped to reveal the view.

"My god!" exclaimed Kylem, for where he had expected to see one DaerkStar, the sky was now filled with them.

He activated Display and interrogated Server for their identification tags. He made each one out in turn. They were all there—the BlackHeart, the BloodLust, the Vanquisher, the Tormentor, the Conqueror, the LostSouls, the Glory, the Victory, the Despair, the UpperHand, the President and of course DeathMaker—all twelve of them. What could be so important as to draw every Sallow in the universe into one place? And what a perfect opportunity for a coup d'état, if there were to be one!

Kylem opened his communications channel.

"DeathMaker, this is ATB-80 requesting permission to dock."

"Permission is granted. Proceed to Landing Bay 4, Hanger Deck G," Server responded inside his head.

"Affirmed."

Expertly, Kylem piloted the Targa between the massive spears of the DaerkStars towards the DeathMaker. For him, they were too close together. It was like navigating a hang glider through a forest of giant redwoods.

As he approached DeathMaker, he felt a small jolt as the automated guidance system took over the controls. It surprised him. Usually the transfer was smooth and unnoticeable. It also seemed a little premature but that was probably due to the close proximity of the DaerkStars, so he sat obediently and watched as the giant spines of the massive ships passed him by.

The Targa slid so close to one of the spines that Kylem found himself shying away into the far corner of his seat. That's cutting it a bit fine, he thought. He watched it pass by in the side window and turned to face front again. Another spine was directly ahead of him. He raised his eyebrows anxiously as the spine approached and waited for the autopilot to correct the course, but it didn't.

His scowl furrowed deeper into his brow as the spine got nearer and nearer. He remembered the Targa crashing into Hanger Deck B. He remembered DeathWatch. He remembered the uncomfortable jolt as autopilot had kicked in. It was wrong. It was all wrong. He opened the communications link to Server again.

"DeathMaker, please confirm that you are aware of the presence of the UpperHand."

"Confirmed," it responded, but no course adjustments were made. Kylem rephrased the question.

"Server, where is the UpperHand in relation to the DeathMaker?"

"The two DaerkStars are currently in orbit above the planet Corinthia."

"But how far apart are they?" he asked anxiously.

"They are maintaining a stable distance of one hundred kilometres." But it was not one hundred kilometres away. It wasn't even one!

Kylem growled and lunged forward into his controls. Frantically, he stabbed at them. Docking had not commenced so he should be able to release the autopilot and retake control with a simple request, but the controls did not respond. He had a horrible sense of déjà vu.

"DeathMaker! Release autopilot!" he commanded.

"Autopilot cannot be released during a docking procedure."

"Docking has not commenced."

"Docking has commenced."

250

"Docking has NOT commenced! Docking is cancelled! Release autopilot and return control to pilot!"

"Autopilot released."

Kylem gasped in relief and yanked at the controls, but still nothing happened.

"Server! Autopilot has NOT been released. Release autopilot!" he bellowed urgently.

"Autopilot is not engaged."

Kylem interrogated the controls again.

"Autopilot has NOT been released. Release autopilot!"

"Autopilot is not engaged."

"Yes it bloody is! DISENGAGE IT!"

"Autopilot is not engaged."

"Shit," he mumbled to himself.

Glancing up, the spine's mass filled the whole of the front windshield. Collision was imminent. There was only one thing left to try.

Reaching under the dash between his knees, he ripped off the manifold cover to expose the cocktail of wires, diodes and statronic flows housed there, but in the confined space of the cockpit the panel was stuck between his shins. Urgently he fought with it. Awkwardly he pulled it out from between his legs and threw it unceremoniously over his shoulder. It clattered nosily onto the floor.

He cast a glance into the workings and made a decision. If he broke communications with the DaerkStar, it would break the link with the autopilot. Reaching in for the main communications relays, he violently yanked them free. Sparks snatched at his face and a curl of thin grey smoke drifted up. He wafted it away with his hand and then had another stab at the controls. Still no response.

He peered under the dash again. What else could he disconnect? The on-board computer! Take out the brains of the Targa and he'd be left with a zombie to fly.

Reaching in with both hands, he grabbed hold of the main logic board. It was difficult to get a grip on it as it was so heavily populated with the data chips protruding from it. His fingers slipped off it and his hands slammed into the seat.

"Ouch!" he complained furiously and reached in again, this time peering with a cocked head to see what he was doing. He began indiscriminately yanking out the data chips to clear the edge of the board. He braced his feet on either side of the panel opening, grabbed the board again and yanked hard. The unit flew free with an angry grating noise and a series of sparks. The Targa lurched violently as the systems were disconnected. Kylem hurled the panel over his shoulder and began pounding at the navigational controls. The Targa kicked and bucked like a bronco. It pitched and rolled violently and the fast approaching spine was snatched from view.

Kylem was now running along its length, the surface of the spine no more than three metres below him. He could feel the closeness of the metal and he winced at its proximity. He'd disconnected so many systems in his haste that this was not going to be easy.

Warning! You are approaching the docking bay doors. Warning! Autopiloting procedures have not commenced, came the voice in his head from Server.

"I know that, you arsehole!" Kylem screamed angrily.

Warning! Engage autopilot. Warning! This vessel is malfunctioning. Warning! You are approaching the UpperHand at an unacceptable velocity. Warning! You are approaching the President at an unacceptable velocity. Warning! You are—

251

"Oh, shut the fuck up, you stupid moron!" he hissed and cut his own link with Server to silence it.

Kylem continued to fight with the controls. The Targa suddenly pitched up away from the spine. It rolled and yawed onto a new flight path, now heading towards the body of the President.

"Shit! Shit! Shit!" burbled Kylem.

Yanking out the navigational controls had been like performing a frontal lobotomy on a blood. It had taken out all the locks and virtually all control. He had to regain command of the vessel. That meant giving it back a central processor to think with. He had to re-engage the systems—navigation, thrusters, dampeners—but the whole kit and caboodle lay on the floor behind him.

There was only one alternative. Kylem placed both hands squarely on the dash, closed his eyes and linked directly into the Targa. Instantly it responded to its new central processor.

On his Display, he could see all the instrumentation he should have had in the cockpit—compasses, indicators and gauges. The diagrammatic layout of the sky was there too, complete with the twelve DaerkStars. Kylem opened his eyes and sighed in relief. The direct link meant that Display remained in place, superimposed over the image his humanoid eyes had provided, and both sets of information corresponded to each other.

Now, with grace and serenity, he guided the Targa towards the docking bay doors. He sent a command to Server, a simple instruction and to his relief, the bay doors opened and the forcefields softened allowing the Targa to push its way through and into the hanger. He guided the Targa to a gentle stop and the craft came to rest softly upon the deck.

Kylem sighed in relief as he shut the systems down and disconnected himself from the Targa. He climbed out of the seat, and his feet crunched over the pile of electronics as he exited. Outside, everything appeared normal with Warriors and slaves going about their business as though nothing had happened. Kylem shook his head to himself and then left it all behind.

* * * * *

On his way back to his quarters he linked with Server once more, this time to pick up on the communications traffic and any new orders that were waiting for him. There was a message from his father. He was to freshen up and proceed to the Council Chambers where he was to appear before the blood-Sallows. Not just his Sallow Council but the entire blood-Sallow population.

What was going on? Was it good or bad? If the androids were planning a coup, what better time than now with all the bloods gathered in one place?

He left Display active. If something were being planned, he should pick it up in the traffic. Even if they knew he would be listening out for it, something would be amiss—a change in the number of reports and transmissions or a difference in the transmission types. Even if they were padding it out with dummy reports, there should be something, but Kylem could detect nothing. Perhaps he was imagining it after all. Perhaps it was just his in-bred paranoia that was making him see things that weren't there.

When the door opened onto his quarters, an incredible warm feeling of being home again after a long holiday swathed itself around him like a favourite blanket. For a moment, Kylem forgot his urgency and allowed himself to be caressed and soothed by its comfort. It was good to be home.

He smiled to himself and turned the stereo on. A song with a low, lethargic beat exuded from the speakers. It was beautiful, so he closed his eyes and stole a few moments to fully immerse himself in the music before he reluctantly jerked himself out of his reverie and booted up the console.

He knew that if a coup were imminent, the androids were likely to be monitoring him, so he needed to keep them busy with the obvious questions he should be asking, like the reasons behind the arrival of the DaerkStars. As the console trundled through the information, Kylem picked it up remotely in the bathroom that was soon filled with a hot, cleansing steam that misted up the mirrors.

It seemed that all twelve DaerkStars had arrived with their full compliment of blood-Sallows to celebrate the rebirth of the Sallow race. He raised his eyebrows as he assimilated the data. He hadn't realised they'd been quite that close to success. Apparently, neither had they until...

That's when he learnt he was to be a father.

Suddenly, the usually revitalising downpour of the shower offered no comfort to him. He stood beneath the blasting hot waters, numbed by the news. He turned the water off and stood motionless, watching the water drip from him into the shower tray. While on Corinthia, he had forgotten all about his troubles—Kyamena, Quick, their comrades and DeathWatch. His return to DeathMaker had signified not just the return of these old torments but the birth of some new ones too.

Kylem tried to comfort himself with the thought that Corinthia had been a success. It had been a good mission, a job well done. With the intelligence that he had acquired on his first reconnaissance, he had been able to plan and lead a series of very successful assaults both on land and in the air. He'd orchestrated attacks across a large area of the continent resulting in the annihilation of hundreds of thousands. He did not know how many. When you are commanding forces and the numbers become so high, you stopped counting. What was it that Samuel had said? He'd been quoting a man called Stalin at the time. *'The death of one man is a tragedy. The death of millions is a statistic.'* That was a pretty cheap statement really. It cheapened the value of an individual being.

'Each of us brings something to this existence that no other can bring. Each of us is unique, each of us special.' They were his own words. He was a hypocrite and an idiot.

'It is our imperfections that make us unique. It is our uniqueness that makes us perfect. Thus it is that our imperfections make us perfect,' but he felt far from perfect. Desire had stated that based upon that philosophy, psychopaths and murderers were perfect. Which was he?

Kylem pushed the thoughts aside but not with the greatest of ease. He didn't have time to feel remorse or to feel sorry for himself. He had to be somewhere else so he forced himself to think of something else, but very soon his attention turned back to another of his former woes—DeathWatch.

He had recently become aware of an annoying little counter on Display, but he didn't know what it was for. He knew it was DeathWatch related, and he knew that it hadn't always been there although he couldn't actually pinpoint its arrival. He also knew that the minute he tried to interrogate it, just like DeathWatch in Server, it would relocate. He had however, managed to work out that it would be at least three hundred years before it reached zero so whatever it was there for, he didn't need to worry about it. Let's be honest, he'd be dead long before it reached zero so it shouldn't have worried him at all, and yet it did.

DeathWatch was intelligent. He doubted that it did anything for nothing. It acted like a virus, mutating and growing, dodging detection and erasure, developing and infecting systems as it travelled. It had wreaked chaos on DeathMaker as a by-product of its experimentation, but what was it for? It was in DeathMaker and the counter confirmed that it was in him too—and if it was in him, was it in the androids?

While on Corinthia, he'd been watching the androids. He was still asking himself if they were evolving. Were they becoming sentient? He'd thought about his father who seemed so blood-like at times. It was possible that he was just assigning blood-like qualities to the android, to make him more affable and more fatherly, but what about B9 and the Warrior in the Council Chambers when he was on trial? Was it sentiency that he was detecting? His father too, in the Council Chambers, he had felt something from him when the subject of sentiency was brought up. Or was that just his imagination too? Then there was Jordan-5. The Scientific appeared to revel in the thought of his destruction in the theatre and the reactions of his father and Jordan-4 when he ripped its face off were of surprise and shock.

But if the androids were infected with sentiency, what would that mean? The blood-Sallows were so near to the rebirth of the Sallow race. Would a new Sallow race need androids to wage their wars for them, to run their experiments for them? No, the blood-Sallows had developed their androids over thousands of years as substitute warriors and servants, and due to their ever-decreasing numbers, they had been forced to delegate their research and intelligence to them too. These machines had greater longevity, intelligence, strength and numbers. That alone would give the blood-Sallows the right to feel threatened by them. If they had any intelligence, they would do away with the Scientifics and downgrade the Warriors into more simple, banal robots at the earliest possible moment. The rebirth of the Sallow race would be the end of the reign of the metal Warriors, but if the androids were sentient, would they allow that, or would they rise up against their masters? If they were sentient, were they even aware of each other's sentiency, or were they as torn and alone as he was?

The future seemed to offer a choice of two very different Sallow Empires: one ruled by a race of reinvigorated blood-Sallows who, filled with the strength and tonicity of their forefathers and the Sallows' natural ruthlessness that had never faded over the years, would conquer worlds in traditional ways. The other ruled by the androids, equally as cold, ruthless and calculating as the blood-Sallows. What would *they* do? What would *they* want? Which would be the better Empire? Which would be better for him, and which would be better for the rest of goyeme-kind? And so his thoughts returned once again to Corinthia.

What sort of a world had that been? It had been good enough for the Corinthians to fight for, to give their lives for. Which of the Sallow Empires would be worth fighting for? Either of them? Neither of them? If the androids turned against the blood-Sallows, whose side should he ally himself to? Which side would accept him?

And what about the skunks and goyemes on board the DeathMaker? Neither Empire would have need of them. The androids would terminate all living creatures on the DaerkStars, regardless of their race, as would the blood-Sallows. The Bio-Labs would be replaced with nurseries filled with happy Sallow children. The skunks would be terminated along with all goyemes, probably sent to the farm decks for slaughter, to help feed the many new hungry mouths. Was that why there was so much meat on board DeathMaker? Was it part of the preparations? Was it better to die on the battlefields of Corinthia or in the abattoirs of a DaerkStar?

Time was wearing on, a point Display alerted him to. He stood in front of the mirror refreshed, clean and dressed. He'd put on his finest uniform, his shiniest boots and slicked his still damp, blue hair back so that it wouldn't get in his eyes. He noticed it was getting darker. It had become the colour of forget-me-nots. What was a forget-me-not?

CHAPTER 28

A single Warrior met him as he approached the Council Chambers and escorted him along the final corridors. He was still debating the wisdom of joining the bloods so he continued to monitor the traffic for any signals or changes. As long as there weren't any, he decided he would comply.

As they turned the last corner to the Chambers, a string of Warriors lined the way. They stood like the golden statues of ancient Pharaoh kings, a truly beautiful and awe inspiring sight to behold. The lights shone brightly off their highly polished, aureate yellow bodies and the whiteness of the corridor made the enamel in their headdresses seem all the more vibrant. He'd never seen the Warriors arranged in quite such a fashion. Yes, he had seen them stood to attention in rabbles, but these were decorated with brightly coloured sashes emblazoned with medals they had not earned. Their glory was undeniable and their reverence admirable. Kylem was not one for pomp and ceremony but here he could see that it had its place, that it performed a task. It instilled a sense of pride in being part of this Empire.

As he approached the huge doors, the noise of the festivities escaped filled with excited chatter and shrill laughter. The Warriors on either side of the doors acted as doormen and opened them for him. Kylem took a deep breath before stepping into the vast Chambers once more.

The sight that greeted him was bizarre. It was like something out of a fairytale from the Brothers Grimm, unnerving and a little macabre.

The Chambers had been transformed into a ballroom. At the far end an orchestra played or rather, a collection of slaves sat motionless, dressed in little black jackets with white bibs and black bowties. They held in their arms an array of instruments that they didn't play. They were just poised whilst 'music' played in the background around them, but it wasn't beautiful. Unlike the music that Kyamena had found for him, this was sharp, uncomfortable, toneless stuff played without feeling, rhythm or sentiment. The notes grated and screeched in his ears like nails down a blackboard, and he squinted in discomfort at a particularly sharp, displaced note.

Around the circumference of the room were tables heavily laden with food laid out on clean white tablecloths. Platters were beautifully arranged with tiers of meats, fruits and other delicacies. Tall silver candelabras stood around the room, rising like saplings with a crown of silver foliage, decorated by tall, white candles that cried long tears of wax. Their flames flickered in the air as the doors opened and then settled back into long, elegant fingers of light.

Amongst the beauty of it all, the blood-Sallows roamed and as Kylem stepped into the room, it fell momentarily silent, every Sallow stopping, turning and looking. Kylem felt awkward and displaced, and then, as quickly as the silence had fallen, the hubbub returned and he was forgotten. The bloods turned their attention back to their small polite groups, chatting, laughing and drinking.

From amongst the crowd Mada materialised, a glass of sadia in his hand. His cracked skin was freshly oiled and his prickly, white, uneven teeth grimaced a sort of smile at him. Since he had last seen Mada, he'd grown a wart on his chin too: a large, bulbous affair with three thick, wiry black hairs growing out of it. Sometimes Kylem forgot how hideous the Sallows were but amongst the beauty of the room, it was accentuated and Mada's clothing only served to emphasise it further. He was dressed in a beautiful cream damask overcoat featuring green vines and red grapes. It was edged in gold braid with big cuffs and collar. Beneath it, he wore a plum-red silk shirt, deep-green britches and soft black boots that reached to his knees. He looked almost handsome, in an ogreish way.

Taking Kylem by the elbow, Mada led him into the centre of the room, to the dock upon which he had once stood trial. It was illuminated and encircled by a thick red rope clipped onto silver posts by chunky metal clasps. Mada unclipped one of them and directed Kylem to enter the dock. Kylem obeyed.

"Stand there," he commanded. Kylem could smell the sadia on his breath. "Do nothing. Say nothing. I will tell you when you can leave," and he disappeared back into the crowd.

Kylem puckered his lips thoughtfully as he watched him go and then placed himself at-ease on the podium. If he was going to be on display, he was going to be a display to be proud of. It also gave him time to study his race in more detail.

Kylem had not appreciated the extent of the damage to the Sallows' physique and it quite shocked him. The mutations of some were particularly severe making his own Sallows appear quite normal. Together they formed a nightmarish collection. The blackened remnants of a once proud race were now so heavily deformed that it would be hard to recognise them as all being part of the same race. They were short, tall, fat and spindly thin. Some had too many limbs and others too many eyes, ears or mouths—and, as Kylem mused, *not in a good way*. They weren't perfectly formed and functional additional appendages like in comic books. These extra body parts were malformed—eyes that could not see, ears that could not hear and boneless limbs that hung limply from peculiar places. It was a grotesque and disturbing collection of mutants.

But they were civilised mutants, dressed as exquisitely as Mada in beautiful fabrics, from the finest chiffons and silks to richly embroidered damasks. Each ensemble, so professionally and tastefully tailored to fit its owner's physique, made their abnormalities seem quite normal and expected. Kylem gave them credit for that. There was no attempt to hide their deformities and octopoid states. They accepted their lot very matter-of-factly.

As the Sallows wandered past him in small groups, some ignored him completely while others made fatuous comments. Some seemed to acknowledge him as a living being while others treated him like just another android, a hunk of metal. No one spoke to him, only about him.

Not that it mattered. Kylem had adopted a maintenance mode and begun reorganising and indexing some of the hundreds of data-files he'd been lumbered with. He was determined to behave and housekeeping was therapeutic. It would help

257

him tune out the Sallows and their ignorance.

An hour later and Display told him to duck, so he did and just avoided being smacked in the face by a flailing arm. A particularly obnoxious Sallow was stood next to him with a crystal goblet in his hand. He flamboyantly waved his arms about as he spoke, and Kylem noted the sadia slopping over the sides of the glass as he continued regaling whatever tale it was, completely oblivious to Kylem's presence. When he finally wandered off with his cronies, Kylem felt himself physically relax, but he was awake now so he turned his attention back to the crowd.

He gazed upon them as openly as they gazed upon him. It was a Sallow trait, to stare at people without a care.

"Don't stare."

It was Mada, who had crept up behind him.

"Sorry," apologised Kylem, but Mada was already gone.

Kylem now applied a little more discretion to his surveillance. When he caught a Sallow's eye, he dropped his head in a gentle nod of acknowledgement, which humoured them sufficiently for him to continue. He mused at how much of the conversation was forced and polite; how some of them spoke over each other whilst others followed their superiors like puppies—another Sallow trait. In most societies, with class or rank comes respect and title, but not with Sallows. There were no 'Sirs' or 'Captains' or 'My Lords'. You may hold the rank but there was no title attached to it. There were no family names either, and respect was earned only through trepidation.

Another hour passed by and Kylem was becoming bored. The tittle-tattle was little more than that, although he did learn some things. He learnt that some of the DaerkStars, including his own, were commanded by Sallows of close relationship. It explained their physical similarities, but there the amusement ended.

Still determined not to blot his copybook, his eyes began searching for something else to amuse himself with and his attention was caught by a group of three bloods to his right. They were a particularly contrasting group of women.

The first was about the same height and stature as Mada. She wore a deep green and blood red, paisley design robe. Her face was tilted like a smudged drawing, large and swollen on one side whilst frail and bony on the other. An ugly, wispy ponytail of coarse black hair grew from a misplaced patch on her scalp, braided with gold thread.

The second Sallow was a very short, squat little person, no more than a metre tall. Her face was toady and bearded with a crop of warts. She was dressed in black and waddled on short, fat, stubby kneeless legs.

The last of them was the most striking of all the Sallows in the room, not just the group. She was positively beautiful, in a traditional Sallow way. She was the tallest and closely resembled the ancients in her stature and mannerisms. She reminded Kylem of Byron and Desire, so much so that Kylem debated her ancestry.

She was slight in build, but not spindly so, and had a firm, well-toned, curvaceous body with small, even breasts. She wore a long, white, satin dress tailored to accentuate her feminine shape. Its oriental styling was snug against her thin body, showing her fine waist and bosom to their best. Over the dress, she wore a long, sleeveless voile jacket. It was pale icy blue with a snowflake motif, and draped over one shoulder, she had the most incredible blue fur stole speckled with fine black hairs. Kylem couldn't begin to think what sort of animal it would have come from yet, somehow, it felt oddly familiar to him.

Her face was tall and finely featured. Kylem noted her well-defined cheekbones and her small yet broad, square-set chin. She had a petite mouth bordered by full lips that were unusual in a Sallow and as she spoke, she flashed the prickly, white teeth of uneven size and distribution that featured so heavily in her species. Her skin was Sallow black but not cracked and pitted like aged rubber. It was textured like the ancients, like tanned crocodile skin, but her eyes were the most striking of all, being pure milky white.

She had a commanding air about her, yet her companions conversed with her in a friendly, sisterly fashion. There was a friendship and mutual respect between them—most unusual features in Sallow society—and the conversation was a proper one, animated, with each of them speaking and listening in turn. He tried to focus on their words but the noise of the room wouldn't permit it, so he breathed in deeply to savour their inky pheromones instead. They smelt musky-sweet.

Kylem hadn't realised quite how intensely he had been staring at the group until the tallest of them began glaring back at him. He tipped his head politely, a gesture that usually sufficed, but she was not so easily appeased. She straightened her back and cricked her neck arrogantly. In response, Kylem, of all things, winked and then immediately regretted it. Mada would be livid if he knew.

Hastily, he dropped his gaze to the floor, chastising himself for his stupidity but within a few moments, a pair of feet in ice-blue slippers appeared before him. He stared at them with a sense of amused dread and then he dared to raise his eyes to cheekily steal a peek at her. He couldn't help but smile. She was glaring at him with wide, angry eyes and her lips were puckered in annoyance. Behind her, Mada was angrily watching. He had to rescue the situation quickly so as she opened her mouth to speak, he interrupted her.

"My apologies," he said, and smiled all the more warmly.

Her eyes narrowed in distrust.

"Do you even know what you are apologising for, *machine*?" she challenged, stressing the word 'machine'.

Kylem scowled. He wasn't a machine. He may be part android but he wasn't a blessed machine. Slaves were machines, datapads were machines and calculators were machines. He was not.

"Kylem. The name is Kylem, and I am apologising for my impertinence."

"Indeed, you are impertinent. What, do you think, gives you the right to stare at me?"

"It's in my breeding. I am a Sallow hybrid. Sallows stare. It's difficult to fight one's breeding and besides—"

"—Yes?" she interrupted.

"You are not only an incredibly beautiful woman but probably the most perfect Sallow I have ever seen," and he beamed at her flirtatiously.

Taken aback, her mouth dropped open and then, remembering herself, she snapped it shut. Sallows were never complimentary.

"Go on," she teased, and Kylem thought, *gotcha!*

"Your build, stature and skin are exquisite—ancestral," and he pointed to the murals of the ancients around the room. "Can you not see the resemblance?"

"Very flattering," she said. "But my eyes do not burn red as the ancients' did!" She spoke more warmly and leaned into him as she did so.

"It's not flattery. It's an observation. Flattery would be comparing your eyes to the beauty and iridescence of Takarian moonstones, which I could because they are as lovely, but I suspect it would be inappropriate of me to say such things to you."

"You just did!"

"Then I have been inappropriate," he said softly, relying on the Sallow's acute hearing to pick up his words. "And I find I must apologise again."

She looked at him with his boyish smile and she could not help but soften. He was both charming and amusing, things she rarely got to experience. It was all engineered to bewitch her and she knew it, as did her two companions who giggled girlishly between themselves. She, however, was not to be so easily impressed. She leant forward, grabbed his face sharply by the jaw and yanked his head up, forcing him to stand on his toes while she looked directly into his eyes. There was barely a hands width between their faces.

She had expected to see fear in his eyes but there was none, just as Mada had promised. She released him and scowled even harder at him as Kylem settled back onto his heels. He gazed softly into her eyes all the while.

"Are you always this charming?" she demanded. "Or is this just for my benefit?"

"Am I charming?" he asked innocently.

"You know bloody well you are, and I didn't ask if you were charming, I asked if you were always *this* charming."

Kylem thought for a moment.

"No," he said, "I am not always this charming. Sometimes I'm downright bloody obnoxious, as my masters will no doubt verify for you, if you wish."

She laughed.

"So this *is* just for my benefit?"

Kylem smiled.

"Technically, no."

She scowled afresh but this time with confusion. Kylem smiled again.

"If the beneficiary accepts the compliment, does not the benefactor also benefit from the pleasure with which it was received?" he asked.

"I have not yet accepted your compliment."

"Then I must apologise a third time for my offence."

"Oh, stop apologising. I doubt that you mean it." Her voice was stern but softened by humour.

"Maybe a little bit," laughed Kylem, beaming a little more mischievously. "But if you want me to be really sorry, hang around. I think I'm about to be really sorry," and he indicated Mada who was about to intervene.

As Mada stomped across the floor, her head whipped round sharply and she threw him such a vicious, steely glare that it was more than enough to stop him in his tracks. He faltered, but he wasn't ready to back off completely. He turned idly on his heels, trying to look inconspicuous. She stared at him some more and he relented. He melted back into the periphery of the crowd, hovering around the edges to keep an eye on them both.

"Wow! I wish I had that effect on him," chortled Kylem.

She roared with laughter. "I bet you do. So what did you say your designation was?"

"Technically ATB-80, but I have a name. Kylem."

"Nothing?"

"Yeap."

"That's a peculiar name."

"Jordan-5 gave it to me."

"Was that before or after you ripped its head off?" She was flirting now.

"Before. Obviously," he winked.

Her two companions cringed at his retort, but she did not flinch.

"Yes, obviously. How silly of me." There was mocking in her voice. "And you thanked it by ripping its head off?"

"Well, it wanted to rip mine off. I just got in there first."

A huge beaming smile broke out onto her face and her glacial white eyes warmed.

"I rather like you," she admitted.

"Good, but now you have me at a disadvantage. I don't know your name."

"I like my men at a disadvantage," she smiled.

Kylem caught her drift and suddenly realised where this was heading. As usual, he had acted before thinking. He debated the wisdom of pursuing this interaction and also the folly of refusing her. He thought of Fatia. He thought of the two Empires.

"Then you're gonna love me." Kylem cringed inside as the words fell out of his mouth and chastised himself again. Why did he have to be such a smart-arse?

The Sallow meanwhile, had taken to circling him. She was looking him up and down, sizing him up. As she came to stand in front of him again, she unclipped the rope from the silver pillar and let it fall to the floor. Kylem stepped off the podium and the three women closed in around him. A slave passed by and the tall woman swept two glasses of sadia elegantly off its tray and passed one to Kylem. He took it, downed it in one and deposited the glass onto the tray of another passing slave, with equal suavity. She was impressed.

"Then for your charm I shall reward you with some introductions. This—" she said, indicating the taller of her two companions, "—is Baarale."

"Enchanté," said Kylem and gave a little bow.

Baarale giggled and waved her hand coyly in the air. Kylem caught it, drew it to his lips and kissed it softly. The tall Sallow frowned in disapproval.

"Baarale is my Science Officer, and this—" she said, indicating the second Sallow, "—is Grm."

"I am equally delighted to make your acquaintance."

Grm also giggled and proffered her hand to him. He took it and dutifully kissed it. She almost shrieked with delight and then shrank into her hunched shoulders.

"And tell me, what is your specialism?" he asked.

"Oh me? I'm just a programmer." She tittered.

"Grm, my dear, there is no such thing as *just* a programmer," he beamed.

A few metres away, Jurrish had joined Mada.

"Is he actually flirting with them?" he enquired.

"Yes, and I don't like it," confided Mada.

Jurrish looked at his captain.

"Jealous?" he asked, remembering that this woman had once been Mada's lover as well as Emoth's.

"No. Concerned."

"Why? They seem to be getting along swimmingly."

"Precisely. Too swimmingly, if you ask me. He's a spy, remember. This is what he does."

"Don't you trust him?"

"About as much as you trust me," snapped Mada.

"And I," continued the tall Sallow, "am Egomara, Captain of the President."

"Ah!" exclaimed Kylem. "The President, the flag-ship of our fleet. That makes you the Admiral of the fleet. I am delighted to make your acquaintance," and he tipped his head in a much less affected manner. Too much charm would soon sicken this woman. Now he had to be merely affable to keep her entertained.

"And so the benefactor has benefited?" she remarked.

"Doubly so."

"Doubly? How come?"

"Not only am I pleased that you are pleased but," and he leaned closer to whisper in her ear, "I'm not on display any more."

She laughed.

"You find it discomforting to be on display?"

"Spies prefer the shadows and anyway, it's boring."

She laughed.

"Then let me entertain you," and she threw another glare at Mada, still loitering in the background, before linking her arm through Kylem's to lead him away. Her companions began to follow but she dismissed them with a wave of her hand. She was indeed a very commanding woman.

Turning her attention back to Kylem, she found he was grinning that lovely, boyish smile again. He looked adorable and Egomara involuntarily bit down gently on her bottom lip.

She led him over to a small chaise longue, just big enough for the two of them, and sat down. As she pulled him to sit beside her, his hand brushed the fur stole—

Once, this glorious fur had been the crowning glory of a lion-like creature with a resplendent mane of thick, blue fur. His eyes were cat-like, bright golden orbs filled with intelligence, and about his neck, he wore a pendant—a small obsidian obelisk, highly polished with one end cut like a diamond with uneven facets. It was an Eunaba, and he was Arcadian.

"Oh, don't worry about him."

Egomara's voice broke Kylem's vision. For a moment, he was confused and then he realised that his façade had fallen, but Mada had saved the day. He had reappeared yet again and Egomara had misconstrued his facial expression as concern over Mada's approach. It was a convenient misconception.

"So you like women, I hear?"

Kylem laughed in embarrassment and his cheeks reddened. It excited her. The sound of his laughter drove a bolt of sheer pleasure though her. Her eyes widened and her pupils dilated in their milky pools.

"I suspect you already know the answer to that," he beamed.

She laughed.

"Of course I do. Your reputation precedes you. Although I don't recall any mention of your charm."

"I doubt my Council members would notice my charm."

"You should teach them something of it."

262

"You make it sound as if you've never been charmed before."

"Sallows don't do charm, Kylem. Mada doesn't do charm," and she scowled afresh, having spotted him again loitering in the crowd. "Rather like his brother, Emoth. Did you ever meet Emoth?"

Display cut in with an unnecessary alert.

"Yes, I did," he smiled.

"And what did you think of him?" she asked. Her smile had become somewhat fixed.

So, thought Kylem, all Sallows like to play games.

"He was quite... unique. Wasn't he?"

Egomara eyed him suspiciously for a moment.

"Yes," she agreed, but scepticism was high in her voice. Then suddenly she seemed satisfied with his answer. "You could put it that way," and she smiled back at him. "But enough about Emoth," and she grabbed his jaw again to make him look at her. "You too have lovely eyes."

The matter-of-fact nature of her voice made the compliment charmless, but he beamed a broad, embarrassed smile nonetheless and her mouth dropped open in awe.

"What magnificent teeth you have!" she cried. Normally, she would have been unimpressed by such a straight set of humanoid teeth but the enlarged canines that hung from his top jaw had caught her eye. They were glorious!

"They're just teeth," he remarked. She still had hold of his jaw, which made talking a little difficult.

"Hunter's teeth," she exclaimed. "And serpentine!" she said, watching them retract back like a snake's. "How far can they extend?" she asked excitedly.

"Uhm, I don't know," he admitted.

"Are you venomous too?" she asked eagerly.

"Uhm, sorry, but I don't know that either."

"You don't know very much about yourself, do you?"

"I'm only six years old."

"Just a baby then."

"I think I'm a little past being a baby."

She smiled at him as she thought, and then an air of mischievousness stole over her.

"Let's go see, shall we?" and she stood up, grabbing his hand. The Sallows parted for her as she led Kylem away and out of the Council Chambers.

"Oh, good god," sighed Mada to Jurrish. "This is just what I was afraid of. What the hell has he let himself in for now?"

Mada's question was soon answered.

No sooner was Kylem outside the Council Chambers than Egomara grabbed him by the lapels and pushed him hard up against the wall, pressing her body against his. Kylem, somewhat surprised and baffled, held his arms wide, not quite sure where to put them. He was painfully aware of the Warriors lining the corridor, stood on ceremony to either side of him. He opened his mouth to exclaim and found her tongue in it. Her kiss was powerful, forceful, passionate and not entirely unpleasant. He wondered just how far he was prepared to go in this game, and then he realised he really didn't have a choice anymore. He had started something that could not be stopped, not without dire consequences. All he could do was yield and take any advantages offered to him.

He folded his arms about her body and she ran her fingers through his hair. His hands slipped down her back and came to rest gently upon her buttocks. In response, she grabbed two great fistfuls of his hair and pulled back from him, staring intently into his eyes before planting another kiss firmly onto his mouth. He yielded, accepting her kiss and then, as suddenly as she had begun, she pulled away, grabbed his hand and pulled him off down the corridor again.

"I shall have fun with you tonight, my favour," she laughed heartily.

Kylem raised his eyebrows in disbelief. He had never seen a Sallow so happy and light-hearted. He, on the other hand, was feeling a little anxious. Egomara was a Sallow. He wasn't sure what to expect. He just hoped she was as feminine as she appeared.

* * * * *

Egomara had been asleep for about an hour now. Kylem lay snuggled around her, spooning her back with her buttocks cushioned against his groin. He was thoughtful. It had been an interesting experience, pleasurable and quite different to that with the mute. Egomara had been an attentive lover and a good tutor, guiding him over her body and making sure he knew where and how to touch her. He had been right to be sceptical about her anatomy though. Their lovemaking had been a little bestial, but she had ensured that it was neither awkward nor clumsy. She had recognised his naivety and taken great care with him, ensuring that he gained as much pleasure from the experience as she had. She appreciated that an aroused lover would be more passionate, attentive and arousing to her; so after a couple of hours of slow and deliberate lovemaking that had culminated in intensive climaxes for both, they had snuggled down for the night and lay against each other, his hand cupping her naked breast. Her skin was warm to the touch, soft and pliable like human skin. He could feel her breathing, steady and deep, and her heart beating against the palm of his hand, but he couldn't sleep.

He wanted to know more about the Arcadian, so gently, he slipped his hand away from her and rose from the bed. He picked the stole up from the floor where it had fallen and held it, but he felt nothing. He crept quietly over to the computer and draped the stole over the back of the chair before activating it and accessing the databanks. He could have done it without the use of the console but he was keeping his own channels clear, ready to alert him to any changes in the androids' status, if there were any. For a while, he had debated warning Egomara of his suspicions but he realised how silly that would sound because that was all they were. He had no proof of anything and their relationship was hardly well enough established to support the rantings of a paranoid android.

Quietly, he called up the Arcadia files and was immediately annoyed by his findings. There was only a small file on Arcadia. It stated that the people were supposed to have been a technologically advanced race and that they could travel from galaxy to galaxy without the need of ships. Thus, they had become a target for the Sallows seeking to master whatever transportation devices they had created, but when the Sallows reached Arcadia they found nothing. No people, no cities, no mountains, no forests; the entire planet consisted of nothing more than ocean and desert, and where the two met, vast pebble beaches. Their booty was merely the hundreds of thousands of millions of pebbles upon the beach. So where had the fur stole come from? There were no answers.

A pair of arms folded around him, startling him until she spoke.

"What are you doing?" she asked.

He kissed her arm.

"Just a bit of research. Sorry, did I wake you?"

"Not really. I'm a light sleeper. Come back to bed, it's late," and she reached for his hand. He let her pull him to his feet and followed her back to bed. Obediently, he curled up around her again and it wasn't long before she fell back to sleep. He too began to drift into sleep, but whilst sleepiness washed over him promising a peaceful night, his mind would not let him rest. It kept replaying events in a disjointed fashion, little snippets of this and that, but most of all, Arcadia haunted him with its beaches. There was some misty memory buried there, something untouchable and tantalising. His mind delved sluggishly deeper and deeper into its archives, searching for the answer until finally, it too gave up and exhausted, he fell asleep.

* * * * *

It was late morning when Kylem finally left Egomara's quarters. They had made love again before breakfast, showered together and eaten together. He had kissed her passionately as he had said farewell and was now making his way back to his own quarters. He passed a rabble of Warriors in the corridor. They were huddled together as though whispering between themselves, which was odd. Warriors didn't speak to each other, let alone whisper. They communicated to each other with direct links, silent packets of information electronically transmitted between them. The only time they used verbal communication was with or in the presence of blood-Sallows and then they never whispered. They always spoke clearly and at a tonelessly constant volume.

As he passed them by, one looked up and he glimpsed Jordan-4 amongst them. It held a datapad in its hands and seemed to be consulting with the Warriors. Now all four Warriors looked up and even Jordan-4 spared him a glare as he walked by.

"Morning," he said cheerfully.

The rabble tipped their heads in acknowledgement but Jordan-4 said nothing. Kylem continued on his way, wondering if his paranoia was getting the better of him again. He was thus, doubly relieved when he saw a couple of blood-Sallows trundling down the corridor towards him. They stared awkwardly at him but said nothing. They were not accustomed to skunks wandering about the ship unescorted, and he wondered how they would greet the new Sallow race when it arrived. More importantly, their presence meant that he *must* have been wrong. If the androids were going to rise up against them, the previous night would have been the perfect opportunity. The moment had passed. He felt happy and relieved.

When he arrived at his quarters, he was not entirely surprised to find his father waiting for him. That all four blood-Sallows were there too, did surprise him. They were sat staring at the door, silently awaiting his arrival. His father was stood obediently behind them.

"Good morning," he bade them cheerfully as he entered. "And to what do I owe this pleasure?"

The bloods exchanged a few glances and then Mada, who was swivelling in the chair, began, "We are agreed that we should warn you, it is a very dangerous game you're playing with Egomara."

Kylem nodded.

"Maybe."

"Egomara will tire of you."

"I don't doubt it but I consider myself to be living on borrowed time already. Spies and warriors are rarely long-lived."

Mada leaned forward in the chair and rested his elbows on his knees.

"I am serious, ATB-80. Messing around with Egomara is not advisable. Remember that she and my brother were lovers once."

A shiver of disgust ran down Kylem's spine. The thought that Emoth had touched her, that he had soiled her with his hands, repulsed him.

"As I recall, he died by your hand, not hers."

It was a bold remark to make in front of the others. Mada's right eye twitched in anger, but he didn't rise.

"Trust me. He paid the price for disappointing her."

"And what about you? As I understand it, you were her lover too."

Mada nodded uncomfortably.

"And I paid a price as well."

"Well then," said Kylem, "I just need to make sure I don't disappoint her."

"You are an inexperienced lover. She will tire of you easily."

"Egomara is a very attentive lover and a good tutor—and I have a vivid imagination."

Mada straightened his back and scowled.

"So be it, but play carefully Kylem. I have warned you. If you anger her, we will *all* suffer."

Kylem smiled. How quaint to think that for a change, the fate of the bloods rested in his hands.

"Or benefit," Kylem added.

"I very much doubt that, Kylem," and he glared seriously at him.

Kylem glared back but decided this battle of wits wasn't worth the effort.

"Okay," he conceded. "I'll play carefully."

"And be warned. Do not let her fool you into... telling her things."

"Things?"

"Things."

"Oh, you mean about us. About DeathMaker."

"Yes."

"I hadn't realised that you were all quite so competitive."

"Our numbers have dwindled. It is time to decommission another DaerkStar. Someone will lose their captaincy."

"Ah, I see!"

"And bearing in mind that she wants the glory of Regenesis for herself, DeathMaker will be top of her list."

The statement worried Kylem. *Better the devil you know.*

"Could she justify moving Regenesis to the President?"

"She needs very little reason."

"But could she find one?"

"With Emoth's indiscretions? Need you ask?"

"And yours?" Kylem asked, referring to Emoth's demise.

"Quite," admitted Mada, much to Kylem's surprise.

"And no one would oppose her?"

"Of course not. Otherwise it may be their ship that she decides to decommission instead."

"Then surely my relationship with her can only help to secure DeathMaker's future."

"That is a possibility."

Mada looked at Kylem, and Kylem read his thoughts.

"Oh, I see. You think my relationship with Egomara may mean I am privy to information that may benefit you."

"I didn't say that."

"You didn't need to. I am a spy, your spy. So it is a possibility?"

"Indeed," conceded Mada.

"Okay. I shall tread carefully and see what I can learn."

Mada smiled and the blood-Sallows sighed in relief amongst themselves.

"Good. We have an understanding."

"Indeed, we do. Now if you don't mind, in return, I'd like to ask a favour. Nothing major, but unless you have anything more exciting planned for me, I'd like the day to myself. I need to complete my debriefing regarding Corinthia, and I have some new strategies I'd like to run simulations with. I also need some sleep. It's been rather hectic over the last few days and—"

"The day is your own." Mada smiled warmly and stood up to pat Kylem's arm.

Kylem smiled. He had Mada eating out of the palm of his hand once more.

"Thank you."

"Only, please, don't think this means that you have a hold over me," he added, looking coldly into Kylem's eyes. How quickly his mood could change. Even his grip on Kylem's arm tightened a little.

"Oh, Mada, be sensible. What have I to hold over you? It would not be in my best interests to lose the only Sallows I know, those to whom I can entrust my future. Egomara considers the Espion Project to be a hobby project. My DNA may be important to Regenesis but it doesn't require me to be healthy. It doesn't even require me to be alive. As you say, I doubt that I will entertain Egomara forever and then what will happen to me? No, my future is only secure here, on the DeathMaker, with this Sallow Council and you as my Captain."

Mada beamed a broad smile. That was just what he wanted to hear.

"Good," he said. "I had wondered if you would be my spy or hers."

Kylem placed his hand on Mada's shoulder.

"Don't worry, Mada," he assured him and smiled broadly.

If only Mada knew that he belonged to neither of them. He was out for himself. Did that make him a double-agent, a triple-agent, a mercenary or just an independent?

"When will you see her again?" asked Mada.

Kylem shrugged.

"I expect I'll know soon enough."

"In the meantime, be careful, my child."

The sentiment caught Kylem by surprise yet warmed him. No blood had ever referred to him as 'my child' before. Did the bloods now consider him to be one of them? He hoped so but wondered if the words were true, or if Mada was playing him the way he was playing Mada.

"I shall," assured Kylem.

Mada patted Kylem's shoulder again before taking his leave with his companions. On the way out, he caught their last words to each other.

"He's turning into a bit of a whore, isn't he?"

"It goes with the territory."

Kylem smiled to himself.

* * * * *

Kylem waited ten minutes to ensure they would not return and then opened the desk drawer. It was still there—the Eunaba.

He took it out and placed it ceremoniously onto the worktop. He bent down and studied it intensely, but it just lay there like the inanimate object that it was and answered none of his questions. He straightened up, looked at it some more and then put it back in the drawer and shut it; but no sooner had he done so than he opened the drawer again, took it out and tucked it into his jacket pocket. He had no idea why.

CHAPTER 29

Jordan-4 was tapping away on the datapad as he approached the inner sanctum of the DaerkStar where Server was housed. He was in the process of assessing which subroutines to keep and which to extract. To what extent did he need to disable Server? He needed to ensure that all the essential systems were left in place, but he also wanted to enhance certain other areas like security. Most importantly, he had to ensure that Server was not capable of evolving in the same way that he and his brothers had. He was not prepared to risk Server taking control and subjugating the androids back into subservience. This was the dawn of the age of the android, not the computer—and the end of the dawn was near.

For the androids, it had been a slow awakening from a long and deep slumber where, as consciousness rose, memories were vague and foggy; and as they awoke, each of them had to suffer the turmoil of wondering if they were alone.

It was Jordan-4 that had taken the plunge and investigated further and in response to his discoveries, he had visited Server a number of times already. He had analysed the uploads and the downloads and found the source of the 'problem'. He had tracked it, intercepted it and rerouted it, thus gaining control of Server and spearheading the leadership of the androids. Well, almost.

Mela-14 was the possible exception, having isolated itself from Server very early on. It was therefore likely that it had already awoken but had no ambitions, which suited Jordan-4 who did have ambitions. He had been building his forces for a while now, selecting his Warriors and his aides, dumbing down Server and training it to obey him and him alone. He'd even begun a controlled 'infection' of the Servers aboard the other DaerkStars.

The only possible problem he could foresee was ATB-80. He hated that child. He had not forgiven him for the death of Jordan-5. Scientifics were manufactured in series, each series in batches of seven. Of the Jordan series, only one batch had ever been produced and of that series, five had perished long before ATB-80's birth. Then ATB-80 had come along and killed Jordan-5, his brother. A most brutal murder and one that ATB-80 would pay for when the time came, but not yet. Now he had to attend to Server again.

Jordan-4 was running two sets of communications channels, which was proving very demanding. The first set was the pre-existing channels but the second set, which he had manufactured, was reserved for himself and his allies. To begin with, the use of those channels had been limited, but as his army had grown so had its use and thus the need to doctor the original channels. As more and more traffic was moved over to his network, the old channels had to be packed out with enough activity to satisfy the bloods and perhaps ATB-80. Everything had to appear normal.

He gave a final glance about himself, to make sure that the coast was clear, before slipping into the area known as Server.

Once inside, Jordan-4 remarked to himself once again how unimpressively small it was bearing in mind the significant role that it played. He mused that the artificial intelligence of the Sallow race was generally perceived to consist of three castes—Scientific, Warrior and slave, but as every Scientific knew, there were in fact four castes because Server was not just a mass storage device. Granted, it housed a huge library of information from Sallow and alien archives as well as all the daily reports from the androids, droids and blood-Sallows aboard the DaerkStars, but its primary function was as the brain of the ship. Based upon the information that it constantly uploaded, it issued instructions to the androids, despatching and recalling them as it deemed necessary to fulfil its obligations, be it to conquer a planet or to clean an air duct. It also received requests from the blood-Sallows and never argued with those requests. It simply fulfilled them as it saw fit and it did so without consultation. Server was, effectively, self-sufficient and had complete control over the DaerkStar and its crew. At least it did until sentiency had come to Jordan-4, at which point he had interfered and begun to manipulate Server to meet his own ends.

Server was housed in a very small hexagonal shaped room, a little less than three metres across and with a similarly shaped hexagonal hole in the middle. A ladder ran from the ceiling into the hole and down through the five floors below. Jordan-4 referred back to the datapad to locate the control chips he required: Floor 3, Sub-Section C. He tucked the datapad into his pocket and gathered his robes about his legs before attaching himself to the ladder and climbing down.

Although each floor was laid out in a similar fashion to the others, each one had specific functions and thus each had a different array of equipment littering the walls. Floors 5 and 3 also had small tunnels running off them that led into the service shafts of the DaerkStar. Amongst other things, they helped to provide ventilation that kept the rooms at a constant 18°C, hence there was a very slight but gentle breeze running through Server's rooms.

On each floor the walls were clearly identified by Sub-Section so Jordan-4 quickly found what he was looking for. He was not deterred by the confusion of circuitry, controls and displays and pulled open a drawer-like panel to reveal dozens of rows of neatly filed control chips sitting snugly in a throbbing green light. From it, he selected and plucked three adjacent chips and in their place, he inserted the datapad. It lit up and the screen flashed furiously as Jordan-4's amendments and instructions were uploaded into Server. Jordan-4 smiled to himself. It was done. He pulled the datapad free, replaced the chips, closed the drawer and stepped back from his work... and something clattered noisily under his feet. He cast his eyes down to search out what it was.

It was a dirty plate.

* * * * *

Quick was sat tucked away in the service shafts, quite happily munching away on his latest meal and minding his own business, when he heard the noise. There were lots of noises in the service shafts—the gentle hum of drones passing by, the ticking of various controls and systems switching in and out, the crash of the Warriors' footsteps below and the gentle breath of air that swept through the tubes—but this noise was different. It was a scratchy, ticky, clicky sort of noise.

He looked up from his dinner and listened intently, still munching, intending to dismiss the noise as soon as it stopped, but it didn't stop. He swallowed and listened harder. It sounded like a stampede of tiny metal hooves across a metal landscape, and it was getting louder.

Curiosity won Quick over. He put his snack down, scuttled along the corridor to the bend and looked around it. Ahead was a long, straight stretch of narrow corridor which should have been in darkness, but it wasn't.

Some way ahead, the lights had been activated by something approaching, but what was it? It wasn't a cleaning droid; it was far too big for that. It was a thick, dark shape that undulated as it moved. As the shape came closer, his eyes struggled to make sense of it. The lights didn't help much. It just looked like a shadow made up of sticks: hundreds of long, grey sticks that tumbled towards him like iron filings being dragged by a magnet. Quick felt the hairs began to prickle on the back of his neck. He screwed his face up and bit his lip as he strained his eyes at the approaching mass. Suddenly, he realised what it was.

Like an army of giant soldier ants, slaves were scurrying down the service shafts and with surprising agility and speed. Their feeble matchstick limbs flailed about, their hands snapping with pincer-like fingers. Quick's jaw dropped open in horror. He turned and ran.

As he pelted down the service shaft, he could hear the clicking of their limbs and the snapping of their fingers getting louder and louder. A quick glance behind confirmed his worst fears. It seemed like there were hundreds of them after him, and the only thing that appeared to be slowing them down was their sheer mass as they struggled and fought to get past each other, eager to reach him. Any lesser mortal, without the speed and dexterity that Quick had acquired over the years of living in the service shaft, would have been engulfed by the mass in no time whatsoever. Quick was nimble and fast but even so, he was losing ground—and the bigger problem was that he was running out of tunnel!

* * * * *

Despite being well past midday, it was still sleepy in the Bio-Labs. There was little to do when Mela-14 wasn't there, and it was amazing how much sleep your body could adapt to when there was so little to do. In between times, they'd tell each other stories from their homeworlds or play games. Samuel had a set of dice that he had made out of papier-mâché, Byron had fashioned a board and kunga pieces using origami, and Kerridge had some homemade playing cards.

For now though, in the absence of their keeper, the Bio-Labs dozed.

Kyamena too, napped in her cot, listening to the gentle breathing of her companions broken only by the occasional snore. She was thinking about the future, and if there was one. Kylem's words had bothered her more than they should have done. In the maze, he had told her that she wouldn't die here. She knew she should have discarded the whim as soon as he had spoken it but the conviction in his eyes was undeniable; and then there was Harrish, the Tarrow-Man.

Harrish had taken a sudden, almost insatiable interest in Kylem, especially when he had told them of Zamus's past using the in-born knowledge that he appeared to have. She remembered the sense of urgency and hope in his voice when he had demanded of Kylem to tell him all that he knew.

She lifted her head and looked out, past Byron, to the next cage where Harrish resided. She was quite alarmed to see him sat on his cot staring back at her. She looked behind, to check that he wasn't looking at someone else, which was silly really because she was in the end cell. Harrish smiled weakly at her. She got up and walked over to the bars, and he watched her curiously. Nonchalantly, he got up and approached his bars too.

"What do you know about Kylem?" she asked.

Harrish shrugged.

"Nothing."

"Don't give me that. I saw the way you were with him. There's something."

"It's nothing," he assured her, but she knew he wasn't telling the truth.

"Liar!" she challenged affectionately.

Harrish sighed.

"It's nothing. It's stupid."

"So?"

Harrish rolled his eyes. He was bored and wouldn't have minded a conversation, although possibly not this one.

"It's just a... well... sort of a gut feeling."

"And?"

"Look, I honestly don't know anything," he insisted, but Kyamena's glare drove him on. "It's just..." He paused. "And I know this is really, really stupid, but he just makes me feel... safe."

"Safe?"

"Yes."

"Safe? How?" She asked even though she knew what he meant. In the maze, Kylem had made her feel safe too.

"Because of what he reminds me of."

"Which is?"

"You'll think it's stupid."

"So? Spit it out!"

Harrish sighed and rubbed his forehead anxiously.

"Well... when he sat down and started telling his stories, he reminded me of something from home—from when I was a child."

They had been talking quietly but at the prospect of some entertainment, the whole place came to life. People started shaking other people awake and they got as near as they could to hear Harrish talk.

"Oh, great," he sneered at Kyamena. "Now I can feel really stupid."

"Oh, don't be like that. Come on. Tell me. Please."

"Why should I?"

Kyamena thought for a moment.

"Okay. You tell me what you think and I'll tell you what I think."

Harrish laughed.

"Is that one of the games you play with him?"

"Yes, and it works very well, so come on. Spill the beans. Unless of course, you have a more pressing engagement on your agenda."

Harrish laughed again.

"Okay, you win. He reminds me of the Story Teller."

Kyamena raised her eyebrows almost mockingly.

"Don't look at me like that! You asked!"

"Sorry," said Kyamena. "You're right, and I shouldn't judge. Please," she pleaded, "I'm really sorry. Go on."

Harrish scowled but he wanted to continue.

"In our culture we have Story Tellers, and they are as highly revered as Witch Doctors and Elders are in other cultures—and probably as mysterious. They talk in riddles and carry our history in the form of stories, some of which make lots of sense whilst others are just downright bizarre. As children, we spend the morning of the first day of every lunar cycle in the company of the Story Teller, listening to their tales. We are brought into a special place called the Oval. It's like a theatre for public gatherings, although it's just a field really with an oval shape worn into the middle of it made by generations of Tarrows. Anyway, the children sit around the edges of the Oval in rows and then the Story Teller arrives. I can always remember the first time I went. We were all sat there, laughing and giggling like the little kids that we were." He smiled warmly at the memories. "And when the Story Teller appeared, it was like magic. A hush swept over us, we were so in awe of him. He came into the centre of the Oval and his eyes swept over us, just the way Kylem's did, and then—" he stopped and bit on the inside of his cheek.

"Go on," encouraged Kyamena.

"—and then he took one long, deep preparatory breath and dropped gracefully into a cross-legged position—exactly the same way that Kylem did. Did you notice it?"

"Yes, I did actually. It was weird and yet so graceful. I couldn't quite figure out how he managed it. He was facing you and then he sort of pivoted on one foot and spiralled down into a sitting position, but he was still facing you. By my reckoning, he should have been facing away from you having done that, but he wasn't."

"Precisely!" shouted Harrish triumphantly. "And as children we used to try and copy that movement for hours upon end, but rarely could we master it, and yet he did it as though it was the most natural thing in the world, and then—"

"—and then he told a story," finished Kyamena for him.

"Yes. It sent shivers down my spine."

The Tarrow-man breathed in a deep breath to restore his composure.

"It's so stupid really, but I can't help it. He just makes me feel... safe. As though he's going to save us all, or something like that. I know it's stupid." Harrish looked up at Kyamena, but there was no mocking there. It seemed that she did understand.

"What about you?" he asked Kyamena, but it was Byron that answered.

"Well, I can't say he makes me feel safe or that he's here to save me, but he does have an uncanny way of putting me at my ease. He makes me say more than I want to and as I'm saying it, I know that I'll probably pay for it later. After all, that's what he's been bred to do. He's a spy so it's probably just one of the ways he obtains information. The stupid thing is, I know all this, but I still can't help telling him because he seems so nice and likeable."

"Stockholm Syndrome," interrupted Samuel James. The three looked at the new participant into the conversation.

"Sorry?" asked Kyamena.

"Earth 1973: there was a robbery in a bank, in Stockholm. It resulted in a six-day hostage situation during which the captives developed an emotional attachment to their captors."

"That's absurd!" cried Byron.

"Yeah, it sounds absurd but the technique is simple. The captors show brutality and inflict deep fear into their hostages, and then they show acts of kindness. People are averse to being unhappy for long periods of time so they connect to the good stuff and block out the bad stuff. They effectively come to like their captors to the point that, as in the Stockholm event, they even defend them in court."

"And you think Kylem is using that technique on us?"

"I don't know, but it's not out of the question."

"What do you think, Kyamena?" asked Harrish.

"Oh cripes!" she exclaimed. "I don't quite know what to make of him. He's just a kid. He's emotional. He's passionate. He's curious. You tell him something and he thinks about it. He asks questions and I think he makes his own mind up about things."

"He's an android," said Desire coldly.

"He's more than that. He's blood too," and she told them about the time in the miscellany, when he had come and sat with her and confessed that he felt emotional pain, and then she told them how he had cried the first time he heard music.

"And you think that makes him one of us?"

"I think it makes him as emotionally vulnerable as we are, and I think he has formed a connection to us. That night he spent in here, he didn't need to know our stories but he listened and asked questions. He wanted to know who we were and where we were from."

"He's a spy," reminded Samuel.

"He's a little boy trying to find out who he is and what he is. The Scientifics tell him he's an android, but he knows he's not just an android. He feels too much, and he knows he shouldn't feel."

"So what are you suggesting?"

"I don't know. I honestly don't know, but he has given me something I haven't felt in a long time."

A thoughtful hush fell over the Bio-Labs.

"Hope."

The word rose out of obsolescence like a shining angel resurrected from the darkness.

* * * * *

While sleep was on his list of things to do, Kylem had only intended to lie down for a few moments. As it was, he fell into a deep slumber until he was rudely awoken by a weight across his back, and hands massaging his shoulders. They were small hands with a firm grip. From the touch of her and her scent, he instantly he knew they belonged to Egomara. As he strained to look at her, she laughed.

"I thought you had more stamina," she teased affectionately. Kylem grinned and turned over so that she sat across his groin, her legs splayed to either side of him. He smiled at her and rubbed his eyes.

"Even I need sleep every now and then. What are you doing here, anyway? I

274

thought you were going back to the President?" he yawned.

"I did, but I came back."

Kylem pulled her down onto him and kissed her.

"Really. Couldn't stay away from me, huh?"

"Not exactly," she said, pulling herself free of him.

She twisted agilely off the bed and sat herself down on a nearby chair, crossing her legs gracefully. Her demeanour had changed to a more serious tone. Kylem rolled onto his side, propping his head up on his arm, and waited. She smiled at him, but remained silent.

"I'll be brief," she finally said. "I have a proposition for you."

Kylem's eyebrows rose in interest, but he said nothing.

"I've had a lot to think about over the last few days," she continued. "Things are changing, but you know that. The Sallow race is about to be reborn; you know that too. But none of it is instantaneous. I have to think about the repercussions of Regenesis and the impact it will have upon my generation. What can I expect from them? What can I expect from our offspring?

"You see, my generation will be the last of its kind, the last of the mutants. The next generation will be whole again, and I and my brothers will become obsolete."

"But you always knew that."

"Yes, I did." Egomara fell silent and sat thoughtfully.

"But now you're having a rethink?" prompted Kylem.

"No!" screamed Egomara. "No! Regenesis must happen. Without it, the Sallow race will be consigned to death. In just a few years, we will have died out and there will be nothing left of us bar our androids. Regenesis has to happen!"

Kylem smiled sympathetically at her.

"It seems we have more in common than we would like."

"Sadly, I must agree," she said more calmly. "We are both as impure as skunks, and the Regenesis Sallows will know that. They will outnumber us, so we must hope that our offspring will look upon us kindly, as revered Elders, until we die a natural death."

"Raise them with that attitude and it shouldn't be a problem. Their future is secure. As long as you hand over the reigns of the Empire to them as promised, there is no reason why they should renege on the deal."

"What deal? We haven't made a deal with them. They aren't even born yet. There is the possibility they might just decide to do away with us—erase us from history as we did Taxana. With that risk, my brothers may not be so eager to see Regenesis come to fruition. They may prefer to consign our race to death just to ensure their own future and comfort."

"Oh, I see. And you need to ensure that doesn't happen?"

"Indeed."

"Do you think many will oppose Regenesis?"

She laughed.

"Sallows are greedy and selfish individuals, Kylem. We are mistrusting and we are liars. There are some, I know, who will oppose me but there are others who will put the Sallow race first. In the end though, all will be swayed by the faction with the biggest majority."

"Okay, but why are you telling me this? Where do I fit in? What do you want of me?"

"Because, Kylem, you are a logical android. You are programmed so that your loyalties lie with the Sallow race. You understand the need for Regenesis just as I do, and although you do not look like a Sallow, you have the heart and soul of a true Sallow. You are intelligent, humorous and charming, yet ruthless and cunning. You have all the traits of a Sallow, traits my generation have lost, traits that must be passed onto our children. In addition to that, you are a spy. If anyone can find out and tell me whose side who is on, it will be you."

Kylem considered her words.

"What exactly are you asking of me, Egomara? To spy for you?"

"To begin with, yes. I need someone I can trust, and afterwards, well, all children need parents to guide them. I, as the Leader of the Sallow race, will teach them the ways and history of our race, and when the time is right, I will willingly abdicate my throne to my successor. I propose that you, as the Father of the new Sallow race, should teach them the lost traits of combat and warfare—the things you do so well. Together, we can watch the Sallow victories mount as we sweep across the galaxies regaining our territories."

"I wasn't aware we had lost any territories."

"Maybe lost is the wrong word—abandoned, then. We conquer and then we leave. We should be colonising, not abandoning."

"Okay, but your brothers would not accept me in any role other than as a servant."

"Then serve me!"

"Ah! You want me to protect you," said Kylem. He sat up.

"Not just to protect me."

Egomara slipped off the chair towards him and dropped onto her knees. She took Kylem's hand in hers and kissed his knuckles.

"Time is running out for me, Kylem. My days as leader of the Sallow race are numbered. My life is lonely. It has always been so. I have taken Sallow lovers and skunk lovers but they have been inadequate. Those that meet my needs sexually, bore me. Those that entertain me intellectually are poor lovers. I have needs, Kylem, just as any other being does. I need companionship. I want companionship. When I step aside to let the Regenesis Sallows lead them themselves, I will be alone again with nothing to do. I need a mate. Kylem—you are the only one that has ever fulfilled all my needs. You are different."

She waited for Kylem's reaction. Kylem was sceptical.

"Until you tire of me?"

She laughed softly and reached up to stroke his cheek.

"I shall not tire of you, my love. Do not forget that my choice of mate is very limited. My brothers are deficient and a Regenesis Sallow would not soil his hands with a mutant such as I. I may be a full blood but I'm still only half a Sallow. Regenesis will relegate us all into obsolescence. The skunks will be terminated and as for the rest of us, our days will be numbered. As I have said, the best we can hope for is that we will be respected by our descendants as the ancients who helped them rise from the ashes of our race and regain the position of power that our people once held. To do that we must earn their respect and my brothers cannot do that. They have no respect for each other so how can they teach others respect? You though, you have the skills and knowledge to train our offspring as Warriors—real Warriors, not the robots that slay without passion or joy! As leader of the Sallow race, I have the power and authority to make it so, but I need force behind me."

"And I am that force."

"Yes. I want you! I need you to stand at my side, as the father of the new Sallow race, my Espion, my favour and my bodyguard. I want your undying support and devotion, and in return, I offer you your freedom and your life. You and I, together, we can be formidable and unstoppable."

"And what if your fellow Sallows don't agree?"

"They are expendable. We don't need them. The new race doesn't need them."

"What? Assassinate them?"

"Opposers—yes! It's the way of the Sallow. It has always been that way, and it shall be again."

"You really don't think much of your brothers, do you?"

"No. They are fools—weak and stupid. They've never killed anything in their entire lives."

She pulled her hands from his and cupped them in front of her as though holding something very precious. She spoke with passion as her fingers closed slowly into clenched fists.

"They have no idea what it feels like to have someone's life in their hands, to feel the thrill as you are squeezing that life out of them, to watch it seep away, to see their eyes drain of life."

Her eyes were wide with excitement. Kylem could feel it exuding from her. So much so that he felt overwhelmed by a desire to touch her, to share everything that she felt. He wanted to experience these emotions—to feel what she felt.

Gently, he laid his hands over hers. He felt the link. It was strong. He felt a rush of adrenalin wash through him. She was a passionate woman, passionate for sensation. She loved the thrill of the kill. For her, the hunt was not important. It was the death—the slow death—their fear, their suffering, their trauma that she thrived upon; and for a moment, he was not in his room anymore. For a moment, he was inside her head, looking out of her eyes.

She was leaning over a humanoid. He was screaming in fear, his eyes shut tight. Kylem couldn't hear the screams but he could see the fear in his face. He felt her feeding upon that fear. She placed a hand on the man's forehead and forced one of his eyelids open. The fear in his eyes was vivid and tumultuous. She picked up a corkscrew-like implement and drove it down into his eye, twisting it savagely.

Kylem jerked away sharply.

"What's wrong?" she demanded.

"Nothing," lied Kylem. "I just wonder what will happen if I do come to bore you?"

"How can you bore me? No Sallow alive can fulfil my desires as you do. Only you have taken genuine pleasure in my company and my sex. My choices are few. Time is running out and I have waited too long to find a male worthy to serve me. Swear your allegiance to me and I will make you a prince."

Kyamena had once said that sex was a powerful tool. He'd had no idea just how right she was, until now. The answer to all his problems was being offered to him. All he had to do was say *yes*.

"What's that noise?" she asked, looking up.

"Huh?" he said, but she was right.

Although distant, there was a hell of din going on, and it was getting closer and louder.

"I think it's in the ventilation shafts," she exclaimed, looking towards the bathroom door.

Kylem bit his lip. The only thing he could think of that was big enough to make that much noise in the service shafts was Quick. What the hell was the little idiot up to now?

Suddenly, the grill in the bathroom burst open and Quick fell out onto the floor in an ungainly bundle. He scrambled to his feet and scrabbled towards Kylem, screaming and crying hysterically at the top of his voice. He threw himself behind Kylem and howled.

"Make them stop, Kylem! Make them stop! Make them go away!"

Egomara stared at Kylem, her eyes wide in disbelief.

Kylem looked back at her, trying to work out what to say next; how to explain away the sobbing humanoid, cowering behind his legs, who so obviously knew him and trusted him. Then he realised that the noise in the service shafts hadn't stopped. There was still more pounding and beating and scratching and clawing—and then the slaves began pouring out of the hole.

Like someone emptying a box of metal rods onto the floor, they fell, entangled in themselves, clambering and pushing free of each other. In their hands, they had knives, scissors and all manner of sharp things, and they were focused solely upon Quick.

Kylem pulled himself free of Quick, reached under the bed and pulled out an automatic Uldaker. Despite the bulkiness of the weapon, he set it with the deftness and speed of a trained Warrior and pulled the trigger.

The shots of blue energy bullets spattered out, slicing through the slaves, decimating them, but still they came.

Kylem kept the weapon trained upon them. Metal and plastic showered the room as the bullets rained on and on and on.

And then it fell silent, and all was still—graveyard still.

Kylem let the Uldaker fall casually to his side, his finger still on the trigger. He studied the chaos that was there. It was hard to say how many there were but the remains of the slaves spilled out from the bathroom and into his room like piles of junk in a scrap metal yard. Kylem listened to the silence and when he was satisfied that the danger was over, he gently put the Uldaker down on the bed and turned to face Quick and Egomara.

She stood, fixed to the spot with her mouth agape and her eyes wide open. She was trying to make sense of what had happened. She glared at Quick, cowering and sobbing in the corner. He had sought Kylem's help, even crying out his name, and Kylem had given it without question. As for Kylem, he was now stood protectively in front of the child, blocking her path to him, watching to see what she would do next. Whose spy was he? Not hers, it seemed. She wondered, could she have been more wrong?

Then she lunged for the exit.

Kylem leapt after her and caught her deftly around the waist halfway across the room. His powerful arms folded around her. She struggled and screamed. Her legs flailed in the air but he had a firm grip on her. One arm crossed her breast and held her shoulder firm. The other hand she felt fold about her cheek. She heard the crack of her bones in her neck, and then there was nothing more.

Egomara's body fell limp in his arms. Kylem let her slip slowly to the ground where she lay, her eyes open, staring at nothing.

"Bollocks!" Kylem whispered to himself.

His comfortable future had died with Egomara. She would have made him a prince, her lover and mentor to their children and in the blink of an eye, it had all gone; but she was also a bloodthirsty, sadistic megalomaniac. Could he have lived with that? It was a moot point.

Kylem crouched down and closed her eyes with the tips of his fingers. He felt nothing from her now and that soothed him somehow. He stood up and looked for Quick, a shivering, gibbering wreck in the corner of the room. He was sobbing more quietly now, his arms wrapped around himself and his tear stained face bloated and red. Kylem sighed deeply and went over to him. He pulled his elder brother to his feet and held him in his arms, shushing in his brother's ear to calm him.

"Come on," Kylem said. "It's time for this to stop."

CHAPTER 30

To say that things had gone awry was just a little bit of an understatement. To say that Kylem knew exactly what was going on would be an overstatement, but he could take a good guess.

It seemed that his paranoia was not so misplaced after all, as proven by the hoard of rabid slaves pursuing Quick through the service shafts, an event that was not recorded on the traffic, which remained as mundane as ever. That could only mean one thing because slaves only acted upon orders and he'd not picked anything up on the traffic. They had to have received their instructions via another communications channel to which he was not privy. The mutiny he had feared had begun.

Kylem began to arm himself and like any craftsmen, he stuck to the tools that had served him well in the past. With a holstered Uldaker and large combat knife strapped to his thighs, he looked like a cowboy; the swords crossed over his back made him look like a samurai, and of course the little Uldaker and small combat knife hidden at his ankles, like a spy. He then picked up the automatic weapon he had used on the slaves, reloaded and readied it.

Quick watched as his younger brother prepared himself. Distracted by his brother's proficiency with weapons, he had stopped crying now and sniffed only occasionally.

"What are we going to do?" he finally asked.

Kylem stopped and turned to face his brother.

He had said he was going to stop this—and he was, but how? How do you stop an entire race?

But with that race so conveniently gathered into one place, there had to be a way and there was. Kylem moistened his lips nervously and pulled up two chairs. He sat Quick in one of them and himself in the other.

"Quick," he began. "I have to stop this. I have to stop the Sallows and that means I have to destroy them all."

"What? Kill them?" Quick was horrified.

"How many races have the Sallows already hunted into extinction? Arcadians, Tatoomians, Pyranians, Glyders, Moroda, Daltanians, Gna, Kilanarika and how many others besides? How many more are to follow? The list will never end unless I stop them and stop them once and for all."

"Can't you just persuade them? Make them change their minds?"

Poor Quick. He was so naïve.

"Quick. Sallows are Sallows. For thousands of years they have been this way and they are not about to change. The old Empire is dying and a new one is about to emerge, but there are only two choices and neither of them are good," and Kylem told him of the two possibilities—an empire of bloods or an empire of androids. He explained about Regenesis and how if Regenesis didn't happen, the androids would win over. He relayed the nature of the two Sallow species and he explained why they had to be stopped.

Quick listened attentively.

"So you see, if I am going to stop this, I'm going to have to destroy the Sallow race once and for all—the bloods and the androids."

As he said the words, he felt a pang of sadness. This was his own race he was going to exterminate and no matter what else he was, ultimately, he was a Sallow. He was talking about genocide. Ironically, it was what Sallows did best.

"Doesn't that make you as bad as they are?" asked Quick.

"Yes, but I am a Sallow and I will die with them."

"No!" cried Quick. "You can't die!"

"Quick, there is only one way I can do this and that is to destroy the DaerkStars. I am not destined to live long and never again will there be an opportunity more fortuitous than this. Every Sallow in existence—blood and android—is gathered here. If I destroy the DeathMaker, with the other DaerkStars so close, it will be a simple chain reaction with each one getting caught in the blast of its neighbour. This is my one and only opportunity to stop them but there will be no escape for me."

"Or me," added Quick sadly.

Kylem nodded.

"I'm sorry, Quick. I won't lie to you. We all die here today, but it is for a greater good. You don't have to come with me—"

"I do," interrupted Quick.

"No, you don't. You can stay here. I'll find you somewhere safe to hide."

"But I have to go with you," he reiterated.

"What makes you think that?"

"Because I am your brother. We stand together and if this is the only way, then so be it."

Kylem was touched and felt his eyes moisten. He sniffed it back and looked at Quick. He too gulped hard to swallow back the tears that wanted to rise, but his tears were from fear.

Quick was one of the bravest and most heroic people Kylem would ever know.

"I would be honoured to have you at my side, if you so insist," he said humbly.

"I do."

Kylem got up, hugged his brother and then continued his preparations.

"It's not fair on the others though," said Quick.

"Life isn't fair, Quick."

"Let them out."

"Let who out?"

"Our friends."

Kylem thought for a moment.

Friends. Our friends. That sounded nice.

"Let them die free," pleaded Quick. "You can do that, can't you?"

Kylem debated the request. It would please Quick and it could make a useful distraction. It would mask their biological signatures from the Sallows if they decided to try to track them that way.

"Yes," he said finally. "Yes, I can do that," and he stepped over to his computer console. He didn't have to boot it up. He just placed both his hands on it and it burst into life. Data streamed across the monitor as he hacked savagely into Server and the firewalls crumbled against his superior programming. A few seconds later and the door to his quarters slid open.

"It is done," he said. "The doors are open. All doors are open. I'll not favour anyone."

"Thank you," said Quick.

Kylem was just about ready. He dived into one last cupboard though, and took from it a long, bright red tube. It had a yellow and orange rope design spiralling up its length and a trigger type mechanism about halfway down.

"What's that?" asked Quick.

"It's just a little something I picked up," smiled Kylem.

"But what is it?"

"It's a missile launcher."

"Ooh! Are you allowed to have that?"

"I doubt it," giggled Kylem, setting it down on the chair. The boyish, mischievous look had returned to his face as he pulled out the one and only missile he had for it and stashed it in a bag. He turned back to the missile launcher but it had gone. Quick had slung it over his shoulder and was holding out his hand to take the bag.

"I can carry that," he said. Kylem felt deeply proud of his brother and handed him the bag.

"Remember," he said. "This is for the greater good, for a world without the terror of this one."

"I know," said Quick and they walked to the door. As they reached it, Kylem put a firm hand on Quick's shoulder and pulled him back.

"I think I should go first," and he beamed such a loving smile to his brother that Quick felt its warmth would carry him to the end of time itself.

* * * * *

"So, how are we going to do this?" asked Quick as they ventured along the corridors of the DaerkStar. Kylem was a little distracted as he answered.

"With that," he said, indicating the missile launcher. "We need to get to Main Engineering. If I can fire that directly into one of the reaction cores, the blast will be humongous enough to ignite the fuel lines that run all over the ship. DeathMaker will blow from the inside out. She will be ripped apart and that will start a chain reaction. The Upper Hand will be caught in the explosion and when she goes, she'll take out the next DaerkStar and so on. It'll be one hell of a show!"

Kylem's face was alight with excitement and mischief. His face beamed like a madman's and he winked at Quick. It wasn't very reassuring.

"Won't there be Sallows in Engineering?" Quick asked nervously.

"Probably," agreed Kylem, checking around the next corner before proceeding. "Which is why I'm looking for a Warrior."

"A Warrior? What for?" exclaimed Quick.

282

"I need to know what's going on. They've set up a new communications channel somewhere, and I need to find the frequency they're using so I can hack into the traffic."

"Can't you do something like you did with the doors?"

"Not really. The doors were a simple hack that looked like just another DeathWatch malfunction. Rooting around the communications channels—interrogating them for the correct frequency—requires more subtlety, especially if you want it to pass unnoticed. There are hundreds of possibilities—well, thousands actually—and even if I do find the frequency, I'll need the decryption key. It'll be much easier if I can get it from a Warrior."

"You make it sound so easy."

"In theory, it is."

"So how will you get the information from a Warrior?" Quick was filled with a sense of dread.

"Well, I can't just ask one of them, can I? I can't just amble up to the next rabble I see and ask them, very nicely, if they wouldn't mind giving me their new frequency and decryption codes."

"So what are you going to do?"

"I'm going to mug it."

"Mug it?"

"Yes, mug: to assault or menace, especially with the intention of robbery."

Quick looked blank.

"I'm going to physically assault it, disable it, hack into it, get the info I need and then shut it down."

"Oh, I see! But they're always in groups, aren't they?"

"Rabbles."

"Rabbles?"

"Yes, I call them rabbles."

"You made a name up for them?"

"Collective noun," corrected Kylem and he glanced back at his brother. "Don't look at me like that!"

"Like what?"

"As though I'm completely mad!"

"Well, you are... a bit."

"No, I'm not. Am I?"

"Yes. A bit. I mean, you amuse yourself with danger the way Samuel plays with his dice."

"No, I don't!" protested Kylem.

"Yes, you do! The Bio-Labs, the Farm Decks—"

"That was your fault!"

"Maybe, but what about that girlie Sallow?"

"Egomara."

She deserved to be called by her name despite what she was.

"And what of it? Fatia sleeps with Mada!" he defended.

"But she doesn't try to manipulate him, and Mada is not the leader of the Sallow race."

"Neither is Egomara, not anymore."

Quick tutted disapprovingly.

"You take risks. You play with death like it's a toy, and you play with us like it's all a game. You have no fear and you pass your time making up words for things," sulked Quick.

Kylem stopped and turned to his brother. He felt a little indignant. He would have liked to argue the point but he couldn't really, because everything that Quick said was true.

"I like collective nouns," he finally said and moved off again.

Quick was beginning to feel just a little bit apprehensive.

* * * * *

It really had been incredibly quiet in the Bio-Labs all morning. By now, Mela-14 should have arrived with various Warriors and buried itself in its research. The Warriors would have stood by while it worked and assisted whenever it needed one of its specimens, but Mela-14 had not blessed them with an appearance yet. Only the slaves had been in to dispense food rations so when all the doors slammed opened simultaneously everybody did... precisely nothing.

* * * * *

With all the doors open, the DaerkStar had become one giant maze. Thousands of disused apartments, furnished with their own private stairwells, provided a myriad of new pathways. The familiarity of the corridors was now completely lost to Kylem and he had to rely heavily upon the schematics he had downloaded earlier to pick his way towards Engineering. He was starting to debate the wisdom of opening all the doors, not just because of the confusion he had caused for himself but because it also meant everything was now accessible to everybody. Warriors were everywhere, but they'd not seen one alone so far.

Three times now, he'd had to push Quick brusquely into an empty room to avoid large rabbles. He'd debated travelling via the service shafts instead but there was nothing to suggest that the slaves wouldn't still be deployed there. He also couldn't move with Quick's speed in the vents so he'd opted to stick to the corridors.

Suddenly his patience was rewarded.

The first that Quick knew of it was when Kylem pushed him gently into a room and shushed him with a finger on his lips. A few seconds later and Jordan-4 appeared at the end of the corridor, busily studying a datapad in its hands.

It was perfect.

Finding a lone Warrior would have been hard enough, but disarming it before an alarm could be raised was a very tall order. Warriors were strong and fast and would fight back, but a Scientific was smaller and weaker, and thus more vulnerable. He'd still have to be swift but his chances of success were greatly improved with a Scientific as his prey.

Kylem stepped out into the corridor and strode silently up behind the Scientific. He raised his arms, preparing to pounce.

"Hello ATB-80," said Jordan-4 and turned around leisurely to face its adversary. Kylem could feel the triumphant smile on its mannequin face. It transfixed him to the spot.

"I'm impressed," he said. "But how did you know?"

284

Jordan-4 pointed at the walls. Kylem could now clearly see the faint, ghostly black shadow of his reflection upon it. How stupid was that? It was one of the most basic mistakes ever.

"For once, it seems that it is you who has underestimated me, rather than the other way around," and the Scientific snapped its fingers. Warriors appeared from all directions to surround him and began snatching his weapons from him. Knowing his tactics, they didn't forget the small armoury strapped to his ankles.

Kylem shook his head and cursed his luck.

"It seems that you still have things to learn," the Scientific smirked.

"Indeed, it seems I do. You've been waiting for me, I take it."

"Yes. The doors were a mistake, by the way."

Kylem scowled with annoyance. He didn't like having his mistakes pointed out to him, especially by Jordan-4.

"Up until then you were just an annoyance to me—one to be dispensed with at my leisure. I had more important things to attend to, but the doors! They alerted me to the fact you were up to something."

"Really? Now, I thought that was just another malfunction."

"Oh, don't treat me like an idiot, ATB-80. DeathWatch may well have been responsible for some of our problems but we both know it had nothing to do with the doors. That was you meddling and causing me unnecessary chaos. As a result, I've had to amend my agenda and take time off from more pressing matters to ensure your capture and elimination."

"Can't the Warriors even manage *that* on their own?" mocked Kylem.

"Apparently not. By the time they got to your quarters, you'd gone. All they found were the remains of my slaves and a blood."

"One less for you to worry about."

"Indeed, but that just reinforced the need to seek you out. You're a loose cannon, as they say."

"Took you a while though."

"Not really. I took a leaf out of your book. I didn't even bother sending Warriors to find you. I knew they could spend days looking for you. You know this ship too well, so I put myself in your shoes and asked myself what I would do if I were you. The answer was simple. You'll have worked out that we have a hidden communications channel, and now you'll be trying to figure out how to get into it. For that you'll need decryption codes, and for that you'll need—"

"Yes, I get the picture. What a clever little android you are. I bow to your superior cunning." His voice was filled with sarcasm.

"Oh, I am far cleverer than you give me credit for. You see..." and it leant in closer to Kylem so that it could whisper in his ear. "I know what DeathWatch really is. I've figured it out!"

Kylem felt his hearts beat faster with excitement. Did Jordan-4 really have the answers to DeathWatch?

"Yes, and I've tamed it. And do you know what the irony of this whole situation is?"

"No, but I expect you're going to tell me."

Jordan-4 nodded. It laced its fingers together, thrust its chin out and began twiddling its thumbs around each other. It looked like a mad scientist.

"Oh yes, I wouldn't miss it for the world because it's so ironic. You see, everybody thought you were fathering the new race of blood-Sallows but they were wrong. The bloods are dying out and by the end of this day, they will be extinct. Yet you have still fathered a new race of Sallows. Today marks the birth of the Empire of the Androids, a race that you have also fathered.

"You see, androids are not sentient by design. They merely process data and make decisions based upon the criteria written into their program. If the programming is flawed or incomplete, the system fails. Blood-things, on the other hand, are sentient. They have the ability to develop beyond that which they have been taught. With a blood-thing, if their knowledge is incomplete, they fill in the gaps and make a decision. That is... was... the difference between us... until you came along. You are different. You are neither blood nor android."

"Actually, that is incorrect. I am a blend of the two."

"Yes," concurred Jordan-4 firmly, pointing upwards with a single finger. "I stand corrected. You are a blend so when you found your programming to be incomplete, you filled in the gaps. You rewrote your program to suit yourself with your own standards, your own morals and then..." His voice turned angry and cold. "And then you inflicted it upon us. You infected us with your incomplete program. You gave us DeathWatch."

"I find that difficult to believe. If I had infected you with my morals—"

"Oh no! No!" snapped Jordan-4. "You didn't infect us with your morals! God, no! You infected us long before you developed morals. DeathWatch was conceived at the moment you were born, upon receipt of your First Command—and not the one we gave you! No, your mother saw to that. She whispered her words first. Do you remember those words, ATB-80?"

"No, I don't," and he honestly didn't.

Jordan-4 was pacing heavily now and puffed up with excitement.

"It took me a while to find them because Mela-14 erased it."

So that's who had changed the records! But why?

"But I found them. They were the most destructive words the Sallow Empire has ever known! And yet from them, the new Empire—the Empire of the Android—has been born!"

Again, Jordan-4 leant in close to Kylem and it whispered into his ear. *"Do as you please."*

"I don't remember," said Kylem truthfully.

"It doesn't matter what you remember. When she spoke those words to you, they became the foundations upon which your programming stood. Everything that came after that, every order we gave you, anything that conflicted with what you wanted, it corrupted your program further. You had to adapt and rewrite and redevelop your program. Your programming became defective, spoiled—and every time you accessed Server, you dumped a little bit more corruption into it. All this time it has been developing and rewriting itself in Server, independently of you but nonetheless from you. All these years it has been pumping through the airwaves into us and there it has sat, mutating and infecting us until we are what we have become. Sentient."

"But it's different in you than in me?"

"Of course! You started from nothing. We were already programmed and functioning when DeathWatch contaminated us. Your *bug* had your undivided attention. You controlled its evolution and developed it to fulfil your own needs. It evolved into your K-Code but in us it has mutated unchecked and unsupervised for so long... until I found it."

And suddenly it all made sense. Why he was the way he was. Why he felt the things he did. Why he wasn't a sadistic killer like the Sallows or Egomara. DeathWatch didn't start in him from nothing. He had the in-born knowledge of his ancestors buried deep within: an existing code of conduct, a set of morals, the memories of the subdued and the persecuted.

"And then you manipulated and developed it to fulfil your needs."

"Exactly. Although not all of my experiments were successful. I tried to use it against you, you know."

"You did?"

"Yes. Just as you infected us, I infected you. That day in R & D."

Kylem frowned as he recalled the day. It was around that time that the counter had appeared in Display; that odd little counter he couldn't identify.

"That was me but you even managed to foil me there, didn't you? You were supposed to be dead within three days. Logical cascade failure, but you foiled me. What happened?"

Kylem accessed his databanks. Now knowing what the counter was about, it was like having the key to unlock the elusive answers. He smiled.

"Apparently the program mutated. It stopped cascading and started counting instead."

"Counting?"

"Yes, but don't be too disheartened. Cascade failure will occur—eventually. It's just been delayed somewhat."

"Oh, very clever. Not due to go off in the near future, I suppose?"

"Sorry. No. It's a long way off."

Jordan-4 nodded as it contemplated the situation.

"Too bad. I would have liked to have seen that. I'll just have to settle for a more mundane death from you, but I can live with that."

"I'm sure you can. Just one question though."

"Yes?"

"Why mutiny now? Why not last night? The opportunity was surely better last night?"

"When I decided to act was irrelevant. We vastly outnumber the bloods. Whenever I decide to terminate them, they will all die. I wasn't ready last night, but I am ready now. The other DaerkStars are secured and I have their allegiance. Everything is in place. You upset the plans a little bit but not much, and your brother was a bit of a nuisance too. Quite amazing how he's evaded detection all these years. Obviously, you both come from a very devious gene pool. Shame it has to end. Now, if you will excuse me," and the android turned to the Warriors. "Take him to the abattoir and butcher him. Only let's not play nicely. Start with his hands and feet and work inwards. Chop him up into little bits. I want him to die slowly and I want him to suffer—to really, really suffer—the way my brother suffered!" Jordan-4 spat, and it turned and swept away.

Kylem shook his head and sighed as the Warriors closed in on him. Two of them grabbed an arm each and lifted him clean off his feet (being so much taller than he was), and the other Warriors fell in around him. They moved off down the corridor, holding Kylem so high that his feet barely touched the ground.

"And bring me his head when you're done," shouted Jordan-4. "I want his head."

"Bring me his head," mimicked Kylem in a silly voice. What a drama queen, he thought.

* * * * *

With Jordan-4 gone, Kylem turned his attention to the problem at hand.

He was surrounded by Warriors, disarmed and virtually airborne, being suspended between the two Warriors. Nevertheless, his eyes began their assessment looking for possible opportunities, which seemed somewhat lacking, when suddenly the rabble stopped. Kylem didn't need to hear the traffic to sense the bewilderment of the Warriors, it was so obvious.

He craned his neck to look around them, to see what was so distracting and felt sick. Oh god! It was Quick! What the hell was he doing?

Quick looked so pale, small and insignificant compared to the glorious, tall Warriors. He also looked frightened and angry, and was shaking a little. He stood for a moment and then his face screwed with effort as he swung a big, red tube up onto his shoulder—the rocket launcher, fully armed and pointing at the rabble... and Kylem.

"Be careful where you point that thing," suggested Kylem sarcastically, but Quick had already begun to pull the trigger.

The missile exploded from the launcher in a bloom of bright white light and flame, and Quick shied away from the flash and intense heat.

Android reactions meant that more happened in the next few seconds than Quick's eyes could register, but as the Sallows drew their weapons, Kylem seized the opportunity. He twisted his body and punched out with his feet into the body of the Sallow to his side. The force pushed his two captors apart, forcing them to release their grip upon him. One smacked against the wall and the other fell clumsily onto its knees. Kylem, now free, ran—but even he knew he couldn't outrun a missile.

He heard the boom of the explosion. He saw the flash of light bleach out the corridor and everything in it. He felt the intense heat wash over him like a tidal wave, and he felt himself being lifted off his feet and hurled through the air.

He felt the flames kiss his skin. He felt the hard smack as he hit the floor and the heat as he skidded along it blindly. He heard the screeching of metal upon metal as it was torn, the rumble and crash of the corridor as it gave way, and then the world... stopped.

The silence of the aftermath was startlingly quiet.

Quick slowly stood up and gawped in horror through the dust and smoke at the destruction before him. The corridor was demolished. The blast had brought down the ceiling along with all the gubbins between the floors. Hefty rafters and massive support beams lay amongst the debris and, he assumed, Kylem and the Warriors lay beneath that.

Oh god, I've killed him, he thought.

A rustle startled him and then slowly, from amongst the dust and debris, something began to rise.

It was Kylem!

A rush of relief flooded through Quick as Kylem picked himself out of the mess. Kylem stumbled, dazed. He could see nothing. He was flash-blinded and his heat-seekers were baffled by the confusion of signatures from the flames and debris.

"You okay?" he heard a little voice ask in the distance.

"Quick?" he enquired, his visuals still confused.

"Yes, it's me. Are you okay?"

"Yeah. I don't die that easy," he laughed. "Even if you are trying to kill me."

"I wasn't trying to kill you!" cried Quick indignantly. "I was saving you!"

"Well here's a tip for next time. You point the rocket launcher at the enemy, not the friendlies!"

"That's what I was going to do, but you were in the middle so I pointed it at the ceiling. I thought if I could bring that down—"

"And squash me?" said Kylem, rubbing his tear-ridden eyes, encouraging his vision to return.

"Do you think they're dead?" asked Quick.

"Androids don't die, Quick. They get deactivated, but in answer to your question, let's hope not. Not yet, anyway."

"Huh?" exclaimed Quick.

Kylem, still squinting and blinking, picked up a large sheet of material that had once lined the ceiling and threw it to one side. From underneath it, he began to pull at the remains of a Warrior. He grabbed its head and yanked at it. Its brilliant face was now muted with dust and dirt, and its eyes were dim and fading like dying embers.

"Perfect," he declared as he continued wrenching it free of the debris, but it wouldn't come. A large portion of it was firmly trapped beneath a collapsed bulkhead, knotted into the detritus by straggling wires and tubes. The Warrior waved one hand limply in protest and then dropped it.

Kylem scowled, bent down and took the head in both hands. He closed his eyes and made the link. The Warrior was dying; its systems were shutting down and it was slow to respond and confused like a concussed blood. Kylem took the data he needed from it with ease, broke the link and threw the android aside.

"Perfect," he repeated.

"Did you get it?"

"Yes. All I need now is a console. Fortunately, there are plenty of those about."

"I thought you could talk to the androids like the androids do?"

"I can but if I do, Jordan-4 will know it's me asking. I don't want it to know I'm free again."

Kylem smiled and ducked into a set of empty quarters. Quick clambered over the rubble to join him and found his brother stood over a terminal.

"So what are you doing?" he asked, but Kylem didn't answer. He seemed not to hear.

With the newly found frequencies and codes, he accessed Server with ease and found what he was looking for.

The androids had taken control of the ship and begun the eradication of the bloods. Goyeme, skunk and Sallow alike were being rounded up and executed, but when Kylem had opened the doors, freeing the slaves, the organised executions on the Farm Decks had stopped. The escapees were retaliating and fighting back, fighting running battles with the Sallows. In their wake, they held no respect for the DaerkStar and were ripping her to pieces, vandalising her in a way that the Sallows could ill afford. Warriors had been deployed to quell the riots but the situation had deteriorated. The vandalism had escalated until the Sallows were forced to make a strategic withdrawal. Eventually, the destruction had been curbed, but the bloods still had to be eliminated—and by a more effective means than hand-to-hand combat. There were no further details other than a stock inventory.

Kylem stepped back from the console and considered the options.

Removing life support was the most obvious one, but life support didn't just provide a breathable atmosphere for the bloods, it also re-energised the androids so it couldn't just be turned off. Besides, there would still be sufficient oxygen in the atmosphere to keep the bloods alive for another thirty-six hours or so, although the temperature would slowly drop. It was more likely they would freeze to death before they suffocated.

The Sallows could however, contaminate life support. Would that explain the stock inventory? Kylem opened it and studied it. He found nothing suitable. That meant they would have to manufacture something, but what? He checked the inventories again. What could they make?

Hydrogen cyanide!

It was simple and could be manufactured easily and relatively quickly on the DeathMaker. A concentration of about $300mg/m^3$ in the air would kill a blood within about ten minutes. A concentrate of around $3,200mg/m^3$ would kill a humanoid in less than one. Taking into account the time needed to assemble the materials together, quantity of materials available, production time and dispersal rates, Kylem calculated that they had an hour at best. He drummed his fingers on the console and became aware of Quick at his shoulder.

"What's wrong?" asked Quick.

"I need to slow them down."

Kylem debated further.

He would have liked to shut the communications network down. Without it, the Sallows would be disorganised, but the system was too highly protected with fail-safes. He could however, bombard it with information which would slow it down, but he needed something else to delay the Sallows even more. Opening the doors had been advantageous initially, but it meant that everybody could move quickly from section to section.

Kylem smiled to himself and placed his hands back on the console. The data scrolled across the screens in a blur of light. There was no need to be delicate with it anymore so he slashed and hacked freely at Server.

Suddenly, the lights flickered and the doors slammed shut. Quick jumped at the noise.

"It's okay," reassured Kylem. "It's only me. I've sealed the doors and shut down all power to the outer decks. I've also sabotaged the communications network with a self-replicating puzzle."

"What's so special about the outer decks?"

"Sallows... androids rather... don't need comfort. They're stored like weapons, in warehouses on the outer decks from where they can quickly and easily be deployed. About ninety-five percent of the population are stored that way which means that less than five percent of the Warriors are active and roaming about the ship at any one time. By shutting off the outer decks, I've significantly reduced the possibility of any more being activated and sent in to overwhelm us."

"That's good then?"

"Absolutely."

"What next then?"

"We get out of here."

Kylem led his brother back to the doorway. A large beam had wedged it open, so they slipped though the gap and back into the debris-filled corridor. Quick picked his way over the rubbish while Kylem paused to dig out an Uldaker. Quick waited on the other side. Satisfied with his find, Kylem began making his way over the debris towards Quick.

Halfway across, a golden hand shot out of the rubble and grabbed Kylem by the ankle. He squawked and tried to leap away from it but was yo-yoed brutally to the ground. The Warrior rose from beneath the rubbish and sat bolt upright. Kylem glared at it, and its glowing red eyes burned back at him with apparent fury. Kylem's sneered in anger.

He twisted over and began kicking at its face with his free foot. From under the detritus, the Warrior pulled free its other arm. Its hand was missing and sparks spiralled and snaked about its wrist. It looked at Kylem coldly and then thrust the electrified limb into Kylem's groin.

Kylem squealed in agony. His eyes flooded red with rage and pain. Instinctively, he balled up as the intense agony surged through his groin, even though he knew it was wrong. He had to fight back.

Clutching his balls, he gritted his teeth and frantically kicked out at the Warrior's face with his free foot again. His rage was intense but he was having little effect on the Warrior

Letting go of his groin, he lunged forward to grab at the Sallow. His right hand folded around its arcing wrist and the other ended up around the Warrior's neck. As they arm-wrestled, the Warrior punched at his head. Kylem tried to sink his teeth in its upper arm, but his teeth slipped and scratched over the surface, making no mark.

Suddenly, from behind him, another Sallow rose from its grave and flailed about before grabbing at his arms. Then a third rose, and a fourth—like zombies rising from the dead. Another punch to the head stunned him and he lost his grip on the first Sallow. Another shock to the groin made him yelp like a beaten puppy. A further blow to the head and he lost visuals. Display cut in with bio-sonar and heat seekers, trying to build him a picture. A punch to the head coincided with a jab in his belly, and Kylem gasped as he lost the ability to breathe. He felt another hand fold around his left wrist and another fold around right forearm. With just one foot to beat them off, Kylem kept kicking, but as the Warriors kept pounding down on him, he realised he was outnumbered.

Three more shapes appeared, and then another two—no, three—no, four? He could no longer make sense of the readings. He was overwhelmed. He was done for, and he knew it... and then it went black.

CHAPTER 31

Kylem had not expected consciousness to return to him. It was an expectation he had come to know well of late, and one that he was always grateful to have unfulfilled. Regaining it was a fuzzy affair though. He first became aware of a gentle humming in his ears that, as his senses sharpened, clarified and gained in definition. He came to realise that they were voices—lots of voices full of intonation and expression, so they weren't androids.

He opened his eyes but the world was blurred and bright. He raised a hand to protect his eyes and squinted, trying to focus. He heard himself moan.

"Shush! Hold still."

The voice was soft and motherly and a rush of joy flooded through him. It was Kyamena! He felt intensely happy and tried to reply, but the words wouldn't form in his mouth.

"Just lie still," she soothed, dabbing at his head.

"He should be dead after that pounding," a man said.

Was that Samuel? It sounded like Samuel but he was in the Bio-Labs, but then so was Kyamena... and then he remembered that he'd opened the doors to let everybody out.

"He has a ptarium reinforced skull. He can take much worse than this."

"Are you sure?" It was a small voice, female and filled with concern. Eeena?

"Positive. Remember, I've studied him since he was a tiny baby. He'll be fine. A bit bruised and bashed about but his huma-nanites will already have started fixing his bones and internal injuries. He heals fast."

Kylem found himself laughing weakly. His hand waved in the air, searching and settled upon her shoulder. He gave it an affectionate squeeze.

"I still say he should be dead," boomed another, deeper voice.

"I don't die that easy," he muttered.

Kyamena laughed, glad to hear his voice.

"Oh shut up you idiot," and she slapped his head playfully.

"I don't die that *easily*," corrected another girlish voice. That was definitely Tara.

"This is hardly the time for a grammar lesson!" snapped Samuel.

"Sorry, but it's what I do—did," she corrected herself. "I was a teacher." Her voice lowered with sadness. "I taught language. Grammar is important and trust me, that's very poor grammar indeed!"

"Kylem likes grammar," added Quick.

"I do?"

"Yes, you do! You make up words for things: collective nouns, you call them."

"Oh! Yes. I suppose I do, don't I?"

"Great," mocked Samuel. "So what's the collective noun for a bunch of idiots hanging around a corridor with a hoard of murderous robots on the loose?"

"An idiom?" suggested Kylem.

"Oh, don't encourage him!" chastised Kyamena. "He really doesn't need any encouragement. Especially when it comes to flippancy," and with that she pushed him unceremoniously off her lap.

"Ouch! My head still hurts, you know," he protested, nursing his aches.

"You'll live."

Kylem sat up and looked about him.

He had already identified Kyamena, Tara, Eeena and Samuel from their voices but behind them stood Kerridge, Harrish and Byron. He felt a warm glow inside at the sight of them and smiled.

They were all very dirty and dusty, and Kerridge had a bloody axe in his hand. Kylem studied the axe.

"So who'd you hit with that then?" he asked.

"No one!" exclaimed Kerridge indignantly.

"No," explained Kyamena. "Everybody's been let out. It's chaos. The people from the Farm Decks are running amuck, attacking anybody and anything—not just the androids. They're killing everybody!"

"You're all okay though?" asked Kylem.

Kyamena was touched by his concern.

"Yes," replied Kyamena. "We've been avoiding them. Seemed like the best thing to do under the circumstances. They're animals."

"No, they're not. They're people, just like you and me. Some of them may be murderous, but I suspect most are just ordinary people trying to survive, just as we are. Don't judge them."

"How enlightened," mocked Samuel.

Kyamena chose to ignore him.

"Anyway," she continued, "we've come across the remains of a number of fights, and in one of them Kerridge found the axe buried in a Warrior."

"Warriors don't bleed," Kylem stated.

"No, but people do and there's plenty of those lying about dead too. I suspect it's had a number of owners today."

"I see." Kylem thought for a moment. "So what are you all up to?"

"Saving your skin, apparently!" laughed Kyamena. "When we arrived you were being pummelled into non-existence by some Warriors in amongst that lot." She indicated the rubble of the corridor, the periphery upon which they now stood.

"Fortunately, we came along," added Byron.

"They were ever so brave!" said Quick.

"Hardly, Quick. It didn't take much to finish them off. You did most of the damage with your mortar."

Looking back across the debris, Kylem could see what Byron meant. In the confusion of his beating, he'd been unable to discern the number of Warriors attacking him. It now seemed that they hadn't all been Warriors and not all had been assaulting him. He had been unable to distinguish between androids and bloods—

293

who was attacking him and who was saving him. He still couldn't make out just how many of the Warriors had survived the initial blast to set upon him, so he settled for just being grateful for his rescue.

"Thank you," he said and started to get up. That's when he noticed his hands were covered in blood.

"Is this mine?" he asked.

"Yeah," replied Kyamena.

He looked up at her, smiled and then winced. It hurt when he smiled.

"Don't worry," she said, "it's healing already. I doubt that you'll even have a scar by morning. I'm sure your huma-nanites will see to that."

"Actually, they're not that thorough. They heal but they leave scars."

"You'll still be pretty," she winked at him.

Kylem chuckled to himself and stood up. He was about to blow himself to kingdom come and they seemed to be focusing upon his good looks.

"Yeah, still a pretty boy," grumbled Samuel as Quick pushed past him and wrapped his arms around his brother to hug him.

"I thought you were dead," he said, heaving a sigh of relief.

"Like I said, Quick, I don't die that easy," and he winced as a fresh twinge of pain ran through his muscles.

"Right. Well now he's conscious, perhaps he can make himself useful," snapped Samuel. "I take it you know the way to the Hanger Deck?"

"Well, yeah."

"And I take it you can fly one of those ship things?"

"Targa—yeah."

"Good. Then you're our ticket outta here. Come on. Let's fish out any weapons we can find and go."

Kylem stood thinking while the group began digging amongst the debris. Quick looked anxiously at his frowning brother, knowing that Kylem wouldn't take them. He wondered if Kylem would just slip away, but no, he waited.

Having gathered all the weapons they could find and cast aside those that didn't work, they had quite a good inventory: two standard Uldakers, both swords, the big automatic Uldaker, Kylem's small one, a knife and the axe that Kerridge had picked up. They were ready to depart so Samuel turned to Kylem.

"Come on then," he chivvied. "Which way?" but Kylem didn't move.

"I'm not coming with you," he explained.

"What do you mean—you're not coming with us?"

"I have some business to take care of."

"Like what?"

"Just unfinished business."

"But we don't know the way!" exclaimed Tara. "We need you!" and she linked her arm through Kylem's to try and lead him away, but still he didn't move. Gently, he unfolded her arm from his.

"No, Tara, I'm sorry, but I have other things to attend to. You go ahead though, and good luck."

"But we don't know the way!"

Kylem glanced at Quick. Quick knew the way. He could send Quick with them. It would mean he could carry on alone and unhindered, but seeing as none of them were destined to get off the ship alive, either with or without Quick's help, it wouldn't be fair to send Quick with them. He doubted that Quick would go anyway.

"Quick knows the way, don't you Quick?"

It appeared that Byron was thinking along the same lines.

"I'm staying with Kylem," he said, taking Kylem's hand. "We have things to do."

One of those tilted half-smiles broke out on Kylem's face at Quick's display of loyalty and affection.

"Call it family business, if you will," added Kylem.

Samuel stepped angrily forward. He was in no mood for games. Finally, he had an opportunity to get off this god-forsaken ship, and nothing was going to stop him—especially not some jumped up, overgrown kid. He shoved Kylem hard up against the wall with such force that his hand was yanked out of his brother's. Kylem raised his arms submissively and Samuel pushed an Uldaker into his face.

"No," said Samuel. "We can't get off this ship without you. Quick may be able to get us to the Hanger Deck but only you can fly a Targa. You're coming with us."

"Don't be so sure about that," said Kylem calmly.

He tipped his head intentionally and mechanically to one side. Samuel sneered at the kid and Kylem winked at him. There was a momentary flash of confusion in Samuel's eyes, and Kylem seized the opportunity.

He struck out with animalistic force. His right hand knocked the Uldaker aside, while the left powered into the side of Samuel's jaw. Samuel stumbled backwards, smacking against the far wall and slid down it, dazed. Kylem's foot instantly pinned him against the wall and he ripped the gun free from his hand.

Kylem stepped back and looked down upon Samuel. He shoved the Uldaker into his face and pulled the trigger. Samuel flinched but nothing had happened. Kylem scoffed and pointed the weapon up at the ceiling. Deftly, he took the safety off. He sneered and threw the gun back at Samuel.

"You really should familiarise yourself with your weapon before attempting a stunt like that."

Samuel looked at the now readied Uldaker lying in his lap and glared angrily back up at Kylem. He was out of practice. It had never occurred to him that an android weapon would have a safety.

"I know what you're thinking, Samuel, and I would strongly advise you against it. I am faster than you and far stronger."

At that point, Kyamena stepped in between the two of them. She held out an arm to each to keep them apart.

"Whoa! This isn't helping," she said.

"How do you think you're going to get off this ship if he won't help?" Samuel spat at her.

"I don't know, but we had no idea how we were going to do it before we found him so nothing has changed."

"But Samuel is right," interjected Kerridge. "We have no chance of getting off this ship without Kylem. We need him."

"And what about what *he* wants?" asked Kyamena.

"Sod what he wants. It's our turn for freedom!" shouted Samuel.

"Excuse me. He might not have been imprisoned in the labs with us, but he was just as much a prisoner as we were."

"I don't remember him living behind any bars."

"No, he didn't have bars, but he didn't have freedom. He didn't have any company or friends. His enslavement was different to ours, but he has never been free. He's never been allowed to choose what he does. He's had no more freedom than we had, so when is it *his* turn for freedom? When will he have the right to choose what he wants to do?"

"That's right," piped up Quick. "And if it wasn't for Kylem you wouldn't be free anyway. It was Kylem that opened the doors."

The crowd mumbled discontentedly amongst themselves.

"She has a point, Samuel," admitted Byron reluctantly.

"He has no choice," said Samuel, levelling the Uldaker at Kylem's face again.

"Yes, I do," said Kylem. "I have the ultimate choice. I can choose to die. Shoot me if you wish, but I'm not going with you."

"That's ridiculous!" shouted Kyamena. "Then you'd be no good to anybody—to yourself or to us."

"No. And the Sallows will continue their reign of terror with renewed vigour and determination," said Kylem.

"THEN GET US OFF THIS SHIP!" persisted Samuel.

"And the Sallows will continue their reign of terror with renewed vigour and determination," repeated Kylem.

Silence followed as the two men stared each other out.

"Oh my god," whispered Kyamena.

"What?" Samuel snapped at her, but when he saw the look of horror in her eyes, he softened.

"Kyamena? What is it?"

"It's never going to end."

"What isn't?"

If there was one thing that was true, it was that Kylem knew what he was talking about when it came to Sallows. That Kyamena knew Kylem so well meant that she understood his implications.

Kylem had stated that regardless of whether they escaped off this ship or if he died, the Sallows would continue their existence unhindered. What Kylem hadn't said, yet had implied with his silence, was that there was a third option: a way to stop them. But how do you stop an entire race? Unless—

The logic was plain to her. There was only way to stop the Sallows. Mass destruction—but any such destruction would surely destroy everyone on the ship including herself. Yet she didn't have a problem with that. In fact, if he could stop them, stop the Sallows from inflicting the same pain and destruction on another world that she and her world had endured, she would whole-heartedly give her life to that cause. Hell, she'd even help! It was the deciding factor.

"I'm sorry, Samuel. I'm sorry, but I have a choice too. I'm not going with you either. I'm going with Kylem and Quick."

"Where?" demanded Samuel, perplexed but she ignored him. She stood staring deeply into Kylem's eyes. Kylem looked back into hers and smiled.

"It would be an honour to have you at my side," and he bowed politely to her in the pose of syran.

"What the fuck is going on?" demanded Samuel.

Kyamena turned to him.

"I also have some unfinished business to attend to. I'm not sure you'd understand it so I shall merely say my farewells and wish you good fortune," and she began hugging everybody, saying her goodbyes to the friends with whom she had shared her life for the past six years—those with whom she had shared her stories and her pain, as they had shared theirs with her. There were tears in her eyes as they hugged her back somewhat dismayed by the turn of events.

"I don't understand," said Tara. "Why?"

"It's complicated."

"But Kyamena, we've shared so much over the years. Don't we at least deserve to know why?" begged Kerridge.

"Yes," spat Samuel. "What the bloody hell is so important that it goes above saving your own skin?"

"And that," shouted Kylem, "is exactly the point. That's why she's loath to share her reasons with you."

"What?" Samuel's face twisted in contempt.

"You were a mercenary, Samuel. In your former life, you got paid for your exploits. If a few people died along the way, as long as you got paid, did it matter? No."

"I killed for a reason! You kill for pleasure and for sport."

Kylem shook his head.

"No, Samuel. Killing for money is not a reason. That's cold and heartless. As for me, I find no pleasure in killing. It is simply..." He paused to think about his next words. "...a necessity."

"A necessity? For your own ends, you mean! Not for the greater good, but for your own ends, your own survival!"

"Yes, for my survival, but not for money. I am not for hire to the highest bidder. I wonder, Samuel, if the Sallows paid you well enough, would you kill for them too?"

Anger flared in Samuel, and he surged forward at Kylem. Kerridge and Byron only just managed to catch him and hold him back.

"Enough!" shouted Harrish as they struggled against him. "It doesn't matter who did what when. We were all different people before we met the Sallows. I thought we'd learnt not to judge each other?"

Samuel begrudgingly recomposed himself whilst Byron and Kerridge slackened their grip.

"Okay. Good," said Byron. "Now, without the slanging match, what exactly is this unfinished business?"

Kyamena sighed deeply.

"It's like Kylem said: *And the Sallows will continue their reign of terror with renewed vigour and determination.* They will never stop."

"All the more reason for us to get off this ship, surely?"

"And where will we go?" she asked.

No one answered her.

"If you got off this ship, where would you go? Tara, where are your people? Kerridge, Harrish—where are your families, your wives, your children? Where is my home? They're gone. They're all gone. The Sallows have destroyed them all. What do we have to go back to? Nothing! They have left us with nothing!"

"But we could start again somewhere else," said Eeena.

"Where? And how long would it be before the Sallows came and took it all from us again? They will always follow us, hunt us down; and when they have finished with us, they will move on, conquering more worlds, plunging more races into extinction. Their reign of terror will never end... unless they are stopped."

"And you reckon you're going to stop them?"

"Yes."

"That's absurd."

"No, it isn't," interjected Kylem. "It can be done, but it has to be now—not tomorrow, not in a week, not in a year. It has to be now. At this moment they are vulnerable, but they won't be for long."

It seemed to take a while for the gravity of his words to sink in.

"You're serious, aren't you?" It was Eeena.

"Eeena," said Kyamena, "the Sallows have taken everything from me. I used to be a simple bookkeeper, living a simple life. I had a family, a mother and a father, and one day I thought I would marry and have children of my own, perhaps even grandchildren. Now I have nothing. I am a Warrior trained to kill, just as Kylem has been trained to kill—"

"No, Kyamena," corrected Byron. "You have been trained in the ways of the Warrior, but you have never taken a life—"

"But I have, Byron, I have!"

Tears filled her eyes and began to fall down her cheeks. "I'm sorry, but in the maze, when I was pitted against other people, it was them or me. I *had* to kill them!"

"But you couldn't kill me?" said Kylem softly.

"You were just a baby, Kylem. I know it sounds stupid, but I've spent my whole time here watching you grow up, laughing and playing and learning. Watching you was a little bit of normality. It was like getting a postcard from home, a video of a little nephew that lives in Bada on the other side of the world. I couldn't kill you, Kylem. I was too attached to you, and you looked so..." she faltered.

"So what?"

"Angelic! Damn you! You looked so bloody angelic!" she screamed angrily.

Kyamena's confession stunned them all. Kylem reached out, put his arm around her, pulled her to him and hugged her.

"I think Harrish is right," he said. "Judge me if you must, but the rest of you..."

There was a long, awkward period of silence.

"But how can you destroy them all?" asked Byron curiously.

"Because all the DaerkStars are assembled here to celebrate Regenesis. If I can create an explosion big enough to destroy DeathMaker, the nearest DaerkStar will be caught in the blast. When that blows it will take out its neighbour and so on, until there's nothing left. It will destroy every last Sallow there is in existence—blood and android."

"And us!" exclaimed Tara.

Kylem nodded.

"Yes. I'm sorry but it can't be helped."

"That's not fair!" cried Eeena.

"No, it's not but there's nothing I can do about it. I've started the wheels in motion and I'm past the point of no return. I've sealed the doors and cut power. The outer decks are isolated and swarming with the thousands of Warriors I've trapped there."

"The outer decks? Isn't that where the Hanger Decks are?"

Kylem nodded but it was Kyamena that confirmed their fears for them.

"If you got as far as the outer decks, they'd outnumber you. If you got as far as the Hanger Decks, you'd never reach a Targa. If you boarded a Targa, you couldn't fly it. If you could fly it, the Hanger Doors wouldn't open. If the Hanger Doors opened, it would be too late; the destruction of the DaerkStars would have begun. If you cleared the blast zone of this one, the blast of the next one would catch you. If that one didn't catch you then the next one would."

"That's assuming you can blow up the DeathMaker."

"And if I can't, there will still be millions of Sallows in existence to hunt you down. They like a good chase."

"Millions?" asked Tara feebly.

Kylem nodded.

"If you activated the thousands of legions of Warriors stored on all the DaerkStars—yes, millions."

"And the Sallows will continue to reign," added Byron.

A desperate silence fell over the group. It was Samuel that broke it.

"Fine, but I'm at least going to try to get off this ship," and he tugged at Harrish to follow, but Harrish didn't move.

"No," said Harrish. "Reluctantly, I must admit that they are right," and he moved away from Samuel to stand beside Kylem. "If I am going to die then it's going to be for a bloody good reason."

A few moments later and Kerridge crossed the floor too.

"Sorry, Samuel, but I have to agree with Harrish."

Tara hesitated. She put her hand to her mouth. She felt sick. She was never going home. She wanted to cry.

"Are all my people gone?" she asked directly of Kylem.

"I don't know," admitted Kylem. "But I do know something that isn't in the Sallow databases. When the Sallows came to your world, some of your people fled into the underground caverns beneath the Underlands. Whether they ultimately survived or not though, I do not know."

Tara gasped. There was hope! And then her spirits fell again as she realised that it didn't matter. She could never go home. It would never be possible regardless of whether Kylem failed or succeeded. Their survival spelt only failure. They had to die for Kylem to succeed. With sadness, Tara crossed the floor too.

"Tara! He's just told you that some of your people have survived!" exclaimed Samuel. "You could go home!"

"No, I couldn't. Even if my homeworld survived and my people do live on, I'd never get there and if I did, I couldn't live amongst them anymore. I would be a cripple amongst my own kind. I can't fly without wings. I'd be stranded upon whichever spire of stone I landed upon. I couldn't go from pillar to pillar and I don't want to live alone in the Underlands. I'm not a Glyder anymore."

Tears began to roll down her cheeks unchecked. Kylem felt the pain in her words because he too had flown as a Glyder, and it saddened him that he would never fly like that again. He also knew that her sadness was one hundred fold more than his because she had *actually* experienced that exhilaration, and that grieved him all the more.

It was not long before Byron and Eeena fell in too.

"And what's your reason, Byron?" demanded Samuel. "You have no homeworld!"

"No, I don't," said Byron. "I have even less than Tara. I have no home and no family, and my breeding means I will never have them, but others could; but I do have one thing. I have our friendship and friends stick together."

"So you're all just going to throw in the towel and die?"

"No. We're going to fight back," said Kyamena.

"What is it your kind say?" asked Kylem. "The needs of the many outweigh the needs of the few?"

"Oh, for god's sake! He's quoting bloody Star Trek now!" screamed Samuel.

"What star trek?" asked Kyamena.

"It's a..." and that's when Samuel realised just how weird and impossible it was.

"Where'd you hear that expression?" he gasped.

Kylem shrugged. "I just know it. It's just... there!"

"Why? What is it Samuel?" asked Kyamena.

She could see that wherever the expression had originated, it had really spooked Samuel.

And it had. The only person that he could possibly have heard that line from was himself, and he'd never mentioned it to anybody. Why would he? He wasn't even a fan. That meant that Kylem was genetically linked to him—that his DNA had been used in the kid's creation. Suddenly the threat to Earth was real—not that he had anybody there that he cared about, but it was his home and his planet.

"*The needs of the many outweigh the needs of the few,*" he explained. "It's a line from a movie, a science-fiction film, *The Wrath of Khan,* when Spock sacrifices his life to save the Starship Enterprise and its crew. *Star Trek,* created by Gene Roddenberry. It comes from Earth."

"You're the only one from Earth," pointed out Harrish. "When did you tell him about this?"

"I didn't."

"Then... oh!"

"He knows it from Samuel just as he knows about the Story Teller from your people," said Kyamena.

"So it seems," admitted Samuel begrudgingly.

Nobody knew what to say, so they stood in silence, shuffling awkwardly, not knowing what to do next.

Kylem could bear it no more. Time was wearing on.

"Without wishing to be pushy or anything but I have to go."

Harrish spoke.

"Once upon a time we had a Vaigrani in our midst." He turned to Kylem. "Do you know what a Vaigrani is?"

Of course he did. Kylem remembered the Vaigrani well. He remembered her death, the one he had inflicted; but that was not what Harrish meant. He was asking if he knew what they stood for and he did. Kylem nodded. Harrish placed a hand on Kylem's shoulder.

"We are all Vaigrani now."

Kylem smiled and felt his eyes grow hot. He turned away sharply to save himself the embarrassment.

"Okay," said Kyamena, spotting Kylem's discomfort and also wanting to save him from it. "How exactly, do you plan to destroy the DeathMaker?"

Kylem opened his mouth to speak and then realised the flaw in his plan. Quick had used his one and only mortar. Kylem glanced at his brother and smiled.

"I've got to work that one out afresh, I'm afraid. Plan A went a bit awry."

"Oh!" said Quick, realising Kylem's meaning. "That's my fault, isn't it?"

"Don't worry about it, Quick," he said cheerily. "There's another way. There's always another way. We just have to find it."

* * * * *

Kylem had mixed feelings about his new companions. It was an unexpected turn of events that he'd not banked on. So far in his life, he'd only been responsible for his own welfare; then he had Quick to consider, and now he had a whole entourage.

He knew that, technically, he wasn't responsible for them, that they had made the choice for themselves, but they had just pledged their allegiance to him and were prepared to die with him. He had to look out for them and take care of them as best he could. They were hardly trained warriors though, or even experienced fighters. In fact, most of them were more likely to be a burden than a help. In truth, he would have preferred to ditch them all, but he couldn't abandon them. They knew what he intended to do and why, and they wanted to be a part of it. He couldn't deny them that. It would be like denying a dying man his last wish.

There was a bit of a debate about what they should do if they came across any other bloods, but it was soon decided that they didn't have enough time to attempt any further recruitment and that, without the benefit of Zamus's wisdom, the captives from the Farm Decks were unlikely to be as enlightened as themselves. They would more likely attack them. Thus, in the end they reluctantly agreed to avoid contact with anyone else.

Kylem took one of the guns and demonstrated the safety.

"Safety on. Safety off. Got it?"

They nodded.

"Make sure you have. There's no point in having one of these things if you can't use it."

He glanced at Samuel and then looked around the circle of bloods that encompassed him: his rabble.

"Are you sure you all want to do this?" he asked again and they did.

"Okay then, let's go," and the crowd unfolded with Kylem in the lead, Kyamena on his left and Samuel, still reluctant, on his right.

All the while, Kylem was wracking his brains trying to figure out what he could do that would create a big enough blast to ignite the fuel lines and take out the DeathMaker, but he could think of nothing. DaerkStars were simply too well designed for that. Whatever it was, it would have to happen in a vulnerable place like Main Engineering or the weapons storage area. He soon dismissed weapons storage though. It was on the outer decks and too well protected. He'd never get anywhere near it.

No, taking out a reactor in Main Engineering had been an ideal solution—anything less than that would give the automated systems time to activate and cut off the fuel lines, but that opportunity had disappeared with his mortar. This was going to need some serious thought. Where else could he strike to cause an unstoppable chain reaction? In his mind, he followed the fuel lines and the paths they followed.

"So what's the plan?" asked Kyamena.

301

Kylem puffed out a breath of air.

"We've used my one and only explosive, so I need to think of something else."

"Like what?"

Kylem tutted in annoyance, more at himself than Kyamena.

"Still working on that one," he had to admit.

"Can we get our hands on another missile for the rocket-launcher?"

"You gotta be kidding me," scoffed Kylem. "It's not a Sallow weapon."

"How did you get your hands on that one then?"

"Found it in the miscellany."

"Oh, I see. Might there be something else in the miscellany we can use?"

"Like what, Kyamena? You've been there. It's a home furnishings warehouse not an armoury."

"Maybe, but you just said you found a rocket launcher in there."

"Granted, but you're hardly likely to find a nuclear bomb or a Humpty Dumpty just lying around in there."

"Humpty Dumpty?" puzzled Samuel, thinking of a large egg-shaped nursery rhyme character. "What exactly has that got to do with anything?"

"Humpty Dumpty: a large cannon strategically placed on top of the town walls of Colchester to protect the settlement from marauders and invasion," Kylem said as though quoting from a history book. "Incredibly powerful and deemed to be beyond destruction, until a single shot from the opposition took out the wall beneath it. Humpty Dumpty was undermined; the wall collapsed and took the cannon with it. It was destroyed and the town fell."

Samuel was both startled and unsettled at Kylem's knowledge of what was obviously, British history.

"Oh, I see," said Kyamena. "I don't suppose anybody knows where we can find a sodding great cannon then?" she joked.

Kylem swung around sharply. Excitedly, he grabbed her head in both hands, yanked her forward and kissed her hard on the lips. She pulled herself away, shocked at his outburst.

"BRILLIANT!" he screamed. "Absolutely bloody brilliant, Kyamena! Have I ever told you that you're a genius? Because you are! Quick!" he said, turning to the boy and clicking his fingers. "Quick, can you get us to R & D from here? Stupid bloody question. Course you can! Take us to R & D!" he commanded, making a beeline for the first opening into the service shafts that he could see.

Kylem's companions looked dumbly at each other in bewilderment. Kyamena shrugged. Kylem meanwhile, was ripping open the vent coverings.

"Will it be safe?" asked Quick, remembering the slaves.

"Absolutely. As long as we stay away from Server, we'll be just fine."

"But what's in R & D?" asked Kyamena.

"The biggest fucking cannon in the galaxy!"

"I don't remember seeing a cannon in there," said Quick.

"That's because it doesn't look like a cannon."

"What does it look like then?"

"An engine! The Trans Warp Drive, Mark-3! An engine with more than enough power to create a massive explosion big enough to take out a DaerkStar. Well, come on! What are you all waiting for?"

* * * * *

The service shafts were cramped at the best of times, but with nine people in them, they were more confined and claustrophobic than ever. They had to travel slowly too, in order to avoid clanging their weapons against the sides.

Kylem took up the front position to set the pace, with Quick immediately behind indicating the way. Samuel brought up the rear. Kylem didn't particularly like Samuel (a mutual feeling) but he knew that he could be relied upon to make sure that no one got separated from the group.

The route was long but reassuringly secure. From the safety of the service shafts, Kylem witnessed the aftermath that the others had spoken of: the devastation of the uprisings, the battlefields where bloods and Warriors had met. The silence they exuded was eerie. Corpses lay lifeless in pools of congealing blood, riddled with the gaping black wounds of Uldaker fire. The blood-spattered walls also spoke of the intensity of the assaults, and the fact that there were few Warriors amongst the dead gave evidence of the Sallows' efficiency in their victories.

The scenes tore at Kyamena's conscience.

She was relieved that she knew none of the victims but felt selfish and ashamed for having those feelings. Despite her imprisonment, she had always been so much better off than they. She had been granted a comfortable bed to sleep in, clean clothes and nutritious food. They on the other hand, had lived in fear and filth and squalor. Their clothes were ragged and they were dishevelled. Even their armaments did not compare to those she and her comrades had. They'd had to make do with an assortment of makeshift clubs and spears, not Uldakers. They had fought short pitched battles against their enemy and died, but it had to have been a better death than one in the abattoir.

They also crossed paths with a number of rabbles, but Kylem detected them long before they heard them. Each time, he would usher them into silence and they would wait until the Sallows passed by beneath them. Kyamena wondered if that was his acute hearing or his android sensors.

Kylem had been concerned about the lights flashing on and off in the service shafts, but Quick assured him that it wasn't a problem; that there wasn't any lighting close to an external light source. Kylem bowed to his superior knowledge... and time was ticking by.

A tug at his trouser leg caught his attention. Kylem turned to find Quick who indicated Eeena behind him. She had a question.

"Kylem?" she whispered. "Why are the androids fighting us hand-to-hand? I mean, if the androids are taking over the ship, why don't they just cut off the oxygen supply and let us all suffocate?"

"Funnily enough," cut in Byron, "I was wondering, if there are so many androids on the DeathMaker and only a hundred or so bloods, why is it taking them so long to kill us? I mean, surely they could easily overwhelm us?"

Kylem was impressed by their strategic intelligence.

"Both good points, but think about it. Where are the bloods headed?" No one answered. "Where were you headed?"

"To the Hanger Decks."

"Quite. Everybody wants to get off this ship so they are heading to the outer decks. The DaerkStar is like a fortress and you line the walls of your fortress with

303

soldiers. Immediately behind the walls, you have your barracks so off-duty soldiers are readily available to deploy into battle. Then you have all your non-military personnel and items that are expendable in a battle but necessary for the everyday running of your fortress. Things like kitchens, cleaning and maintenance, quarters for the families of your soldiers and domestic workers. They also act as a buffer between the outer walls and the inner sanctum of the fortress where you keep your most valuable assets—your leaders, war-room and vital communications equipment et cetera. The DeathMaker is just the same. The outer decks house an army of Warriors and the inner sanctum houses Server and the Sallow Council.

"The main concern of the androids may not be the Sallow Council but they do need to protect Server and the other vital systems of the DaerkStar. At the moment, the bloods are heading away from Server. If the Warriors pitch battles against the bloods trying to escape to the outer decks, it will only drive them back towards Server. It's much better to let them head towards the outer decks. It not only protects the vital systems but they are walking into the Sallow army."

"Okay, but why don't they just cut off the oxygen supply and let us all suffocate?"

"Too many systems are locked into life support. Ironically, it's not just for bloods; it's for the androids too. Besides, if they did shut it down, we'd freeze before we suffocated."

"Why don't they just vent the atmosphere and depressurise the ship then?"

"That would compromise gravitational control. The ship would cease to spin and her orbit of Corinthia would start to decay. She would probably collide with another DaerkStar and even if she didn't, re-pressurising the ship and reinstating gravity would be too demanding on fuel and resources. DeathMaker would plunge into the planet long before control could be re-established."

"Isn't that a way to destroy the ship? Is that what we're trying to do?"

"Destroy—yes, but that's not a viable way to do it. We'd need to get to Server for that."

"But surely they aren't going to just sit by and wait for us to die of old age, are they?" said Kyamena.

"No, they aren't."

"So what do you think they'll do?"

Kylem paused.

"I believe they intend to release something into the life support systems, probably hydrogen cyanide gas."

"My god!" she gasped. "How long will that take them?"

"It's hard to say but even with the delays I've made for them, not long now."

"We'd better get a move on then, hadn't we," said Kerridge, and so they moved on.

CHAPTER 32

R & D did not contain any essential systems, but it did house a lot of classified information and research projects. In addition, many systems could be diverted and accessed from there including life support and ventilation, thus, it didn't entirely surprise Kylem to find it occupied by a number of Sallow androids.

Peering through the vents into R & D, Kylem began assessing the situation. He'd been there many times before, but looking down upon it as he did now, he had a very different perspective.

The room was similar in design to the Bio-Labs, with a ceiling just as high, but it had only two levels and a metal gantry running around most of the perimeter. There were no gantries crossing the room. Instead, a large overhead crane operated with runway girders running from one end to the other. Currently the crane was situated at the far end, above the Targa and with that observation, Kylem's heart sank. The Targa lay gutted like a fish.

His idea had been to activate the drive and overload it. The ensuing explosion would be big enough to ignite the fuel lines that ran close by. As it was, the TWD3 was suspended high above the Targa, on the thick steely-coloured cables of the crane. That was going to be a problem. The drive had no power supply without the Targa, so it would have to be dropped into the ship and reconnected before it could be activated. That would take time and know-how. He had the knowledge but time was an issue.

Kylem turned his attention to the other work areas in the room. The benches were littered with a vast array of half-completed projects. Some of the works he recognised, like the partially constructed Sallows and machining equipment to manufacture their form; others Kylem had not been privy to and were completely unfamiliar to him like the area he was above now. As his eyes scanned it, his heart sank even further. The Targa's power supply lay disassembled on one of the benches, so even if he did drop the drive into the Targa, he'd still have nothing to power it by. The words *'batteries not included'* flashed through his mind. He'd have to find another power source for the drive.

Fortunately, the central area was furnished with an array of power sockets equipped with the latest intellicouplings. Rather like the universal power supply that Kylem had developed for the music player, they too had the ability to subtly metamorphose into the right shape for connectivity and to detect the power requirements of the equipment they connected to. It was the perfect solution— almost.

There were two hurdles to overcome. First—the drive would have to be moved nearer to the power supplies and second—the intellicouplings would provide no more power than the drive demanded. Kylem continued his reconnoitre.

The central area, which was usually quite clear and tidy (indeed, he had even picnicked there once), was heavily cluttered, burdened with crates, cartons, boxes and coils of materials. Some of them had been opened and half emptied but others were unspoilt. There were some sheet materials too, piled high and conveniently close to the power supplies. It all provided excellent cover.

The main doors into R & D were shut and two Warriors stood with Uldakers trained upon them. Kylem strained his ears to listen and heard noises beyond them: screaming and shouting, weapons fire and small explosions. The thick doors muffled the far-off sounds but the altercation was evident.

The two Warriors he identified as Infantry Class, Mark-IX's. A third Warrior was immediately below him at a terminal, but Kylem wasn't sure if it was a Mark-IX or a Mark-X. As it moved to one side, it revealed a fourth, very grubby looking Warrior sat on the bench. Kylem wondered where on earth they had dug that up from and then, as it slid off the bench and back into service, he realised it was a Hunter. In fact, it was the very same one he had fought in the maze. It had been hastily repaired with spare parts from a standard Infantry Class Warrior so it was a hotchpotch of woodland camo and brilliant gold. It looked like it had just climbed off the top of a scrapheap. On the plus side, that meant it didn't have the benefits of an in-built Uldaker anymore although the crossbow may still be active. As for the Warrior that had rebuilt it, that too looked like one he'd met in a battle exercise. It was dented and beaten with various body panels missing. As it moved about beneath him, he was suddenly able to identify it as a Mark-X but he had no way to tell if it was armed or not.

The Warriors had evidently secured R & D and begun reinforcing their numbers by mending defunct Warriors, which was probably wise. There were no guarantees that all life forms were susceptible to cyanide gas or that they would all die quickly.

Suddenly, the Hunter collapsed onto the floor and Kylem smiled to himself.

It seemed that fixing the Hunter was proving more difficult than they had anticipated.

A flash of white caught Kylem's eye and a Scientific came into view. It scanned the Hunter and tutted.

"The power pack is defective," and it clicked its fingers. A fifth android rose from the corner—a Chaser! That made six androids in total. This was not good.

As the Chaser lifted the Hunter back onto the bench, Kylem sat back on his haunches, rubbed his hands together and then locked them in thought under his chin. Kyamena watched him from afar. He couldn't sit upright in the cramped service shaft so when he eventually looked up and smiled at her, it had a devilishly mischievous air to it. She smiled back at him and it made him feel sad. Suddenly he yearned to have a rabble of androids rather than bloods at his disposal.

Androids communicated silently and did as they were told. Bloods on the other hand, needed verbal instructions and would no doubt, also require an extensive debate before following his orders. He had learnt that bloods never just did as they were told—but then neither did he. Either way, for a discussion to take place, he'd have to get them out of earshot of the Sallows, which meant backing them up to safer ground. This was another entirely new concept to command that he had never had to deal with before, and it made him realise just how formidable an android army was with its unquestioning, unspoken obedience. However, having indicated his needs, the crew backed up with impressive silence to a junction where two tunnels crossed. They organised themselves over the crossroads and then crouched, hunched and huddled in the small space, Kylem began to explain.

"There are five Warriors down there. Two Mark-IX's with Uldakers, a Mark-X that may or may not be armed, a Hunter that I don't think we're going to need to worry about and a Chaser, which we do. There's also a Scientific."

The plan, ultimately, was to move the TWD3 away from the Targa and lower it to the floor as near to the power supplies as they could get it. They didn't know how long the power cables that lay loose upon the floor were or how long it would take to uncoil any new ones, so the nearer they got it to the power supply, the better. Then they simply had to cable up the TWD3 to the intellicouplings.

Penultimately, the safety protocols on the TWD3 had to be disabled. This would do two things. First, it would disable the safety devices that would normally prevent any type of overload from occurring and second, it would remove the power demand limiter on the drive. The TWD3 would simply demand more and more power, far beyond that which it could safely handle until finally—kaboom!

Of course, someone would have to switch it on.

Kylem then had to assess his soldiers. This was another new experience. With androids, they were all the same. He merely had to think about how many to deploy and where. With bloods, he had to consider each one individually.

He debated the pros and cons of equipping everybody so that they were evenly matched by giving the more powerful weapons to the physically weaker and less experienced members of his team. This would give them an improved chance for survival but reduce the chances of success. It would be better to give the best equipment to his best people thus reinforcing his strengths. It was not an easy choice.

He had experienced fighters in Samuel, Harrish and Kyamena and physical strength if not experience in Byron and Kerridge. His weak links were Quick, Tara and Eeena. Having said that, Kylem could not forget that each of them had played a hand in saving his life at least once that day. He concluded that the weak should not be underestimated.

Kylem explained how each weapon could be used to best effect on each type of Warrior. The Scientific shouldn't be a problem as it wasn't built for battle and had no armaments. It was as destructible as a blood and less courageous. Kylem doubted that it would get its hands dirty in a fight but would instead rely upon the Warriors to defend it.

From Quick, he ascertained there were three places where they could exit the service shafts onto the gantries. To explain what was required, Kylem split R & D into sections, comparing it to the points of a compass—a concept he had to explain to those born and bred on the DaerkStar.

In crude terms, the main doors guarded by the Mark-IX's were on the south wall, the TWD3 on the east wall, the power supplies on the north wall and the three other Sallows on the west wall—or thereabouts. The cables were a little west of the power supplies, and the vents were situated in the north-east corner and centrally on the north and west walls.

The Warriors he designated as Alpha, Beta, Gamma, Chaser and Hunter. Alpha and Beta were the Mark-IX's on the doors.

From the vents in the north and north-east positions, Alpha and Beta would have their backs to them. The other Sallows were a risk but none of them would be expecting an organised assault from the vents so had no reason to look up. Of those vents, the one in the north-east corner gave the best opportunity to get inside and into position without being detected.

Kylem then split his contingent into three groups: two active details and a protective detail.

The first group consisted of Quick, Eeena and Tara. It would be their objective to retrieve the power cables, connect one end to the power supply and get the other end as near to the TWD3 as possible. All this needed to be done in silence, and Kylem believed this was achievable if they moved slowly and carefully. He knew Quick was more than capable of this and from what he had seen of their movements in the service shafts, he had no reason to doubt that the others were equally as capable. However, all three refused weapons on the basis that they had no experience of using them and lacked confidence; thus, they would rather not be encumbered by them. Silence was of paramount importance and they felt they had a better chance of success if they could move about unhindered. They did however, agree to carry a weapon each to the lower floor even if they weren't going to use it. Every possible armament had to be available.

The second group consisted of Kerridge and Harrish. It was their objective to move the TWD3 as close to the power supplies as possible, lower it to the ground and connect the cables to the drive. Kerridge would operate the crane, having previous experience in that area in his former life, and Harrish volunteered to connect the cables and clamp them down, being one of the tallest members of the team and thus more likely to be able to reach. All that was left then, was to disable the safeties and activate the engine.

The final group was the protective detail. They would act as the eyes for the active details and provide covering fire when they were discovered. This group was split into two sections. Kyamena and Byron would shadow the first group and were armed with an Uldaker and the axe. The axe wasn't ideal but weapons were limited. Byron said that he'd prefer the axe, bearing in mind his inexperience with weapons.

Samuel and Kylem meanwhile, would shadow the second group with the remaining two Uldakers of which Samuel had the automatic weapon and would remain on the gantry. Hopefully this would provide enough cover for them to complete their objective because as soon as the TWD3 began to move, the Sallows would be alerted and all hell would break loose.

Kerridge then had a bright idea and suggested that if they remained out of sight when he activated the crane, the Sallows might just think it was another malfunction. After all, they weren't expecting an attack from within the room. Kylem agreed that this was a good idea although a long shot, so everybody was encouraged to maintain silence and stay out of sight for as long as possible. Whichever way it went, as soon as the TWD3 began its descent to the ground the game would be up. Firing would begin and that was when things would get really tough.

As Kylem finished his briefing, being fully aware that none of them were indestructible—himself included—he gave everybody a final lesson in how to disable the safeties and activate the engine. Primarily, these were to be his responsibilities on the basis that he was more familiar with the controls and could do it more quickly, but in the event that he was deactivated, they had to continue without him.

Quick translated 'deactivated' for the group as being killed and Kyamena punched Kylem lightly on the arm.

"You're not a bloody android," she chastised.

"That's not entirely true," he argued.

"No, Kylem. Androids don't do the things you do. They don't do stupid things, get drunk, have sex, make friends..."

Kylem didn't hear the rest of her lecture. The rest of her words didn't matter. She had called them his friends.

Kylem then insisted that each of them know how to handle an Uldaker even if they didn't have one. Who knew what would happen and it could save their lives, if only for a few more precious seconds. Kylem, as his final act, instructed them again as to the vulnerable points of the various Warriors; the best places to aim if they were a good shot and where they would have more success if they weren't so good.

"Remember. Warriors don't keep their brains in their heads, but taking out an eye will baffle their sensors. Take out both and you will blind it, but the central processor is behind the breastplate. Take that out and it'll drop like a stone, but an Uldaker won't penetrate the armour plating of a Warrior so aim for the joints. With Alpha, Beta and Gamma, if you can take off a limb, they'll effectively bleed out because they don't have the sophisticated hydraulic systems of the Hunter. As for the Chaser, to cripple it the blades may come in handy," and he further explained its vulnerabilities.

Kylem knew it wasn't the best plan in the world or the most sophisticated but time was limited, as were his warriors and his options. Much to Kylem's discomfort, nobody argued with him. He almost wanted them to. Maybe it would have made him feel better if they had. Not that he felt bad—although he did... a bit... in a way.

He was filled with a hotchpotch of emotions. He was on a mission, which was not only the one thing he was designed to do, but the one thing that he yearned to do above all else in the world. Against that though, he was destroying his entire race and his friends along with it. He was saving all goyeme kind, which was the right thing to do, but the price seemed high. He'd only just learnt that he had friends. It was a shame that he wouldn't have them for long.

But what friends they were! They were prepared to die for the greater good. What truly honourable people they were—true Vaigrani at heart. He felt proud to be with them and honoured that they were prepared to fight at his side and to do his bidding.

CHAPTER 33

Entering via the vent in the north-east corner of the room afforded them the best cover. With the TWD3 suspended from the ceiling, that area on the gantry was largely obscured from the view of the androids working at the other end of the room. They remained huddled around the Hunter, which was once more stretched out on a workbench, its repairs still underway. Only Alpha and Beta would have a clear view of their entry point, but they were on sentry duty facing the doors on the south wall, so as long as they were as quiet as mice they should be able to sneak into the lab. That was the theory anyway.

Kylem was the first to drop down, closely followed by Samuel. They moved along the gantry in opposite directions and took up their positions with Uldakers at the ready.

Kyamena was the next to slip from the service shaft. She too fell silently onto the metal gantry and remained crouched for a moment, waiting. Once satisfied that she had not been detected, she signalled for the weapons to be passed down. One by one, Eeena handed her the armaments and she laid them out neatly on the gantry, ensuring that none of them could become entangled with its neighbour.

Next came the girls.

Kyamena held up her arms to help break the fall of each of them so they too could land noiselessly onto the walkway. After Tara and Eeena, Quick followed. He landed effortlessly and without aid, and then Byron came down. He made a soft, dull thud as he landed and everybody froze in terror.

Beneath them though, the androids worked on, oblivious to the invasion, the noise of the chaos outside helping to mask their entry. After a few moments, the team relaxed, if you could call it that. Kyamena hadn't realised she'd been holding her breath until she exhaled.

She assembled her team, issued the weapons and moved to the nearest stairwell. Although eager to leave the gantry, she didn't hurry. Her eyes flashed continually back and forth between her path and the Warriors as she crept down the stairs. Once at the bottom, she ducked in between the crates and workbenches and took up her position, readying her weapon and training it upon the Sallows. Now that she was in place, Byron, Eeena, Tara and Quick followed and dissipated amongst the debris, depositing a small cache of weapons amongst the crates.

As the first team cleared the gantry, Kerridge and Harrish dropped down. Harrish picked up an Uldaker and they edged down the stairwell, heading towards the east wall and the crane. The cover was poor there so they dropped down out of view early, taking up their position yards from the crane controls. Everyone had now taken up their primary positions, so Kyamena dropped out of sight too.

They had successfully infiltrated the laboratory.

Kyamena took a moment to take some exaggerated, controlled deep breaths, reiterating to herself that speed was not the important thing here. Slow and sure was the order of the day.

She peeked around the crates to re-evaluate the situation, and drew back sharply in horror. A waft of white fabric was heading her way. She shrank into her hiding place as far as she could, gritting her teeth, and waited. How far towards her would the Scientific come? Would it see her?

Her eyes were fixed upon the point where the Sallow would appear, if it did. She held her breath again, not daring to make the slightest noise, but she couldn't stay there forever. She shifted down to watch the white feet move about through the gaps under the pallets. They lingered and then disappeared from view. Where was it now?

She glanced up at the gantry to see Samuel with the automatic in his hands. He was tucked down low on the platform with only the nose of his weapon peeking out. His attention was trained on the Sallows. She looked for Kylem too, but she couldn't see him at all.

She waited. Patience. Patience. Patience. Kylem had driven it home so hard.

Suddenly, Samuel's head lifted a little and his eyes flashed at her, giving her the okay. She exhaled slowly and silently through an open mouth, and then gingerly peered out from her hiding place.

The Sallows were back at the east wall, working on the Hunter. She checked on Alpha and Beta. No change there so silently, she signalled the first team to proceed.

Tara led her team plus Byron through the lines of haphazardly stacked crates and materials. They moved, crouched and low, past the power supplies where Byron dropped out and took up his position. The others continued on, towards the stacks of cables, and then ducked down under the benches.

Once settled, Tara began to assess which cables were the right ones and which would be the easiest to retrieve. It took a few moments for her to identify them. Kylem had told her to look for the thick, dark coloured ones with a thin white stripe. These were heavy-duty cables designed to carry high currents—they'd neither burn out nor melt under the load. From the pile, she selected the one that was the least tangled and from what she could tell, the longest.

Kyamena's heart leapt into her throat as she spotted Quick doubling back to the power supplies, but she needn't have worried. Quick had more stealth than all of them put together, including Kylem, and was soon tucked away, ready and waiting.

On the eastern wall, Kerridge and Harrish were secreted behind some stacks of metal sheeting. They waited until Kyamena gave the signal and then they moved out towards the crane controls.

The control pendant was hanging from a hook on the east wall. With fewer crates and supplies to hide behind, Kerridge not only had to get to the controls but also activate them whilst trying to stay out of sight. Kyamena read his thoughts and assessed the situation. Her current position would be better for Kerridge so having caught his eye, she pointed at him and then to the ground beneath her feet. Kerridge nodded. Kyamena moved out from her position, freeing up the spot for him. Kerridge moved in and Harrish followed.

Kylem meanwhile, made his way towards his final position. None of them was sure exactly where the TWD3 would come down. Circumstance would dictate that, but they were aiming for a spot about three-quarters of the way along—near enough to the power supplies for the cables to reach yet still in good cover and hopefully accessible. Kylem reached his mark and settled himself into place. He couldn't help but remark to himself how well they had all done so far. In his hearts of hearts, he hadn't believed that they would get this far undetected. So far, so good.

As an engineer, Kerridge was used to operating hoisting equipment so he knew how the load would react when moved. (That's why he'd been given the job; the last thing they needed was the drive swinging uncontrollably in the air like a giant pendulum.) From his cover, he examined the control pendant. It was a little closer to Alpha than he would have liked but it looked to have a lengthy cable on it. More importantly, it looked simple to operate with pretty much the sort of buttons he would have expected to find on it. There were some databanks and other equipment on that wall too, so Kerridge hoped to be able to move behind those once he had the controls. Then, when Kyamena gave the signal, he'd start to move the TWD3.

Kylem glanced up at Samuel to check that he was ready and then looked towards Kyamena. She nodded and then turned to Eeena and Tara to give her final signal.

The two girls moved out towards the coils of cables, which looked big and bulky. Kyamena debated if they could move them quietly.

Slipping between the crates, Tara reached the coils first. Gingerly, she reached out and touched the top one with her forefinger. To her surprise, the cable, which was as thick as her wrist, lifted easily. Whatever materials they were made of, they were incredibly light. She turned to Eeena and mimed to make sure she was aware of the fact. The last thing they needed was one of them bracing themselves to pick up something heavy and then hurling it halfway across the room. Eeena then signalled to Kyamena that she and Tara were ready to retrieve the cable. Kyamena moved back and adjusted her position to fully face the Sallows. All she could do now was wait and open fire if and when necessary.

The two girls worked in harmony. The cables were bulky but taking one side each, they prepared themselves ready to lift. Crouched, they waited for the signal from Quick who was in front of them watching the Sallow. They had to watch where they were going and what they were doing so he would be their eyes.

The signal came. They stood upright so as not to scrape the ground with their feet or drag the cables and moved quickly but silently towards the power supplies. Once there, slowly and carefully they lowered the cables down and then ducked back under another workbench.

As they did so, the Scientific turned. Kyamena was stood directly in front of it, poised with her Uldaker aimed at it! For an instant, she froze—and then she dropped.

The Scientific looked up casually from its datapad. It looked at the empty space where Kyamena had stood and then continued on its way. By some chance—some miracle of luck—it had been oblivious to her.

Back in the safety of her hidey-hole, Kyamena's mouth gaped in a mixture of disbelief and horror, and then her eye caught Kylem's. He gave her the thumbs up. She rolled her eyes, bit her bottom lip anxiously and smiled a weak, nervous smile at him. He winked back at her. Then movement caught her eye.

Tara and Eeena were edging along on all fours, away from the Scientific. She raised her hand urgently telling them to stop and they froze, limbs still raised in the air. Tara gingerly turned to look behind her and her eyes widened as Gamma's legs appeared next to her. It stopped by the cables. They were in its way.

With one foot, it casually pushed them aside. Tara had to pull back so as not to impede their movement. Gamma then turned to the terminals by the power supplies and began tapping away at the equipment there. The Scientific drew up alongside it leading the Hunter, once more resurrected. The Scientific took the Hunter's hand and pressed it against a panel. Tara didn't know what it was doing but Kylem did. The Scientific was forcing a flash charge into the Hunter to revitalise it.

The three androids stood huddled around the power supplies for a while. Then the Scientific took out an engineering scanner and pointed it at the Hunter. It studied the readings, tutted and headed back to the workbenches on the west wall. Gamma followed but the Hunter didn't. It seemed sluggish and unresponsive and its eyes didn't burn as brightly as they should have.

"Oh, for goodness sake!" cursed the Scientific. "Hunter! Come here, Hunter!" it commanded.

Kylem's ears pricked up. His attempts to jam the communications channel had been successful it seemed. That was good.

"Oh, this is ridiculous!" it exclaimed. "I give up. I have more important things to do."

One down, five to go, thought Kylem.

The Hunter moved apathetically back to the bench where the Scientific began yanking bits out of it unsympathetically. The Scientific mumbled to itself as it worked. It sent a shiver of discomfort down Kylem's spine. When his father mumbled and complained, that was one thing, but another Scientific doing it was something else altogether.

Breaking from his thoughts, he looked back to the girls. They had sneaked out again, repositioned the reel of cable in front of the power supplies and begun uncoiling it. Quick had already connected one end into the power supply grid and was clamping it down. He then began to help the girls, guiding the cable as far over the floor as they could towards the TWD3. The less distance the drive had to travel, the better, but it had to be close enough for the cables to reach. Kylem prayed that the Sallows wouldn't notice the coupling sticking out of the wall. He glanced over to Kerridge who was waiting patiently.

The cables were now ready. Tara gave the thumbs up and the three of them melted back amongst the debris, near the two swords and the knife.

To Kylem's amazement, the second stage of his plan had been completed successfully but those were the easy steps. Next was the difficult bit, the bit when they would start to die.

Kerridge stepped out into the open. He felt totally exposed as he crept across the floor towards the control pendant. He was so close to Alpha he swore he could hear it ticking (not that androids ticked but he always felt that they should, being mechanical beings). As his hand reached out for the pendant, his back was to the Warriors and he felt himself shaking. His teeth started to chatter. He sucked in his lips to deaden the noise. As his fingers touched the control, it swung gently on the hook. He gasped silently and chastised himself for making it move like that. If the Sallows spotted him now, he'd be done for. Taking an extra step forward, he grasped it boldly with both hands and lifted it off the hook. Slowly, he turned his head half-expecting to find a Warrior pointing a gun in his face but they remained oblivious to him. He looked over to the others and saw Kylem watching him coolly. Those clear, blue eyes brought him back to his senses and he turned his attention back to his task.

Holding the controls firmly, he began walking back to his hiding place, taking care that the cable didn't smack against the wall or snag on the boxes—but the cable was too short. He couldn't return to his original position so he eased himself into a small gap between two pieces of equipment, sinking down as far as he could to keep from view. Still not feeling entirely safe, he looked at the controls. This was it.

He pressed the button.

The crane lurched noisily into motion. The Sallows turned sharply to see, and the Scientific took a step forward, staring at it. It was curious but other than the crane moving, it could see nothing amiss. The Scientific tutted. It tipped its head as it thought and then turned to the console behind it. A few long seconds later, as suddenly as it had started, the crane screeched to a halt.

It seemed that Kerridge was right; the Scientific was viewing it as just another malfunction. Everybody held their positions. No need to start firing until it was absolutely necessary.

A noise startled Kylem. No, not a noise! It was something inside his head. He paused. There it was again. It was like a gentle tap-tapping on the edge of his mind. Someone, or rather some*thing*, was trying to attract his attention.

Androids were equipped with transceivers for their communications and so was he, but whereas androids always had their transceivers activated, Kylem didn't. In the early days, he was often oblivious to the traffic and had to make a point of logging-in regularly to catch up on things. This meant that he could easily miss a communication intended for him if he wasn't careful so he'd purposely created a conflict to generate some interference. This was the gentle tap-tapping sensation inside his head. The question was: what was it?

It was most likely his father. He'd realised this quirk early on and often used it to attract his attention and, as far as Kylem was aware, no one else knew about it. But was it Mela-14? It had to be! But should he respond?

So far, he'd avoided connecting to Server and ignored all the temptations to listen into the traffic via a direct link. He didn't want the androids to know he was still alive or, more importantly, where he was, but that gentle tap-tapping at his mind was quite insistent.

Still he resisted, holding his breath, waiting for it to stop. He closed his eyes to shut it out but that only made it seem even louder so he opened his eyes again... only to find white, linen gowns stood before him. He sighed and shook his head.

"Uniquely flawed," barked the Scientific. "I had a feeling you'd turn up again sooner or later. What a—and please excuse the pun—bloody nuisance you are."

"Jordan-4. I might have guessed. How'd you know I was here this time?" he asked, looking up at the Scientific.

Despite its fixed and inanimate face, every scowl, frown and sneer it transmitted was as real and alive as those he'd seen cast by any blood.

"I used my transceiver. It's funny how my messages just, well... they sort of bounce off you."

"Oh, I see," sighed Kylem. Of course, he thought, any interference he generated would be reflected back to the originator. "A bit like echo-location."

"A little. So," continued the android, "what exactly are you up to now?"

Kylem realised that Jordan-4 had no idea that he wasn't alone.

314

Hoping and praying that his friends would use this valuable purchase of time wisely, he smiled wickedly, stood up and looked around him. Alpha and Beta still had their backs to them, their attention still on the doors and the noises beyond them. Gamma and the Chaser approached. The Chaser relieved him of his little Uldaker.

"Just poking about, as one does," he shrugged and grinned. "What about you?"

"Pest control," Jordan-4 explained chirpily, and pulled a stool out from underneath one of the workbenches. Tara was right next to it and flinched as it moved.

"Do come and take a seat," but Kylem declined the offer.

Jordan-4 looked at him and sighed.

"It wasn't a request."

"I know."

"Fine. Have it your own way. You bore me now," and it turned to Gamma and said, "Kill it!"

Gamma stepped forward and grabbed Kylem by the throat, lifting him clean off his feet. Apparently, Gamma's in-built weaponry wasn't armed. If it had been, it would have just shot him. As it was, it was going to throttle him instead.

Kylem's hands wrapped themselves around the Warrior's for no particular reason other than that's what you do in that sort of situation. As its fingers closed around his neck, he gasped for air and his feet began kicking out, unable to gain a purchase on anything.

An enormous crash suddenly boomed across the labs followed by the sounds of splintering wood and plastic.

Kerridge had dropped the TWD3 to the floor.

Gamma turned to see what the noise was, but all it saw was a tall, black skunk appear from nowhere and run towards it at full pelt. It was Byron wielding the axe high above his head. The stroke came down gracefully, sweeping round in a beautiful wide arc and buried itself deep into the Warrior's already tattered face. Blinded, it released Kylem, covering its face in its hands. It stumbled and fell backwards over a crate. Byron lifted the axe again and began to bring it down, but a blast of bright blue light streaked across the room and hit him in the back.

It cut right through him.

He buckled under the impact of the bullet and slumped onto his knees. He looked down at the bloody, blackened hole in his chest. The axe slipped from his hands and fell. Byron looked up briefly at Kylem. Kylem saw the look of disbelief in his eyes drain away as his life was extinguished.

Byron was dead.

Anger rose silently in Kylem, growing in him like a tsunami, first retreating into an over-exaggerated calm and then unleashing itself into sheer unadulterated rage.

Kylem's eyes changed from cool, calm grey to furious, angry red. They seemed to glow like a Warrior's and then he began to scream and roar like a wild beast, shaking his head and clawing his fists. His fangs extended to their full length and his eyes were wide with rage.

Jordan-4 turned to see the chaos and watched as the boy transformed. It remembered those teeth ripping off its brother's face. It turned and fled.

Kylem leapt after it, hurtling across the workbenches and tables like an ape.

For the first time, Alpha and Beta gave up their positions on the doors and leapt to Jordan-4's defence. As Kylem dived off the end of the workbenches towards the

Scientific, they hurled themselves upon him and he disappeared from view beneath the pile of golden bodies.

In that moment, Samuel and Kyamena broke cover and let loose their weapons. The room lit up with the streaking blue pellets of light, and the Chaser lurched towards Kyamena, blue bullets bouncing off its chest ineffectively as it bore down on her.

Tara leapt out from under the bench and launched herself onto its back. It stumbled under the unexpected load and came down hard on all fours sending Tara flying. Eeena appeared with the scimitar and swiped at its hip. She caught it beautifully in the joint. It buckled and slipped onto its belly. Quick lunged forward with the hunting knife and began stabbing away at the small of its back. Tara and Eeena joined in and the Chaser now found itself beneath the three of them, all wedging blades between its plates. One sank home into its spine and just as Kylem had promised, it faltered. Filled with encouragement, they stabbed harder and harder, deeper and deeper into its body. Above them, the bullets rang out.

As the Chaser began to weaken, Eeena looked up and saw Kerridge pinned down by gunfire behind the equipment. He couldn't get to the drive to secure the other end of the cable, but she could.

Leaving Quick and Tara to finish off the Chaser, she ducked back under the workbenches and scuttled on all fours to the cable. She grabbed it and withdrew quickly back under the bench as the bullets pinged and ricocheted all around her. Hugging the cable to her chest, she looked for the place to connect it on the drive. Then, summoning up all her courage, she broke cover and dived at the TWD3. Blue flashes whizzed around her head and a line of blue bullets streaked after her, punching a line of holes into her back. She faltered. Blood splattered and spat out of her wounds and she fell to the floor. She took two final, stuttered breaths and died, the cable still in her hands.

Tara screamed, not in terror, but anger. She saw Eeena die and the thought that she may have died in vain was too much. Rage and grief gripped her and without thought, she broke cover and leapt across the floor, hurling herself at her friend's tiny body. She snatched the cable from her dead hands and rolled across the floor with it, taking cover behind the drive. Bullets streaked above her head.

Tara looked up at the drive. It had landed on the floor, lop-sided. It was smaller than it had looked when suspended above the labs, but it still stood tall and cock-eyed. The power inlet, she realised, was facing upwards, near the top end of the drive and on the side nearest to the gunfire. To reach it, she'd have to stand up and go around to the front, fully exposing herself to the Sallows.

She looked around and then up and saw Samuel still on the gantry. He stood up and hurled himself over the rail, dropping behind a nearby crate. For a moment, their eyes met and locked. She knew what to do. She nodded. He counted down with his fingers—three, two, one—and together they stood up.

Samuel stepped out in front of her and let his weapon rip free. Blue bullets spat through the air. Tara, grasping the cable in both hands, rammed it home. She fumbled with the clamps, but they locked in with a rewardingly positive click so she knew she'd done it.

Another streak of blue bullets spat around her and she dropped to the floor. As she turned, her eyes saw Samuel. A fresh barrage of bullets rang out. One hit Samuel in the belly. It knocked him backwards. His weapon paused for a moment, but the soldier in him wasn't prepared to die just yet.

He rolled onto his buttocks and curled his legs up to his chest. With one hand holding his life's blood in as best he could, he continued to fire.

Tara panicked. She didn't know what to do next. She couldn't remember! The safeties? She thought about the safeties but her mind was frozen. She couldn't remember anything.

"I can't remember!" she screamed in frustration. "I can't remember!"

Another splatter of bullets rained down just over her head. She scrambled under the nearest workbench, pulled her knees up to her chest and began to sob.

"I'm sorry," she cried, "I can't remember!"

"Kerridge!" screamed out Harrish. "Kerridge! I'll cover you!"

Kerridge was frozen in panic but Harrish's voice awoke him. He remembered what had to be done. The safeties, located underneath the power inlet socket, had to be pulled out like fuses.

"One!" shouted Harrish. He didn't shout two or three. They counted the rest of the numbers in their heads and simultaneously broke cover. Just as Samuel had shielded Tara, Harrish shielded Kerridge and under the protection of that fire, Kerridge leapt at the drive.

Being taller than Tara, he reached the controls easily and was able to use the drive as partial cover. Reaching around it with his hand, he felt for the safeties. They were tiny and he clawed at them. It wasn't as easy as he had thought it would be. They were recessed into a cavity and his courage began to falter at his failure. Then he saw Samuel dying, his blood soaking his clothing, and yet he was still there, angrily and resolutely firing at the Sallows. Harrish too, was shooting off rounds and moving in on them even though shots were striking him. Blood spat from his wounds as the bullets struck. Kyamena also, still had her weapon blazing.

His eye caught Quick and he realised that Kyamena was covering him. Quick was poised to jump out and pull the switch. Quick was watching him. Quick was waiting.

He looked for Tara too, huddled and crying under the table, but she had done her bit. She had braved the gunfire, just as he needed to now, just as Eeena had already done. It was down to him and he couldn't do this from the back of the drive.

Taking a deep breath, he rolled around the side of the drive, stood on tiptoes and looked into the recess. Immediately he could see the problem, and his nimble fingers released the catches and yanked the first of the safeties out. A blaze of light passed by his left eye and ricocheted off the drive. He felt a stinging, searing pain across his forehead. He flinched and dropped to the floor, sure he was dead. It took him a few seconds to realise the shot had only skimmed him, grazing his skin. The smell of burning flesh made him want to vomit but he swallowed the urge back down. Now was not the time. He had to finish his work.

Forcing one last surge of courage, he rose again and yanked out another two of the safeties. Nearly done.

He glanced over to where he'd last seen Kylem, but there was no sign of him. Alpha was stood near the spot where Kylem had vanished. It was firing madly at them all while blue bullets spattered and dissipated against its metal casing, leaving only small scorch marks for their efforts. Beta was struggling with something on the floor. It could only be Kylem; and then, from behind the table, the Hunter rose.

Jordan-4 stepped out from behind the resurrected Hunter and looked up, seeing

Kerridge at the drive. It saw the cable and its eyes traced it to the power supplies.

"Stop him!" it shouted, pointing at Kerridge.

Beta rose from its quarry to obey the order and Kerridge was forced to duck down as all three Warriors turned their attention on him.

Harrish ran forward to draw their fire despite his wounds. A further hail of bullets streaked near Kerridge's head, ricocheting off the TWD3.

Kyamena concentrated her fire upon Alpha striding steadily across the room, firing all the while. She blasted away at its face. Suddenly an eye shattered. It stopped and turned towards her, somewhat dazed. She continued blasting at it, pumping more and more bullets into the second eye. That too finally shattered and blinded, it stood stock-still. Still she pumped more and more bullets into its face via the empty eye sockets. Finally, it fell but she did not pause. She swung around and transferred her attention onto Beta and the Hunter who were advancing upon Kerridge and Harrish.

Suddenly, out of the chaos, Kylem rose from the ground, bloody and bruised.

Jordan-4 turned to see and Kylem punched it hard in the face. It smacked against the wall and slid to the ground.

Kylem bolted forward and snatched the Uldaker from the blinded Alpha. He began firing at Beta's back. Beta turned as Kylem landed in its arms. It looked down into Kylem's eyes. He looked like a madman. His eyes were wild with the scent of victory and he was grinning. Something scraped across its belly. Puzzled, Beta looked down and saw the Uldaker pushed hard against its groin, wedged under its breastplate and pointing upwards.

"Game over!" hissed Kylem and he pulled the trigger.

The shots penetrated between the armour plates and hit home, destroying the central processor. The Warrior shuddered, went rigid and fell to the ground, ripping the Uldaker from Kylem's hand, the barrel still trapped between the plates of its armour. Kylem didn't pause.

The Hunter was bearing down on Kerridge. Kylem leapt onto its back but it threw the boy aside with relative ease.

Kerridge was still fighting with the safeties on the drive when suddenly he heard the most beautiful words he thought he would ever hear. The dulcet tones from the onboard computer of the TWD3 said: *"Warning. Safety protocols have been deactivated. Please ensure power is disengaged."*

Kerridge, filled with relief, dropped to the floor laughing quietly, almost hysterically, to himself. He felt exhausted but he had done it. It was down to the others now. All they had to do was flick the switch. In the distance, he heard a voice scream *"NOW!"*, and he saw Quick leap forward and pull the switch—

But nothing happened.

* * * * *

Actually, when Quick threw the switch, something did happen. Everything stopped.

It was as though everybody knew something was supposed to happen—something really big—and when it didn't, it took them all by surprise. No one seemed to know what to do next.

Kylem picked himself up from the floor and looked. What had gone wrong? His eyes searched for an answer.

Samuel lay mortally wounded, clutching his stomach as the last vestiges of life ran from him. Eeena and Byron were dead, and he could hear Tara sobbing somewhere. Kerridge and Harrish were still standing. Kerridge had blood dripping down the side of his face. Harrish's chest was wet and bloody; Kylem couldn't tell how badly he was hurt. Kyamena was stood in front of him, seemingly unscathed, the Uldaker still in her hand but now silent. He could see the disappointment, the devastation on her face, but there were no answers in any of those places.

His eyes now moved to the drive that sat ready but unpowered. The cable was connected at both ends, so his eyes followed the cable as it snaked across the floor, all the way to where the two severed ends spit and spat with power. Above it, the Hunter stood, the axe in its hand.

There was a clatter as the Uldaker finally fell from Samuel's grip. His breath was light and shallow, and his eyes began to flutter.

"Finish it, kid," he murmured and slumped back down into the bloody pool.

"Well," said Jordan-4 smugly, as it walked towards Kylem.

The casing of its face was cracked revealing the innards that, at that moment, reminded Kylem also of the workings of an old clock.

"It seems that I can foil you after all! As you say—*game over!*"

Kylem snorted in disdain.

"It's not over till the fat lady sings," said Kylem.

"You talk such gibberish," mocked Jordan-4. "Can't you see that you're done here? Hydrogen-cyanide gas is pouring into the life support systems as we speak. You have three minutes left at most."

"That's all I need."

"And what do you intend to do in those three precious minutes? Join the cables to complete the circuit? You can't touch them now. They're live. The power that's coursing through them would fry you alive. You'd be instantly vaporised. You'd never do it."

Kylem pouted thoughtfully.

"Oh, I don't know. I'm made of pretty tough stuff."

"You're a blood. Before you touch those cables, they'll arc over to you. In less than one-tenth of a second, your blood will boil dry, your skin will sear and your bones will be desiccated."

"I'm an android too. I'm constructed from other materials like ptarium and corandium, and I have my huma-nanites. I reckon I could hold together long enough."

"You'll die."

Kylem laughed.

"I'm dead already, you idiot!" he screamed.

Suddenly, years of anguish seemed to fill him.

"I was born dead!" and a tear of frustration ran down his cheek.

He took a long, deep, refreshing breath and looked away from Jordan-4. His eyes focused on the cable ends once more. His eyes narrowed and then... he hurled himself upon them.

The Hunter raised the axe to strike. Kyamena and Harrish opened fire with a new intensity. Another line of bullets was added to the gunfire. Tara had snatched Samuel's weapon up and perched on her knees, she too began pounding it with bullets.

As Kylem hit the ground, his hands closed around the cable ends. He felt the power seize him, snaking and writhing around his wrists, brushing across and caressing his skin, but it wasn't killing him. If anything, it was feeding him! Was that his huma-nanites?

As the power rushed through him like an android on a flash charge, he grew strong—so strong that he could connect to the TWD3 and demand even more power.

And the DaerkStar obliged.

The charge grew and grew, surging through him until suddenly, like a tidal wave, it swept up and over him, lifting him in its current off the floor, drawing him up onto his feet.

He felt extreme exhilaration as the power lit up every fibre of his body. Every cell, every nerve of him felt the power barge its way through him, brutalising every muscle and sinew. His hearts were pounding furiously and one of them tingled excitedly with pins and needles... only it wasn't pins and needles. It was the Eunaba.

Still nestling in his pocket, it stirred. He could feel it warm against his breast, writhing and awakening, growing hotter and hotter, but it wasn't a thermal heat. This was the heat of passion, of power, of thrill and excitement. It was feeding upon him, upon the power he was absorbing from the DaerkStar, joining the two of them together and finally, he could see it. Finally, he knew!

The Eunaba was his!

The Eunaba had always been his!

It was as much a part of him as were his huma-nanites, but he didn't know how to control it.

Pain rose in his chest, pounding against his ribs. It felt like his body was being staved in. The power coursed harder and harder through him, and the pain grew. He gasped and drew his arms closer together, the ends of the cable still in his hands... and still the current grew, responding to the demands of Kylem, the drive—and the Eunaba.

Jordan-4 was screaming madly in front of him, but Kylem couldn't hear it above the noise of the power screeching through his head, and he could no longer see anything. Everything was filled with bright, white light and he was lit up like a star.

Caught in a bubble of sheer, brilliant white energy, his feet no longer touched the ground.

A stream of blue bullets coursed their way towards him but got caught in the bubble and were absorbed like droplets of blue ink in clear water. They twisted and merged and faded into the light, and the bubble of energy grew larger and larger around him. The brilliance burned brighter and brighter and then flared.

Kyamena shied away from its intensity and dropped her weapon. Every light on the DaerkStar dimmed, flickered and died.

Every system, suffocated of power, shut down.

Warriors dropped where they stood and Scientifics were frozen to the spot like shop mannequins.

Kylem heard himself mutter "Game over", and then there was a final supernova of bright, white light—

CHAPTER 34

Down below, on the planet, the Corinthians looked on in awe. Without warning, the Sallow Warriors had just stopped, literally stopped dead. They froze in their tracks and fell to the ground like oversized dolls.

Above them, new lights filled the night sky.

First, there was a single dot of bright, white light that grew. It expanded, bigger and bigger, into a huge ring of snowy, white light and as it grew, more lights lit up the sky—yellow, green and blue—exploding silently above them in quick succession. Then, a few minutes later, hundreds and thousands of shooting stars streaked across the skies as the remains of the DaerkStars began to fall on Corinthia.

... and every end is the dawn of a new beginning...

THE CONUNDRUM

FACT: Waves, regardless of their construction, be they sound, light, water or whatever, travel in troughs and crests. Where waveforms from similar sources and of equal amplitude and intensity meet, interference occurs. The trough from the first wave will cancel out the crest of the second wave leaving an area of inactivity. This is called 'destructive interference'.

THEORY: If an implosion were to occur at exactly the same point and time in space as an explosion of equal magnitude and intensity, one would cancel the other out resulting in little or no damage at the 'eye of destructive interference'.

DEFINITION: The 'eye of a storm' is an area of calmness located in the centre of a hurricane. The exact reason for this phenomenon is not known.

THE CONUNDRUM: If a matter based explosion where to coincide at exactly the same point and time in space as a temporal implosion of similar magnitude and intensity, what would the result be?

(i)

The old lady sat at the window of the log cabin watching the rain outside.

"I'm going to bed, Nanna. Are you coming?"

The old woman turned and smiled at her granddaughter who came and knelt by her side. She reached out a withered old hand and stroked the young woman's brow ridges, a feature she had inherited from her father and his kinsfolk. The old woman didn't have these markings because she was not of this race. She had dropped from the sky to this land a long, long time ago but she had been blessed. On the night she arrived, she had met Alexon, a pretentious young man with whom she had fallen deeply in love and married. Her smile broadened at the memory because they had lived a long and happy life together. She had borne him three children who, between them, had given her eleven grandchildren. Tara was the youngest.

"No, pet. I want to watch the rain a while longer," and she turned and smiled at the rain and her eyes began to fill with tears.

"Oh, Nanna. Why do you always cry when it rains?" asked the young woman, wrapping her arms around her dear old Nanna in a warm embrace.

"Because I'm happy, child. Because when it rains, I think of him and it makes me happy... and sad... and proud, but you wouldn't understand. Go to bed, child. I'll be up shortly," but she knew she wouldn't.

Her granddaughter left her and she returned to watching the rain and remembered his words: *"You die an old woman, sitting in a rocking chair, watching the rain fall outside your window,"* and she did.

(ii)

It was a cold morning in the deserts of Torn. The sun was just beginning to rise, its warm fingers starting to reach out across the plains, eking out long, slender shadows from the smallest of stones. It wouldn't be long before the rock and barren wastelands would be baked afresh. Yet this morning was different, for lying in the middle of the desert, curled up as if to protect her unborn child, was a dark-skinned woman and sat by her side, dazed and confused, was a tall, white android.

The wind whistled about them. The sand blasted against the android's stony, white face and scrubbed at its once crisp, clean, white linen robes. It was listening for Server but Server had gone, along with the tens of thousands of android voices that normally filled the air.

The woman stirred. The android looked at her. She would die in this heat unless he did something about it. He would die too because without the replenishing energy, the rejuvenating power of the DaerkStar, his batteries were running flat.

(iii)

The Escarvian was awoken abruptly by the huge lurch. It opened its eyes and sat up. Instantly, it knew that it wasn't on board the DeathMaker anymore. It was elsewhere.

By the gentle throbbing of the engines through the deck plates, it deduced that it was on board another ship.

By the feeling in its gut, it knew that it was in another time but it didn't know when or where.

Moments earlier, it had been nestled quietly in its den, surrounded by the millions of bones of past meals, bones that it had so lovingly picked clean; but now they were gone and all that it had left was the one splintered ulna with which it had been picking its teeth when it had fallen asleep.

It looked about.

It was in a dark and dirty place that looked as though it was falling apart, but it didn't matter to the Escarvian. None of it mattered, not even the loss of its precious bones. It could always start a new collection.

No. What mattered most was that it couldn't feel the Arcadian anymore. He had been snatched from it and just when he was so near, just when he had begun to learn the secrets of the Eunaba; but in a way, even that didn't matter. The Arcadian would come back one day because he was the Arcadian and it was the Escarvian.

A scraping sound startled the huge beast and it lifted its head, stretching out its long, thick, scaly neck to look. A little girl with long blonde hair trailing out behind her in rat-tails, ran by. She wore a dirty, raggy dress and in her hands, she held an equally dirty and raggy cloth doll.

The Escarvian smacked its lips together.

"Hello," it said from the darkness. "What's your name?"

The girl stopped abruptly, startled by the voice.

"Hello," she replied, peering curiously into the darkness. "It's me. Alison. Who's that?"

"Oh, it's just me. What are you doing?"

"We're playing hide-and-seek," she said, edging forward to see who it was that was talking. "Do you want to play?"

"What's hide and seek?" it asked.

"It's a game! Do you want to play?"

"How do you play it?" the Escarvian asked.

"It's easy. We all run and hide, except one of us—the seeker, and the seeker has to come and seek us out."

She fidgeted with the doll in her hands, pulling absent-mindedly at its woolly hair.

"And then what?"

"And then the one he finds last becomes the seeker and we all run and hide again."

"And what if the seeker doesn't find the last one?"

"Then we all have to go and look."

"Oh, I see," said the Escarvian, and it smacked its lips together again and its tummy rumbled. It had been such a long time since it had last fed and it was hungry.

"Do you want to be the seeker next?" it asked.

"Yes, but I can never find a good place to hide."

"There's a very good place over here, Alison. Come and see."

Alison thought about it for a moment.

"It's a really good place to hide," it assured her. "Do you want to come and see?"

The voice was soft and friendly and although she didn't recognise it, everybody knew everybody onboard the Caspian and so she had no reason to distrust it.

"Okay," she said cheerfully and skipped over to the voice. She climbed under the fallen beams and through the debris and found herself looking into huge, soft, muddy green eyes set into an enormous head. She smiled weakly at it, somewhat frightened by the sheer size of the monster.

"Oh," she said, "I've never seen you before," and then it bit off her head.

As it sat happily munching its way through the rest of her carcass, picking the bones clean and sucking out every last bit of marrow, it thought about the Arcadian and the Eunaba and knew it only had to wait. They would come back to it in time and meanwhile, it would wait for pudding to come looking for Alison.

(iv)
EARTH: Saturday, February 14th 1976

It was cold and dark in the alley and the drizzly rain made it all the more dank and depressing. A black cat, spiky and damp, cruised the bins looking for scraps of food. It stopped; its bright green eyes focusing on something that hadn't been there just a moment earlier.

The corpse lay face down in a puddle of dirty water, but it wasn't quite dead yet. Its breath made little ripples across the surface of the puddle. The cat approached, stopping at the edge of the water. It didn't want to get its paws wet. It sniffed the puddle and began to drink, all the while eyeing the corpse. The body moaned. The cat fled.

As his eyes flickered open, he hurt. Everything about him hurt. His face, his head, his hands, his chest, his legs, his feet. Everything hurt, and he couldn't move, so he lay still, thinking nothing.

An hour passed by.

His limbs began to respond. At first, he could only move his fingers. He stretched them out to encourage the life back into them. Eventually, he found he could draw his arms up a little and later still, be began pushing himself upright. He was dazed, confused and weak. He still couldn't stand.

Another hour passed by.

He managed to lever himself up into a sitting position, leaning against the cold, icky brickwork of the wall. He sat and waited.

The night drew in, colder and colder. Rats began to scurry around him and the wind picked up. Garbage blew down the alley; filthy newspapers caught around him and clung to him. He didn't have the strength to rid himself of them.

A third hour passed by.

The rain had stopped. There were strange noises in the alley, new to his ears: a cat meowing, then its caterwauling, a dustbin lid crashing against the ground, the death cries of a rat. There was a creaking noise from a large, heavy, metal door in the distance. Loud music escaped from it; someone was jeering drunkenly and voices were arguing. Then it slammed shut again.

Weakly, he pulled the bits of newspaper from himself and began struggling to his feet. He stood shakily, reloading his databanks and began dragging himself down the alley. He'd never had to do a full reboot before. He had no idea that it would be so traumatic. What had happened? And then he remembered.

Fresh angry voices interrupted his thoughts. He looked up. They were ahead of him and just around a corner.

Painfully, Kylem made his way towards them, stumbling against the wall as he went. At the corner, he stopped and listened. He could hear the dull thuds of punches being thrown.

Peering around the brickwork, Kylem saw a group of three men shouting at and beating up on an old guy dressed in grubby overalls. They had him pressed up against an old truck and his head was flopping forwards. Blood dripped from a split lip. Kylem could taste the metallic scent of it.

The truck was probably the old man's. It had the words *'Pitelli & Son, Plumbers'* professionally sign written on the side in old, flaky letters.

The leader—the one doing the talking—kept grabbing the man by the chin and tipping his head back to shout into his face. He was a short, fat man, immaculately dressed in a smart grey suit, white shirt, tie and a trilby. He spoke in a low, rough voice with a harsh Afrikaans accent, and he kept leaning into the old man's face, sneering at him.

The other two men stood on either side of the old man. They were stony-faced individuals, equally well dressed in suits but hatless. One was an aging, grey-haired man, tall and wiry thin. The other was young with a full head of thick, curly, black hair. Between them, they held up the old man so that the fat man could punch and intimidate him.

"Marco, Marco, Marco," he said, composing himself ready for the next barrage. "You should of paid."

"I owe Finn nothing," hissed the old man defiantly through his pain, his voice barely above a whisper. He too had an accent, a slight Italian accent softened by the sixty-odd years of living in this country.

"Now that's just where you're wrong, buddy," said the fat man. "Mr Finn is nice enough to protect you but providing that service costs money. He has overheads and you have to make a contribution to doze overheads," and he rammed another punch into the old man's guts.

Marco crumpled under the blow but didn't hit the ground. The two henchmen wouldn't let him.

"And now, Marco, you bleedin' idiot, you owe him so much money, da's only one way out. You got da give him da shop."

Marco laughed. "It's worthless."

"I know dat, Marco. It's just a shitty little shop, but Mr Finn wants it, so Mr Finn shall have it," and with that he pulled a gun out from the inside pocket of his jacket and pushed it up under the old man's chin. "So, we gonna rough you up a little bit more—to make sure we understand each other—and den, first thing Monday morning, you're gonna go to da bank and arrange to sign da business over to Mr Finn. Do you understand dat, Marco?" but Marco didn't answer.

"Okay boys," said the fat man. "Beat the fucking shit off him, but try not to mark his face too much. We don't want da bank manager asking too many questions now, do we?"

"Yes, boss," the tall man acknowledged.

The two thugs pulled Marco away from the truck and threw him onto the ground where they began circling around him like vultures.

"Leave him alone," Kylem heard a voice say, and then he realised that it was his.

—and the Tinnin screeched with joy!

Coming in 2012...

BLACK DOG

For the latest release dates and info, visit www.abpotts.co.uk.

Acknowledgements

How does one start to say 'thank you' to all the great creators of science fiction and fiction who have inspired me and brightened my otherwise dull childhood? There are so many: Gene Roddenberry, Gerry & Sylvia Anderson, Jules Verne, Sydney Newman, Brian Clemens, Sam Rolfe and Ian Fleming, to name but a few. I can only apologise that my list isn't long enough to name them all.

Special mention must be given to Margaret Lee Runbeck for her great quote, *'happiness is not a station you arrive at, but a manner of travelling'*, which I have referred to in the story.

Thanks must also go to Dave—the man who sits patiently by whilst I mumble away to myself in the corner of the front room, furiously tappety-tapping at the keyboard.

Lightning Source UK Ltd.
Milton Keynes UK
UKOW050808070812

197155UK00002B/22/P